MOONDROP MIRACLE

JENNIFER LAMONT LEO

Moondrop Miracle by Jennifer Lamont Leo

Published by Mountain Majesty Media

PO Box 638, Cocolalla, ID 83813

ISBN: 978-1-7337058-4-4

Copyright 2020 by Jennifer Lamont Leo

Edited by Robin Patchen

Cover and interior design by Hannah Linder

Author photo by Cary Burnett

For more information on this book and the author, visit https://www.jenniferlamontleo.com

Library of Congress Cataloging-in-Publication Data

Leo, Jennifer Lamont

Moondrop Miracle / Jennifer Lamont Leo 1st ed.

Printed in the United States of America

MOONDROP MIRACLE

March 1988
Chicago, Illinois

S leet slashed against the tall damask-draped windows of the
Gold Coast apartment, casting gloomy shadows over
Constance Sutherland's face as she sat at her dressing table.
Already she regretted her decision to speak at the Young Entrepreneurs of Tomorrow banquet. The miserable evening would be much
better spent in the coziness of her own firelit library than shivering in
some drafty banquet hall. Now, making matters worse was a notice in
the newspaper that a local TV station would be featuring, on this very
evening, a retrospective of the films of the late Gilda Miller, Connie's
favorite actress. She'd have to miss it. *Hell's bells.*

When her dear friend Sonja Atwater had called and asked
Constance to speak, whatever had possessed her to say yes? What
nugget of wisdom could she possibly offer these vibrant young women
about to sail forth with their freshly minted degrees, ready to conquer

the world? The very vitality of today's young women made Constance feel old and well past her prime.

Or perhaps it was just the incessant rain that was making her feel like a bowl of yesterday's oatmeal. The pounding of it against the windows carried her mind back to a similar storm, nearly sixty years earlier, on a dark Tuesday that had changed her life forever.

She turned away from the window. Mustn't dwell on the past. Mustn't let her mind slip away. Mustn't give in.

In any case, she'd given her word. And even though one would hardly blame an octogenarian for declining to go out on such a blustery evening, Constance was not one to shirk a commitment.

With a sigh, she lifted her tortoiseshell comb as if it were a weapon and gave a few firm strokes to her silvery hair, still shiny and falling into the soft chin-length waves that had been her signature style for years.

A gentle rap sounded at the door, and the housemaid carried a tray into the bedroom and set it on the dressing table. "I thought you might appreciate a hot cup of tea, ma'am, before you head out."

"Thank you, Elsa. That's very thoughtful."

"Are you sure you ought to go?" Elsa frowned at the dripping windows. "Looks right nasty out there."

"Of course I'll go," Constance said with a note of mild disapproval, as if she hadn't just been entertaining those exact thoughts herself.

"You look lovely. I remember how much your husband liked you to wear blue."

"Yes, he did." A bittersweet pang tweaked Constance's heart. She handed Elsa the newspaper. "If you're staying in, you might want to catch this Gilda Miller film festival on television. I'm sick about missing it."

Elsa took the paper and glanced at it. "You don't have to miss it. Just record it to watch later. That's why your son gave you that VCR last Christmas."

Constance waved her hand impatiently. "I can't ever get that darned gizmo to work right. Too many buttons."

"Don't worry. I'll set it up for you," Elsa promised. "You can watch it later when you get home, or tomorrow. I know how much you liked Gilda Miller."

"Thank you." As Connie took a grateful sip of the steaming tea, a buzzer sounded from the front hall. The cup clinked as she set it in the saucer.

"That will be the doorman to tell us the car is here. Please call down and have him signal the driver I'll be ready momentarily." Under her breath she added, "I do hope the Young Entrepreneurs haven't sent along a chatterbox this time."

"Yes, ma'am."

After Elsa left the room, Constance took another sip of tea, checked her evening bag for the index cards on which she'd jotted some notes for her speech, and glanced once more at the mirror. At eighty-one, she was still blessed with the graceful, almost regal bearing of her youth. Above a long pale blue silk shantung skirt, her silver-and-blue beaded top shimmered in the lamplight and nicely complemented her coloring.

Before leaving the bedroom, she applied one final swipe of lipstick and slipped the tube into her bag.

"Remember to sparkle, old girl," she told her reflection and smiled in spite of herself.

Within moments of pulling away from the curb, it became apparent that the Young Entrepreneurs had indeed sent a chatterbox.

"Oh, Mrs. Sutherland, I can't even tell you what an honor it is to meet you in person." The red-haired, alabaster-skinned driver blurted the words as she weaved the Volvo in and out of city traffic on rain-slick streets.

Constance clung to the armrest and tried not to flinch visibly as the side-view mirror of a cab passed within a hair's breadth of her window.

"When Mrs. Atwater asked for a volunteer to pick you up for the dinner, I begged and begged and begged to be chosen."

"How kind," Constance said, wishing she'd do a little less begging and a little more steering.

"I can't wait to hear what you have to say. Why, you're simply a legend."

What should have been a fifteen-minute drive took no more than ten, thanks to the woman behind the wheel, who drove as fast as she talked. Constance could hardly keep up with the woman's plans to start some sort of a computer technology business. Fortunately, the girl accepted her noncommittal responses without question, hardly stopping to breathe. The car lurched to a stop at the curb in front of the elegant Palmer House Hotel. The legend emerged shakily and gratefully accepted the capable arm of a uniformed doorman, who escorted her into the lobby while the driver handed the keys to a parking valet. In the light and warmth of the gilded lobby, she regained her bearings, glad to be back on *terra firma*.

"This way, Mrs. Sutherland." The redhead caught up to her and gestured toward an escalator rising to a crimson-carpeted mezzanine. Together they rode the escalator, Constance stepping careful to keep the hem of her long skirt from catching in the machine's gnashing teeth. It would never do to fall and break a hip in front of all these people.

The mezzanine was crowded with women milling around outside the ballroom. Some of them gathered in small whispering clumps, sliding glances her way, and she looked down at her outfit to make sure nothing was askew. Several ladies murmured greetings as she passed. Some of their faces looked familiar, but her escort hustled her along before she could place any of them.

"They're waiting for us."

Constance halted. "Miss—MacDonald, did you say? Before we go in, I'd like to stop and powder my nose."

"Oh, um, sure. The restroom is right down that hallway." The girl hesitated. "Do you want me to go with you?"

"I'm not *that* elderly, dear." Constance added a smile to soften the words and headed toward the ladies' lounge.

Satisfied that her appearance was in order, she let Miss MacDonald guide her through the ballroom to the speakers' table. In the low light of the room, she made out her place card. She'd only been seated a moment when a shrill voice pierced through the dusky gloom.

"Connie, darling! I'm so glad you've come, and on this beastly night, too."

"Sonja." Constance's heart lightened at the sound of a familiar voice. An elegantly dressed woman not much younger than herself, but apparently a good deal more spry, slid into the empty chair next to her and the friends embraced. "Thank you for inviting me, although, truth be told, I don't know what I have to say to these young women that they haven't heard a thousand times before."

"You're too modest." Sonja grasped Constance's hand and squeezed it. "Why, the girls insisted I invite you. You're a legend in your own time."

There was that word again. *Legend.*

Introductions were made around the table. The other speakers for the evening, both decades younger than herself, included a prominent neurosurgeon who'd founded a medical technology company and a banking executive whose name Constance had seen on the business pages of the *Tribune.* Four bright-eyed members of the Young Entrepreneurs' board, including Miss MacDonald, filled out the table of eight.

Over shrimp cocktail and French onion soup, Constance and Sonja got caught up. Sonja explained her mentoring role with the Young Entrepreneurs of Tomorrow, a position she'd taken on after retiring as professor *emeritus* at a local university.

"Goodness, you're as busy in retirement as you ever were," Constance remarked.

"Oh, I love working with the young women." Sonja's eyes sparkled. "They have the whole future ahead of them. Kind of makes me feel young again. And what about you? I'm *dying* to hear about the new Pearlcon facility that just opened in Hong Kong."

Connie started to explain, but just as the entrée was served, Sonja was called away to look after some detail of the production. Connie turned her attention to the conversation elsewhere at the table, which had turned to higher education.

"More women should be encouraged to major in STEM fields," the banker said.

"STEM?" Constance tested the unfamiliar acronym on her tongue.

"Science, Technology, Engineering, and Math," the neurosurgeon explained. "It's a new acronym gaining traction in the universities. Too

5

many women today are opting for the liberal arts, taking the easy way out. How can we ever make headway in a man's world if we don't tackle the same hard subjects they do?"

"Women are trapping themselves in a pink-collar ghetto," the banker asserted. "This alarming situation needs to change. What do you think, Ms. Sutherland? It is Ms. Sutherland, isn't it?"

"*Mrs.* Yes, that's the name I use professionally." It was simpler that way.

"Well, what do you think? Do you agree that women are trapping themselves in a pink-collar ghetto?"

"*Ghetto* seems a strong word, don't you think?" Constance said. "Not all women are cut out for science and math. Not everyone wants to compete toe-to-toe with men."

"Women who shirk doing a man's work are letting down the sisterhood," the neurosurgeon declared. "Of course, you made your fortune in a pink-collar field," she added with a nod toward Constance. "But times have changed. STEM is the wave of the future."

Feeling a bit pounced upon, Constance straightened and addressed the woman directly. "While it's true that few fields are more 'pink-collar' than the cosmetics industry, there are of course a great many women scientists working in Pearlcon laboratories around the world. We wouldn't have much of a company without them, would we?" She dabbed her lips with a white linen napkin, taking a moment to plan her next words. "Many women can and do excel in science and math. But a woman shouldn't feel she has to become like a man to achieve success."

"We don't need to become *like* them. We need to become *better* than them," said the banker with what sounded like a sneer.

"What field did you take your degree in, Mrs. Sutherland?" asked the neurosurgeon.

"Oh, I never went to college," Constance said. "After high school, I attended a year of finishing school. Then I married and had a child. I didn't start my career until later."

"Finishing school?" The neurosurgeon could not have looked more astonished if Constance had claimed Stateville Prison as her alma mater. The doctor and the banker exchanged a glance, clearly wondering why such an undereducated woman was speaking at an event aimed at soon-to-be college graduates. Constance wondered herself. "It's a wonder your business succeeded as it has," the neurosurgeon concluded.

"I didn't know it would succeed at the time. All I knew was that I had to do it. And eventually, I became most interested in offering women opportunities that didn't seem to exist anywhere else."

All at once, the face of an old classmate flitted across Constance's memory. *Julia Harper. That's who these women remind me of. Good old Julia with her no-nonsense leather brogues, mannish hats, and leaflets proclaiming the rights of women and whatnot.* The memory amused Constance so much, she almost missed what the banker was saying. A few minutes later, she wished that she had.

"Thank goodness times have changed," the banker said. "Maybe foregoing a proper education was acceptable back then, but it certainly isn't a viable option these days. After all, very few people have a rich daddy to bankroll their business. Most of the young people here tonight are not women of privilege, such as yourself."

The woman had hurled the word "privilege" as if it were an accusation. *Rich daddy, indeed.* Heat rose in Constance's chest and spread to her face. Why were these rude women attacking her? Where was Sonja? Whatever was keeping her? Constance felt her sparkle melting faster than the ice cream served for dessert. It took everything she had not to snap back some witty barb and put the women in their place. In her mind she heard Aunt Pearl's voice say, *Don't stoop to their level, Connie. A gentle answer turns away wrath.* So she said simply,

"Apparently, you haven't heard my story. Perhaps my speech will fill in some of the gaps for you. I suggest you listen carefully."

Before her tablemates could respond, the lights dimmed. Sonja stepped behind the podium and introduced the neurosurgeon as the first speaker.

The room grew warm. Constance slipped out of her wrap and folded it over the back of her chair. It was too dark to read the index cards in her bag, so mentally she reviewed her speech, noting portions she could skip if the hour grew late but reminding herself of the one point she absolutely had to make to these impressionable young females.

JENNIFER LAMONT LEO

For heaven's sake, be glad that God made you a woman.

As the neurosurgeon droned on about entrepreneurial opportunities around today's highly specialized wellness environments—apparently no one called them "hospitals" anymore—Constance let her mind drift back to her own youth.

She had not cared about college. At twenty-one, she'd had no greater purpose in mind than marrying Winston Sutherland III and having fun. Lots and lots of fun. Aunt Pearl had been the one who had longed to go to college—and been denied the opportunity.

But God had other plans for both of them.

May 1928
Chicago, Illinois

Brrring!
The jangle of the telephone in the hall awakened Connie Shepherd from a sound sleep She opened one reluctant eye, then blinked it shut again. *Hell's bells*. She'd forgotten to close the curtains before she went to bed. Now, the spring sunshine streamed through the tall windows, straight into her eyes. Half asleep, she grabbed the down pillow and pulled it over her head in a futile attempt to block out the noise and light.

Mercifully the jangling stopped. Connie had nearly slipped back into blissful sleep, hoping to resume a pleasant dream involving a trip to the beach and wading in the waves of Lake Michigan alongside the dreamy actor John Gilbert, when a gentle tap sounded at her bedroom door.

"Miss Connie." The low voice of the housemaid broke into her reverie. "Miss Connie, you're wanted on the telephone."

"I'm sleeping," she murmured into the pillow.

Tap, tap, tap. The volume louder by a notch. "Miss Connie."

She groaned, flung back the thick, cozy blanket, and swung her legs over the edge of the bed.

"Gracious sakes alive," she said to the door. "Who could be so rude to be calling at this hour?"

"It's your mother calling from Florida. Long distance," the voice added, as if that additional detail would make Connie's feet move faster.

Muttering a quiet oath, Connie grabbed her silk robe from a nearby chair and shoved her feet into quilted satin slippers. She shuffled out to the hallway, where a housemaid stood next to a small table holding the stick and receiver. Connie accepted them and grumbled, "Thanks, Helga."

"It's Hilda, miss." The maid turned and headed down the hallway, her footsteps silent on the thick carpet.

"H'lo," Connie slurred into the mouthpiece.

"Connie?" Opal Shepherd's bright voice crackled over the line. "Are you all right, darling? You sound terrible."

"I just woke up. Perhaps you've forgotten the time difference."

"Even so, half the morning's already gone. Why are you still in bed? Are you ill?"

Was she ill? Connie had a fuzzy recollection of stumbling home very late—or very early, depending on how you looked at it—from another evening spent trolling the South Side jazz clubs with Winston and the rest of their crowd. That would explain the tiny people drilling her skull with jackhammers.

"I'll be fine," she mumbled *Fine after a couple of aspirin and half a pot of strong coffee.* When would she learn that cocktails made her sick, no matter how fashionable they were among her crowd?

"Well, it's high time you were up and about. Goodness, Connie, you're going to sleep your life away."

Connie shifted the receiver to her other ear. "Did you call for some other reason than to roust me from my warm bed? Is everything all right down there in the land of sunshine?"

"Everything's fine here. But listen, darling. I need you to do me a tremendous favor."

"What is it?" Her mood was not conducive to favors.

"I've been trying to telephone your Aunt Pearl since yesterday and haven't been able to reach her."

Connie yawned. "She's probably just out puttering in the garden or brewing up who knows what in that laboratory of hers."

"That's what I thought, too," her mother said, "but last night I called and called, even late at night when she should have been tucked safely in her bed, and still received no answer. I'm getting worried. She's all alone out there on the farm with nobody but her cats. What if something's gone wrong in the laboratory? Remember that little incident with the nitroglycerin."

Connie rubbed her forehead. "Who could forget? Certainly not her neighbors."

"She's not always as careful as she should be."

"That's an understatement."

"Or she might have had a heart attack or a stroke, or an accident riding on that motorcycle, or ... oh, anything at all." Mother's voice took on a wheedling tone. "So, darling, would you mind driving out to the farm this morning to make sure she's all right."

"I don't know. I have such a busy day planned."

"Doing what?"

Connie had no answer for that. Instead she said, "I'm sure you're overreacting. Why don't I just keep trying to telephone from here?" *From the comfortable confines of my cozy bed.* "You know she'll turn up eventually. She always does."

"I'm sure you're right. But just in case, would you do me this one teensy favor?"

Connie sighed with great drama. "Oh, I suppose so"

"Thank you. I'll feel so much better knowing she's safe."

"How are things in Florida? Is Daddy making money hand over fist?"

"Don't be vulgar. But, yes, the real-estate market seems to be recovering from that terrible slump. Your father's just putting the finishing touches on some property transactions, and we'll be on our way home well before the wedding. You'll be all right on your own until then, won't you? Not too lonely? Now don't forget to call me as soon as you get to Pearl's. We're still at the Nautilus. You have the number."

After a hot, steamy bath, Connie felt more human. She even started to look forward to the outing, in spite of her initial reluctance. She loved any excuse to take her sleek automobile out on the road. A fast, windy ride on a fine spring day would clear her head.

She dressed in a matching pink-and-gray argyle skirt and sweater, then stood before her mirror, positioned a pink cloche over her wavy blond bob, and added a swipe of rosebud lipstick. In the breakfast room, she poured a cup of strong coffee from the pot on the sideboard, spread a piece of toast with marmalade, and devoured them standing up—a breach of etiquette that would have driven her mother around the bend had she been there to see it.

"I'm headed out to the farm, Robbins," she told the butler when he came in to check on her.

"Very well. Shall I call Parker and have him bring the car around?"

"I'll drive myself. Looks like an A-plus day."

As she pulled her shiny Hudson out of the garage onto leafy Astor Street, her spirits rose. The May breeze tugged at her stylish cloche. Ever since her beloved Daddy had given her the roadster for her eighteenth birthday three summers ago, it had been her prized possession, especially when the weather was fit for driving with the top down. The cream-colored chassis sported a collapsible roof, wine-red leather upholstery, glistening chrome, and more horsepower under the hood than Connie would ever require on the streets of Chicago. Without taking her eyes from the road, she felt the admiring glances of other drivers. She maneuvered skillfully through the traffic-clogged city streets. By the time she was speeding out of the city limits on Route 20, she felt her cares—including her vague concern about Aunt Pearl's welfare—floating away on the breeze.

Gradually, skyscrapers gave way to fields and small towns. Aunt Pearl's farm lay about an hour's drive northwest of the city. Connie quickly calculated that she could drive out there, assure Pearl was safe and sound, give her a stern lecture about answering her telephone in a timely manner, maybe enjoy a quick bite of lunch, and head back to the city well in time to change clothes for dinner with Winston. They'd been invited to his boss's house, and, much as Win liked to tease her about her tendency toward tardiness, he wouldn't be laughing if she made them late for dinner with the top brass at his company.

At last she pulled off the main highway and started down the muddy road leading to Aunt Pearl's farm. She slowed the Hudson to a crawl to avoid damaging the tires on the ruts and potholes. Poor Parker would have quite a chore later scraping mud off the car, but it couldn't be helped, not as long as Pearl insisted on living in the back of beyond.

Connie had always had a soft spot in her heart for Pearl, the eldest of the three McCabe sisters: Pearl, Opal, and Ruby. Ruby, the youngest, had gone off to India as a missionary. Connie's mother, Opal, since her marriage to real-estate magnate Marcus Shepherd, spent most of her time conforming herself to the dictates of Chicago society and making sure her daughter conformed as well.

And then there was Pearl. Thwarted in her plans for a career in the sciences, Pearl taught school until she married Stewart Russell, a dairy farmer she'd bumped into, quite literally, while on a schoolteacher's tour of the Louisiana Purchase Exposition. They'd settled happily on his large dairy operation outside of Chicago. Connie had only dim memories of Stewart, who'd died of influenza in 1918. After his death, Pearl kept the farm but gradually sold off the cows and acreage until little more was left than the farmhouse, a few outbuildings, and a great big red barn. And Pearl's cats. Lots and lots of cats.

It was in the barn that Pearl spent most of her time. She'd converted it into a makeshift laboratory, where she concocted potions and tinkered with inventions to her heart's content. So the barn was the first place Connie expected to find her as she steered the mud-spattered Hudson onto the property and parked under a blossoming apple tree.

"Hello? Aunt Pearl? Are you here?" Connie stepped delicately on the dirt path leading to the barn, realizing too late she ought to have worn sturdier shoes. The barn door hung open. She peered in, her eyes adjusting to the dimness. A sudden movement made her back up a step, but it was only a friendly gray tabby leaping down from a cobwebbed windowsill to greet her. Connie's gaze landed on a large dusty wooden table piled high with glass beakers, steel instruments, Mason jars containing who knew what, and thick reference books. Next to the table sat an unidentifiable contraption, a hulking barrel-like structure strung haphazardly with tubes and wires. But no sign of her aunt. To her relief, Pearl's pride and joy, a shiny red Indian Scout motorcycle, leaned on its kickstand near the door, allowing Connie to strike "motorcycle accident" off her mental list of possibilities.

With growing concern, Connie picked her way up the path to the farmhouse. Peeling white paint gave the cottage a shabby air, but the flowerbeds overflowed with brilliant tulips and hyacinths, forsythia the color of sunshine, and lilac bushes soon to burst into bloom. Connie banged on the door, then tried the doorknob. Locked.

On the bottom porch step, a black cat stretched lazily in a spot of sunshine, while an orange one snoozed on the step above. A calico lay curled up on a wicker chair in the shade.

"I don't suppose any of you three could clue me in to Pearl's whereabouts," Connie muttered as she sank onto the top step and wrapped her arms around her knees, considering her next move. Pry open a window? Summon a neighbor for help?

Moments later, she heard the clatter of an automobile engine. She turned to see an ominous black Dodge pulling off the road, the words "Sheriff Patrol" lettered in glaring white on the side of the wagon. With a pounding heart and rapidly dwindling confidence in Aunt Pearl's capability to handle any situation, she hurried down the steps, scattering cats every which way.

This couldn't be good.

❧ 3 ❧

A tall grim-faced deputy stepped out of the cruiser as Connie flew down the path toward the police wagon, fearing the worst.

"Deputy, what is it? What's happened to—"

Before she could finish the sentence, the rear door opened, and out popped Aunt Pearl, a sweet-faced woman dressed haphazardly, as usual, in a faded house dress and flour-sack apron, stray silver hairs escaping her bun. Her face lit up.

"Connie, dear! How lovely to see you," she said, her smile bright as sunshine, as if being delivered home in a paddy wagon was an ordinary occurrence.

Connie nearly melted with relief. "Aunt Pearl, are you all right? Where have you been? We've been worried sick."

"Of all the ridiculous things," Pearl huffed, brushing past the deputy. "I was working in my laboratory last night, minding my own business, when two officers of the law burst onto my property and hauled me off in the middle of the night like a common criminal. Didn't even give me time to remove my apron."

"What on earth?" Connie looked to the deputy for some kind of explanation.

"You her daughter?" he asked.

"I'm her niece."

"Well!" Pearl lifted her chin. "In any case, Connie, I've been at the police station all night long, explaining to the good officers the profound difference between bootleg whiskey and my latest contribution to science."

Connie glared at the deputy.

"You must admit, miss, that it looks mighty suspicious," the deputy said, squinting into the haphazard laboratory. "We don't come across too many widow ladies who operate fully equipped, er, laboratories in their barns."

"Well, now you know *one*," Pearl said.

The deputy dipped his head. "Sorry again for the inconvenience, ma'am. It won't happen again."

"See that it doesn't, or I'll have words with the sheriff myself," Connie snapped, hoping she sounded authoritative.

The deputy touched the brim of his hat and opened the door of the cruiser.

"Wait here a moment, deputy," Pearl said. "I have something to give you."

"Yes, ma'am."

Pearl strode toward the barn. While they waited, the deputy grinned at Connie and gestured toward the Hudson. "That yours? She's a beauty."

Connie nodded.

The deputy's grin deepened, displaying a dimple. "Say, maybe you and me could take her out for a spin sometime."

"I hardly think so."

Pearl returned and handed a small unlabeled jar to the deputy.

"When you get back to the station, give this remedy to that nice Sheriff Blake and tell him to apply it to his arm with a cotton ball, morning and night." Her tone was motherly. "That rash of his should clear right up."

"Yes, ma'am. Sorry again for the trouble."

"No harm done."

Pearl and Connie watched as he backed the cruiser down the rutted driveway.

"What was that you gave him?" Connie asked.

"It's my latest invention. A miraculous tonic, clears up everything from dandruff to diaper rash. For heaven's sake. Moonshine, indeed. Have you *ever*." Pearl slipped her arm through Connie's. "Come into the house, dear, and I'll make us some lunch. You look as if you could use some meat on those bones. I'm afraid I don't have anything fancy, just some ham and cheese."

"Are you sure it's no trouble? You must be exhausted after your ordeal."

"Nonsense. You can't drive all the way out from the city and then not stay and rest a while. I didn't realize you'd be visiting today, but I'm very glad you've come. Just sorry I wasn't here to greet you when you arrived."

"Mother rang from Florida," Connie said. "When she couldn't reach you, she became worried and called me."

"Oh, darling. I'm terribly sorry to put everyone through such inconvenience."

"It's no bother, truly." Connie patted her aunt's hand. "I'm just glad you're all right. I wonder who called the sheriff and made such a silly accusation."

Pearl harrumphed. "I'll bet it was that busybody, Agnes Pratt. She lives up the lane and always has her nose in everybody's business. She's never taken a shine to me, not since the first day Uncle Stewart brought me home."

"How could anybody not take a shine to you?"

"I think she carried a torch for Stewart." The diminutive woman glanced up at Connie. "Anyway, I'm glad you're here. Do you know, the Lord brought you to mind just the other night?"

"Did He?" Connie smiled indulgently at her aunt. Pearl was one of those rare individuals to whom God was a real, live being, not just an abstract concept, as Connie had been taught. To Pearl, God was neither silent nor remote. He was as constantly present in her life as her cats. She was known within the family for being on personal speaking terms with the Divine. This was one of the reasons, among several, that the socially conforming Opal described her sister to others as "unconventional."

Connie, like her parents and just about everyone else she knew, confined thoughts of God to Sunday mornings. The Shepherds attended a fashionable church in the city, and Connie went with them if she hadn't stayed out too late the night before. It wasn't that she didn't believe in God at all. After all, some cosmic force must have set the world in motion and kept it spinning all this time. But she didn't have intimate and familiar conversations with God the way Pearl did. Now she said lightly, "Do tell. You've got me on tenterhooks. What exactly did God say about me?"

"He didn't say anything. Not out loud." Pearl sounded impatient, as if Connie ought to know these things. "He speaks to us through the Bible prophets, not through people today."

"Of course. Sorry. But you said He told you something about me."

"I said He brought you to mind. It was just an impression that came up while I was praying for you."

"You pray for me?"

"Every night."

"That's so sweet." An unexpected glow warmed Connie's chest. In a strange way, she envied her aunt's faith, even if she didn't quite share it.

Pearl continued. "As I prayed, I saw you standing up in front of a crowd of people. You seemed to be leading them in some way. Urging them to march forth into battle or something."

Connie snorted. "Me, leading a crowd into battle? Goodness. That's unlikely, isn't it?"

"As I said, it was just an impression." Pearl shrugged. "I suppose it could have just as easily been caused by a touch of indigestion. But I prefer to believe it was the Lord."

"Funny duck." Connie squeezed her aunt's shoulders with affection. In the sunny, cluttered kitchen she said, "Do you mind if I telephone Mother in Florida? I'm sure she's pacing the floor, waiting for my call."

"Of course, dear. I'll just go and take a quick bath and change my clothes. I must look a fright."

Connie cranked the black telephone hanging on the kitchen wall. She sneezed just as the operator said, "Number, please." Darn cats.

"Excuse me, operator. Winter Garden, Florida, please," she said into the mouthpiece. "Mrs. Marcus Shepherd at the Nautilus Hotel. Reverse the charges."

By the time Pearl returned to the kitchen dressed in a fresh frock and apron and smelling sweetly of violets, Connie had related the whole story to her mother, endured a few blistering remarks about Pearl and her "confounded experiments," gracefully exited the conversation, and set about assembling sandwiches and heating water for tea.

"That's better." Pearl peered at Connie. "Your eyes are red, dear. Are you catching a cold?"

"Just my cat allergy acting up. Don't worry, it's mild."

"Oh, I forgot about that. Perhaps we should eat out on the porch."

"Good idea."

Pearl carried plates and cups to a little table set up on the porch. Connie followed with the teapot and a plate of sandwiches.

"Looks delicious," Pearl said. "Maybe you picked up something useful at that fancy finishing school, after all"

"Maybe one or two things," Connie said with a grin. "But not sandwich-making. That I learned from Mrs. Blake, our cook."

"I keep telling your mother she should ship you off to a real college. Aren't you just aching to go back East to Bryn Mawr or Radcliffe? Or even stay closer to home. I've heard the University of Illinois has an excellent science program."

"I don't want to study science or anything else." Connie toyed with the crust on her sandwich. "I'm glad to be done with school. I was never very good at it."

"You're such a bright girl, Connie. I hate to see you waste time on ... whatever it is that you're wasting time on."

"Who says I'm wasting time? Goodness, I'm getting married in two weeks. Why would I want to go to college?"

"Why, to learn things, of course. When I was your age, I would have given anything to go to college. I planned to be the next Marie Curie. As a girl, I looked up to her example." She sighed. "What I would have given to follow in her footsteps."

"So why didn't you go? To college, I mean."

"My father—like yours, I gather—wasn't a big proponent of higher education for women. And even if he had approved, there was no extra money to pay for tuition. So, I taught school instead. Back then you could teach school with only a high school diploma." She bent and scratched the ears of the black cat that was rubbing its head against her ankle. "I always thought I'd go to college later, after I'd taught for a few years, but then I met your uncle, and life took a different path."

"Do you mind?"

"Mind? No, I suppose not. I loved my life with Stewart, and he left me well cared for. But there's always a part of me that will regret not pursuing higher education. The road not taken and all that."

"What about your sisters? Did they want to go to college?"

"I was the only one. Opal married well, of course, when she managed to land your father."

"I don't know if I'd put it quite like that," Connie said. "I understand Daddy was quite smitten."

"Oh, of course, they married for love," Pearl said quickly. "I didn't mean to suggest otherwise or to make her sound like a social climber. The demanding life of a society matron suits her perfectly."

Connie couldn't decide if Pearl was being sarcastic or not, so she let it go.

Pearl continued, "I simply meant that, like you, she hadn't been interested in college. And neither had Ruby, although she did attend the Bible institute for a year to prepare for the mission field." A wistful note sounded in her voice. "I was the only one who truly yearned for more education. It's hard for me to understand why every young woman wouldn't want it, if the opportunity presented itself."

"Well, I'll be marrying Winston exactly two weeks from today," Connie said firmly. "My future is all sewn up."

Aunt Pearl leaned forward in her chair. "What does Winston do for a living? I'm sure you've told me, but I've forgotten."

"He's in investments," Connie said, fiddling with the salt shaker.

"Investments," Pearl repeated. "What does that mean? Is he a banker?"

"Well, I don't know, exactly. Sort of, only he's with an investment firm, not a regular bank." Connie shrugged. "He never talks about business with me. I know he's a junior partner in Carruthers & Mullin, and the company just moved their offices into one of those great big new skyscrapers on LaSalle Street, and he works very long hours, but he seems to enjoy it. They must like him, too, because they keep giving him fat commission checks."

"So the Lord is prospering him."

"Carruthers & Mullin are prospering him," Connie drawled, and knew she'd said the wrong thing when Aunt Pearl's expression stiffened.

"Everything good comes from the Lord, Connie. I've been telling you that since you were a very little girl."

"Yes, yes, I know."

"And you love Winston."

A glow spread across Connie's chest. "Yes, I do. He's everything I've ever dreamed of. Smart, handsome, successful ... and he makes me laugh."

Pearl set her lips firmly as if choosing her words. Finally she said, "Even so, you really should learn more about what your husband-to-be does all day long."

Connie plucked a cat hair from her skirt. "Mother says it's the man's job to earn the money and the woman's job to spend it."

"That sounds like Opal." Pearl set down her teacup "Honestly, Connie. How do you expect to be a supportive wife to your husband if you don't even know what he does?"

"I support him," Connie protested, flailing about for a specific instance to back up the assertion. She hadn't given the matter much thought, but in that instant vowed to learn more about Winston's work.

Pearl cocked her head. "Exactly how long have you known Winston, dear? If you don't mind my asking."

"We met a year ago at Gwendolyn and George Carpenter's wedding. I was a bridesmaid and Win was an usher. He'd attended boarding school back East, you see, living with an aunt in Boston. Then he'd stayed on for university, only moving back to Chicago when he got hired by Carruthers & Mullin."

"I see," Aunt Pearl quirked an eyebrow. "So you haven't known him all that long, then."

Connie squirmed. "Long enough."

"Have you had enough time to make sure, sure, sure that he's truly the right man for you?"

"What do you mean?"

"I mean, do you have things in common? Besides dancing and having fun, although that's important too, of course. For example, does he know the Lord?"

More God talk. Connie was tiring of the sermonette.

"His family attends St. Lucian's, same as ours."

"Do you share the same values? The same general goals in life?"

Connie's patience reached its breaking point. "Of course we do. For heaven's sake, Aunt Pearl. What have you got against Winston?"

Pearl blinked. "Nothing. I don't even know the man." She paused as if to collect her thoughts. "I'm sorry if I sound like a meddling old woman. I just want you to be happy, that's all."

"I am happy," Connie said. The words came out sounding more snappish than she'd intended.

Pearl reached across the table and patted the back of Connie's hand. "I'm sure it will all work out. Marriage is a noble calling, and if you're sure Winston is the one, I support your choice wholeheartedly. But I can't help but think that a girl should also have her *own* purpose, too. Her own way to use her gifts and talents in God's kingdom."

"I will use my gifts in making our home and raising our family."

"Of course you will." Pearl's expression grew misty. "My time with Stewart was short. Too short. I don't regret a minute of our life together. But I also wish I'd had the chance to study and become a real chemist, too, or maybe an engineer, instead of just tinkering out there in a homemade laboratory."

So that's what's behind this, thought Connie with relief. *Aunt Pearl regrets her own choices and is projecting her disappointment onto me. The poor dear. Best to change the subject.* She swallowed her last bite of sandwich and dabbed her mouth with a napkin. "Speaking of laboratories, what is this mysterious new project you're working on? The one that cures absolutely everything, and has the vice squad hauling you off in the middle of the night?"

A grin lit Pearl's face. "Oh, my dear, it's something I'm extremely excited about. There's never been anything like it. It's one of my best inventions."

"Like the soup spoon with a fan attached?" Connie didn't even try to mask the skepticism in her voice.

Pearl lifted her chin. "Think of all the poor souls who are injured each year by sipping steaming broth." She slapped her palm on the table for emphasis. "I still think that a soup-cooling device could be a practical tool." Seeing the expression on Connie's face, she thrust out her lower lip and muttered, "With a few adjustments, that's all. Just a few minor adjustments."

Connie crossed her arms. "And what about Felix Fizz-Water, the world's first soda pop for cats?"

Pearl pressed her lips together for a moment. "You can't win them all."

Connie started to say something clever, then changed her mind. Dear Aunt Pearl looked so earnest. She deliberately softened her tone. "What is this marvelous new invention, then?"

Pearl stood and set her napkin on the table. "It's that amazing skin remedy I was telling you about. The one I sent along to the sheriff. Come along and I'll show you. Here, these will save your dainty shoes." Connie slid her feet into the muck boots Pearl provided and followed her out to the barn.

"The Pride of Frankenstein," she muttered as they entered the jerry-rigged laboratory. The worktable and the shelves behind it bore skinny glass tubes, fat glass jars, stirrers, chemical bottles of dark amber glass, isopropyl alcohol, pipettes, notebooks, flasks and beakers. A scattered pile of books and papers cluttered the tabletop and poked out of the drawers of an ancient wooden filing cabinet. Connie wrinkled her nose at the smell, a curious combination of old wood, hay, alcohol, formaldehyde, and livestock, even though the dairy cows had been sold off long ago.

Pearl snapped on a pair of rubber gloves and handed an extra pair to Connie, along with a set of safety goggles. "Here, put these on. Better safe than sorry."

"I'm glad to hear you say that," Connie said. "Remember the incident with the nitroglycerin."

"Won't make that mistake again." Pearl nodded toward a shiny red fire extinguisher hanging on the wall. The large gray tabby jumped up onto the worktable, purring loudly. "Now, Newton, you know you're not allowed up on Mama's workbench." Pearl gently lifted the tabby and set her down on the rough plank floor. To Connie she whispered, "We'll be welcoming some little ones soon. She's in a family way."

Connie sneezed and glanced at her wristwatch. "So what's the project?"

Pearl straightened her shoulders, and Connie caught the gleam in her eye.

"Feline De-Flaker."

"What?"

"Feline De-Flaker. You see, Edison had developed the most terrible case of dandruff," Pearl explained. "He's a black cat, as you know, and the dandruff showed up terribly on his coat. It was very embarrassing for him."

Connie smiled. "Was it really? How could you tell? Do cats blush under all that fur?"

"They blush in their own way," Pearl said, a bit defensively. "Anyway, I tried scads of different solutions and nothing was effective. I've been experimenting with it all winter. Then just last week, I had a break-through."

"Do tell."

"Fenugreek." She whispered the word, even though they were alone in the barn.

"Fenu-what?"

"Fenugreek. It's an herb. Your Aunt Ruby in India sent me some for Christmas. I didn't care for the taste, but when I tried using it in my cat-dandruff formula, it worked like magic. It's expensive, so I've started growing some indoors, over there." She gestured to a small greenhouse structure set up next to a window.

"What do you mix it with?"

"That's a trade secret." Pearl winked. "A little of this, a little of that ..."

"And it works?"

"Edison's coat has never been so shiny and sleek. Completely flake-free. Here, try some."

Pearl dipped a cotton ball into the liquid and dabbed a little on the back of Connie's hand.

"Mmm. Nice." She inhaled the attractive scent. "Smells sort of exotic. I'm impressed. So, are you going to take it to market?"

Pearl laughed. "I don't think so. I'm not much of a businesswoman. For now I'll just use it on my own cats. Maybe someday I'll sell it to Dr. McGee, the local veterinarian. Maybe he can do something with it. Here, take some home." She capped the small vial and handed it to Connie, who slid it into her skirt pocket.

"Thanks. My friend Gwendolyn has a cat. Maybe I'll give it to her."

"Remember, it's good for people skin, too."

"Seems a shame to keep it all to yourself if it works. You should at least get the formula patented." Connie glanced again at her wrist-watch. "Oh, my. I need to get back to the city. There's a company dinner at Winston's boss's house. He'll never forgive me if I'm late again."

They walked to the house. Connie pulled off the muck boots and set them on the porch. She kissed her aunt on the cheek.

"Next time, you must take me for a ride in this fancy automobile," Pearl said with a glint in her eye as Connie slid into the driver's seat. "Looks like it goes like the wind"

"It does, and I will." Connie raised her voice to be heard over the engine. "Next time. Meanwhile, be a dear and stay out of jail, will you?"

"Have a good time at the party tonight." Pearl waved as Connie backed down the driveway. "Remember to sparkle!"

4

Directing her gaze across the snowy linen expanse of the Carruthers' dining table, Connie confirmed to herself that the youngest associate of Carruthers & Mullin, Financiers, was far and away the best-looking man in all of Chicago. She resented the dreary formal-dinner etiquette that seated her apart from her fiancé. Happily they'd soon be dining together, in their own beautifully appointed dining room, for the rest of their lives. She could hardly wait.

Between two tall flickering tapers, she caught Win's eye and smiled. He winked back and made a subtle thumbs-up gesture over the leg of lamb, signaling his approval. His wavy copper hair glinted under the glow from the chandelier. Her insides melted like warm butter. Oh, how she hoped all their children would be redheads!

"So, as I was saying," droned the gentleman seated at Connie's right, operating under the misguided assumption that she found his life story as fascinating as he did, "my maternal grandmother's side, the DeLacys, produced a four-star general, two state senators and a Supreme Court judge, and on my grandfather's side, the Von Hoffen-roods, ..." Connie stifled a yawn and toyed with her fork, being not as fond of lamb as Winston was.

To her left, Mr. Fitzwater Abercrombie gave new meaning to the term "silent partner," barely speaking a word throughout the interminable meal. Apparently his abundant fortune, neatly recorded on the books in Carruthers & Mullin's vault, did all the speaking required.

Of the thirty or so people seated around the table, the only other person besides her own fiancé who seemed even remotely interesting was that young lawyer—Connie'd forgotten his name—who'd recently traveled to Spain. As Connie and Winston planned to visit Spain as part of their honeymoon tour, Connie hoped to get some tips from the man on what to see and where to dine. But he was seated at the far end of the table, beyond shouting distance.

Connie chafed at her situation, marooned between two such dreary partners, but also understood that her husband-to-be was a rising star on LaSalle Street. He'd received two promotions within the past year at the investment bank. And she further understood that Winston's rising-star status meant that her future held countless client dinners much like this one. She may as well get used to them, to consider them as practice sessions for her hostessing skills, if nothing else. She'd long observed the way her mother charmed and flattered her father's clients with finesse. She understood the importance of making Winston look good to his boss, colleagues, and clients like Fitzwater Abercrombie and... and the other man, whose name slipped from her mind like syrup off a stack of pancakes. Mr. Waters? Mr. Winters?

Windbag, more likely. Mr. Pompous A. Windbag.

Connie snorted at her own private joke. A bit too loudly. Quickly she lifted her napkin and dabbed delicately at her lips as if suppressing a cough. She couldn't even glance at the gentleman to her left, lest she spasm into giggles. Would this dinner never end? Later in the evening she'd get her reward. She and Win would make their escape, scoot out of there, catch up to their friends at some noisy nightspot, and dance until dawn. But until then, she had to play the part of dutiful wife-to-be.

While Pompous Windbag paused in his discourse to chew a bite of lamb, Connie strained to hear what Win was saying to the bejeweled society matron seated next to him. She caught the words "Saint Lucian's" and "Drake Hotel" and knew they were discussing the wedding. How she wished they could swap dinner partners. She loved to talk about her wedding but suspected neither Pompous Windbag nor Fitzwater Abercrombie would appreciate the finer details of bridesmaids' frocks and table decorations.

At the head of the table, Mr. Carruthers stood, cleared his throat, and tapped a spoon against a crystal goblet.

"May I have your attention, please?"

Conversation hushed, and all heads turned his way.

"As you know, Carruthers & Mullin ended our fifteenth fiscal year on April thirtieth," he intoned. "And I'm pleased to share the news with all of you, our most loyal shareholders and longtime clients, that fiscal 1928 has been a banner year for our company. Never before in our history have profits and earnings been so high."

Excited murmurs and a smattering of applause broke out among the guests.

Mr. Carruthers grinned and lifted his hand for quiet. "We couldn't have achieved this success without the hard work of everyone on our staff. In particular, I'd like to recognize one young man who has worked above and beyond the call of duty." He reached down and picked up a small rectangular black box from next to his plate. "After only two short years with the firm, this employee has proved himself responsible and diligent and has singlehandedly brought in a higher share of new business than anyone in recent memory. On behalf of Carruthers & Mullin, as a token of our appreciation, I would like to present this commemorative fountain pen to Mr. Winston Sutherland."

The table broke out into enthusiastic applause. Connie thought her heart would burst. A beaming Winston stood and made his way to the head of the table, where he accepted the gift and pumped Mr. Carruthers' hand.

"Thank you. Thank you so much."

Connie watched his face as he talked, saw the glint in his eyes under the chandelier's glow. When Aunt Pearl had said "remember to sparkle," she could have been speaking about Win, but he didn't need any reminding. A thrill of pride ran up her spine. She knew that success at business meant everything to Winston. He worked hard and deserved this honor. And he played hard, too. Evenings, he took Connie dancing at jazz clubs across the city. He played polo, golfed, fished, and hunted. He had great and loyal friends. He was the perfect man for her, the perfect husband.

"Congratulations, Mr. Sutherland," Mr. Carruthers was saying. "Keep up the good work, and you're likely to become a full partner in the firm one day."

As Winston returned to his seat, he caught Connie's eye and grinned. She blew him a kiss.

Mr. Carruthers concluded his speech with a few more remarks about the strong state of business. His words barely registered with Connie in her pride over Winston's success. She could hardly wait until they were alone and she could tell him so.

❧ 5 ❦

Connie's opportunity to discuss all things bridal came after dessert, when the ladies trailed their hostess, Bertha Carruthers, into the adjoining drawing room. The gentlemen stayed behind at the table to smoke cigars, swap tall tales from the treacherous jungles of the financial district, and beat their starched-shirted chests. Winston winked at her as she passed, looking pleased as a peacock to be seated there among his senior colleagues, enjoying the attention.

The women gathered in small clusters throughout the large and elegantly appointed drawing room, exchanging pleasantries in low voices.

"I've been very eager to speak to you, Miss Shepherd," Bertha Carruthers said, motioning for Connie to sit next to her on a striped satin loveseat. A maid in a black dress and white apron circled the room with a tray, offering little glasses of sherry to the guests. The pesky little obstacle called Prohibition never seemed to affect the personal liquor cabinets of people as wealthy and influential as the Carruthers family. With her headache from the previous night still fresh in her memory, Connie recoiled internally from the tray, but in the circles in which she and her family moved, after-dinner sherry was the done thing. She accepted a glass to be polite, pretended to take a dainty sip, and seated herself on the sofa.

"As you've just heard, my Harrison is quite enthusiastic about your Winston's prospects with the firm," Mrs. Carruthers confided chummily. "He tells me your young man is every bit as talented a financier as his late father was."

"Oh, Winston is absolutely devoted to the firm." Connie's heart warmed at hearing such high praise of her man. As a founding partner of the firm, Harrison Carruthers's opinion mattered very much to Winston's career prospects. Connie might not have had much of a head for business, but she understood who the key players were, and Mr. Carruthers was the keyest of players.

"And we were both so delighted to receive an invitation to your wedding," the bespectacled matron continued, her voice taking on the fluttery tone that weddings seemed to bring out in some women. "We've not yet had the opportunity to dine at the Drake, but we hear it's 'all the rage,' as you young people say."

"I'm looking forward to it," Connie said with suitably modest understatement, "but there's still so much to be done. My list of tasks is a mile long."

"If you're anything like your mother, you'll zip through it in no time. She and I serve together on the hospital board, you know. I've never known such a champion at organizing charitable events." She made a sweeping gesture with her arm, silver bracelets jangling. "And your father, too, so clever at real estate. With all this new building and development going on, Chicago won't remain the 'second city' for long, will it? We'll soon be giving New York a run for its money."

"Yes, ma'am, we certainly will." *And Winston and his firm will be at the center of the boom.*

"Speaking of real estate development, Connie," brayed Sally Meade from her nearby perch on a brocade armchair, "have you had news from your parents? They're still in Flahrida, aren't they?" The way the older woman pronounced "Florida" grated on Connie's nerves, but she politely replied, "Yes, ma'am."

"I do hope your father's Flahrida interests are panning out. Real estate speculation can be such a dicey proposition, don't you think? I heard there's been trouble in the market."

Connie caught the note of condescension under the woman's casual remark. Since when were her father's business dealings any concern of Sally Meade's?

"They're expected home quite soon. I'll give my mother your regards," she answered brightly through clenched teeth. With a twinge of irritation, she suspected that Drusilla Sutherland, Winston's widowed mother and a bosom chum of Sally's, must have been gossiping about her family's affairs. Again.

Drusilla had moved to Boston to live with her sister after both had been widowed. Even so, she managed to keep her nose in everyone's business back in Chicago, thanks to Sally. Both women, from established and wealthy Chicago families, had made it plain that they considered the Shepherds to be inferior *nouveau riche* social climbers. They'd always cheerfully accepted Marcus Shepherd's generous financial support of their causes. And they'd been happy with Opal Shepherd's tireless work on their boards and committees, but they had never fully accepted them, a mere tailor's son and grocer's daughter, into their lofty social circle. Connie's father didn't care as long as they called on his real-estate expertise and rewarded him handsomely for it, which they did. But though Opal never complained, Connie sensed her mother cared deeply. And it hadn't helped matters any when Drusilla's son, Winston, had chosen Connie over Sally's daughter, Zoe, disappointing both mothers' marital ambitions.

The whole affair was silly. Winston, though he might have occasionally danced with Zoe at parties and proms after his return from back East, had never seriously considered her a potential marriage partner. If he had, Connie never would have dated him in the first place. She wasn't a man-stealer. As for Zoe, if she minded not landing Winston, she never let on. She was, in fact, to be one of Connie's bridesmaids. But her mother, Sally Meade, was a piece of work, as Connie's mother would say, and the prospect of having Drusilla Sutherland as a mother-in-law was enough to make a person take a large gulp of sherry. Too bad she didn't care for sherry.

To her relief, the drawing room door swung open, and the

gentlemen filed in, reeking of cigars. Pompous Windbag led the charge, pontificating loudly on some subject or other. Connie seized the momentary disruption to excuse herself from Mrs. Carruthers and make her way to Winston's side. He was speaking with the young lawyer, a tall man who looked to be in his late twenties. Win turned slightly at her approach.

"There you are, darling. Have you met Mr. Adam Deveare? Adam, my fiancée, Constance Shepherd."

"I haven't had the pleasure." Connie extended her hand. "How do you do, Mr. Deveare. Are you with Carruthers & Mullin?"

"No, ma'am." The man had a wide, pleasant smile that Connie found appealing.

"I thought you might recognize the name, darling," Winston said. "He's with Deveare and Associates, your father's law firm."

"Oh, *that* Deveare. Yes, Lloyd Deveare has represented my father for years."

Adam grinned. "Miss Shepherd. So you're Marcus Shepherd's kid?"

She laughed. "That's right. And it's Connie, please."

"Adam." He had a refreshing candor that blew the stuffiness straight out of Mrs. Carruthers's late-Victorian drawing room.

"Have you met my father?" Connie asked.

"I have, and he speaks very highly of you."

"Is that so? Well, I'm not surprised. After all, I am his favorite offspring," Connie teased. At Adam's raised eyebrow she added, "Of course I'm his *only* offspring."

He laughed, a hearty, non-lawyerly laugh that made her like him right away.

Winston broke in. "We understand you and your wife have recently returned from Spain."

"Just me, actually. I'm not married. But, yes, I had business to attend to in Barcelona."

"Would you mind telling us about your visit?" Winston said. "We're headed there ourselves in a few weeks and would love an insider's perspective on where to—"

All at once, from halfway across the room, Windbag's booming baritone drowned Winston out.

"I don't know what this world is coming to," he blustered. "At Easter break, our eldest daughter, Desdemona, came home from that blasted women's college and announced she wants to pursue a career in banking. Banking!" He thrust out his chin in defiance. "No question, I put my foot down. No daughter of mine will be getting a job in a bank."

"Can you imagine?" Mrs. Windbag bustled up like a disgruntled pigeon to stand beside her husband. "Our sweet darling girl, proposing to do such a daring thing?"

Connie had never been a crusader for women's rights. If anything, conversations and newspaper articles championing this or that cry for justice generally bored her. But something about the Windbags' outmoded attitudes, so firmly stated, raised her hackles. She tilted her head and asked in her most innocent voice, "Why shouldn't she? Has banking suddenly become a dishonorable profession?"

Several guests chuckled, as she'd meant them to. Across the room, Sally Meade's mouth tightened into a thin, hard line. Connie could imagine the story she was forming in her mind to tattle to Drusilla: *Do you know what your future daughter-in-law said to the Pompous Windbags?* Connie smiled. *Let her tattle.*

Mr. Windbag looked at her, surprised, then broke into a chortle. "I hope not, my dear, or else several men in this room will have crossed over to the dark side. I only mean that women shouldn't sully themselves by working in the business world. Especially pretty young women like my daughter. And you." His leering smile set Connie's teeth on edge.

"Besides, it injures women's health," Mrs. Windbag added, her indignation rising to match her husband's.

"What does?" Connie asked.

"Working in business All that wheeling and dealing. Most taxing on the"—Mrs. Windbag lowered her voice to a stage whisper— "the female constitution."

"More sherry, anyone?" Mrs. Carruthers bolted erect on the silk sofa and cleared her throat loudly, as if to say there would be no talk of female constitutions at *her* dinner party. "Gentlemen, you must be parched." She signaled to the maid, who made another round with the decanter and glasses.

"Well, I, for one, find the business world absolutely fascinating," Connie said. It was an outright lie, but she felt a sudden mischievous urge to shake up these stuffed shirts. Why shouldn't this Desdemona person work in a bank, if that was what she wanted? "Maybe the business world could use a few more women working in it, to balance things out."

Sally Meade looked appalled. "I'm sure what Miss Shepherd means is, she's excited about Winston's work and wants to learn all she can to support him in his career." She shot Connie a warning look.

An awkward murmur trembled through the room as guests affirmed the value of wifely support. It was true, of course. Connie had no more mind to pursue a career than to fly a rocket ship to the moon. Still, it irked her that they thought she couldn't do so, if she wanted to. As if there were something wrong with it. *Goodness, I'm starting to think like Aunt Pearl!*

Tired of holding the unwanted glass of sherry, she discreetly positioned herself next to a tall potted palm and poured the contents of the glass into the soil. As she did so, she noticed the young attorney, Adam Deveare, striving to suppress a smile. Indignation rose in her chest. What did *he* have to smile about? Was he laughing at her?

Determined to change the subject, she turned to him and forced the corners of her lips upward.

"Mr. Deveare was just about to tell us all about his trip to Spain," she prompted. "Do go on."

The young lawyer cleared his throat. "Ah, yes. You'd asked about Barcelona."

Ever the skilled hostess, Mrs. Carruthers deftly inserted a remark about an exhibit at the Prado she'd read about in a magazine. But despite the fact that she kept her gaze fixed on Adam as he offered his opinion, Connie's interest in the topic had flagged, along with her patience for stuffy dinner parties. She slipped her arm through Winston's and squeezed, signaling she was more than ready to leave.

When Adam had shared all he seemed inclined to, Winston took Connie's empty sherry glass and his own and set them on a tray.

"It sounds like a magical place," Connie said to Adam.

"It is. I hope you both have a wonderful time on your trip, and I hope to see you again. Perhaps you'll have occasion to accompany your father to our offices. If so, we'll all have lunch."

She couldn't imagine ever doing that, but smiled warmly. If she ever did need a lawyer, Adam Deveare seemed a good deal more fun than his staid father.

Winston steered her toward their hosts. "I'm afraid it's time we were going. Morning comes early."

Mr. Carruthers nodded his approval. "I appreciate a young man who's at his desk at nine o'clock sharp."

❧ 6 ❧

Minutes later, Connie snuggled into the leather seat of Winston's Nash sedan as he navigated traffic. At a stoplight, she said, "Let me see your new pen."

He reached inside his dinner jacket, pulled out the narrow box, and handed it to her. She lifted the dark blue-and-silver fountain pen and turned it over in her hands, admiring the way it gleamed in the light from the passing streetlamps. "It's a Waterford. And look, it's engraved. 'In gratitude from Carruthers & Mullin, Financiers.'" She smiled up at her fiancé's noble profile. "I'm so very proud of you."

"Aw, it's just their way of telling me I'd better not slack off," Win joked. Then he furrowed his brow slightly. "Darling, you had me worried there for a moment tonight."

She widened her eyes. "I did?"

"I feared you were about to spout a slogan and start campaigning for women's rights."

She tilted her head. "What do you mean?"

"All that talk about women becoming bankers and such. You were a bit—forthright."

"Oh, for heaven's sake." She replaced the pen in its box and snapped it shut. "I just don't see why the idea of Desdemona Windbag—"

"Winbeck."

Connie blinked. "What?"

"Their name is Winbeck." Win glanced at her and tried to suppress a grin—without success.

"Why does supporting the idea of Desdemona *Winbeck* working in a bank suddenly make me some kind of foaming-at-the-mouth radical?"

"It doesn't. But remember, these men are of an older generation. They're not used to all these newfangled ideas like women in the work-place. But, let's face it, some women simply aren't cut out for marriage and family life. I don't see why they shouldn't be allowed to find a place in the business world."

Connie sat back, appeased. "I wish more men felt as you did."

"I'm just glad you aren't one of those women."

She slid him a glance. "Why not?"

Winston shrugged. "Women like that are unfeminine."

Connie stared at him. "But what if it were me? What if I wanted to pursue a career like Desdemona?"

"You?" He started to chuckle, then stifled it when he saw the look on her face. "Then I doubt we'd be getting married, sweetheart. You wouldn't be the Connie Shepherd I know and love, who is too pretty and sensible to want a job in business. Besides, who would be left to run the household?"

"Why, the staff, of course."

"But somebody has to look after the staff."

They drove in silence for a while as Connie mulled this over. He was right. Wasn't he? The thought of pursuing a career in the business world had never crossed her mind before. So why was she arguing about it now? The whole topic was making her feel cross and off-balance.

"Darling," Win said calmly after several minutes. "In the future, perhaps it might be best if you didn't stir up such controversy at these professional events."

She sat back. "Me? I didn't stir up anything. Mr. Winbeck did. I merely offered my opinion."

"Still, it would have been better, I think, if you hadn't joined in."

Her brow furrowed. "I'm not allowed to have an opinion?"

"Of course you are," he soothed. "You can say anything you want to. To me. In private. Not to a room filled with men who hold my future in their hands—and who, it must be said, know a lot more about how the business world works than you do."

"I may not be a businesswoman, but I'm not a complete ninny," she sputtered. "I do pay attention to what's going on in the world."

"Now, darling, don't get in a lather. Nobody is calling you a ninny. You're quite clever, actually."

"I'm not in a lather." But for some reason, being called "quite clever" didn't land right, either. It sounded patronizing. Or maybe she was just tuckered out from her spirited defense of Desdemona Winbeck's right to stand on her feet all day in a teller's cage.

"All right," he said gently "Let's not argue." After a pause he added, "Say, George said everyone was planning to meet up at that new joint on Clark Street. They say the band is the gnat's eyebrows. Shall we try to catch up?"

She was on the verge of saying no because she was too tired and had a headache, both of which were true. But all at once the prospect of music and dancing made her energy surge, and she nodded.

"Sounds like the cat's meow."

7

After being granted admission by the bouncer at the door, Connie and Winston stood at the entrance to the dimly lit speakeasy tucked away in the basement of an Italian restaurant, where presumably prying eyes wouldn't find it. Through the haze of cigarette smoke, Connie scanned the sea of dancing couples until she spotted Gwendolyn Carpenter and Cyrilla Morgan seated with their husbands at a far table. Zoe Meade was there, too, her normally brown hair dyed a startling henna-red.

As they wove their way through the crowd, she felt her pep returning despite the late hour. It felt wonderfully refreshing to be among old friends, to let loose a little after the constrained atmosphere of the Carruthers's dinner party. Friends since grammar school, these women knew her better than anyone, apart from her own family.

The husbands clustered at one half of the table, the women at the other. Connie folded herself gracefully into the booth on the women's side while Winston sauntered over to shake hands with the men.

"Quick, girls, pour me a cup," she said, feigning exhaustion. "I'm absolutely parched."

Gwendolyn's pale, slender arm passed her a teacup containing something that was decidedly not tea. Connie sniffed it, wrinkled her nose, and handed it back.

"I mean *real* tea, not rotgut whiskey," she clarified.

"*Tea*-totaling tonight, are you?" Cyrilla quipped with a grin. Her auburn hair had been disciplined into stylish marcel waves all over her head.

"Last night's rum punch punched me in the gut," Connie admitted. "No alcohol for me tonight."

"How was the dinner party?" Zoe asked.

"Too many stuffed shirts and not quite enough chocolate tart." Connie stretched her arms overhead. "Winston received a commendation for his hard work. They gave him a lovely pen."

"To sign more lucrative deals with, no doubt." Gwen said. Light from the wall sconce over their heads glinted off the honey-brown waves of her hair.

"He's certainly good at what he does," Cyrilla chimed in. "He talked my husband into making quite a sizeable investment. I must admit, it made me nervous at first. But so far the returns have been handsome, so"—she lifted her teacup—"to Winston."

All the ladies clinked their teacups together and said in unison, "To Winston."

Connie glanced to see if her intended had noticed the toast in his honor, but he was saying something to George Carpenter, shouting in his ear to be heard over the blare of the music.

"How are the arrangements coming?" Zoe asked, tapping her cigarette against an ashtray. "Are you all set to walk down the aisle to eternal wedded bliss?"

Connie ignored her bored tone and sat forward. "I met with the Drake's caterer yesterday to go over the menu. How many times do I have to say 'no smoked salmon'? I don't care if Gloria Swanson just served it at her umpteenth wedding. Salmon gives me hives."

"Sounds fishy to me." Cyrilla lifted a sardonic eyebrow.

Gwendolyn pushed out a laugh as Connie groaned in mock despair.

"There, there, dear. Help is on the way. We've just ordered a fresh bottle of champagne," Gwendolyn said in her usual take-charge manner.

"None for me," Connie said. "I'll get a headache."

"I'll have hers." Zoe helped herself to a canapé from a tray in the middle of the table.

"Careful, darling," Gwendolyn warned. "That bridesmaid's gown has to fit perfectly in a few weeks."

With a reluctant sigh Zoe set the canapé on the edge of her saucer and pushed the saucer aside.

"Don't waste it. I'll take it." Connie, the proud possessor of a fashionably boyish figure, reached for the cracker. Zoe gave her a dark look. "You're so lucky. You can eat whatever you want and not gain an ounce."

Connie shrugged. "For now, anyway."

"I'm so excited you chose the Drake for your reception." Gwen's crystal drop earrings sparkled whenever she moved her head. "Everyone's been all abuzz about it ever since the *Trib* ran your engagement announcement."

"Oh, that," Connie groaned. "Could that photo of me have been any more gruesome?"

"Oh, stop it with the false modesty," Zoe grumbled. "You've never taken a bad photograph and you know it."

Before Connie could form a retort, Gwendolyn broke in. "You've never looked lovelier."

Connie smiled her thanks. She didn't know what was making Zoe so prickly tonight, but whatever it was, she hoped her friend would get over it soon.

Zoe pulled a lipstick from her small beaded handbag then shut the bag with a snap. "I must say, you seem awfully calm for someone who's getting shackled soon. If it were me, I'd be nervous as a cat." She formed an "o" with her lips and carefully applied the lipstick, using the blade of a butter knife as a mirror.

"Not me," Gwen exclaimed. "I'd be over the moon—if I weren't already happily married to George, of course," she added quickly. "That adorable new house ..." She turned to Zoe. "Have you seen the house yet? Cutest little fairy-tale cottage you ever did see."

Cyrilla snorted. "Fairy-tale cottage with five bedrooms."

Zoe gave an unimpressed shrug. "It's nice enough, but it's way out in the suburbs. Awfully far away from everything."

"For goodness' sake, Zoe, it isn't Planet Mars," Gwendolyn said. "The commuter train goes straight there, and besides, anyone who's anyone has an automobile these days."

Zoe responded by helping herself to another canapé from the tray, and this time she didn't set it aside but took a defiant chomp.

Gwendolyn wound her long necklace of topaz beads around her fingers. "Has Julia Harper responded to the invitation yet, Con? I haven't seen her since graduation, and it would be wonderful to catch up."

"I don't know," Connie said. "I'll have to check the guest list. I'm sure Mother's been keeping track."

Cyrilla grinned. "Ah, Julia." The table went quiet as each woman conjured up a memory of the infamous Julia Harper. Julia chain-smoking cigarettes and, worse, blowing smoke rings. Julia sneaking out to unapproved dances, where she shimmied in a way no product of the Rockingham School for Girls should shimmy. Julia teaching the other girls how to coax lip rouge into the fashionable bee-stung shape, when the housemother was nowhere around.

Zoe's mouth jerked to one side, drawing out a momentary resemblance to said housemother. "She was forever getting into mischief, but for some reason she always seemed to escape punishment. A gentle slap on the wrist, if anything."

"And how!" Gwen concurred. "If it had been one of us caught smoking behind the gymnasium, you'd better believe our parents would have been summoned. Or worse."

"I think the dean was a little scared of her," Connie said.

"Whatever happened to dear Julia?" Zoe asked.

"I don't know. I'm not sure where she's living now but I sent her an invitation via her parents. I'm sure she'll come if she can."

"Perhaps she's in Paris, pursuing modern dance or whatnot," Cyrilla said.

"That sounds like something Julia might do," Gwen said. "She was always three steps ahead of the rest of us. I figured she'd end up in

Greenwich Village or someplace, among all those bohemian free-love people."

"Anyway, I hope she got the invitation," Connie said. "It's hard to keep track of all the details. My brain feels ready to explode."

"At least you have your bridesmaids well in hand," Cyrilla soothed. "We're all set to float down the aisle, graceful as swans." She slipped Zoe a sidelong glance.

Zoe released a delicate burp. "Wouldn't it be refreshing to talk about something else for a change? No offense, Con, but if I hear one more word about gowns or caterers, I'm going to scream. We've been talking about this wedding for months."

"Just as we talked about my wedding and Cyrilla's wedding for months." Gwendolyn tapped her brown Turkish cigarette over an ashtray. "Your turn will come."

Zoe's mouth set in a thin line.

"In any case" Connie said briskly, "Zoe is right. Let's talk about something else."

"Right you are," Gwen said. "What say we grab those men of ours and dance?"

"I'm going to powder my nose." Zoe set off in the direction of the ladies' room.

Connie touched Gwen's elbow. "What's with Zoe tonight? She seems a bit snappish."

"She's always been jealous of you, ever since we were tykes. Probably even worse now that you've landed the catch of the season."

Connie laughed. "Oh, surely not."

Gwen's eyes widened. "Sure! Don't you remember how she used to imitate you in school? She'd buy the same dresses as you, joined the same clubs. She even liked Winston for a time, remember? And tonight she's sniping at you for every little thing."

"So it's not just my imagination." She paused. "But we've all outgrown those childish rivalries, haven't we? Besides, according to Winston, they're just pals. Practically grew up in each other's shadow, before Win went off to boarding school."

"That doesn't mean she didn't have her jaunty beret set for him, before you came along."

"Oh, applesauce—" Connie started to say, but Gwen hushed her as Zoe rejoined them.

"You two ought to see the ladies' room," she announced. "They've redecorated it. It's gorgeous. Except the flowery scent they're using is overpowering." She threw a glance at Connie. "Not unlike your perfume."

"Let's dance," Gwendolyn suggested quickly before Connie had time to take offense.

By the time Connie dragged Winston out onto the dance floor, he was leaning on her a bit too heavily.

"Win, you're listing to starboard," she hissed.

"I'm the greatesht invesshtment banker Cruthers 'n' Mullin have ever ssseen," he slurred drunkenly into her ear.

"I'm sure you are, darling." Perhaps he'd consumed more sherry at the Carruthers's than she'd realized.

"We're gonna be ssso rich. Sssooooo rich."

She patted his shoulder and tried to get him to stand up straight. "We're already rich, darling. Say, why don't we sit this one out?"

"Lesss celebrate."

"We are celebrating." She gently turned him about-face and eased him back to their table. When George and Gwendolyn also returned to the table, out of breath and with faces flushed from dancing, Connie confided, "Win's in no condition to drive. Would you mind giving us a lift home on your way?"

"Happy to," George said. But at least another hour passed before he and Gwen were ready to leave, an hour in which Connie had to prop Winston up and poke him now and then to keep him awake. *Some celebration*, she thought darkly.

At last they called it a night and said good-bye to their friends. George poured Winston into the backseat of his Chrysler, and Connie slid in beside him. To cover her embarrassment, she conversed brightly with Gwen about nothing of any importance as they drove across the dark city.

George pulled the car up to the entrance to Connie's apartment building on Astor Street. He parked next to the curb, stepped out, and came around to open her door. She glanced at Winston, snoring in the other corner of the backseat, dead to the world. Clearly there was no point in telling him good-night.

"I don't understand it. Winston drinks all the time when we go out, but I've never seen him get like this," she muttered in apology.

Gwen swiveled around from the front seat and reached over to touch Connie's arm.

"I know, sweetie. It must have been all the excitement, the commendation and everything. Plus, he probably mixed a few different liquors over the course of the evening. That can be hard on the old innards."

"I'm so embarrassed. He will be, too, when he sobers up."

Gwen laughed lightly. "Don't be. I could tell you many a story about times George has had a little too much. Don't worry about Win," she added. "He'll sleep it off at our place, and George will take him back to fetch his car in the morning."

"Thanks. Well, good night."

Connie forced a smile, but inside she burned with humiliation. All their friends enjoyed drinking cocktails. So would she, if they didn't make her ill. After this morning's headache, she knew her limits. But she'd never before seen Winston this affected. Three sheets to the wind and all those other ugly phrases used to describe drunkenness scrolled through her mind. How many times had her father mentioned that one mark of a true gentleman was his ability to hold his liquor?

She thanked George and Gwen again and swept into the marbled lobby. After greeting the night doorman, she sought the comforting enclosure of the elevator. She entered the apartment quietly out of habit, then remembered her parents still were out of town. Quickly she flipped on the lights, revealing the luxurious, perfectly appointed living room that reflected her mother's taste down to the last Miessen vase. The apartment looked like something out of a magazine but always felt empty and cold when her parents were away, as they often were. She didn't much like staying there alone with only the servants for company, preferring to go out with her friends as much as possible.

As she walked down the hallway toward her room, she rationalized Winston's behavior. The liquor wasn't the problem. Everybody in their crowd drank liquor. Her own father and mother drank liquor. But she couldn't shake the fact that, if she knew, Aunt Pearl would surely disapprove. The thought made her cringe. She loved Aunt Pearl and hated to think she was letting her down by marrying Win. But marry him she would. He was intelligent, charming, good-looking, and treated her like a princess. Most of the time. She wasn't going to let this one night of overindulgence spoil her dream. Getting drunk wasn't characteristic of Winston, and he'd surely regret it in the morning.

Yawning, she changed into a silky peach-colored gown, robe, and slippers and padded into her bathroom. As she reached for the jar of cold cream, she gasped to see her reflection in the vanity mirror. Gingerly she touched her sunburned nose, glowing bright red like a circus clown's even through her face powder. *Hell's bells.* Had she looked like that all evening? What must everyone have thought? What had she been thinking, driving all the way out to the farm that afternoon on a sunny day with the top down? Goodness, why hadn't one of her friends said something? Now her nose would flake and peel and she would look ghastly in her wedding photos.

With rising panic, she searched the medicine cabinet for first-aid salve but found none. Maybe her mother had some. Passing through the bedroom, she caught sight of the argyle skirt she'd earlier tossed onto a chair. She remembered Aunt Pearl's tonic. She reached into the pocket of the skirt and fished out the little vial.

Back in the bathroom, she opened it and took a sniff. The fragrance was pleasantly spicy, almost woodsy.

"What harm could it do?" she said to her reflection, feeling reckless. "It's not Elizabeth Arden, but if it's good enough for Edison the cat, it's good enough for me."

She smoothed cold cream onto her face and wiped it off with a tissue to remove her make-up. Then, she picked up the vial, spilled a few drops onto a cotton ball, and dabbed it on her nose. The solution felt cool and soothing, and the redness started to fade almost immediately. *Well, I'll be.* She gave her reflection a critical look. *I guess if my nose is still attached to my face in the morning, then Aunt Pearl may have come up with a winner this time after all.*

She crawled into bed with a firm resolve not to worry any more about Winston. He'd simply over-imbibed, that was all. He'd spend the night safely at Gwen and George's house and face the morning a little worse for wear. He'd be embarrassed, would apologize profusely, and soon the whole incident would be forgotten. With that, she put the whole issue out of her mind.

But in the moments just before sleep, Aunt Pearl's words swirled through her head. *Are you sure he's the right man for you?* Was her aunt on to something? Or were hers just the words of a lonely widow who regretted her own choices in life?

8

A few days later, Connie and her bridesmaids gathered at Marshall Field for a final fitting of their gowns, followed by a chatter-filled lunch in the Walnut Room. Then Connie drove back alone to Astor Street. She turned into the circular drive in front of the apartment building and left the Hudson for the building's valet to park in the garage. When she entered her family's apartment, she nearly tripped over a towering heap of tan leather luggage lining the black-and-white tiled front hall. At last her parents were home!

"My darling girl! There you are." Her mother, dressed in a chic lilac jersey traveling suit, sailed forth and greeted Connie with a kiss on the cheek. She returned the embrace and inhaled a reassuring whiff of her mother's Mitsouko perfume.

"Welcome home, Mother. And right on time, too. I don't think I could have held out a minute longer. How was the trip?"

The older woman waved her hand as if clearing the air of a bad memory. "Horrible traffic on the Dixie Highway south of town. We should have accepted Lloyd Deveare's offer to fly us up in his firm's aeroplane. But you know how skittish your father is about flying." She linked arms with her daughter and drew her toward the sitting room.

Connie glanced around. "Where is Daddy now?"

49

"He headed straight for the office as soon as we arrived." Mother glanced heavenward. "You know how he is." She tugged the silken rope against the wall that signaled the kitchen to send up tea.

"Yes." Connie nodded, swallowing back disappointment that her father hadn't delayed checking in at the office until he'd greeted his only daughter. "Winston is the same way, especially now that he's trying so hard to make a good impression on Mr. Carruthers. Business comes first."

"Your Winston is an ambitious young man, and there's nothing wrong with that." They seated themselves on a blue tufted silk sofa. "You'd do well to make friends with Mrs. Carruthers. She's the type of woman who can open doors for you."

"I do think we made a good impression," Connie said. "Thankfully, we left before Winston ..." She paused and bit her lip.

"Before Winston what, darling?"

Connie hesitated. Her mother thought the world of Winston, and Connie didn't want to tarnish his image in the eyes of her parents.

"Nothing. Just something silly. It's just that he ... he had too much to drink the other night. He couldn't drive home and had to spend the night at Gwen and George's."

Her mother's penciled brows lifted, and for a moment Connie panicked. Had she said too much? Broken her mother's trust of Winston? But then the older woman smiled. "Is that all? Well, darling, I suppose a man can be silly once in a while when he's celebrating such a grand achievement. It's not like he makes a habit of it." Her mother patted her hand. "It's natural for you to feel a little on edge, this close to the big day. Now, tell me what else has been going on. I want to hear all about everything. We've time before dinner to have a quick chat."

"You chat, I'll listen," Connie replied. She leaned back against the cushion, relieved to no longer have to worry about Winston and his drinking. If her mother said it was all right, then it was. "I've been chatting all afternoon. Dress fitting and lunch. You'll be happy to know the gown fits perfectly."

"Oh, lovely. And the girls?"

"They're all set." She paused to gather her thoughts. "I must say, though, Zoe Meade seems a little, well, off her feed."

"In what way?"

"She's been acting quite spiky toward me lately. I almost regret asking her to be a bridesmaid. It's just that we were school chums for so long, and I couldn't very well invite Cyrilla and Gwen without including Zoe too."

"Be patient with Zoe, dear," Mother counseled. "Piles of money, to be sure, but she simply hasn't grown up with the advantages you've had in other ways. She's rather plain, poor thing, and her father was a gambler and her mother must be a trial to live with, I'm sure. I'm afraid poor Zoe hasn't had the most stable of upbringings." She reached for the teapot on a side table, which the maid had delivered a moment before. "And Winston's mother? Have you received any word from her?"

"Only that she'll be arriving two days before the wedding and staying with the Meades."

Her mother was silent for a moment, then said, "I know you're not particularly fond of Drusilla, sweetheart. But getting along with your mother-in-law is even more important than making a good impression on people like the Carruthers."

Connie examined her lacquered fingernails. "I know that."

"No matter what happens with Drusilla, you will try, won't you? She's a lonely woman since her husband died. And her opinion still holds sway here in Chicago, even though she's living in Boston now."

"Of course."

Mother patted Connie's knee. "That's my girl. And thank you again for looking after Aunt Pearl." She shook her head. "All that to-do over nothing. My sister is a dear, but no more eccentric creature ever existed."

"I don't know about that," Connie said. "I think she's a marvel."

"You would. You're so much like her, in some ways."

Connie cocked her head. "In what ways?"

Her mother fluttered a manicured hand. "Oh, I don't know. The way you both disregard convention when it suits you. The way you go your own way without a care about what others think."

"I care," Connie replied defensively. "Just not as much as you do, maybe."

Her mother stood. "Well, you don't get anywhere in this world without making the right people happy. And now, my darling girl, I'm going to change out of these traveling clothes and have a nice, hot bath while you relax. I'm certain your father will be home for dinner and you can have a good chat with him then."

As her mother swept out of the sitting room, Connie thought about what she'd said. Was pleasing people really the key to getting along in the world? And did "people" necessarily include Drusilla?

❧ 9 ❧

On the first Saturday in June, Connie appeared through the large wooden doors at the back of the sanctuary at St. Lucian's, one glove-encased hand linked through her father's arm. Her gown of white *peau de soie* was cut in the latest style with a straight bodice, a low waist, and a modern knee-length skirt that caused an excited gasp to ripple through the congregation. The lace-edged scoop neckline revealed her one touch of tradition: a string of pearls that had once belonged to Great-Grandmother Shepherd. The train flowed a silky white river behind her. An elaborately beaded band placed low on her forehead anchored a long veil of embroidered chiffon.

At the chancel gate, Winston stood with his groomsmen, all handsome and dignified in gray morning coats and striped trousers. If the lot of them had spent the previous night carousing until dawn, as some stag parties were reputed to do, Connie couldn't tell. Her heart nearly burst with happiness as her father transferred her hand from his arm to Winston's.

The ceremony passed in a dreamlike blur. Two hours later, standing at the base of the blue-carpeted staircase in the Drake Hotel lobby, Connie lifted her head in what she imagined was a regal position, dropped her shoulders, and pulled in her midsection, all the while smiling until she thought her face would crack. One arm looped gracefully through Win's. The other ached under the weight of her cascading bouquet of white roses and gardenias. Who knew flowers could be so darn heavy?

"Perfect. Hold it right there." The photographer thrust his head under the black curtain and lifted the flash tray in one hand. With a flash and a bang and a puff of powder, the camera captured the image of the radiant bride and groom. When the photographer emerged from under the black curtain and gave her the thumbs-up, she relaxed. Winston rubbed his jaw.

"I think that's enough for the time being," the photographer said. "I'll shuffle all this equipment and meet you upstairs."

Sighing with relief, Connie cast a weary smile at Winston. She hoisted the bouquet in one hand and lifted her train with the other. Taking their time, they headed up the staircase to the second floor.

The high-ceilinged ballroom was packed pillar to post with the cream of Chicago society. An orchestra played light, buoyant dinner music that suited Connie's mood as she and Winston inched toward the head table, pausing to greet guests as they went. When Winston was waylaid by a gentleman she didn't know who seemed eager to discuss business, he shot her a look of apology. She continued ahead, eager to get off her feet. Once seated, she took a long sip from a goblet of ice water. The liquid felt soothing on her parched throat.

Moments later, Connie's new mother-in-law approached the table.

"May I?" Drusilla took the empty seat next to Connie. "You look lovely, my dear. As always."

"Thank you."

Drusilla sighed. "It's easy enough to get married. The trick now is to stay married."

Connie prickled with annoyance at Drusilla's patronizing tone and scrambled to say something positive. "Thank you for the wedding gift, Mother Sutherland. It was very generous of you."

Drusilla had paid the down payment on their new suburban home. Now she waved a hand as if brushing away the gratitude. "It was the least I could do to help my son and his bride get off on some kind of solid footing." Her words landed as a criticism, though Connie immediately regretted the thought. At least Drusilla was making an effort to be kind.

Her new mother-in-law continued. "I do hope you're not terribly disappointed that I've decided to live in Boston for the time being, even though my son assured me I would be most welcome to live in his home." She paused, her gaze fixed fishlike on Connie's face. Connie took care to keep her expression absolutely neutral, even though her insides spasmed at the thought of having Drusilla come and live with her and Winston. He'd never even mentioned such a possibility. "I'm sure he explained to you that my sister relies on my companionship and has requested I stay on with her. And now that Winston's dear father has passed on, there isn't much left here in Chicago for an old woman like me." She coughed delicately.

"I do understand," Connie said evenly. "Surely you'll come for a visit, once all the decorating is finished. It's such a mess now, plasterers and painters everywhere."

"I wouldn't dream of imposing on newlyweds," Drusilla said airily. "You'll have enough trouble to contend with without a mother-in-law installed in the guest room."

Connie watched as Drusilla returned to her own table. What did she mean by 'trouble'?

When Winston returned with glasses of fruit punch, spiked no doubt with the contents of the flask in his vest pocket, Connie said lightly, "Darling, your mother just said the most extraordinary thing."

Win smirked. "That doesn't surprise me. What'd she say now?"

"That she hoped I wasn't disappointed that she'd chosen to live with her sister in Boston instead of with us."

"That's good news, isn't it? The house all to ourselves?"

Blood rushed to Connie's head. "I didn't realize her living with us was even a possibility." She paused to gather her thoughts. "What if she'd said yes? What if she'd taken you up on your offer?"

Win's jaw tightened. "What if she had? We've plenty of room."

"Yes, but you didn't talk to me about it first."

He blinked. "It never occurred to me that you'd mind."

"Mind? Of course I'd mind."

He glanced around the ballroom teeming with guests. "Sweetheart, I don't think now is the time—"

"Now is the perfect time."

His expression remained neutral. "Oh, come now. Would it really be so horrible? After all, she is a widow, and I am her only son. It wouldn't be that unusual an arrangement. Lots of families do it."

"But why us? It's not as if she's destitute. She has scads of money." Even as she said it, she felt mean-spirited and cold-hearted. But she had never been very good at hiding her true feelings.

"Money has nothing to do with it," Winston said. "My father did leave her well provided for. She just hates living alone. Why do you think she travels so much and lives with her sister between trips?"

Connie swallowed. A fog settled over her brain as she struggled for words. "I don't want to sound unkind. I do feel for her. Really, I do. But I ... Well, I don't think you should have made such an important decision without talking it over with me first."

His voice remained steady. "I'm sorry. Of course if you object, then it's out of the question."

"Really?" All at once a healthy dose of guilt gushed in alongside the relief.

"Really." Winston slid a hand under her chin and lifted it for a kiss. "You're my wife now. You come first."

Connie sighed. "It's—it's not that I don't like your mother." *Yes, it is,* her conscience whispered. *She's never been anything but rude to you.* "It's just that she's so very ... so very ..."

"No need to explain. Mother can be a handful. She's quite strong-willed."

That's one way of putting it. "Thank you for understanding. I hope you're not angry with me."

"Angry? I could never be angry with you."

Connie melted into the reassurance of his kiss. She didn't want to start out married life at odds with her mother-in-law. But neither did she want to share her home with a harpy like Drusilla.

"Excuse me, you lovebirds." Gwendolyn collapsed in her chair with a swish of pink silk moiré. "Don't let me interrupt."

Winston grinned. "We won't."

She leaned toward Connie with a conspiratorial grin.

"Did you see who's here?"

Connie swept the air with her hand. "Gwen, in case you haven't noticed, there are five hundred people here."

Gwen's eyes widened. "Table eight. Julia Harper!"

Connie gasped. "Julia came? Oh, how wonderful. I must go say hello." She stood. "Excuse us, darling. There's an old school friend I must say hello to."

Gwen stood too. "Wait for me. I can't wait to hear what mischief she's been up to."

Winston lifted his glass in their direction. "Cheers!"

"Come on." Gwen grasped Connie's hand and pulled her through the crowd. "You won't believe it."

"Won't believe what?"

"You'll see."

As they crossed the room, Connie searched the crowd for a flamboyantly dressed flapper, probably sporting some outrageous hairpiece or, even better, a feather boa, maybe with a long cigarette holder in her fingers. The Julia she'd known in school liked to dress for attention.

Instead, as they approached table eight, she saw a plain-looking woman sitting alone, sipping—or rather gulping—a glass of water.

Gwen stopped and said with a note of triumph, "Connie, darling, you remember our old friend, Julia Harper."

Connie blinked in surprise. "Julia?"

The woman before her bore little resemblance to the Julia Harper of yore. She wore a sturdy light-blue cotton dress more suited to an outing of the Camp Fire Girls than a fashionable wedding. Her hair was shorn in a no-nonsense bob, her face scrubbed clean of make-up.

She stood. "Connie! Congratulations, dear!" She pulled Connie into an enthusiastic hug. "Sorry I'm late. Had to stop and patch a flat."

Connie gasped. "On your car?"

"On my bicycle."

So, the devil-may-care prankster of their school days was still on an unconventional path—just in an unexpected way. Connie recovered quickly.

"Julia! So glad you could make it. Let's sit a moment and get caught up. Tell me what you've been up to."

Gwen excused herself. Connie signaled, and a waiter brought a tray of punch cups. Julia downed hers in two gulps and grabbed another one.

"I barely scraped through the Rockingham School by the skin of my teeth," she said cheerfully. "My parents were at their wits' end, practically locked me in the house to keep me from getting into more trouble. But the summer after graduation, they let me enroll in a painting class at the Art Institute to give me something constructive to do. Wouldn't you know, I loved it. I buckled down, worked hard, and at the end of the summer, I transferred to the university."

"So, you're still a student?"

Julia nodded, spearing a pickle with her fork. "And a teaching assistant. Probably be there the rest of my life. I love university life, though I suppose I've become a bit of a bluestocking."

That explained the get-up. And the bicycle.

"And how about you, Connie. What are you doing these days?"

"Well, I'm married. Obviously."

They shared a laugh. Then Julia said, "And what do you do?"

Connie paused. Hadn't she just answered that question? "Well ... besides the wedding, we're settling into our new home." Pause. "My husband's in investments."

"That's nice. But what do *you* do?"

"Me?" Connie wasn't sure what Julia was asking. She was Win's wife. Wasn't that enough?

Apparently not. "Haven't you some community involvement? Some career? Some cause you feel strongly about?"

"Oh. Sure." Connie's mind flitted over the various clubs and committees her mother was so deeply involved in. Mother had urged her to get involved, too, but Connie hadn't followed up with any of them. "Well," she said falteringly, feeling put on the spot, "one has only so much time."

Julia nodded. "You know, since you and your friends have time on your hands, we could use help at the women's betterment society. In July we celebrated the eightieth anniversary of the first Women's

Rights Convention at Seneca Falls. Now we need to follow up with the ladies who attended the anniversary party. Mailings to be stuffed, events to be organized, that sort of thing. Sounds right up your alley, if you like organizing parties."

"Oh, I don't think so," Connie hedged. "I'm awfully busy."

Julia pursed her lips. "Well, if you ever tire of tea and shopping, let me know. Here's my card."

Connie thanked her and slipped the card into her white beaded bag.

Gwen returned and touched Connie's shoulder. "Time to go back to our places. Dinner's about to be served." As they made their way back to the head table, Connie murmured, "I would never have recognized her if you hadn't pointed her out."

"If dressing like a Boy Scout is what it takes to be taken seriously in life," Gwen replied firmly, "then I'll stay frivolous, thank you very much."

❧ 10 ❧

While their guests feasted on roast duck and caviar, Connie and Winston barely ate a bite, thanks to a steady stream of interruptions by well-wishes and the photographer. In the excitement Connie didn't have much of an appetite, anyway. After dinner, the orchestra swung into a waltz.

"I believe this is our dance." Her father smiled and extended his hand to Connie. She took it and followed him onto the parquet dance floor.

"You look incredible," he murmured as he swept her into the waltz.

"Thank you, Daddy." She smiled up at him as he spun her around in a turn.

"Happy?"

"Happy."

"I'm so proud of my little girl."

A lump formed in her throat. Caught up in building his business, her father hadn't had much time to play with her or spend time with her as she was growing up. To finally have his undivided attention on the very day she'd be leaving his home felt bittersweet. She savored the moment.

Her father relinquished her to the arms of her groom, and the room fell away as they waltzed dreamily around the dance floor. All too soon, the best man, George Carpenter, cut in. For the rest of the afternoon, Connie whirled from gentleman to gentleman, and back to Winston in between. When she didn't think she could dance another step, she relaxed into Winston's arms. His coppery hair shone in the soft glow of the chandelier.

"Isn't it about time for us to say our good-byes?" he murmured.

"Silly. We have to cut the cake first. And I have to toss my bouquet."

"Well, let's get cracking," he said with mild impatience. "Shall I tell the staff we're ready for the cake?"

"You go tell them," Connie said. "I need a moment to catch my breath."

She kissed him on the cheek and headed for the balcony.

The tall French doors leading to the balcony stood wide open on the glorious June afternoon. She stepped out and drew a deep breath, savoring a few minutes alone. In the distance, Lake Michigan sparkled in the lowering sun. Chicago always looked its best on a clear, early summer day, and while she eagerly anticipated their honeymoon in Europe, she couldn't think of any place in the world she'd rather live.

"There you are." Her brief moment of respite was cut short by her mother scurrying forth in a froth of salmon-colored tulle. "What in the world are you doing out here, all by yourself? You mustn't neglect your guests."

"I'm not. I just needed a breath of fresh air."

"You'll have plenty of time to breathe after everyone's gone home. Come now."

With a sigh, Connie turned to follow her mother back into the reception.

"Oh, Connie." Aunt Pearl burst through the French doors wearing her best dress, a mint-green organza and a matching flowered hat and gloves. The ensemble was charming, if slightly out of date—not unlike Pearl herself. "Darling, I'm so glad I caught you alone. I wanted to speak to you in person."

"She's not alone, Pearl," Mother said in an exasperated tone. "She has a roomful of guests to attend to. Can't this wait?"

Pearl smiled apologetically at her sister. "This will only take a moment. I promise."

"I'll be right in, Mother."

Her mother pursed her lips. "You two! Mind you don't linger out here all day."

Connie promised. When Mother had gone back inside, she bent to embrace her aunt, who kissed her on the cheek. Then, Pearl drew a white envelope from her small green handbag.

"Here's a little something for you, dear," she said quietly. "If you don't mind, I'd like you to open it now instead of waiting until later, so I can explain it."

"Oh, you're sweet." Connie took the envelope and lifted the flap. Inside was a card decorated with wedding bells, and within the card was a folded slip of paper. At first Connie assumed it was a check, but closer inspection revealed a page of notes written in Pearl's spidery handwriting. Puzzled, she glanced at her aunt.

"What's this?"

Aunt Pearl lowered her voice, even though they were the only two on the balcony. She whispered confidentially, "It's the formula for Feline De-Flaker."

"The formula?" Connie stared at the paper, confused. "But I don't understand. Why are you giving it to me?"

"It's your wedding gift."

"I see that, but—"

Pearl leaned closer, her expression serious. "I was praying to our Lord about you last night, and the idea came to me to give it to you."

"Divine inspiration?"

Pearl's eyes grew wide. "I couldn't say for sure," she whispered. "But it was quite a coincidence, don't you think? The idea coming to me right in the middle of my prayer?"

Connie fought back a grin. "That is quite a coincidence. Well, thank you for the formula."

"Not just any formula. Feline De-Flaker. The message was very specific."

Connie didn't know whether to laugh or to question her aunt's sanity. "Was it? You had a vision to give me a formula for curing cat dandruff?"

Pearl waved a hand. "It sounds ludicrous, I know. But I think—I think this formula is much more important than it seems. I don't know why." She glanced upward. "But He does. He's a Lord of infinite wisdom, our ever-present help in times of trouble."

A shiver tickled Connie's spine. Twice in one day—her wedding day, of all days—people had mentioned the possibility of trouble. She was glad she wasn't the type of person to believe in omens.

"Thank you." She examined the paper. "I—I don't know what to say," she added truthfully.

Pearl grinned proudly. "You keep it somewhere safe."

Connie glanced up. "But this isn't your only copy, is it?"

Pearl shook her head. "Oh, no. I kept a copy back in the laboratory." Her eyes sparkled. "After all, I have to keep turning out batches for the Hoosier Grove sheriff. He can't seem to get enough of it. Obviously, I haven't told him it was initially developed for cats." She stood proudly, as tall as five-feet-one would allow. "Of course, I'm also giving you that china gravy boat that belonged to Grandma Heloise. As a wedding gift, that should be conventional enough to satisfy even your mother. And you used to admire it so when you were a little girl. But this"—she tapped the paper in Connie's hand—"this is just for you. A girl should always have something to fall back on. You never know when it might come in handy."

Though Connie could not imagine a time or circumstance when she'd need to mix up a batch of Feline De-Flaker, the realization that her aunt was concerned about her well-being warmed her heart. "I'll keep it safe," she promised. She folded the slip of paper, slipped it back into the card, and slid the envelope into her white beaded bag. Arms linked, aunt and niece together walked back into the party.

After all the cake-cutting and bouquet-tossing, the bridal party stepped out onto the sidewalk to find the sky had darkened. A strong wind whipped the waves of Lake Michigan into a seething mass of whitecaps. Laughing, Connie snatched at her veil, which threatened to blow away down the street. Then, amid a shower of rice and good wishes, she and Winston rode off to begin their new life together, oblivious to the thunder rumbling in the distance.

❧ 11 ❧

Two months later, after the new Mr. and Mrs. Sutherland had returned from their honeymoon trip to Spain and the south of France, Connie, her mother, and Gwendolyn spent a slow August afternoon seated around the long dining table in Connie's new home. All the mullioned casement windows had been cranked open to catch whatever breeze was available, and an electric fan whirred on the sideboard. At one end of table, and on the carpeted floor around it, sat piles of wedding gifts. In assembly-line fashion, Connie penned thank-you notes to her wedding guests while her mother pronounced each gift and its sender and Gwendolyn stamped and sealed the envelopes.

Mother picked up a square box, lifted the lid, and gasped.

"Oh, my word."

Connie glanced up from the note she was signing. "What is it?"

Her mother put her fingers to her lips to stifle a giggle. "You tell me." Gingerly she lifted a grotesque, grimacing ceremonial mask from the box.

Gwendolyn laughed out loud. Connie joined her.

"I'll bet it's from Aunt Ruby," Connie said. "She's always finding strange things overseas."

Mother checked the enclosed card. "No, it's from Lizzie Quick. Something she picked up on one of her safaris, no doubt. That poor spinster is always traipsing off on some adventure or other."

"Poor thing indeed," Gwendolyn droned. "Scads of money and no family responsibilities to keep her at home. However does she manage?"

The older woman examined the mask from all angles. "Why she thought anyone would want this terrifying visage leering down at them from the wall is beyond me." With a shudder, she placed the offending item back in the box and firmly closed the lid.

Connie uncapped her fountain pen. "Dearest Lizzie," she read out loud as the nib flew over the card. "How can I ever thank you for your imaginative gift, which has brought such smiles to all of our faces?"

She finished the note, signed it with a flourish, and passed it to Gwendolyn for sealing. Then she laid down her pen, stretched her arms overhead, and sighed. "Time for a break. We've been at it for hours."

"You've been at it for forty-five minutes," her mother said briskly.

"Well, it seems like hours." Connie pushed back her chair. "Come on, Gwen, let's go bother Ingrid and see if there's anything good to eat in the icebox."

"Oh, no, you don't," her mother said sternly. "Ingrid has enough to keep her busy without you two getting in her way."

Connie sighed and sat back down. Mother had helped her hire a combination housekeeper-cook named Ingrid Swenson and a gardener-handyman named Sam Crocker, both of whom were so efficient, there was little for Connie to do around the house. With her mother hiring the staff and her mother-in-law putting up the down payment, it was hard to think of it as *her* house, even though she'd done the lion's share of the decorating herself.

"One full hour, and then you can take a break," Mother continued. "Your guests went to a lot of trouble to get you these gifts. The least you can do is show your gratitude. "

She was right, of course. Connie sat back down. "Oh, I almost forgot. There are some envelopes in my evening bag. It's over there on the credenza."

Gwendolyn found the bag, opened it, picked out the envelopes, and handed them to Connie's mother.

"Looks like one is already opened."

"Oh, that's from Aunt Pearl."

"A check?" Mother pulled the card from the envelope.

"No. She gave me the formula for one of her inventions."

Mother's brow puckered. "Whatever for?"

Connie shrugged. "She said she thought it might come in handy someday."

Her mother read the slip of paper in the card. "Feline De-Flaker?" Her color rose. "Of all the ridiculous things to give your only niece on her wedding day." She sniffed. "Trust Pearl to come up with something completely and utterly useless. For heaven's sake, you don't even own a cat."

"Oh, I don't know." Connie took the card from her mother and ran her finger over the embossed design on the front. "I think it's sweet. How many china gravy boats does a girl need, after all? Besides, that little sample bottle of De-Flaker she gave me did wonders for my complexion."

Mother's eyes widened. "You put it on your face? Darling, what were you thinking?" She heaved a sigh. "That glowing complexion of yours, my dear, comes from being a joyful newlywed. With maybe just a little help from Elizabeth Arden. Definitely not from something intended to relieve cats of their dandruff. The very idea!" She wrinkled her nose in distaste.

"It will make a nice keepsake." Connie slid the paper back into her evening bag before handing the bag to her mother. "If I ever get around to making a scrapbook, I'll paste it in there. Then maybe someday when I'm old, I'll run across it and remember dear Aunt Pearl and her crazy inventions."

"Oh, well. She did also give you that gravy boat." Her mother's slim shoulders gave a resigned shrug. "Frankly, I think it's an ugly thing, painted with all those garish Victorian roses. But you've always loved it so."

"It belonged to Grandma Heloise, and then to Aunt Pearl," Connie said simply. And for her, that was reason enough to treasure it.

Mother rolled her eyes. "Well, let's hope she remembered to include the saucer. With a scatterbrain like Pearl, one never knows."

❧ 12 ❧

Connie lounged against the pillows, lazily admiring the way the November sunlight filtered through the bedroom curtains, forming lacy patterns on the wallpaper and glinting off the silver hairbrush-and-mirror set, small jar of hairpins, and jewelry box that sat atop the polished cherrywood dresser. Winston emerged from his dressing room wearing a white oxford-cloth shirt and well-cut gray trousers. He strode to the dresser, slipping a necktie under his collar.

"Still in bed?" He had a gift for stating the obvious. "Looks like a beautiful day. I should think you'd want to be up and about."

She yawned and stretched. "I don't know what's wrong with me. I've been so tired lately."

But she knew exactly what was wrong with her.

She was bored to distraction.

To hold down expenses—Winston was still just a junior executive, after all—she'd passed on hiring a chauffeur. Sam, the gardener, could serve as one in a pinch, and besides, one of her favorite pleasures was driving herself around town in her sporty little roadster. But one could only drive around so much. Even driving out to Aunt Pearl's wasn't the fun lark it used to be. Her aunt focused all her attention on her latest laboratory creation, reluctant to stop and visit and leaving Connie to keep company with the cats. So she'd stopped going.

She'd busied herself all fall with decorating their new home. She was especially pleased with how the living room had turned out, with its sophisticated peach-and-gray color scheme and straight, sleek lines. So much more up-to-date than the overwrought antiques favored by her mother and Drusilla. But now the house was nearly finished, except for Winston's study, and the gardens were mulched over for the winter. There simply wasn't as much to do. Or rather, there were plenty of things to do— shopping excursions, lunch with the girls, riding in the park—but for some strange reason the thought of doing them made her limp with fatigue. Frankly, she hadn't felt like herself for at least a week, maybe two.

She watched in the mirror as her husband looped the ends of his tie, one over the other.

"I'm thinking hunter green for your study," she said. "Or maybe a dark red. Not a red-red. More like a claret, or maybe brick. And chocolate brown leather for the sofa, with brass studs. Would you like that?"

"*Mhm*," he mumbled, giving the knot on his tie a final jerk.

"Which one?" she pressed. "The green or the red?"

"Whichever you think is best, darling. It really doesn't matter." He ran a comb through his short hair, still slightly damp from the shower.

"Of course it matters," she said crossly. She thought about it for a minute. "What do you think of a hunting theme for the artwork, horses and hounds and whatnot? Or is that too cliché?"

He lifted his gray suit jacket from the wooden valet next to the dresser, then turned to face her. "Honestly, I have no opinion. I leave it all in your capable hands." He peered at her with concern, as if noticing her for the first time. "Do you really not have any reason to get up?"

She picked idly at the edge of the blanket. "Bridge. But not 'til after lunch."

Win slipped into his suit jacket. Then he came and sat on the edge of the bed and folded Connie's hands in his. He smelled of soap and Brylcreem.

"You really should get involved in some things."

"What things?"

"I don't know. Wifely things," he said. A mild edge of irritation crept into his voice. "What are other men's wives involved in? Doesn't Mrs. Carruthers serve on the hospital auxiliary? Isn't Mrs. Mullin on the museum board? Surely there's something you can sink your teeth into. It would be good for my business, you know, for you to make an effort, to make friends with the right kind of ladies."

"I have plenty of friends."

"You need to widen your circle."

She flopped back against the pillows. "But I'm so tired."

"You're tired because you need to get out in the fresh air and sunshine." He stood and fastened the buttons on his suit jacket, leaving the bottom button fashionably undone. "Come on, lazybones. Up and at 'em."

"But nothing sounds interesting to me."

"Pick something." He leaned over and kissed her on the cheek, then stood. "I love you. See you tonight."

Moments later, she heard the front door close and Win's bright whistling as he headed toward the Burlington & Quincy commuter train station. She pictured him in his gray suit, beige trench coat and gray hat, blending in with all the other prosperous men in beige trench coat and hats. He'd spend long hours at his desk in the Chicago offices of Carruthers & Mullin. Doing what, she wasn't exactly sure, but it would involve files and papers and important people contacted on the telephone. At lunch he might entertain a client at the Union League Club. In the evening, he'd return home, often quite late, tired and without much to talk about. But she could tell he was pleased with their life together, and it was clear that business was going well. They were, as her mother said, settling in.

Now, turning onto her side and leaning on her elbow, she looked out the window at the autumn leaves, now fading to dry, dull brown.

Oddly, in spite of living the life she'd always dreamed of, Connie felt as if she were fading, too. What could she do to pull herself out of the doldrums? Perhaps she should plan a party. A small surge of energy sparked up her spine. Yes, maybe a party would liven things up. Now that the upheaval of painting and staining and hanging artwork and installing things was done and dusted, she and Win could invite their friends over to admire the house in its finished state.

She did love the house, an impressive Tudor Revival that resembled an illustration from *Grimm's Fairy Tales*. She loved the leafy suburb, its curved streets winding placidly through the mature trees. The only flaw that Connie could see in the house was that Win's mother had given them the down payment as a wedding present, which made Connie feel beholden. She wished they could pay Drusilla back the money, but since it had been a gift, the only thing was to accept it graciously. She knew she ought to feel grateful, not resentful. But she had trouble feeling the house was truly hers, even though Winston had put the title in her name alone. "In case anything should happen to me," he explained. She'd been touched by the noble gesture, but didn't think too much of it. Didn't responsible husbands do that sort of thing all the time? Besides, nothing would ever happen to Winston.

Behind the house was a flagstone terrace where Connie and Win loved to sit on summer evenings, watching the fireflies dance in the gathering dusk and listening to the chirp of crickets in the lawn.

But that had been in summer. Now in late fall, with the green-and-white striped awnings rolled up, the gardens mulched over, and dead leaves scuttling over the terrace, the house didn't seem quite as inviting. But perhaps their friends would enjoy gathering indoors around the stone fireplace just as much.

The prospect of a party energized Connie, and she roused from her torpor enough to sit up against the pillows and reach for a pink-covered notebook and pencil she kept in the drawer of the bedside table. Aunt Pearl had given her the notebook "to write your dreams and goals in." Connie couldn't think of any dreams and goals. Life was pretty much exactly the way she'd wanted it. But she'd used the notebook to record paint colors and furniture layouts and window measurements. Now, she turned to a fresh page and wrote "Christmas Party" across the top.

There was a soft knock at the door, then Ingrid came in bearing a breakfast tray.

"Morning, Mrs. Sudderland," she chirped in her singsong Swedish accent.

Connie set the notebook aside and eagerly accepted the tray. She picked up her fork. But all at once the sight of coddled eggs made her feel queasy.

"No breakfast this morning, Ingrid," she said abruptly. "Please, take it away."

The housemaid's brow furrowed. "Is something wrong? I think I made them yust the way you like."

Connie waved her hand. "It's fine. I'm just not hungry, that's all."

"Can I get you something else?"

"No, thank you."

With a puzzled frown, Ingrid reached for the tray. Connie gently laid her hand on the housemaid's rough one. "Thank you," she said with sincerity. "I do appreciate your kindness." She made a mental note to put a jar of hand cream by the kitchen sink.

Ingrid nodded and took the tray away, softly closing the bedroom door behind her. Connie lay back on the pillows, her tummy roiling.

She hoped it wasn't the flu. Getting sick was the last thing she needed.

❧ 13 ❧

A week before Christmas, a gentle snow fell outside the Enchanted Forest exterior of the Sutherland house. In the cozy library, Connie and Winston and their closest friends gathered around a ceiling-tall Christmas tree festooned with glittering baubles, silver garlands, and tiny electric lights. Connie looked around the room in satisfaction. Gwen and George had made the trip, of course, and Cyrilla and Jim had come, leaving their daughter with the nanny. Even Zoe Meade was there, complaining about the distance even though the Carpenters had invited her to ride in their car.

All eyes were directed toward one wall, where Winston had erected a silvery-white screen that Carruthers & Mullin used for presentations. Now he stood behind a home-movie projector, fiddling with the knobs and reels on his newest toy as grainy black-and-white images flickered.

"And this was in Biarritz," Connie explained as images of herself in a bathing costume, wading through the surf, flashed across the screen. "We stayed at Le Pavillon Royale, and one morning we saw John Gilbert at breakfast. Unfortunately we didn't have our camera with us."

"Really?" Cyrilla sounded breathless. "Is he as good-looking in person as he is on the silver screen?"

Connie assured her that he was.

The men seemed less than impressed by the sighting of the matinee idol. Instead they crowded around the projector.

"Eastman Kodak." Jim Morgan squinted as he examined the machine. "What kind of film does she take?"

"Sixteen millimeter," Win said. "Something new for home use. They call it safety film, It's supposed to be less apt to burst into flame than what the studios use."

"Let's hope so," Connie murmured to Gwen. "After all the work we've put in to getting this place ship-shape, I'd hate to have to start all over."

As the last bit of film clicked through the reel, everyone blinked as Connie switched on lamps. "Well, we've had our dinner, and you've all been so patient to sit through our honeymoon pictures without complaint. What do you say we have coffee now and open presents?"

The guests murmured in agreement. As they rearranged their chairs, Connie rang a small silver bell. Ingrid appeared, looking sharp in a crisp new black-and-white uniform and a starched cap perched on the crown of her blond head.

"We'll have our coffee now, Ingrid."

"Yes, ma'am." The housekeeper left the room and returned a few minutes later with a cart holding a silver coffee pot, cups and saucers, cream and sugar, and a platter of decorated Christmas cookies and her fast-becoming-famous Swedish *pepperkakor*.

"I'd give anything to visit the south of France. You're so lucky." Zoe groaned, taking a decorated sugar cookie from the platter. "What a romantic spot for a honeymoon."

"It was glorious," Connie agreed, "except the summer sun can be brutal at times. Most days we went to the beach in the morning and took a siesta in the afternoon, when the sun was at its peak."

"And then danced until dawn under the stars," Win added with a wink at Connie.

"Spain was even worse," she said, stirring her coffee. "I thought I'd burn to a crisp."

"Well, you must have done something right, because you came back looking healthy and happy, not at all sun-scorched like those of us who spent the entire summer on the golf course or the polo grounds."

Gwendolyn shot a look at her husband. "I swear, darling, with all the time you spent out on the course, your skin is going to be like leather before you're thirty."

George Carpenter merely shrugged.

"I envy you, Connie," Cyrilla said. "I don't dare spend any time in the sun at all or I freckle like an Irish milkmaid."

"Freckles are adorable," Connie insisted. Privately, she thanked her little bottle of Feline De-Flaker, which had turned out to be the perfect antidote to sunburned, peeling skin. She'd returned from her trip with a complexion smooth, soft, and fashionably suntanned. But how she managed it—with her trusty little vial of Feline De-Flaker— would remain her little secret, for now. Perhaps she'd share it with the other ladies. Someday.

That wasn't the only secret she had. She and Winston had recently learned they were expecting a special blessing the following summer. A secret he wasn't ready to share just yet. Not before she'd had a chance to tell her mother. And not before she'd gotten used to the idea. She'd never even owned a dog, and now she was going to be responsible for another human being for the next eighteen years or so. The prospect was daunting, and she had no many questions. She wanted to ask Cyrilla, the only mother in the group, for advice, but there was no way to tell Cyrilla without everyone else finding out. Anyway, she hadn't yet started to show, and if any of her friends had noticed a certain round-ness to her face and figure, they'd been too tactful to say so.

The rest of the evening passed amid much laughter, joking, and the ripping open of colorfully wrapped packages. Winston, lubricated by ample whiskey from the discreetly disguised liquor cabinet, distributed the gifts, making funny remarks with each presentation. At one point he made a rude remark about Zoe's new frizzy hairstyle. Connie cringed, thinking he might have had too much to drink, but Zoe laughed, so Connie let it pass.

The men murmured in appreciation for leather-bound books and boxes of cigars. The ladies, too, exclaimed over their gifts.

"Wherever did you find such exquisite scarves?" Cyrilla asked, lifting a brilliant peacock blue-and-tangerine scarf from its box. "Each one is different, and there's nothing like them in the shops around here."

"I had my Aunt Ruby ship them over from India," Connie said. "She'd sent me one for my birthday last summer, and I thought you'd all love the rich colors."

"We do," Gwendolyn said. She slipped a crimson-and-gold scarf around her neck and stroked the soft silk. "Thanks to you *and* to your Aunt Ruby."

"Missionary life certainly seems to agree with her. She included a long, chatty letter about all the goings-on over there. She included some boxes of tea, too, and an assortment of Indian spices. I handed all that off to Ingrid for the kitchen."

"You and Win ought to go and visit her," Cyrilla said. "From what I hear, India is quite fascinating."

"Couldn't possibly get away for that long," Winston said before Connie could formulate an answer. "Besides, Europe was quite exotic enough for me."

Connie felt a slight twinge of disappointment. Their European trip had whetted her appetite for more travel. Apparently, Winston didn't feel the same.

When all the gifts had been opened and all the eggnog consumed, the guests began taking their leave. Ingrid appeared with coats and scarves. Amid all the thanks, good-byes, and see-you-soons, Connie overheard George say something to Winston about investments.

"Think you can cut me in?"

"I'll see what I can do, old buddy." Win clapped his friend on the shoulder. "Call me at the office right after the first of the year."

After everyone had gone, Connie and Winston returned to the library. Win walked to the liquor cabinet and poured himself a nightcap.

"I think you've had enough to drink," Connie said mildly. "That joke you made about Zoe's hair almost crossed the line."

"She took it in good fun," he said. "Want me to pour you one?"

She shook her head. He settled into his favorite upholstered chair with his whiskey in one hand and a cigar in the other. As he reached for the matchbox, Connie flung open a window in spite of the frosty chill that seeped in.

"You men and your cigars," she chided gently.

"Aw, baby." He reached for her as she passed and pulled her down onto his lap. "Give a fellow a break. It's almost Christmas."

She flinched. She hated when he called her baby. He only called her that when he'd had too much booze. It was as if he became a different person when he drank. When he was sober, he was dignified, neat, self-possessed. When he drank, he became sloppy and slurred his words. She wondered why she hadn't noticed that when they were dating. And the cigars! At least her father had the decency to smoke, when he smoked at all, a fragrant applewood pipe.

She stood abruptly. "Sorry. My condition must make me extra sensitive to smells." She took a seat in her own wingback armchair. "What was George saying to you on his way out? Something about an investment?"

"Just some stocks he wants me to purchase for him. Something that's doing particularly well in the market at the moment."

"What sort of stocks?"

He puffed his cigar. "It's complicated, baby. The details would only bore you."

Connie straightened up and turned to look him in the eye. "No, they wouldn't. I want to know about your work, about what you do all day long in that great big skyscraper."

"I arrange my paper clips into neat, symmetrical rows."

"Be serious."

"I am being serious." He took a sip of whiskey. "A man doesn't want to come home and talk about his work. It's my job to earn the money and your job to spend it."

Shades of her parents. "But I want to be involved in your work, too, if only you'd let me." *It would bring us closer*, she thought but didn't say.

Winston laid aside his glass. *If he tells me one more time not to worry my pretty head about business, I'm going to scream.* But instead, he stood and yawned broadly, stretching his arms over his head.

"I'm beat. Coming up?"

"In a minute."

After he'd gone, Connie slowly circled the room, extinguishing candles, turning out lamps, and picking up stray bits of wrapping paper and ribbon, even though Ingrid would give the room a good going-over in the morning. Her husband's response to her interest in his business had cast a faint pall over the evening. She was familiar with the attitude. Her father had it, rarely discussing business topics with his wife or daughter. But Connie was bored with bridge and shopping. Learning something about Win's work would engage her mind, give them something to talk about after dinner. Who knew? She might even prove to be useful to him. She had good ideas sometimes.

His reluctance to discuss his business with her was annoying. She wanted to be a real part of Winston's life, not pushed into the background. She wanted her marriage to be more of a partnership than her parents' had been.

She felt a rush of guilt at that thought. Of course, she meant no disrespect to her mother. But a lifetime of sitting home, or filling her day with shopping and club meetings while her husband was away working all the time, didn't hold much appeal.

She patted her slightly rounded belly. Things were about to change, anyway. And maybe this baby would prove to be the one thing she and Win would have, or ever need to have, in common.

❧ 14 ❧

As January of 1929 wore on, Winston stayed later and later at the office. Darkness fell early, and Connie felt the gloom keenly. She started eating her dinner in the kitchen on evenings when Winston wasn't home, just to avoid sitting all alone in the chilly dining room. She nibbled at the tasty meals Ingrid prepared and tried to make small talk as the housekeeper bustled around, cleaning up the kitchen for the evening. Ingrid's responses were always polite, even friendly, but she didn't stop her washing and wiping, even for a minute. Connie wished she'd sit down and have a cup of tea with her, or play a few hands of rummy. One evening she said as much.

"Can't tonight, Mrs. Sudderland," the housekeeper said in her lilting accent. "My nephew is starring in a play over at the high school. Then we're taking the whole family out for hot chocolate after." She smiled at Connie. "You want to come, too?"

"Oh, no, thank you," Connie said quickly. She couldn't picture herself sitting in a school auditorium among a sea of doting parents.

"All right. See you tomorrow." In her sturdy cloth coat with her purse slung over her arm, Ingrid left through the back door, closing it behind her.

Connie envied the Swenson family gathering, which she imagined would be filled with much laughter and joking. Her own grand house stood silent and dull by comparison.

And hot chocolate suddenly sounded wonderful. She rooted around in the pantry for cocoa but, finding none, settled for a glass of plain milk instead. She switched off the light and, in spite of the early hour, went upstairs to get ready for bed. She turned the pages of an Agatha Christie novel until she felt sleepy, which happened rather quickly these days due to what her mother referred to as her delicate condition. At least when she was sleeping, she didn't feel quite so lonely. Maybe that was one of the good things about having a baby. She would never feel alone again.

A few days into the new year, Connie and her mother braved the gray slush of Michigan Avenue, doing their best to avoid being splashed by passing motorcars. Stamping their boots on the thick floor mats, they pushed through the heavy revolving door of Marshall Field. Ever since Connie and Winston had shared the thrilling news of their pregnancy with her parents over Christmas dinner, Mother hadn't been able to talk of anything else.

"What's the rush?" Connie had said when her mother had suggested a shopping trip. "The baby won't be here until August. Why don't we wait for a break in this ghastly weather?"

"Nonsense. January is the time to get the very best selection of spring maternity clothes, while all the shops are filled with resort wear. Besides, your father and I will be leaving for California in a few weeks and won't be back until June. Trust me, you won't feel like shopping in the heat of summer when your figure is at its most cumbersome."

There was no arguing with her mother when she got an idea in her head. So here they were, trawling the Michigan Avenue shopping district for bonnets and booties in the middle of a biting Midwestern cold snap.

By eleven o'clock Connie had two new maternity dresses and a pair of plain soft kid slippers.

"They look so ... grandmotherly," she remarked with a dubious glance as her mother handed them to her.

"You'll appreciate them when your feet swell," Mother said.

"Great. Something else to look forward to."

Passing by the millinery department, a stylish hat caught her eye.

"Oh, look! Isn't this the most adorable thing?" She pointed to a mannequin wearing a deep green cloche with a plaid velvet ribbon.

A pretty sales clerk, her dark hair cut into a fashionable Louise Brooks-style bob, shot a dazzling smile at Connie.

"Would you like to try it on? It would look lovely against your blond hair."

Mother grasped Connie by the elbow. "Come along, Constance Anne. We're not here to look at hats today." The rare invocation of her full name compelled Connie to obey.

"Thank you. Another time," she called to the clerk as her mother steered her away. "I'll be back soon to get a better look at that cloche, Miss ... er, Miss ..."

"Rodgers. Dot Rodgers." The clerk's dark eyes sparkled in apparent amusement at a grown woman being herded around by her mother.

"Miss Rodgers. Mind you don't sell it out from under me."

"For goodness's sake, Connie, stay focused." Mother propelled her daughter past Millinery and up to Infants' and Children's Wear, which was completely foreign territory to Connie. She was grateful for her mother's guidance through the bewildering world of bottles and bassinets. But, after what felt like hours of cooing over tiny shoes and caps and sleepers, she was more than ready for a break and said so.

"We'll go up to the Walnut Room," Mother said decisively, linking one arm through Connie's. The other was laden with shopping bags.

The large, elegant restaurant on the seventh floor was filled with lunchtime customers. The dark walnut-paneled walls that gave the Walnut Room its name, along with expansive windows showcasing the cityscape, provided welcome relief from the bustle of the sales floor. Connie ate all of an enormous roast beef sandwich, and a bowl of chowder besides, then asked the waiter for a dessert menu.

Over dessert, Mother described the upcoming trip to California.

"In past years, of course, we've gone to Florida to escape the cold, But your father wants to scout some fresh territory. The Florida market has dried up, but lots of prospective buyers will drive out to California over the spring holidays. Plus, it will be our first cross-country trip in his new Phantom. And he's refusing to bring Parker, preferring to do the driving himself." She stirred a cube of sugar into her coffee. "You and he are so alike in that way. Frankly, I don't see what the attraction is. Driving upsets my nerves."

"I don't know. Being in the driver's seat makes me feel more ..." Connie struggled to find the right words. "In control, I suppose. Independent."

Her mother sipped her coffee, then gently set the cup onto the saucer. "Well, independent or not, I do hate leaving you here in your delicate condition, darling. Especially since this is your first baby. Are you sure you won't come with us?"

"Thanks for the offer, but Win's very busy at the office these days. I'm afraid he can't take the time off to take vacations. And I don't want to be away from him that long."

Her mother smiled. "Still newlyweds, wanting to spend all your spare time together."

Connie fidgeted with the edge of her linen napkin. "I'm afraid I want to spend more time with him than he does with me."

Faint lines appeared on her mother's brow. "What do you mean?"

"I mean he spends every minute at the office. When he's not at the office, he's asleep."

The older woman's face relaxed into a smile. "Is that all? You must remember that Winston is an ambitious man, just like your father."

"That's just it," Connie protested. "I've always wished that Daddy were home more, that he'd spend more time with me. And now I've gone and married a man who does the same thing."

"You can't be selfish, dear. Keep in mind that men like ours work hard for *us*. For their wives and children. You mustn't ever complain, but support him. Be a team."

"I want to be a team, if he'd let me."

Her mother reached across the table and patted her hand. "Give it time."

Connie settled back in her chair as the waiter delivered dessert. "I suppose you're right. Anyway, I'll soon be busy decorating the nursery. It's the one room I didn't anticipate needing this soon, and I want to get it all set up and ready well before the heat of summer hits."

"Good idea." Mother lifted one carefully tweezed eyebrow. "I can see you still have plenty of energy, the way you're attacking that pie. Goodness, Connie. You'd think it was our last meal."

"I'm eating for two."

"That old saying about expectant mothers eating for two is a suggestion, not a rule," her mother admonished. "If you're not careful, you'll have a hard time getting your figure back after the baby's born."

"I don't care. I've never been so hungry."

Mother peered at her daughter with concern. "You're certain you'll be all right without me?"

"I'll be fine. You'll be back well before the baby's born." Connie licked the last few crumbs off her fork. "You mustn't worry. If I do need help, I can always phone Aunt Pearl."

Mother snorted. "I don't know what good that would do, darling. Pearl's never had any children of her own."

"She used to help Uncle Stewart with the calving."

Mother wrinkled her nose in distaste. "For heaven's sake, Connie."

Connie shrugged. "I'm only saying she's not completely ignorant about the birthing process."

Mother laid her napkin beside her plate. "If you're quite finished with this vulgar talk, we should go."

As they stood and collected their things, Connie impulsively hugged her mother. "Thank you for all the gifts for me and the baby," she whispered, her throat suddenly tight. "I'll be fine while you're gone, but I'll miss you very much. I'm glad you'll be home for the big event."

"Goodness." Mother's cheeks reddened. She patted Connie's arm while at the same time gently pushing her away. "Such a public display of affection."

But Connie could tell by the sparkle in her eyes that she was pleased.

❧ 15 ❧

On the day after Valentine's Day, Connie's parents left on their automobile trip to California. Connie had motored into the city early for breakfast and to say good-bye, so it wasn't until she returned home and turned on the radio that she heard the shocking news: seven men found shot to death in a North Side garage. The announcer called the event the St. Valentine's Day Massacre and blamed gang warfare.

Safe in her suburban living room, Connie shuddered as she listened to the report, then clicked the radio off in disgust. Gangsters who'd grown rich and powerful through Prohibition were ruining her beloved city, making it a dangerous and ugly place. She couldn't help but wonder if the hooch Winston stockpiled in the liquor cabinet didn't somehow support this criminal activity. She planned to discuss it with him, if ever he were home long enough to have a decent conversation.

Winter melted into spring, then summer. By June, Connie felt as awkward and clumsy as a hippo at Lincoln Park Zoo. Her back ached, her feet swelled, her belly felt heavy, and the unrelenting heat only made it worse. Even at night, with the electric fan whirring, she found it hard to sleep. All the magazine articles touted the blissful joys of pregnancy and motherhood, and she did look forward to the motherhood part, but frankly she could hardly wait for the baby to be born just so she could feel like her old self again.

One Tuesday morning following another poor night's sleep, Connie stood in her bedroom with Ingrid, feeling crabby as a disgruntled toddler. As the summer morning heated up quickly, so did her temper.

"It's no use. Everything in the closet is hopeless," she moaned, tossing yet another rejected blouse onto the bed. "Nothing fits this hippopotamus of a figure."

"Now, Mrs. Sudderland, you're yust feeling out-of-sorts on account of the heat." Ingrid's voice with its musical accent had a soothing effect on Connie's nerves, like cool water running over hot stones. "How about this one?" The housekeeper reached into the closet and pulled out a maternity blouse that Mother had shipped from California, crisp cotton in blue and white stripes with a white eyelet collar and cuffs on the short, airy sleeves. She held it toward Connie with a patient smile. Slightly mollified, Connie reached for the loose-fitting garment, slid it over her shoulders, and buttoned it up the front.

"I suppose it will have to do," she muttered, studying her image in the mirror. "At least for wearing around the house."

"Why don't you go downstairs? Is cooler. I'll put away these things," Ingrid soothed, sliding the rejected blouse onto a hanger. "There's some lemonade chilling in the icebox. I'll bring some right out as soon as I'm done here."

Connie was too tired to put up a fuss. "You're an angel."

She left the housekeeper to return the discarded clothing to closets and drawers and lumbered her way downstairs and out to the shady back terrace. The temperature in the backyard wasn't much cooler than it had been up in the sweltering bedroom, but, under the shade of the oak trees with a light breeze rustling the leaves, it felt more comfortable than sitting indoors.

She sank heavily onto a lounge chair, thankful her parents were due back from their trip any day. She missed her mother. Mother would sympathize, would understand what Connie was going through, would rub lotion on her legs and lay cool cloths on her forehead. Not that Ingrid wouldn't also do those things—Ingrid was an absolute saint when it came to looking after her—but there were times when a girl simply needed her mother. She thought of telephoning Aunt Pearl for sympathy, then nixed the idea. Much as she loved Pearl, sometimes her high energy could be exhausting.

Connie laid her head back against the striped cushion and closed her eyes, thinking of nothing and listening to the chirping of birds and the buzzing of crickets until she dozed off. She was awakened by the muffled ringing of the front doorbell, sounding very far away. She glanced at her wrist, forgetting for a moment that she'd stopped wearing a wristwatch when her hands and arms had swelled. She sighed. It was probably Gwen or Cyrilla, checking up on her, delivering yet another adorable romper or stuffed animal that they "just couldn't resist." While Connie appreciated their thoughtfulness, she felt too listless to deal with visitors, even her closest friends.

Through the open French doors she heard Ingrid's soft footsteps approach the front door and heard her greet the visitor. She couldn't make out the words, but the low rumble of the voice told her the visitor was male. *Ugh*. A salesman. No matter. Ingrid would send him packing. She started to drift off again.

"Excuse me, Mrs. Sudderland."

Connie opened her eyes to see Ingrid standing at the French doors, wide-eyed, wringing her hands. "There's some policemen here to see you."

Connie's head snapped up. "Policemen."

"Yes, ma'am."

"What do they want?"

"They asked for you."

"Very well." Connie hoisted herself to her feet and lumbered inside, smoothing her rumpled hair as she passed the mirror over the sideboard. As she crossed through the dining room and library toward the front hall, her first fleeting, crazy thought was that Aunt Pearl had gotten herself into some kind of hot water again. But no, that would involve the Hoosier Grove sheriff, not the local police. Or maybe it was Winston in trouble. After all, he was always so secretive about his work, brushing off her questions about it. Perhaps he'd skirted the law in some way, as he did with the liquor. Maybe this was about the liquor! No, that was silly. Anyway, if he *were* in trouble, the police would be visiting him in his office at Carruthers & Mullin, not here at their home. And they'd be asking for Winston, not her. Yet, Connie couldn't imagine what other circumstance would bring law enforcement to their doorstep. She quickened her step.

"Hello, officers," she said, a bit breathless from the effort. "How can I help you?"

The two blue-uniformed cops glanced awkwardly at her belly, then at one another. One removed his hat, revealing a shock of red hair. The other followed suit.

"Are you Mrs. Winston Sutherland?" the red-haired one asked.

"Yes."

"Are you the daughter of Mr. and Mrs. Marcus Shepherd?"

A rock of apprehension dropped in Connie's stomach.

"Yes. What's this about?"

"Ma'am, I'm afraid we have some bad news. There's been an accident."

All Connie remembered later was the ringing in her ears and her difficulty breathing as she slumped heavily against the dark oaken door frame. The policeman's words swam up to her as if through the deep waves of Lake Michigan.

"......Oklahoma...rain-slick road...automobile accident...dead at the scene...jurisdiction...so very sorry..."

Her parents. Dead. Both of them.

A loud ringing echoed through her head. Her knees buckled. Somehow, Ingrid must have gotten her up to the master bedroom and telephoned Win, because sometime later Connie found herself lying in her bed, staring at the ceiling. Winston peered at her from an armchair pulled up to the bedside, concern creasing his brow. Ingrid hovered near the door like a guardian angel.

"Darling, I'm so, so sorry. Are you all right?" Win's expression held concern and compassion.

Connie felt a cold clutch around her ribs as the policeman's words tumbled back through her mind. *Accident...dead...*

Tears began streaming down her face. She turned her head away without responding.

She would never see her parents again. Her baby would never know them.

When she tried to sit up, her head reeled. "Shh," Winston said, gently touching her shoulder. At last she mustered up the energy to speak.

"We—we must telephone Aunt Pearl. We must let her know."

"I already have," he said. "She's on her way. Now, try and get some rest."

Evening had fallen when she awakened again to the sound of commotion downstairs. Moments later, Aunt Pearl appeared at the door, still wearing her hat. Her eyes were red-rimmed but resolute.

"I'm here to stay and help until the baby is born," she announced heartily.

"What about Aunt Ruby ..." Connie started to say.

"I've sent a telegram. Don't you worry about a thing, sweetheart." Aunt Pearl said in a take-charge voice. "We'll muddle through this thing together. Let's just keep putting one foot in front of the other."

In her deep grief, Connie had no inkling what the next moment would bring, much less the next week or month. But upon hearing Aunt Pearl's sturdy voice and seeing her face, she somehow knew, deep down, that she would keep on living.

❧ 16 ❧

The next few days passed in a hazy blur of numb sensations punctuated by bustling bursts of activity. Connie spent much of her time lying on a couch or on the terrace while the household bustled around her, hushed but hurried. How would she'd go on without her parents' love and strength to lean on? But of course she *had* to go on. The tiny new life curled inside her belly changed everything.

Flowers and telegrams arrived practically hourly. From her home in Massachusetts, Drusilla Sutherland sent a huge bouquet of gladioli and lilies that made Connie's eyes water. The flowers were accompanied by an offer to come to Illinois for an extended visit, which Connie urged Winston to decline.

"Just not yet, darling," she pleaded. "I'm not feeling up to it."

"Maybe she can wait and come after the baby is born."

Connie didn't reply, but she didn't think that would be a good time, either. Frankly, no time would be the right time for a visit from her mother-in-law. She hated feeling that way but couldn't seem to help herself.

On the morning of the funeral, Connie sat alone on her bed. Though dressed and ready, she wanted to put off as long as possible the moment when she'd have to go downstairs and start accepting hundreds of well-meant murmurs of condolence. A knock sounded at her door.

"Come in."

Aunt Pearl slipped into the room, carrying a large, leather-bound volume. She handed it to Connie.

"I picked this up for you while I was downtown buying stationery," she said. "I thought it might bring you comfort in the days to come."

Connie turned it over in her hands. "A Bible." She glanced up at her aunt. "I already have a Bible."

"Let me guess," Pearl said, taking a seat on the coverlet beside her. "You have a fancy little Bible with fragile onionskin pages, silk ribbons, and miniscule type that's practically impossible to read."

"Why, yes."

"And let me further guess that you were given it on your confirmation, that the bishop signed the inside cover with a pompous flourish, and that it sits on a shelf gathering dust."

Connie cleared her throat. "How did you know?"

"Because I have one too, given to me at my confirmation. A gracious gesture, but useless when it comes to daily reading. Now this —" she reached over and thumped the cover of the book lying in Connie's lap—"This is what you need. It's a proper study Bible, with notes and commentaries and good strong print. You can read it every day without straining your eyes."

"Thank you."

"I want you to promise me you'll read it."

"I will," Connie promised. "If it means that much to you, I will."

"I want it to mean that much to you." Aunt Pearl stood. "And now, my dear, it's time to go."

Connie set the Bible aside, and together they descended the stairs to the waiting limousine. A solemn and dignified two-coffin funeral service was held in the ornate sanctuary of St. Lucian's, where a year earlier Connie and Winston had joyfully recited their wedding vows. Before the service began, as the organ played muted preludes in the background, Connie sat erect and composed, automatically parroting phrases of thanks as mourners approached to express sympathy.

A member of the church choir whom Connie had never met performed a solo, something about sheep grazing in pastures, surely meant to be soothing. Then the minister spoke kindly words about Opal and Marcus, praising their fierce dedication to the church, which rang false and hollow in Connie's ears. Yes, the Shepherds considered St. Lucian's to be their family church, where births, weddings, and baptisms took place. Connie had attended Sunday school there and had been mildly entertained by the Bible stories, especially the more thrilling ones about hiding baby Moses from the scary Egyptians and the lovely Queen Esther standing up brave and tall for her people. But regular church attendance had not been a habit in the Shepherd household, despite the generous checks her father wrote in support of purchasing a new pipe organ or funding a home for unwed mothers. As the minister spoke fondly of her parents, Connie knew he didn't really know them as real people. They were simply names on a donor list. For their part, Connie suspected her parents' generosity was more motivated by a sense of *noblesse oblige* than true Christian charity, and she wondered if that was good enough.

Good enough for what? She didn't know.

Something about the sermon didn't land quite right. The minister said all the right things, spoke eloquently about the importance of being charitable here on earth before entering what he called "the hereafter." But Connie found little comfort in his words. He didn't sound certain that it was a real place, much less provide any information on how to get there. She sensed something was missing from his explanation, but she didn't know what. It seemed like just a bunch of pretty words strung together, meant to be reassuring but in fact hollow inside.

After the service, Mother and Daddy were buried side by side near other Shepherd relatives at Forest Home Cemetery. For days, people came and went from Connie's house, murmuring condolences and bearing more food than their small household and even the staff could possibly eat. As it was, Connie had to force herself to swallow, her throat tight with unshed tears. Only at night, after the callers had gone home and Aunt Pearl and Winston had settled themselves in front of the radio, did she find time alone to bury her face in her pillow and sob, as she'd done every night since the police had shown up to break the news. In spite of her promise to her aunt, the thick leather Bible remained on her nightstand, unopened.

In the days that followed, everything seemed slightly off kilter. She found it impossible to work up enthusiasm for anything, including impending motherhood.

"You have to think about your *flickebarn*," Ingrid said one afternoon a few days after the funeral. She set a plate of chicken salad and grapes on the kitchen table where Connie and Aunt Pearl were seated, then pulled out a chair and joined them. Since Aunt Pearl's arrival, certain formalities of employer-servant protocol had been abandoned in favor of comfort and companionship.

Connie pushed the plate aside. "I'm tired of thinking about the baby," she said. "I don't think I'm strong enough to be a parent. Not without her own mother to lean on and learn from.

"Well, refusing won't make you any stronger." Aunt Pearl snapped her napkin and set it on her lap. "In any case, you're plenty strong, and you're not alone. You have Winston, you have me, you have Ingrid, and above all, the Lord is with you. He won't fail you."

Connie's mind struggled to find some connection between Aunt Pearl's confident words and the cotton-candy platitudes spouted by the minister at St. Lucian's.

Ingrid nodded. "Listen to your aunt, Mrs. Sudderland. What she says is the truth."

"So you two are ganging up on me," Connie said, amused.

"You bet we are," Aunt Pearl said, pushing the plate toward her.

"Bet that baby girl's hungry as can be, even if her mama turns up her nose at my good cooking," Ingrid added.

Too tired to argue, Connie picked up a fork. "You two keep saying it's a girl. How do you know?"

Aunt Pearl shrugged. "Just a feeling. That's all."

"Me too. Yust a feeling." Ingrid and Pearl grinned at each other. It gave Connie pleasure to see the two women becoming friends.

On a hot July morning, Connie found herself in the stuffy office of the family's lawyer, Lloyd Deveare, for the reading of the last wills and testaments of Marcus Shepherd and Opal McCabe Shepherd. She sat between Aunt Pearl and Winston, her ungainly body wedged into a stiff armchair. Mr. Deveare faced them across the wide expanse of his desk.

"The generous legacy that your parents have left you is a tribute to their financial acumen as well as their sterling character," the lawyer remarked, peering at Connie from under bushy white eyebrows as if daring her to deny it. She nodded miserably. She would have willingly endured poverty and deprivations of the worst kind if it could mean having her parents back.

"And to my daughter Constance, the remainder of my estate..."

Both wills contained much the same wording, although Mother's designated some specific family heirlooms and pieces of jewelry to go to her sisters, Pearl and Ruby.

"Always so thoughtful," Pearl murmured. Connie glanced over, as "thoughtful" wasn't among the usual adjectives Pearl used to describe her sister, but she seemed sincere as she smiled and touched an embroidered handkerchief to her eye.

Mr. Deveare went on to list the assets Connie now owned. Painstakingly, he explained each investment, each stock, each bond, although it was all mostly mumbo-jumbo to Connie—legal jargon that she had difficulty translating into concrete terms.

A generous provision was made "for future grandchild (or grand-children)," to be administered by Connie and Winston until such child reached the age of eighteen.

"That will come in handy when she wants to go to college," Pearl whispered in Connie's ear. Just as Pearl was confident that the baby would be a girl, she took as established fact that the child would pursue higher education.

Connie's mind wandered as old Mr. Deveare droned on, thinking of the innumerable chores that lay ahead. The Astor Street apartment still needed to be emptied, her parents' belongings either transported to her own house or sold at auction or donated to charity—valuable clothing, jewelry, antique furniture, paintings, as well as ordinary household items. The bank and brokerage accounts had to be dealt with somehow. Her father's new Phantom had been obliterated in the wreck, but he'd also owned an older automobile that would need to be sold, unless Winston saw value in keeping it. And then there was the household staff. What would become of them? Such decisions made Connie's head pound. How would she cope with it all? Her inner turmoil must have been visible on her face because Aunt Pearl reached over and patted her hand as if to say, *One step at a time, dear. One foot in front of the other.*

At last, the reading came to an end.

"Do you have any questions?" Mr. Deveare asked, looking at Connie. She shook her head. The lawyer slid several pieces of paper across the polished mahogany desk and showed her where to place her signature. When she'd done so, Winston reached past her to pick up one set of papers, neatened the stack, and slid them into his briefcase. The other set would stay in the lawyer's files. They all stood and shook hands, the lawyer uttering the usual condolences.

As they exited the law firm's office onto steamy Madison Street, Win suggested lunch. Pearl heartily agreed, and Connie let herself be propelled to a nearby restaurant. The interior was hushed, dim and cool, a relief from the blazing sun and bustling sidewalk outside.

When they were seated and had ordered drinks, Win cleared his throat.

"Well, that went as well as could be expected, don't you think?"

Connie nodded as she perused the menu. None of the items listed looked remotely appealing. The heavy smell of something frying slapped her in the face. Her stomach tilted sideways, and she closed her eyes for a moment to quell the seasick feeling. She set the leather-covered menu aside.

"I don't have much of an appetite," she said. "I'll just have soup."

"You will *not* just have soup," Aunt Pearl huffed. "You have the baby to think of. And hot soup sounds unappetizing on a scorching day like this one."

Connie waved a listless hand in surrender. "You choose something for me, then."

Pearl turned her attention to the menu, adjusting her bifocals for a better view. Connie let her mind drift over the long list of tasks still before her. *I suppose tomorrow will be a good a time as any to start clearing out the—*

"—and I know exactly where to invest it," Win was saying in an energetic voice.

Connie emerged from her reverie. "Invest what?"

"Your inheritance," Win said, sounding a little impatient. "Some interesting new opportunities have just opened up at the firm. Haven't you been listening to me, darling?"

"Of course," she fibbed. "Go on."

"This applies to you too, Pearl, if you have money to invest," Winston said.

"Count me out," Aunt Pearl replied. "I've just enough to live on comfortably."

Winston turned back to Connie. "As I was saying, there's this new type of mutual fund that's ... "

She tried to listen, but the unfamiliar financial terms became jumbled in her head. Finally she said, "I don't know, Win. I think my father would have preferred something more conservative. Why can't we just keep the money where it is?"

Her husband frowned. "What do you mean, keep it where it is?"

"Wherever it's currently invested."

He snorted. "Knowing your father, it's sitting in some stodgy old slow-growth account somewhere." He leaned across the table and took her hand in his. "These are exciting times, baby. There's big money to be made, but we have to get in on the ground floor. Leap while the iron is hot."

"Leap from the ground floor?" The mixed metaphor brought a tentative smile to Connie's lips, in spite of her bleak mood.

"From the frying pan into the fire, more likely," Aunt Pearl murmured. Winston didn't appear to hear her. Instead he looked beseechingly at Connie as if waiting for a reply.

"Tell me again what these investment opportunities are all about," she said. "I promise to listen."

"I won't bore you with the details, darling." He picked up a menu and flipped it open. "Suffice to say, the market's never been better, soaring to new heights. Opportunities are endless. And speaking confidentially" —he leaned forward—"our investments so far are making us quite rich."

"We're already rich," she snapped.

He flinched at her outburst.

Across the table, Aunt Pearl snorted.

"I'm sorry, Win. I am glad for you, truly," Connie said, more gently. She laid a hand on her midsection. "This baby is making me grumpy. What I meant to say is, I know you're handling our money admirably well. I do wish to understand your business. I'm sure I could make sense of it, if you'd only explain it to me."

He smiled indulgently. "Forgive me, darling. What I need is for you to trust me to handle our business affairs. You have enough on your plate, what with the baby coming, without worrying about stocks and bonds. Let me take care of it. What do you say? I can have all the funds transferred this afternoon."

"For goodness' sake, Winston, give the girl time to think," Aunt Pearl said.

He ignored her.

Connie felt too weary to make any more decisions. "Go ahead," she sighed. "Do whatever you think is best."

Win sat back, a wide grin lighting his handsome face. "You'll be very glad. You'll see. You know you can always trust me to take care of you. What say we order?" He lifted an arm to signal the waiter.

Connie sighed again. She believed him. She knew she had nothing to worry about, that their future security lay firmly in Winston's capable hands.

But if that were so, then why couldn't she shake the feeling that, when it came to certain aspects of their life together, she was always on the outside looking in?

❧ 17 ❧

In spite of Pearl's and Ingrid's unwavering prediction that the newest Sutherland would be a girl, Connie delivered a boy in August of 1929. His full name, quite a hefty moniker for such a little peanut, was Winston Scott Sutherland IV. Connie had thought it might be nice to name him Marcus, after her father, but Sutherland family tradition prevailed.

"I wouldn't have expected any different," Aunt Pearl huffed. "I suppose when you marry into a family like the Sutherlands, you give up such frivolous luxuries as the ability to name your own child."

To distinguish him from Winstons I, II, and III, the new parents decided to call their son Scotty.

"Or Scott, when he's older and goes to school," Winston asserted. But Connie had trouble imagining the little fellow as anything other than her sweet baby boy. The breathtaking magnitude of her love for him, from the very first moment the nurse had placed him in her arms, shocked her.

"Could he be any more precious?" she sighed to anyone who would listen, admiring his copper curls, his sweet rosebud mouth.

Aunt Pearl stayed on throughout that fall. She was a great help in caring for Scotty, getting up if he was fussy early in the morning so

Connie could sleep in, playing with him, getting him dressed, and freeing Connie to get her strength back and Ingrid to concentrate on her housekeeping tasks instead of childcare.

"You're going to spoil him with so much attention," Connie teased.

"Oh, piffle. It's impossible to spoil a child this young," Aunt Pearl said. "Besides, it's my right as a great-aunt. He's like the grandchild I'll never have."

Connie was grateful for her aunt's presence and pleased to see how well she and Ingrid got along. She frequently found them together, heads together over some household task or other, and she found herself sticking around to talk to them, eager to share in their easy laughter and warm, motherly companionship. As a mother of three herself, Ingrid was capable of giving advice on situations neither Connie nor Pearl had a clue about, such as burping and diaper rash.

One afternoon, Connie entered the kitchen to find both women giving Scotty a bath in the white porcelain sink. Aunt Pearl lifted him from the sink while Ingrid wrapped him securely in a blue terrycloth towel that had been warming on the radiator. Then she carried him to Connie and handed him over with a smile.

"Here he is, clean as a whistle."

Connie cuddled her child and breathed in his fresh, soapy scent. His eyes blinked sleepily.

"Time for bed, little one."

As she dressed Scotty in a clean diaper and flannel sleeper, Connie marveled at how she felt more comfortable around these older women than she did her own fashionable friends. Gwen and Cyrilla continued to invite her to luncheons and shopping excursions, but these outings held less appeal than they had before. Maybe that was a side effect of motherhood—it made staying home seem more attractive than anything else.

Winston, on the other hand, was seldom home. As the autumn wore on, he worked longer and longer hours. Connie could hardly remember the last time they'd gone anywhere together with their friends, or even just the two of them. On the rare evenings when he was home, he spoke in clipped tones, tension creasing his brow. Frequently he became annoyed and short-tempered about the disruption caused by the new baby, and, even worse, by their long-term houseguest.

"Exactly how long is she planning to stay here?" he complained to Connie one evening in the privacy of their bedroom shortly after tripping over one of Aunt Pearl's slippers left inexplicably in the hallway. "I keep finding her things or the baby's things all over the place."

"Aunt Pearl's never been very tidy," Connie admitted. "Between her and Scotty, the clutter is sometimes a bit more than Ingrid's able to keep up with."

"Ingrid shouldn't have to keep up with such chaos," Winston said in exasperation. "She has enough to do around this place without picking up after Pearl every minute. I've never met anyone so scattered and disorganized. "

"*Shh.* Lower your voice. She might hear you."

"I don't care." But he did lower his voice.

"Aunt Pearl has been a tremendous help with the baby," Connie added, hoping to get her husband to look on the bright side. "She plays with him and keeps him amused for hours ... much longer than I'm able to."

Win grunted. "How much amusement does a newborn need?"

From her side of the bed, Connie watched him change into neatly pressed striped cotton pajamas, then hang his jacket and trousers in his closet. He carried the rest of his clothes into the master bathroom to send down the laundry chute. Glancing at his well-shined brogues and wingtips lined up like soldiers on a rack in the closet, Connie thought it was no wonder Pearl's tendency toward clutter got on his nerves.

When he emerged from the bathroom, she gave him an engaging smile. "I'll speak to Aunt Pearl," she promised, but in her heart she knew it wouldn't do any good—not for long, anyway. Pearl was Pearl and unlikely to change her helter-skelter habits, much as she might wish to. Still, Winston had been so tense lately, quick to take offense and fly off the handle at every little thing. He needed to have some patience.

For her part, Aunt Pearl had been slow to warm up to Winston. As much as he disapproved of her personal habits, she disapproved of his drinking, which had gotten heavier of late. Not that Pearl said as much out loud, but Connie could read her aunt's face—the faint scowl, the pursed lips—whenever Winston's breath stank of whiskey or he slurred his words.

Connie felt caught in the middle. But for her sake and for Scotty's, she needed to keep the peace. Aunt Pearl would go back to her own place someday, probably sooner than later, but Connie wanted to put off that day as long as possible. Taking care of a baby was a lot of work, and she didn't know if she'd be up to the task without her aunt's help. It didn't seem fair to ask Ingrid to add childcare duties on top of cooking and cleaning.

On a stormy Tuesday afternoon in late October, a driving rain slashed against the mullioned windows of the library. Connie felt stifled and suffocated with an unexplained sense of foreboding, as if all the air were being sucked out of the room. She tried reading a magazine but soon lost interest and tossed it aside. She swiped an imaginary bit of dust from the immaculate end table. Finally, in spite of the pouring rain, she wrapped herself in a raincoat and called for Sam Crocker to bring around Winston's Nash sedan. This was not the kind of weather to drive out in her sporty little Hudson.

Aunt Pearl appeared in the arched doorway leading to the hallway, holding a drowsy Scotty. She clucked her tongue. " Whatever would make you want to head out in nasty weather like this? I should think you'd catch your death."

I have to get out of this house or I'm going to scream, Connie thought, but she only said, "I need to find a Halloween costume for Scotty before the Morgans' party. You're included in the invitation, so you might want to think about a costume for yourself."

Pearl's face lit up. "Oh, how fun! I'll have to dream something up."

"I've no doubt you will. You have a knack for creative ideas," Connie said. "Frankly, I'd rather skip the party, but I've already told Cyrilla we'll come. She promises it will be a good, old-fashioned family frolic, with bobbing for apples and taffy-pulling and such." Gently she stroked her son's red-gold curls. "Even though Scotty will remember none of it, maybe a night out be good for all of us. Winston has been working so hard at the office. He deserves a night of fun."

"And so do you," Aunt Pearl said. "You need to get out of the house more."

Connie laughed. "I never thought those words would apply to a social butterfly like me. Former social butterfly," she said, and kissed Scotty's velvety cheek.

She heard the car's tires swish on the brick driveway. Leaving Aunt Pearl and Scotty to cuddle together by the warmth of the fireplace, Connie took an umbrella from the rack in the foyer and hurried to the sedan.

"State Street, please, Sam," she said as she slid into the backseat.

"Yes'm."

The car wove through quiet streets in the direction of Chicago. As they passed through the business district of their suburb—little more than the commuter train station and a few shops that had cropped up around it—Connie noticed a small crowd gathered on the sidewalk in front of the bank, huddling under umbrellas and rain hats.

"Odd that so many people are out in this weather, isn't it?" she remarked to Sam, then didn't give it another thought as she considered costume possibilities for Scotty. Wouldn't he look adorable as a clown? Or as a little lion, with a fluffy mane and tail?

The car threaded through increasingly heavy traffic as it approached the city. The wiper blades made a gentle *swish, swish* sound that soothed her frazzled nerves.

Within half a block of State Street, Sam brought the car to a halt behind a line of stalled traffic.

Connie leaned forward. "Can you see what's causing this back-up?"

"No, ma'am. Traffic seems worse than usual, for this time of day." He peered through the windshield. "Looks to be something going on over there." He pointed to a crowd of people swarming the sidewalk in front of one of the city's major banks.

"Golly," was the only thing she could think of to say.

As they drew nearer, they saw a mounted policeman ride through the crowd. Connie cranked open her window. "Excuse me. Can you tell us what's going on?"

"Better move along," the policeman hollered in a rough voice.

Connie shivered as droplets of rain hit her in the face. She rolled the window back up. An inexplicable sense of panic rose in her inside her chest. "Let's go home, Sam. No Halloween costume is worth risking life and limb in this crowd."

When they got home, she shrugged out of her coat and propped open her dripping umbrella on the tiled floor to dry. She found Pearl sitting in the library, no longer holding Scotty. Instead she leaned toward the crackling cathedral radio, frowning and adjusting the dials.

"Aunt Pearl, you'll never believe the crowds we saw—"

"*Shh*." Pearl looked at her, wide-eyed. "They're saying there's been a run on the banks."

"Maybe that explains what was going on downtown," Connie said. "I'm going to call Win." She hurried to his study and picked up the telephone. But, despite countless attempts to connect to the Carruthers & Mullin offices, the line remained busy. She returned to the library. They would just have to wait.

Ingrid served their supper on trays so they could keep listening to the radio. When Winston finally came home later than evening, his complexion looked pale and wan. After putting Scotty to bed, Connie sought him out in his study. He was standing next to the steam radiator, sipping a scotch and wearing a look of utter despair.

"What's the matter?" she said as she hurried over to him. "You don't look well. Won't you please sit down and tell me what's happening?"

He gave her a blank stare, as though he were surprised to see her.

"Are you sick?" She put a hand to his forehead. He brushed it away.

"Just a rough day today."

She knew it had to be more than that. She sat in an armchair. "Does it have anything to do with the crowd outside the bank downtown? Is it true what they're saying on the radio? Has there been a run?"

He didn't respond, but she knew by the look on his face that the situation was serious.

"But not *our* bank, right, Win? Not Carruthers & Mullin?"

"No, not Carruthers & Mullin," he said woodenly. "Not yet, anyway. I have to go back to the office." He set down his glass, stood, and put on the damp raincoat that he'd flung across the radiator.

Connie stood too. "But what about your dinner?"

"Not hungry." He kissed her forehead. "Don't you worry about a thing. Everything will be all right." But his voice sounded flat, wooden, as if he were repeating lines from a script.

Desperate for reassurance, Connie clutched at the lapels of his raincoat. "Winston Sutherland, if you tell me again not to worry about business, I'll—I'll..."

But before she could complete her thought, he'd gently removed her hands from his coat and headed back out into the storm.

❧ 18 ❧

The Morgans' Halloween party was, to say the least, subdued. Their normally elegant Lincoln Park townhouse was decorated in an improbably cheerful harvest-hoedown theme with pumpkins, hay bales, shocks of corn, and even a giant scarecrow in one corner. A small orchestra gamely scratched out "The Little Brown Jug" and "Turkey in the Straw," but no one was dancing. The promised apple-bobbing and taffy-pulling took place, mostly for the sake of the children, as few of the adult guests exhibited a party spirit.

After her abandoned attempt to shop on the day the newspapers were now calling "Black Tuesday," Connie had not gotten back out to find cute Halloween costumes. Instead, she outfitted herself, Scotty, and Aunt Pearl in pirate costumes easily scrounged together from old clothes, printed scarves, hoop earrings, sooty eye makeup, and a couple of eye-patches cut from a discarded black silk blouse. Winston, arriving late straight from the office, didn't even attempt a costume.

Connie sat on a sofa strewn for the occasion with printed muslin feed sacks. She held Scotty in her arms and thought that they'd have been better off staying home, except that Jim and Cyrilla Morgan were such good friends. Gwen, Zoe, and a few other women sat in armchairs nearby. Aunt Pearl stood near the orchestra, tapping her foot in time to the music.

"I still don't understand exactly what happened. Explain it to me again." Dressed in a flouncy, crinolined square-dance dress with her hair in ribbons, Cyrilla looked surprisingly at home amid the corn shocks and gourds.

"Sweetie, it's not that complicated," Zoe said with a condescending air that befitted her regal Cleopatra costume. "Share prices on the New York Stock Exchange collapsed. What we're left with is unprecedented chaos."

"Well, I know that, but doesn't the market go up and down all the time? Won't it just go back up eventually?"

"It's the 'eventually' that's the problem," Gwen said. "If things don't return to normal soon, there will be bank closures and other messes to contend with. In fact, the repercussions are already happening here in Chicago."

Cyrilla turned to Connie. "Winston works in finance, right in the thick of it. What does he say?"

"Do tell," Zoe said, leaning forward, her hands curled around a mug of warm apple cider. "How is the illustrious firm of Carruthers & Mullin faring?" There was something mocking in her tone.

Connie glanced around for Winston, hoping to signal him to come over and reassure her friends, but he was across the room, engaged in what looked to be an intense conversation with Jim Morgan and George Carpenter. Cheeks burning, she concentrated on adjusting Scotty's little headscarf, avoiding her friends' pointed gazes. All her friends had invested money in Carruthers & Mullin at Win's urging—or their husbands had. Connie had no idea how much they'd invested, but she thought it prudent not to tell them that her husband was spending day and night at the office "to mop up the mess," as he put it. Instead she merely echoed the phrases he kept repeating at home.

"He says it will blow over. He says we shouldn't panic, that it's just a hitch in the system, and it will correct itself in a few days or weeks and everything will be back to normal." Her friends' silence telegraphed their doubt. She didn't quite believe it herself and felt great relief when a housemaid appeared and interrupted the conversation by passing around a platter of cinnamon doughnuts. As soon as she could do so politely, she said, "Well, we've got to get this little one home to bed," collected her family, and went home.

The day after the party, the doorbell rang. A few minutes later, Ingrid came into the dining room where Connie and Pearl were having breakfast. Winston had already left for work.

"Telegram for Mrs. Russell," Ingrid said, handing a yellow envelope to Aunt Pearl.

Pearl tore it open and read. A frown of concern passed over her face.

"What is it?" Connie pressed.

"It's from someone at the missions board headquarters. Ruby is very ill. She's been asking for me." Pearl looked up, her face ashen. "I must go to her immediately."

"What? To India?" Connie couldn't believe it. But in a flurry of telegrams, telephone calls, and packing, a sea voyage was arranged. Pearl's farm and her brood of cats would be looked after by her neighbor, Agnes Pratt, as well as the local sheriff who, it sounded like, seemed to have taken something of a shine to Pearl after the incident of the moonshine allegation. A few days later, aunt and niece said their good-byes in the front hall as Sam Crocker carried Pearl's bags out to the sedan.

"I don't suppose there'll be any chance you'll come back for the holidays?" Connie said.

Pearl tugged on her gloves. "Oh, no, dear. Goodness, I'll have just have gotten there by then. Lord knows how long I'll need to stay." She held Connie's gaze. "Are you sure you don't want me to leave you some money?"

"Of course not," Connie insisted. "Win's still employed, you know."

"I know, but many others are losing their jobs. A little extra cash may come in handy someday." Pearl adjusted the tilt of her hat in the hall mirror. "If not, you can use it to buy yourself something pretty."

"I won't hear of it. You need that money for your trip."

Sam Crocker poked his head in the door. "All set, ma'am? It's time to go, if you want to catch that train."

"Yes. I'll be right there."

A sudden sense of panic seized Connie. "Oh, Aunt Pearl, I don't know how I'll manage without you." She hated the quiver in her voice. The last thing she wanted to do was to make her aunt feel guilty about leaving.

"You'll do just fine." Pearl patted Connie's cheek. "You've been handling everything from Scotty's baths to his diaper changes. And you have Ingrid on hand, too, for help. She's quite fond of Scotty, you know, and she's a mother herself, so you have nothing to worry about."

"I know. She's a dear. But I feel awkward asking her to help with the baby on top of all her other tasks."

"I'm confident things will all work out," Aunt Pearl said cheerfully. She hugged Connie and kissed her cheek. "God's in control."

Connie closed the front door behind her aunt and leaned against it. She was perfectly capable of taking care of her own baby. Of course she was. But the holidays were approaching. If the previous year was any indication, the Sutherland social calendar would quickly fill up with parties and shopping and entertaining clients. Perhaps it was time to hire a new household employee, a full-time caretaker for Scotty.

"The Morgans have recommended an agency that hires out nannies," she mentioned casually to Win over breakfast the next morning. "I have an appointment to meet with them next week."

Winston snapped his newspaper. "A nanny? What for?"

"Why, to take care of Scotty, of course, now that Aunt Pearl's gone. Remember? We talked about this."

He stared at her. "Can't you take care of him?"

"Of course I can," Connie said, exasperated. "What kind of a question is that? I only think it's time he had a full-time caretaker, so that when I'm tied up at bridge club or something, or when you and I go out together in the evenings, he has someone familiar to stay with." She felt a little ridiculous, explaining to her husband what a nanny was for. After all, he'd been cared for by a nanny of his own when he was growing up. Connie couldn't picture Drusilla, her imperious mother-in-law, changing a diaper.

"I don't think we should be adding more household staff at this time, that's all," Win said, folding the newspaper. "Business has been, well ... off ... since the crash."

"I know. But you said the problem was temporary. Is it worse than you thought?"

"Nothing you need to worry about, darling. It's just that money is still a little tight because of the volatile stock market. Until it settles down, we need to be less extravagant than usual about our spending."

"Are you saying we need to tighten our belts?"

"Just temporarily," he assured her, stirring his coffee. "Just until the market corrects itself. You get my drift, don't you?"

"I suppose," Connie said, wondering vaguely where Winston picked up a phrase like "get my drift"—surely not in a white-shoe firm like Carruthers & Mullin.

She had memories of her parents talking about having to save money in the early days of their marriage, when her father was first getting his real-estate business off the ground. But by the time Connie had come along, her father made good money. She couldn't remember him ever denying her anything she wanted.

The memory of her father brought a lump to her throat. She took a big swallow of coffee and then a bite of buttered toast, chewing it slowly. She straightened her spine. She knew how to cut back on expenses, even though she'd never had to before. Fewer luxuries. She'd get her nails manicured less often, maybe dare to show up in the same gown on more than one occasion. Plucky heroines did it all the time in the storybooks she'd loved as a girl. And Connie Sutherland was nothing if not plucky. She and Win would be all right. In fact, her heart cheered a little at the prospect. It would be a sort of game, seeing where she could cut back on expenses and save money.

"Perhaps we should skip buying Christmas gifts altogether this year," she suggested in a sudden spirit of brave sacrifice. "Or buy them only for Scotty. Not for all of our friends, like we usually do."

But Winston, looking alarmed, nixed that idea immediately.

"We mustn't let on, Connie. I want our friends to think everything is going fine with us. No need to air our problems in public. Our temporary economizing will be our secret. Agreed?"

"But I'm sure everyone in our circle's been affected by the downturn to some extent," she reasoned. "Everybody's probably in the same boat as we are. Even the Carpenters and the Morgans and the Meades."

"We're not 'everyone.'" Win dabbed his upper lip with a napkin. "I make my living investing other people's money. We need to keep up appearances or clients will start to worry. You do understand, don't you?" She must have looked skeptical, because he reached across the table, took her hand in his, and looked earnestly into her eyes. "I'm not trying to be less than honest. It's like this. People place their confidence in investment counselors based in large part on the image we project. The way to keep clients calm is to constantly reassure them, both verbally and otherwise, that everything's going to be all right. Don't you see? I can't give them that assurance if I don't look prosperous, if my family isn't well dressed and my home looks run-down—if I can't afford to buy even simple Christmas gifts. We just have to be a little more careful with our money for a while, that's all."

"But *is* everything going to be all right?" She noticed the newly formed lines on his forehead and around his eyes, heard the note of anxiety in his voice. Something sounded off to Connie about Win's logic, as if they were expected to act roles in a play or try to give a false impression.

"Just until the market corrects and the money starts flowing again," he said calmly, as if talking about an approaching rainstorm in the forecast. "It's just a matter of time before things are back to normal. In the meantime, we need to do our best to look confident and carefree, or even more clients will start hammering on me to give them their money back."

Clearly, he was under a strain at work and didn't need additional stress at home. Connie dutifully instructed Ingrid to cut back on the groceries and other behind-the-scenes household spending in ways that wouldn't be obvious to their friends. She knew she could trust Ingrid to be careful with money and mindful of the household accounts. Less leg of lamb and more macaroni started appearing on the Sutherland dinner table. Connie began keeping meticulous care of her clothing, hand-washing items to make them last longer, items she would normally have instructed Ingrid to send out to be laundered. She even hired a local seamstress to adjust the hemlines of her skirts to accommodate changing styles rather than buying new ones. She told herself that, to everyone's eyes—everyone who mattered, anyway—the Sutherlands were a prosperous, well-to-do young couple with no money worries. There was no need to broadcast their circumstances far and wide.

❦ 19 ❦

Searching for Christmas gifts for their friends, Connie left Scotty home in Ingrid's care one December afternoon and found herself wandering up and down the aisles of Kroch's bookstore in Chicago's Loop district. She'd decided that books would be the ideal gift for everyone on the list. Books weren't terribly expensive—not compared to the costly cigars, silk scarves, and perfumes they'd given in the past—yet they were a thoughtful gift, entertaining and intellectually stimulating. *Well, most books anyway*, she thought as she hastily returned a copy of *The Harlot's Revenge* to the shelf.

She chose a couple of Agatha Christies for the mystery lovers and a selection of Zane Grey stories for the men. For Gwendolyn, who adored bridge, she found a book of plays by a master card player. She even selected a charmingly illustrated Beatrix Potter children's book for Cyrilla's daughter, and, at the last moment, slipped a second copy onto the stack for Scotty, whom she hoped would enjoy Peter Rabbit when he got old enough to appreciate stories. At last she carried her towering stack of selections up to the cashier's counter.

"This will be a charge, please," she told the clerk. "The account is Sutherland."

The clerk looked at his ledger, then at her, then at the ledger again.

Finally he said *sotto voce*, "I'm sorry, Mrs. Sutherland. We can only accept cash today."

"Cash?" she repeated, confused. "Well, naturally, I haven't any cash with me. Normally I just put purchases on my husband's account."

The bespectacled young clerk shifted uncomfortably, avoiding her gaze. "Those are my instructions, ma'am. I do apologize."

Heat rose in Connie's face. "May I please speak to the manager?"

The clerk signaled across the room, and soon an older man with a mustache bustled over. When clued in to the situation, he said with a patronizing smile, "Mrs. Sutherland, I'm sorry to say your account has been in arrears for some time. I'm sure that, as soon as it is brought up to date, all will be well."

With other customers lining up behind her, Connie turned away, embarrassed and perplexed. There had to have been some mix-up. Why would Win let the bookstore account, of all things, fall behind? What other bills were going unpaid?

When her husband got home that evening, she confronted him, recounting the afternoon's excruciating experience at the bookstore and ending with "Why hasn't the account been paid? I felt so humiliated."

Winston's shoulders hunched. "I'm sorry that happened. But as I told you earlier," he added with strained patience, "we've fallen a little behind in some of our accounts." His face looked gray and waxen.

"You told me business was off," Connie said. "You didn't mention anything about falling behind on our accounts."

"I thought I did," he said in a monotone. "That's why I asked you to be prudent in shopping."

"What could be a more prudent gift than a book?"

"No need to worry," he repeated. But his voice had a flat quality to it, as if his mind were elsewhere. The dark rings under his eyes had deepened even since that morning.

"But I *do* worry, Win. How are we going to pay the bills? Not to mention that we *still* have no gifts for our friends, and our party is coming up."

"Cancel the party."

"What?" She couldn't believe what she was hearing. "What happened to keeping up appearances?"

He scrubbed a hand across his face. "Connie, I've been working around the clock. I'm too worn out to think of hosting a party here. Can't you just go out with your friends for lunch or something?"

She crossed her arms. "Well, a little advance notice would have been appreciated. I've sent out all the invitations."

Her anger must have been evident, because he softened. "Go back to Kroch's tomorrow afternoon and buy the books," he said quietly. "I'll pay the account first thing in the morning."

"As if I have nothing better to do than make multiple trips to the Loop," Connie muttered. It was a petty thing to complain about, and she knew it. But it was better than asking him for the bald truth about the state of their bank account, which didn't bear thinking about.

The next morning, the doorbell rang as Connie was pulling out her address book, preparing to call her guests to tell them the party was canceled.

"Is a delivery for you, Mrs. Sudderland." Ingrid entered the bedroom carrying a large box, which she set on the bed. "From Marshall Field's."

Connie opened the box and shook out its contents, a dark green taffeta gown with a matching velvet bow on the bodice. It was her Christmas dress, the one she'd intended to wear to the parties and dances. Who was she kidding? Half the parties had been canceled, now including her own. Ongoing turmoil from the crash had certainly squashed what was left of the holiday spirit. The last time she and Winston had been out socially had been the Morgans' Halloween party.

She held the dress up in front of her and swayed in front of the full-length mirror, loving the way the deep green complemented her blond hair and fair complexion. For a moment, she hugged the garment against her ribcage and closed her eyes. Then, with a sigh, she handed the gown to Ingrid

"Please send it back."

"Are you sure? Is very pretty. Don't you like it?"

"I've changed my mind."

She returned to flipping through her address book as the house-keeper boxed up the gown and took it out of the room. Then, she slammed the book shut. If this was what belt-tightening felt like, it was not going to be fun. It was not going to be fun at all.

Later she sat in the little booth by the kitchen, telephoned each friend on the guest list, and explained with regret that Winston was feeling under the weather and the party would have to be canceled. Each of her friends sounded sympathetic, and they made plans to meet for a quiet ladies-only lunch at the Walnut Room.

"Will we still exchange gifts as usual?" Cyrilla asked.

"Of course," Connie insisted. "Just the ladies this time." But as she hung up the phone, she worried. She couldn't face the embarrassment of going back to Kroch's, even if Winston had cleared up their account by now. Other than books, what sort of gift could she produce on short notice that would please her friends and keep them from suspecting the state of their finances?

Deep in thought, she caught herself nibbling the cuticle on her thumb and chided herself, hearing her mother's voice in her head. A lump formed in her throat. She stared at her hands, which had gone unmanicured for too long and looked a fright. The least she could do to honor her mother's memory was to maintain proper grooming standards. Maybe a few drops of Feline De-Flaker would help the cuticle situation.

But what would help with the gift situation? She flipped through her address book as if it held the answer in its pages.

Suddenly her head snapped up. She stared unseeing out the window. Could the solution to her problem be a solution? Literally?

Her mind flitted back to the words Aunt Pearl had spoken at her wedding reception when she'd handed over the handwritten formula for Feline De-Flaker.

A girl should always have something to fall back on. You never know when it might come in handy.

Connie could give gifts of Feline De-Flaker to her friends. She'd have to call it something else, of course. She envisioned the group gathered around a Christmas tree while she handed out around pretty little cut-glass vials tied with festive ribbon. She could practically hear her friends' murmurs of appreciation at such an attractive gift.

Feeling more cheerful, she hurried upstairs. She rummaged through the shelves in an upstairs closet until she found the quilted satin-covered box containing her wedding memorabilia. Pushing aside the dried flower petals and bits of ribbon, she found Aunt Pearl's card with the handwritten recipe still folded neatly within it. She read over the recipe, then pressed it to her chest. Dear Aunt Pearl! How could she have known that her eccentric gift would come in so handy?

🦋 20 🦋

That evening Connie insisted on helping Ingrid with the after-dinner clean-up in an effort to hurry the process along. The sooner the housekeeper went home, the sooner Connie could take over the kitchen.

Ingrid raised an eyebrow at this unaccustomed audience to her tidying but said nothing. After washing and putting away the dishes, wiping the counters, and sweeping the floor at what seemed to Connie an unreasonably meticulous pace, the housekeeper untied her apron and hung it on a hook, then shrugged into her coat.

"If you don't need anything else, I'll be leaving now."

"Nothing else," Connie chirped. "Just maybe an apron."

Ingrid raised her eyebrows but opened a drawer and pulled out a clean cotton apron. Connie tied it around her slim waist.

"You're planning on making something special, Mrs. Sudderland?" Ingrid asked, her expression doubtful.

"Not really. Just a little ... experiment. Now you run along home." She made a shooing motion with her hands.

Ingrid looked skeptical but picked up her bag. The moment the back door clicked shut, Connie crossed the kitchen, flung open the spice cabinet, and started pawing through it.

Winston, who'd come into the kitchen in search of coffee, watched her for a few minutes. Finally he said irritably, "What are you looking for?"

"I'm looking for that dried herb that Aunt Ruby sent us in her Christmas box last year," Connie said as she lifted a jar, examined it, and put it back in the cabinet. "I had no idea what to do with it, so I gave it to Ingrid. I don't think she knew what to do with it either."

"Maybe she threw it out," Win suggested unhelpfully.

"Not Ingrid. She's too thrifty." Connie continued rummaging among the boxes and jars.

"You should have asked her about it before she left."

"I didn't want to have to explain, in case—" She gave a little yelp of joy and pulled out a small waxed paper packet containing the dried herb. She held it up with an air of triumph.

"Tada! Here it is. Look!" She stared at the packet as if it contained pure gold dust.

"I'm looking."

"It's fenugreek. This is the herb Pearl showed me at the farm the day she was brought home by the sheriff."

Win scratched at his temple. "I thought you said your Aunt Ruby sent it."

Connie took a mental breath. "She did. She sent some to both Pearl and me. Apparently it's native to the region where she's stationed in India. Anyway, it would be nearly impossible to find outside of some gourmet shop, and it's no doubt expensive to boot. I'm thrilled to have it."

"I see," he said, his expression as doubt-filled as Ingrid's had been. Then he shook his head. "No, I don't. You've lost me. Why is this stuff so important?"

She walked toward him and held out the packet. "Smell it."

He took a whiff and blinked.

"It's pretty strong. What are you going to do with it? Not try to cook something." He looked vaguely alarmed.

"Why not?"

"Darling, you haven't cooked anything in your life. Have you?"

"I make a mean tuna fish sandwich. I'll show you sometime." She winked at him. "Anyway, I'm not going to cook anything, even though Aunt Ruby wrote in her Christmas card that it goes especially well with lamb and poultry. I'm simply going to whip up a batch of Feline De-Flaker."

"Feline what?"

"Remember? Aunt Pearl wrote the formula in the card she gave us at our wedding. You—*we*—laughed about it at the time."

His expression remained blank.

"Never mind. It's not important." She clutched the packet to her chest. "But this magical little ingredient plus the rest of Aunt Pearl's formula means I can give Christmas gifts to my friends without spending hardly a dime."

He cocked his head. "Go on."

"I'm going to mix up a batch of Feline De-Flaker and give it to them in fancy little bottles."

"That should thrill them," he said without enthusiasm.

"Only I won't call it that. I'll call it ... I don't know, something else. Something more appealing. Something that sounds more like a glamorous skincare product." She paused. "Any ideas?"

He frowned. "Let me get this straight. You're going to give Feline De-Flaker to your friends for Christmas? But none of them have cats. Do they?"

Connie sighed. "It's not for their cats, silly. It's for *them*. For their complexions. That's why I need to call it something else."

He lifted his hands in a gesture of surrender. "You're not making any sense. Start over."

She drew a deep breath. "As Christmas gifts, I'm going to make some skin tonic for our friends. Aunt Pearl intended it for cats, but it smells heavenly and works wonders on the skin."

"People skin."

"Yes."

"Just making sure." Win looked skeptical. "Does it really work?"

"It clears up the complexion, fights blemishes, heals sunburn—it's worked on me, hasn't it? You've had no complaints." She cast a critical glance at her husband's chin. "You might want to try some as a shaving lotion."

He pulled out a kitchen chair and sat. "So your plan is to mix this stuff up, put it in pretty bottles, and give it to the girls for Christmas."

"Yes. "

He grunted. "What else is in it? Besides that stuff." He gestured to the packet Connie held.

"Oh, several things. But this rare herb is the key ingredient. Without it, it won't work."

He sat back and crossed his arms. "And you're planning to mix up this potion yourself?"

"Yes."

"Where?"

"Here in the kitchen."

He cocked an eyebrow. "Sounds like you've got everything worked out."

She cringed inwardly. "Not really. Just making it up as I go along. Who knows ...? If it goes over well, maybe I can even sell it."

"*Sell* it?" His jaw dropped.

"Well, why not? Since we're going through a rough patch, with your income constrained, it might turn out to be a way to help make ends meet."

He flinched. A short silence hung in the air between them. Then, he scraped back his chair and stood.

"You think it's a good idea?" she pressed.

"Whatever you say. Do what you want."

"Would you like to help me? We could do it together. It'll be fun."

"I'm going to read the paper." As he left, Connie breathed a prayer of thanks that he hadn't put up more of a protest. He didn't seem very enthusiastic about her plan, but he hadn't forbidden it, either.

She turned and faced the stove as if seeing it for the first time, which was not too far from the truth. She unfolded the recipe from the pocket of her wool dress and smoothed it out on the counter. She bent down to read it over once, twice, then stood, hands on hips, and surveyed the cabinets.

"Now, if I were Ingrid," she asked herself, "where would I keep the stock pot?"

She started searching and pulling ingredients from the pantry to mix with the precious packet of fenugreek. Pearl had used some sort of a machine to boil the mixture—the mysterious conglomeration of pots and tubes the police had mistaken for a moonshine-brewing still. Obviously Connie had no such elaborate contraption at her disposal. But, following Aunt Pearl's directions, she figured could make do with a stock pot and some saucepans.

However, a closer reading of the formula revealed several other ingredients besides fenugreek that Connie couldn't locate in the pantry. She substituted some ingredients for things she found around the kitchen. The result stank to high heaven and looked just as nauseating. Her next attempt turned out even more vile.

Until the wee hours of the morning, she worked to perfect the formula. Only Scotty's cries for feeding or changing were able to wrestle her away from her kitchen and force her to get an hour or two of sleep. It wasn't until she'd completely run out of fenugreek did she admit defeat.

A trip out to Aunt Pearl's farm to stock up on ingredients was in order. She desperately needed instruction, too, in the making of the formula. But Aunt Pearl wouldn't be back from India for months.

As she climbed wearily up to bed, she knew there was no getting around it. She'd have to confide in Ingrid after all and enlist her help and kitchen expertise to get this project off the ground.

❧ 21 ❧

The next morning after Winston left the house, Connie bundled Scotty into his snowsuit for the hour-long drive out to the farm.

"I'd love it if you'd come too, Ingrid," she said before the housekeeper had a chance to take off her coat. "I'd appreciate the company. It'll probably feel a bit lonely out at the farm with Aunt Pearl gone."

"Sure thing, Mrs. Sudderland. If that's what you want."

Sam Crocker drove them out to Aunt Pearl's in the sedan, which was more reliable on snowy roads than the little Hudson. Connie and Ingrid sat in the back with Scotty snuggled between them. On the way, Connie explained the purpose of the errand. She told about her aunt's gift of the formula for Feline De-Flaker and her own discovery that Feline De-Flaker was an excellent remedy for human skin ailments.

"You've seen how tight things are for us financially," she said finally. "You've helped us cut back on expenses."

"Yes, ma'am. Things are tough for people all over."

"So, you see, I need Christmas gifts for my friends, and I've decided to give them Feline De-Flaker. I had that packet of fenugreek from Aunt Ruby, and I tried to mix up a batch using a few substitutions, but apparently I'm hopeless in the kitchen." Her voice trailed off, and when Ingrid didn't argue, she gave a sheepish shrug. "So we'll collect the proper ingredients today from Aunt Pearl's laboratory, and maybe that contraption she uses, too. And then I'm hoping you can help me figure it all out."

"I'll be happy to try."

The tires crunched on the drive leading to Pearl's house. Fortunately the snow wasn't deep enough to get them stuck. Connie leaned forward and spoke to the driver.

"Would you mind watching Scotty for a bit, Sam? I'll get him settled in the house, and you can wait with him there."

"Yes, ma'am. Happy to spend time with the little man," Sam said, ever genial.

He followed Connie up the snow-covered porch steps. Ingrid came last, carrying Scotty. Connie found the spare key fastened under the lid of the milk box. They entered the kitchen and Connie flicked on the light.

"I'll go change the little one," Ingrid said, and disappeared into the next room with the baby.

"If you find something to eat, you're welcome to it," Connie told Sam, "and feel free to make yourself some coffee." She pulled some items from her handbag. "Here's a bottle and some cookies for the baby if he wakes up."

"Don't you worry about us," he said. "We menfolk'll get along just fine."

Ingrid returned with Scotty. Sam held him in one arm and jangled the car keys with his other hand. The baby gurgled happily.

With her son settled, Connie led the way to the barn-turned-laboratory. Ingrid trotted beside her, their boots crunching on the snow, their breath forming frosty clouds.

In the drafty barn, Connie tugged off her gloves, then reached in her purse for the folded paper containing the formula. She scanned the list of ingredients.

"I think she keeps most raw ingredients over here," she said, indicating a wall of dusty shelves laden with glass jars and cardboard boxes. "Let's have a look. You read off the ingredients."

Ingrid followed her through the building as she collected the various ingredients in small bottles, peered at labels, then placed the bottles in a basket.

"You know, Mrs. Sudderland, you can buy most of these ingredients in Chicago. There's a wholesale supplier you can go to."

Connie looked at the housekeeper in surprise. "Is there?"

"Sure. My cousin goes there to get supplies for her beauty shop, but they carry other things. Ingredients for making perfume and such. Could save you some money. If you want, I'll ask my cousin who she recommends."

"I'll probably only make it this one time. But thank you."

At last, Connie set the rustic, jar-laden basket on the wooden workbench. "I think that's it. Let's keep a careful tally of everything we're taking so I can pay back my aunt. And I'm afraid I don't have quite the proper equipment." She eyed the tubular contraption. "I hope Aunt Pearl won't mind if we borrow this thing. I doubt it will even fit in the car. We'd better get Sam to help us."

"We won't need it," Ingrid said confidently. "I know what that machine is for. My uncle has one." She paused, and Connie chose not to inquire further into what her uncle might use such a thing for. Making moonshine, most likely, judging from the deputies' reaction to it, but that was none of her business.

Ingrid continued. "For small batches like ours, whatever equipment we have in the kitchen at home should do yust fine."

"All right." Impressed by her housekeeper's acumen, Connie double-checked the ingredients list, then said, "I think we're ready. We'd best be heading back. It looks like it might start snowing again."

Sam drove home carefully along slick roads. Snuggled in the back with Scotty, Connie found herself enjoying a companionable conversation with Ingrid.

"You've been such a help to me today. I really appreciate it. Perhaps when we get home, you can help me mix it up. If you don't mind staying late, of course."

"Thank you for the invitation, Mrs. Sudderland, but I need to get home to my family," Ingrid said. "Is my boys' birthday today. We're celebrating with a cake and candles."

The reminder that Ingrid had a family of her own waiting for her at home always caught Connie by surprise, even though she'd known the woman's circumstances all along. It just seemed natural to think Ingrid's whole existence rotated around the Sutherlands. Connie felt herself blush at her own presumption.

"Of course." She sifted through her mind to recall some detail about her child. "Um ... how old is he now?"

"*They* are seven," Ingrid said with a proud grin.

Twins. Twin boys. Right. Plus the older girl, Sonja. "Well ... tell them Mr. Sutherland and I send them our best regards."

Best regards sounded stiff and formal for seven-year-olds. Connie sat awkwardly, making a mental note to keep a few small, impersonal gifts handy for such impromptu occasions as this. How foolish to not remember even the most important details about Ingrid's family. But Ingrid only smiled and said, "Thank you, Mrs. Sudderland. I'll do that."

"And your husband? He's doing well?"

Ingrid's face clouded. "He's gone."

"Gone?"

"Gone to find work, he said. In Detroit, with some big automobile manufacturer. But that was over a year ago, and I have not heard from him since."

"Oh, Ingrid. I'm sorry to hear that." How could she not have known that such drama was taking place in the life of her very own housekeeper? Ingrid was always so even-tempered, so cheerful. Connie felt ashamed at her own lack of concern for her employees' private lives. After all, they were practically family. Weren't they?

"Is all right, Mrs. Sudderland. Me and my boys and Sonja, we're doing all right. My mother lives with us and keeps us all in order. And the Lord's been good to us."

In the warmth of the car, Connie felt drawn to talk to Ingrid as if she were not an employee but a friend. In that moment she vowed that, as long as she had people working for her, she would always take an interest in them as people, not just as machines sent to do her bidding. It had been a long time since she'd enjoyed some good girl talk. Ever since the Halloween party, she'd felt her friends avoiding her. Their understandable anxiety about the money that Winston had invested on their husbands' behalf inevitably cast a cool shade over the friendships. And there wasn't a thing Connie could do about it. But maybe the upcoming Christmas luncheon would provide an opportunity to clear up any misunderstandings.

"There's one thing I haven't thought of yet—a name for the product. I have to make up some pretty labels to put on the bottles, and 'Feline De-Flaker' is out of the question. Any ideas?"

Ingrid tilted her head. "I'll think about it. If anything comes to mind, I'll let you know."

The following afternoon, before Winston came home from work, Connie joined Ingrid in the kitchen. She watched as the housekeeper, following Aunt Pearl's written instructions, completed each step in the process, then repeated the steps herself. She saw where she'd gone wrong the night before and how to do it correctly. When they were finished, they had two batches of transparent, mint-green Feline De-Flaker packaged in large mason jars. The kitchen smelled appealingly of mint and spices.

"Now leave it sit for a few days, out of the sunlight," Ingrid instructed. "Then it will be ready to use."

Connie stored the jars in the pantry and dutifully left them alone. The evening before her friends were to meet for their annual Christmas lunch at the Walnut Room, she carried one of the mason jars over to the sink, wondering how to make the clear green liquid look like a gift worthy of the finest retail establishment.

She stared at the jar for a moment, then went to the dining room and opened the glass-fronted china cabinet that held a number of small decorative etched-glass bottles. The collection had belonged to her mother, and, while they were pretty, Connie had no other use for them than to display them in the cabinet. She pulled out three and carried them to the kitchen.

She heated water in a saucepan until it boiled, then dipped the bottles in the water with tongs to sterilize them, a method she dimly recalled from a Rockingham School home-economics class. She wasn't sure whether skin tonic required sterile bottles, but better safe than sorry.

She did some more ferreting around in the cabinets, found a funnel, and used it to carefully pour the solution from the mason jar into each crystal bottle. The end result was a pretty collection of sparkling bottles, each containing six ounces of Feline De-Flaker. She smiled in satisfaction.

Hours later, long after Winston had come home, eaten a silent supper, and gone to bed, Connie sat in the rocking chair in the nursery. "I hope the girls will love it," she murmured to Scotty as he drowsed in her arms. "But I can't call it Feline De-Flaker. We must think of something else to call it."

She rocked and rocked. "The name should probably have the word "pearl" in it, to credit Aunt Pearl for her invention. Something pretty and feminine, like ... *Parfum de Perle.*" She wrinkled her nose. "No, on second thought, a pearl's natural perfume is probably anything but pleasant. More like briny and clammy." She thought some more.

"Maybe *Eau de Pearl*—'pearl water.' No, that's even worse." She shuddered, and thought some more.

"How about Pearl's Potion?" Scotty grunted in his sleep. She smiled. "Well, at least that's an honest answer."

Outside the window, the moon emerged from behind a cloud, illuminating the nursery and lacing the walls with the shadows of tree branches. Connie leaned back in the rocker and sighed. It was hopeless. She'd never think up a good name that would capture the essence of Feline De-Flaker and make it sound romantic and appealing.

"I'm thinking too hard," she scolded herself, conscious that she only had until the next afternoon to come up with something. In any case, with such a lovely liquid packaged in pretty crystal bottles, her friends needn't suspect a thing about the Sutherlands' straitened financial circumstances. Winston had promised the setback would be only temporary, and she had full confidence in him. But until such a turnaround happened, they had to muddle through.

"We're going to get through this somehow," she thought, "but a miracle wouldn't hurt."

She rocked in the dark, holding her baby, deep in thought. The low-burning embers in the master-bedroom fireplace crackled and glowed through the open connecting doorway. Through the mullioned window, the winter moonlight threw patterned shadows across the floor.

"See the pretty moon? *Moonlight*. That's a good word, isn't it? Mysterious and romantic." She whispered the word again, trying it out as a product name. "We could call it Moonlight … something. Moonlight in Paris. How do you say moonlight in French? *Claire de lune*. Like the song." She shook her head. "Maybe Liquid Moonlight." She chuckled softly. "That sounds a bit too much like moonshine, doesn't it? What's another M-word? Miracle. Moonlight Miracle. That's good." Suddenly a burst of inspiration crossed her mind. She sat upright, causing Scotty to stir and his eyes to fly open.

"No … not moonlight. Moon*drop*. Because it's drops, you see. Drops of liquid. That's what we'll call it." Scotty's big round eyes returned her gaze. "We'll call our precious elixir … Moondrop Miracle."

❦ 22 ❦

In the twinkling lights from the towering, glittering Christmas tree at the center of the Walnut Room, Connie and her friends enjoyed a festive lunch and opened their gifts to one another as if it were any ordinary Christmas. The walnut-paneled walls of the famous restaurant were festooned with fragrant evergreen boughs and holly, and the tables were filled with last-minute shoppers.

But, under the surface merriment, Connie felt a pang of loneliness. She missed her mother as she recalled their outing to the Walnut Room of the previous winter. How excited she and Mother had been, talking about the future without a care in the world.

With a shake of her head, Connie forced her thoughts away from the past and into the present. She exclaimed with joy over a silk scarf given to her by Cyrilla, a carved wooden jewelry box from Zoe, and a silver baby rattle from Gwendolyn.

"This is much too nice to let him chew on," she said, admiring the rattle's gleaming silver. "Perhaps I'll hang it on the tree instead."

"Baby's first Christmas ornament," Cyrilla remarked.

Gwen's mouth curved up in a smile. "Whatever you think is best."

Now, it was Connie's turn to be the giver. She handed a small wrapped package to each woman. They eagerly ripped the paper.

"It's a tonic for your complexion," she said. "I made it myself from a family recipe."

"What a thoughtful gift, Connie," Gwendolyn exclaimed. She turned the little crystal bottle over in her hand so it captured the light. "You say you made it yourself?"

Connie nodded, pleased that the first reaction to her endeavor was positive.

"Aren't you clever," Zoe drawled, holding her bottle up to the light. "Whatever is it called?"

"Moondrop Miracle." Connie pointed to the neck of the bottle, where she had tied a silk ribbon with a card attached onto which she'd handwritten the name in her best penmanship. "You dab it on at night before bed, and, in the morning, your face is clear and glowing."

"Well, if it's what you've been using on your own face, I'll take a gallon," Cyrilla said. Everyone laughed. "What's in it?"

"Why, moondrops, of course, " Connie said coyly. "And a little bit of magic." She felt satisfied that she'd made her friends happy, and none was the wiser regarding their reduced circumstances. Win would be pleased when she told him about it.

As they finished their desserts, she said, "I'm so glad we were able to get together. This has given me a real pick-me-up."

"Me too," said Cyrilla. The others murmured their agreement.

"Thanks for being so understanding about canceling our traditional Christmas party," Connie said. "Frankly, neither of us felt enthusiastic about hosting the party this year."

"I don't blame you," Gwendolyn said. "It's been a hard year on all of us."

"Win's absolutely exhausted. He's been working day and night."

Cyrilla's face lit up. "Has he? Oh, that's wonderful news. He's landed on his feet, then."

Connie glanced at her friend. "Huh?"

"I knew it wouldn't take him long," Gwendolyn added.

Connie's brow wrinkled in confusion. "Wouldn't take him long to do what?"

"To find another job."

"What's he doing now?" Zoe asked.

Chilly tendrils wrapped themselves around her chest. Her friends knew something she didn't. Trying not to reveal her ignorance, she fought to keep her voice light and carefree. "Oh, you know ... the same, but a lot more of it. He's almost never home."

"Well, that's a relief," Cyrilla said. "We were all so devastated when Carruthers & Mullin went belly-up. So unexpected, a white-shoe firm like that. It was all over the papers, impossible to miss."

And yet I did. Connie heard a rushing sound in her head. She didn't trust herself to speak.

Cyrilla and Gwendolyn exchanged glances.

"Are you all right, darling?" Cyrilla said to Connie. "You're pale as wax."

"I-I'm all right. I just—perhaps something I ate doesn't agree with me. We'd better go."

Zoe made a lame joke about the stork while the four women stood and gathered their belongings. On the way out of the restaurant, Gwendolyn motioned for the others to go on ahead and pulled Connie aside.

"Say, Con. You didn't know, did you? About Carruthers & Mullin."

"Not in any detail," Connie admitted. *Not in broad brush strokes, either.* "Win hasn't talked about it much." *Or ever.*

Gwen linked her arm through hers. "That's great news that Winston's working, though. So many breadwinners are taking it on the chin these days."

When she got home from lunch, Winston was home. His unsteady demeanor and bloodshot eyes told her he'd been drinking. Again. He leaned against the door to the library, jacketless, his tie askew.

She dropped her handbag on the front-hall table and removed her coat and gloves.

"Hello, darling," she said, her voice remarkably steady. "What are you doing home in the middle of the afternoon?"

He eyed her but didn't say anything, as if he were sizing up how much she already knew.

She sniffed. The stench of whiskey surrounded him. "Another liquid lunch, I take it."

He shrugged. She turned to face him squarely. "Is there something you want to tell me, Win?" she prompted. "About your job at Carruthers & Mullin?"

A look of alarm flickered across his face, then he turned sheepish. "How long have you known?"

"For about an hour, give or take."

He slumped against the doorjamb, as if the effort of holding himself upright exhausted him. "They closed their doors. Threw us all out of work."

"When did this happen?"

"Three weeks ago."

"Three wee—" All the breath rushed out of her body. *Breathe. Just breathe.* She regained her composure, then said, "Where have you been going off to every day?"

"I've been out pounding the pavement, trying to find another job. No such luck."

"Why didn't you tell me?" she screeched. "You should have told me."

"I thought I could find something before you found out, so you wouldn't get all upset, but nobody's hiring. Nobody. Believe me, I've tried."

She fought down the panic that rose in her chest. "We'll figure out something. Maybe I could get a job."

"You?" Win snorted. "What kind of a job could you get? You have no skills. Besides, I don't want my wife working. How would that look? Like I'm a poor provider, that's what. Like I can't provide for my family. We don't need the whole world to know the Sutherland family has fallen on hard times."

"Now is not the time to care about how things look," she snapped. "I could get a job in a shop or something."

"I forbid it. It's shameful enough to be out of work myself. I will not have my wife out working in public." She'd never heard him sound so stern.

"I suppose we'll have to fall back on our investments then. I've been hoping we wouldn't have to touch them, but now ..."

The look on Winston's face made her stop talking mid-sentence.

"No."

"Baby—" He held out his hands in a pleading gesture. She backed away.

"Not our investments too."

Mutely he nodded.

She swallowed. "All of them?"

"All of them."

"The inheritance from my parents?"

He nodded.

"Scotty's ..." She could barely get the words out. "Scotty's college fund?"

"Worthless now." He reached up and grabbed his hair as if ready to pull it out. "It's gone, Connie. All of it."

"You mean to tell me there's nothing left? There must be some mistake."

His silence told her there had been no mistake. The room tilted. The enormity of their situation sucked the wind out of her lungs. Shakily she sat in a chair and tried to gather her thoughts.

They'd lost everything. Everything. Her entire fortune had evaporated right before their eyes. How could this have happened?

Somewhere underneath the panic rising like a tide in her chest, she knew exactly how it had happened. She'd trusted him. Believed him when he said he'd take care of her forever. Believed everyone she'd ever known who'd told her not to worry her pretty head about money. Because now that it was gone, not worrying about it seemed like a frivolous luxury indeed.

She had no idea what was going to happen next. But of one thing, she was certain.

Winston Scott Sutherland III would be of little help in getting them out of trouble.

❧ 23 ❧

Christmas Day of 1929 came and went with no discernible celebration at the Sutherland home. Connie thought of going to church but couldn't muster up the will. If it weren't for the fact that she and Ingrid had put up a tree and draped a few decorations here and there before that fateful luncheon at the Walnut Room, there would have been no indication that the holidays had happened at all. *Thank goodness*, Connie thought, *that Scotty is too young to know the difference.*

In her Christmas letter to Aunt Pearl, she'd made no mention of Winston's job loss or their reduced financial circumstances. She'd only mentioned making Feline De-Flaker as Christmas gifts for her friends —rechristened the more melodious Moondrop Miracle—and thanked Pearl for giving her the recipe. Now she wondered if was time to come clean to her aunt so she wouldn't be in for a shock when she came home. *If* she came home. Her last letter mentioned she wouldn't return to the States until summer at the earliest. Connie missed her terribly. Even so, Aunt Pearl had enough to worry about with her sister's poor health. She didn't need the added burden of wondering whether all was well back in Illinois.

Gwendolyn, bless her heart, had invited the Sutherlands to dine on Christmas Day.

"It'll just be us," she caroled over the phone.

But Connie had declined. "Scotty has a sniffle. I think we'd better stay home."

"Perhaps New Year's, then."

"Perhaps. We'll see. Merry Christmas to you and George," she said as cheerfully as she could manage and hung up the phone feeling regret mixed with relief. She knew dinner would have been an uncomfortable prospect for Winston, with the specter of the questionable investments looming over the table. He was still begging her not to share the bald truth of their reduced circumstances with their friends, but it would be impossible to keep it secret if they spent any time together. Gwendolyn knew her well enough to sense immediately that something was seriously wrong, if she hadn't already suspected.

Released from the need to pretend he had a job, Winston seemed to lose all hope of finding another one. Most days, he sat alone in the library, a glass of whiskey in his hand, rumpled and unshaven. Her normally fastidious husband had seemingly lost all pride in his appearance, looking increasingly like the tramps who rode the rails from town to town, begging for food. Connie was grateful that at least the Sutherlands hadn't had to resort to riding the rails. Yet. They'd managed so far to pay the mortgage, thanks to a cash infusion from Drusilla—a humiliating experience Connie felt forced to accept.

"You'll find another job," she said confidently to Winston as they sat in the library with winds howling outside. They'd limped through the holidays, but now she'd regained some of her equilibrium after the seismic shock of finding out they were broke. Now, with a new year upon them, she was ready for action. "You need a routine. Get up, get showered and dressed, and look for a job as diligently as if you were going to the office."

But her husband, once so disciplined and self-controlled, seemed unable to pull himself together, slumping further into despair. The telephone began ringing at odd hours, and he held hushed conversations behind the closed door of his study. When he did leave the house, she never knew where he was going nor when he would be back.

Whenever she asked, he muttered some gruff reply that told her nothing.

With the help of her father's lawyer, Lloyd Deveare, she'd already sold off most of the household goods that had any value, like the polished walnut piano, the cherrywood dining set, and the china, silver, and crystal. But even those fine-quality items didn't bring in as much cash as she'd hoped.

"There's not much of a market for high-end antiques in this current slump," Mr. Deveare explained. "If you can hold out a while longer, you may be able to get a better return."

But she wasn't able to hold out—not with a baby to feed and clothe and a household to run and creditors lurking around every corner. So she'd accepted what proceeds she could get and paid off the bookstore and the grocery and other places around town that had been extending her family credit for weeks. With the modest amount left over she opened a new bank account, under her own name, for emergencies, vowing never to touch it unless absolutely necessary.

Inevitably the slashing of the household budget meant letting go of staff. On a frigid winter day, she sadly gave Sam Crocker his notice.

"You're a good man, Sam. A hard worker and a loyal employee," she said past the lump in her throat as they stood in the warm kitchen. "You'll be able to find work in no time—at wages you deserve." She desperately hoped her prediction would pan out.

At first she couldn't bear to let Ingrid go, too. The thought of taking care of the baby and the house all on her own was too foreign and frightening to contemplate. But, as the bills piled up, and feeling at the end of her tether, she broke down in the kitchen and confided to her housekeeper.

"Oh, Ingrid. We're in trouble." She slumped over the kitchen table, head in hands. On some level, she knew it was deeply inappropriate to unburden her troubles on the hired help in this way, but she didn't know who else to turn to. Besides, since their trip together out to Pearl's farm before Christmas, Ingrid increasingly felt more like a friend to Connie than an employee. "I don't know what to do."

"You need money, Mrs. Sudderland?" Ingrid's voice was brisk. "I got some saved up in the bank. Is not a lot, but I won't see you and your family put out of your house."

Connie's heart was touched by the kind gesture. "No. I mean, yes, we do need money, but no, I don't want to borrow money from you. I'm afraid I can no longer afford to pay your wages. I'll have to let you go at the end of the month." She could hardly keep her voice from cracking as she shared the bad news.

From her seat across the table, Ingrid nodded, ever stoic. She placed her warm, rough hand over Connie's. "You and Mr. Sudderland have always been fair to me. More than fair. And I know for a fact that Sam felt the same way. So whatever it is you're going through, I want to help you if I can." She paused a moment, then said, "Remember I told you about my cousin Lotte who owns a beauty shop? She's been after me to come work for her. I been putting her off because, well, let's yust say Lotte can act a little crazy sometimes. Real bossy, you know? Gets on my nerves. Plus, I've been so happy working here, I didn't want to work for nobody else."

"I appreciate that. More than you know." Connie sighed heavily. "I'll hire you back just as soon as I can afford to. I just wish I could think of some way to earn some money."

Ingrid's voice was soothing. "Now, don't you fret, Mrs. Sudderland. The Lord will provide. I seen it happen time and time again."

Connie gave a bitter snort. "Unless the Lord can restore my husband's job or find him another one quickly, I don't see how He can help. "

"He might do so, or He might answer in some other way. You got to have faith. You got to be prepared that the Lord's answer might look different than what you are expecting." Ingrid gave Connie's hand a gentle squeeze. "You're a smart woman, Mrs. Sudderland. You're young and strong and smart. You got a good head on your shoulders. All gifts from the Lord. You yust keep watching. He's going to take care of you." She paused. "May I make a suggestion?"

"Certainly."

"You're a Christian woman, right?"

"Well, yes. I mean—yes." What a funny question. Of course she was. Wasn't she? She'd been baptized and confirmed at St. Lucian's. Those were the qualifications. Weren't they?

"Then pray to the Lord that He will use you wherever and however you can do the most good."

"Do good?" Connie tilted her head. "As in charity work?"

Ingrid lifted a shoulder. "Maybe, maybe not. Ask Him to show you where you can be the most useful. You might be amazed to see doors open up for you."

"I'll certainly do that," Connie replied out of politeness. She didn't see how praying would solve anything. The way Ingrid talked about God, as if she knew Him personally, reminded Connie of Aunt Pearl. It wasn't how people talked in the polished pews at St. Lucian's.

"And anodder thing," Ingrid continued. "Make a list of good things that happen to you. Every single day, five things you're thankful for. Write them in a little notebook. Maybe that pretty pink notebook you plan your parties in."

Connie snorted. "What good will that do? I need cash, not happy thoughts."

"Give thanks with a grateful heart. The Lord provides for you. Like the Good Book says, 'Let the peace of God rule in your hearts.' Yust try it and see."

Skeptical as she was, Connie could find no objection. "All right. I will," she said at last. She was ready to agree to anything to ease the sorrow of losing Ingrid.

"You should consider starting to go to church, too," the housemaid said finally. "My family attends a good one. Is only a few blocks from here."

"I already belong to a church," Connie said defensively. *Although I rarely attend*, she added silently. *And I don't know how much good it would do, anyway.*

Ingrid jotted a note on a scrap of paper and slid it across the table toward Connie. "You come for a visit. If you don't like it, you don't ever have to come back. But I think it would do you good to be among the people of God."

After the housekeeper left for the evening, Connie went to the nursery to check on Scotty. As she gazed at her sleeping baby boy, she muttered, "Two weeks. Two weeks until the end of the month and I lose Ingrid and have to somehow hold this family together. Winston's in no shape to help me. I may have been able to dance through life this far, but if I don't learn how to stand on my own two feet, we're going to lose this house. And maybe even this family." She swallowed hard. "Lord, if you're listening, please help me."

$$\maltese \quad 2\,4 \quad \maltese$$

Over the next two weeks, Connie soaked up as much information as she could from Ingrid about running a household. Among other household tips and tricks, the housekeeper showed her how to stretch a dime here and a nickel there at the grocery by selecting cheaper cuts of meat and less-than-perfect produce. She taught her how to use the washtub and clothesline and iron, how to scrub the bathrooms until they sparkled, how to sweep the carpets and clean the mirrors without leaving streaks. The pride and delight Connie had taken in her showpiece of a home diminished as she learned the work that went into maintaining so many rooms.

Remembering Ingrid's encouragement to be thankful, she tried every day to express gratitude for her blessings. Every night before bed, she dutifully recorded in her notebook five things to be thankful for. Her healthy, happy baby. Warm beds to sleep in. Cans of soup in the cupboard. Sometimes it was hard to come up with five things, but she found the little ritual did lift her mood and help her to focus on positive things instead of her own fears and anxieties.

On Ingrid's last day of employment, Connie sought her out to say good-bye and hand over her final pay envelope. The two women stood in the middle of the kitchen and embraced.

"I'll miss you, Mrs. Sudderland," the housekeeper said with a quiver in her voice.

"Oh, I'll miss you too, Ingrid. And please, no more 'ma'am' or 'Mrs. Sutherland.' From here on out, I'm just Connie."

"Yes, ma'am." They both laughed. "Sorry. Is a habit." Ingrid dabbed at her eye with a corner of her apron. Then her face brightened. "About my cousin's beauty parlor—"

"Yes?"

"I'm starting work there on Saturday. Would you like me to ask her if she'd carry a few bottles of Moondrop Miracle? Yust to see if they sell?"

"Oh, Ingrid, that's a fine idea. Why not? It would be a great help."

When she left the Sutherland house that evening, Ingrid carried in her bag a few bottles of Moondrop Miracle left over from Christmas.

The next afternoon, Connie ached to get out of the house and away from her husband's creeping depression. She wanted so much to help him, but he'd grown ever gloomier over their financial losses with each passing day. She shrugged into her coat, then popped her head around the door of the library and told Winston, "I'm going out for a little while. Scotty is asleep upstairs."

He grunted from behind his newspaper.

She glanced out the window. "The front walk needs shoveling. I'd appreciate if you'd do it, now that Sam's gone. It would give you some fresh air and exercise, and you'll still be nearby if Scotty wakes up."

He issued another grunt. She left the house and walked through the quiet, slush-filled streets toward the small business district of her suburb, breathing deeply of the wintry air. As long as she was out, she thought she might see if there were any help-wanted signs posted in any of the storefront windows. Just to look. Maybe there'd be some job Winston would be willing take on. Or possibly for herself, if she could convince him to agree to her working. In any case, one of them needed a job, and soon.

As she walked, she ran through her options. What kind of work was she qualified to do? She wasn't artistic or musical. She 'd never tried to teach anybody anything, and the sight of blood made her woozy. She could learn stenography, or she could clerk in a store.

Couldn't she? Deep down, she feared Winston was right. Maybe she had no marketable skills. Besides, she still had Scotty to care for. Even with Winston home all day, she felt uneasy about trusting him to care for their infant for more than an hour or two at a stretch.

There was also the problem that she'd never looked for a job in her life. She wasn't even sure how to do it. Did one simply ask, or was there some kind of protocol involved, some kind of etiquette?

Reaching the main street, she wandered up and down the small business district without seeing a single "help wanted" sign. But this was a rare opportunity to visit the shops alone, without Scotty in tow; she might as well try her luck. Squaring her shoulders, she approached a sturdy brick edifice with "J. P. Dornbusch, Pharmacist" etched on the glass. She paused in front of the drugstore, debating whether or not to go in. She'd entered it once or twice to pick up some cough drops or a magazine, but it had never struck her as a place to shop regularly, the kind of place where a woman like her would choose to spend her money. That could be a good thing, if it meant never running into her friends, if she were hired. She wouldn't mind for her own sake, but it would mortify Winston for their friends to see her working as a shop clerk.

She pushed open the door and entered. The shop was poorly lit and smelled musty. She suspected that, if she ran her gloved fingertip over a shelf, she'd find it covered in dust.

"Good afternoon," she said to the plump, bespectacled man behind the counter. He gave a slight, stiff bow.

"Good afternoon."

"Are you Mr. Dornbusch?" She gestured to the sign on the glass door.

"Yes. How may I help you?" He tilted his head so as to peer at her over the top of his spectacles.

"I... Well, I—" She found Mr. Dornbusch's cold demeanor intimidating, and her bravado faltered. She gestured at random toward the nearest shelf. "I just wanted to have a look at the, um, bandages here."

"What for?"

"Excuse me?" That seemed a rude question indeed. What business was it of his?

"What type of bandage do you need?" he asked, a little more slowly, as if she were hard of hearing.

"Oh. Just—just a small one, I suppose." Could she be any more ridiculous? *Just ask the man!*

He moved around the counter and walked toward the display. "Then I recommend the self-stick adhesive brand. They've improved a lot over the last few years."

"Have they?"

He handed her a small box with a picture of a bandage on the front. She stared at it, trying to untangle her thoughts.

"And if you also need mercurochrome, it's in the next aisle over," he said.

"Mercurochrome," she repeated. All at once, Aunt Pearl's strident voice sounded in her head.

For heaven's sake, Connie. Say to the man what you've come here to say.

Setting the unneeded purchase on the counter, she cleared her throat. "I just happened to be walking past and found myself wondering if you might have any job openings," she said lightly, as one might ask for shampoo.

The proprietor lifted a woolly-caterpillar eyebrow. "What sort of job?"

"Oh, you know—whatever needs doing." *Aack.* She had no idea what she was saying.

"I've no need of a saleslady, if that's what you mean," he said gruffly. "I can handle everything myself."

"I see."

He reached for the box of bandages in order to ring them up, but she took it from his hand and placed it back on the shelf.

"I've changed my mind."

Dejected, she trudged back out to the sidewalk. One by one, she went into each of the small businesses that lined the suburb's modest business district, asking the same question: Were they hiring? She hated doing so without Winston's approval, hated sneaking behind his back, but she was running out of options. In the end it didn't matter anyway. The hardware store, the grocery, the little movie theater—one by one, they turned her down. No experience, no training, no jobs to be had. *Times are hard,* said proprietor after proprietor. As if she didn't know. With as much dignity as she could muster, she exited each store, her heart a little heavier than when she'd entered.

Across the street from the train station was a coffee shop. She went inside and paid a dime for a cup of coffee. As she sat at the counter and breathed in the comforting steam of the beverage, she prayed. But instead of praying for a job, any job, she tried Ingrid's way: *Lord, where could I be of the most use?*

As she prayed, the image of the forlorn drugstore kept popping into her mind. She pictured the section devoted to beauty products, the dusty shelves, the lackluster inventory. She saw with clarity that she *could* be of use there. She might not have known much about retailing, but she did know what women liked when they shopped for personal-care items.

Summoning the spirited optimism of Aunt Pearl, with a dash of her late mother's genteel boldness as well, she straightened her spine, left the coffee shop, and marched straight back to the drugstore. The bell over the door jangled vigorously as she pushed open the door. She strode across the plank floor and banged her handbag on the counter.

"No, Mr. Dornbusch," she said with force, "I'm sorry but I won't accept it."

The proprietor looked up from his account book with a startled stare. "I beg your pardon, madam?"

"I won't accept that you don't need help. In fact, you are *not* handling everything yourself. Not well, at least." She lifted her chin. "I'm sorry to be so direct, but that's the honest truth."

Mr. Dornbusch's eyes widened in owlish surprise behind his spectacles.

"Look at this place." She made a sweeping gesture with her arm. "Your shop is dark and dreary. Your shelves are dusty. Your displays are in disarray, and your selection of ladies' grooming products is a disgrace. No woman worth her salt would choose to shop here. If you expect to make it through these hard times, you're going to need to sharpen your game. Clearly you *do* need someone to help you."

His ample cheeks reddened. "Madam, unless you have a background in pharmaceutical science, I don't see how you can be of any use to me."

She took a bold step forward. "Sir, I may not have a background or training in science, but I have a thorough background in shopping. I know the kinds of products ladies are eager to buy. I also know the kind of experience they want to enjoy when they're out shopping, and believe me, this isn't it."

The man appeared too startled to summon a response. She took pity on him and softened her tone a notch, adopting a more winsome approach.

"Look, Mr. Dornbusch. Times are tough all over. Many of the ladies who used to shop at the big department stores downtown can't afford to patronize them anymore, yet they still want and need their beauty products. They'll be looking to smaller retailers like yourself to fill the gap. To be their hero in a time of need."

Mr. Dornbusch's shoulders seemed to straighten a little at that notion.

Thus encouraged, Connie redoubled her effort. "Now, I know for a fact that women need to find less expensive alternatives to the products they were accustomed to buying at top-level stores. But they don't want to feel as though they're slumming. If you want to attract a decent clientele and keep them from going downtown to Marshall Field or Carson Pirie Scott, you're going to have to improve how you do things. I'm the woman you need."

Mr. Dornbusch appeared flustered by the flood of words, but when he collected himself, he leaned against the counter, arms crossed.

"If I agree to hire you," he said gruffly, "you'll get no special treatment. You're just like any other clerk ... if there were any other clerks."

"Suits me fine," she said, and meant it. "Hire me on. Let me handle the ladies' products and do some improvements to make the store more attractive overall. That'll free you up to handle the pharmacy work you do so well." No harm in tossing in a final appeal to his ego.

Finally Mr. Dornbusch agreed. "A trial run, mind you."

They went back and forth a bit more over the details, but, in the end, Connie left the shop with a part-time job and a small spring in her step. Now, all she had to do was break the news to Winston that she'd be a working wife now—a valued contributor to the household income. Most people would think this was a good thing, but Winston had a funny way of looking at the matter.

Mentally she calculated how to spend her wages. She wouldn't be making much, but it would at least be some money coming in. She determined that once Winston was over the shock of her getting a job, they'd sit down together and hash out a budget to make the most of every penny. They'd get so much farther if they worked together as a team.

When she approached the house, her steps slowed. The front walk remained unshoveled. Connie's annoyance churned. *So much for working as a team*. She trudged up the snow-covered steps and tugged open the front door. A blast of steam heat from the radiator in the foyer greeted her.

"Win?" she called as she removed her coat and boots. "Win, the least you could do is shovel the walk. The snow is up to my knees. Win?"

She found him in the library, sprawled in his favorite chair, snoring. Beside him lay his discarded newspaper. A wail from upstairs sent her racing up to the nursery. She picked up Scotty and soothed him. After changing the baby's diaper and settling him back into his crib, she charged downstairs.

"How could you be sleeping in the middle of the day? Have you been drinking?" She slammed the library door behind her. "You're supposed to be taking care of your son."

"What? Huh?" Win blinked groggily. "Where's Ingrid?"

"Need I remind you that we had to let her go? Taking care of your son is your responsibility. How long had he been crying?"

"He was crying?" Win rose unsteadily to his feet. "Is he hurt?"

Exasperation gripped Connie's throat. "Winston, how could you not hear him? Thankfully, he only needed changing. But something truly terrible could have happened."

"But it didn't. Right?"

"But it could have." Connie's voice rose. "How can you be so irresponsible? Goodness, you can't even shovel the walk."

"Where were you?"

"Out looking for a job. I was successful, too." She stood tall. "I'll be working at Mr. Dornbusch's drugstore, starting tomorrow."

Winston's face reddened under the stubble. "Working in a drugstore? Oh, that's rich. My wife out in public, working at a job. Just advertise to the whole neighborhood, why don't you, that your husband can't support you."

Connie flung up her hands. "Well, what do you expect me to do? You can't. Or rather, you won't, at least not at the moment. You'd rather sit here and feel sorry for yourself. Sam is gone, and Ingrid as well. If you won't look for a job, the least you could do is help out here at home."

She expected him to argue back. Instead, to her horror, he slumped back into his chair and put his head in his hands. "I've failed you."

She squelched the twinge of sympathy that rose. "I can't stand here any longer and listen to your self-pity. You haven't failed me. Contrary to what you seem to believe, I didn't marry you for your money. I married you because I loved you. *Love* you. For better, for worse, for richer, for poorer. Or have you forgotten?"

He said nothing, only gave her a look of defeat.

"The person you're failing is yourself," she continued. "You're not even giving yourself a chance to find work. Where is the strong, confident man I married? Get up, get dressed, and get moving. While you do that, I'll feed Scotty and get him settled, then fix us some dinner. Together, we'll put together a plan."

After feeding the baby, giving him a bath, and putting him in his playpen, she went into the kitchen, slipped one of Ingrid's aprons over her head, and tied it around her slender waist. She warmed up a can of chicken noodle soup and a few slices of toast for Winston and herself. She had not yet mastered cooking but was determined to improve her skills.

Eventually Winston shuffled in. She ladled soup into bowls, and they sat at the oilcloth-covered kitchen table. He hadn't shaved, but he'd showered and put on fresh clothes, which was an improvement. Her heart ached to see him like this. He had always been perfectly put together and in control, groomed like a matinee idol. Now as he lifted the soup spoon with a shaky hand, steadying his elbow against the table, the disheveled, puffy-faced fellow sitting across from her was like a different person, a stranger. She turned her focus to her own bowl. After they ate, she cleared the dishes, then sat down with a notepad and pencil.

"First, let's write down all our expenses. Mortgage, utilities, groceries ..." The pencil scratched furiously across the paper. Every little item in their daily life had to be addressed. Her pencil traveled down the list as she crossed off everything she could do without, naming them out loud. Win sat listlessly, silently. Finally, after crossing household staff off the list, she said,

"Without any hired help, I suppose we'd better consider moving to an apartment house."

Of all the suggestions, that one perked him up. "I don't want to move."

She tapped the pencil. "Neither do I, but we can't keep up otherwise."

"Mother's investments weren't as hard-hit as ours. She'll help us with the mortgage."

"I don't want to accept your mother's money. I'd rather move into a hovel than accept charity from her."

"It's only temporary. Just until the market—"

She flung the pencil onto the table with a clatter. "The market, the market! I'm so sick of hearing about the market. We need money *now*."

Win spoke just as firmly. "Not the house."

"But we can't keep up with it! It's not just the mortgage. Who's going to clean it? Who's going to sweep the carpets, and keep the furnace going, and mow the lawn in summer? When we can't even keep the darn walkway shoveled?" Tears of frustration pushed at the corners of her eyes. She brushed them away with an angry fist.

"If we sell the house, if we let the world know how poor we are, we'll never live it down."

"Nonsense. We'll simply find out who our real friends are, that's all."

Win's voice turned soothing, placating. "Not the house. Anything but that. Please. I'll help. I promise."

Connie sighed. After a moment she picked up the pencil. "First of all, we're not poor. We're broke. There's a difference. Poor is permanent. Broke is temporary. We'll get back on our feet. I know we will. I'm just not sure how." She picked up the notepad and eyed the list with ruthless determination. "So not the house. Yet. But everything else is on the chopping block. Let's see what else we can cut."

❧ 25 ❧

Because she felt her husband couldn't be trusted to watch the baby, Connie hired Ingrid's daughter, Sonja, to babysit for the few hours a week she was at work at the drugstore. A recent high-school graduate, Sonja was a good-natured, cheerful girl, similar to Ingrid in personality. But unlike her petite, plump mother, Sonja stood tall, rawboned, and awkward, with an unruly shock of blond hair that seemed to go every which way in spite of her halfhearted attempts to tame it with an oversize barrette. Her skin bore the angry red marks of adolescent acne. Ingrid had confided to Connie that the girl lacked confidence. But when Ingrid brought her over to meet the Sutherlands, Sonja took to Scotty immediately, holding him tenderly and cooing over him. Based on the smiles he offered, he liked her, too.

"You don't have to worry about a thing, Mrs. Sutherland," Sonja said as she rocked Scotty in her arms. "I grew up helping to care for my younger brothers. I know all about babies."

"A stern caretaker, too, she can be, when the situation calls for it," Ingrid added, smiling with pride at her daughter.

"Well, that's wonderful, Sonja," Connie said warmly. "I'm sorry that I can't afford to hire you for more than a few hours a week. That's as far as my wages will stretch. But I can't afford *not* to hire you, either.

My husband is ... well, he's too preoccupied with other concerns to take adequate care of the baby."

"Oh, we women are better with the babies, anyway," Ingrid asserted with a dismissive wave of her hand. "Men are all thumbs when it comes to the little ones."

Connie directed her smile at Sonja. "You'll take your meals with us, of course, whenever you're working. And you're welcome to raid the icebox anytime for whatever you may find there. Maybe over time we can figure out some other way to boost your compensation. "

"That's all right, Mrs. Sutherland," the girl said. "My mother tells me you are a wonderful woman to work for, and that means a lot. I'm happy to take care of little Scotty."

Connie felt herself blush and cast a grateful glance at Ingrid.

"Is true," the older woman said kindly. "I wouldn't have said it if it wasn't true."

It took Connie a little while to learn the ropes of working in the drugstore, but soon Mr. Dornbusch was trusting her to know her way around the shop and help customers find what they were looking for. After a couple of weeks, he even left her in charge for short stints while he ran an errand or went home for lunch.

"I suppose it's not bad to have some help," he admitted grudgingly after the first week, "but don't go changing things around too much. There's no room in the budget for useless frippery."

When she wasn't helping customers, Connie turned her decorative eye to sprucing up the product displays. First she stripped each shelf of its inventory and gave it a good scrubbing, then polished each box, bottle, and jar before placing them back in neat rows. She washed the dusty windows until they sparkled and took the curtains home and washed them as well, drying them on stretchers the way Ingrid had taught her. Instead of spritzing the air with cheap perfume, she brought from home some of the more delicate lavender water Ingrid had used when ironing sheets. The light lavender scent went a long way toward dispelling the musty air. Before long, the store became a more pleasant place to shop and, more important, to linger. Connie knew that the longer a customer stayed in the store, the more likely she was to buy something. That was certainly true of herself and her friends.

Meanwhile, Scotty seemed happy in Sonja's care. Feeling guilty about paying the girl so little, Connie expressed gratitude by giving her Moondrop Miracle in a little crystal bottle. While she didn't want to embarrass the girl by mentioning her blemishes, she couldn't help but hope that Moondrop Miracle would improve her complexion.

"Oh, thank you, Mrs. Sutherland," Sonja gushed, admiring the bottle. "I've never had anything so fancy."

Winston continued to sit home and drink, when he wasn't going out to destinations he didn't share with Connie. To drink more, she guessed.

One afternoon while she was dusting shelves at the drugstore, the bell over the door tinkled. She glanced up to see a familiar face.

"Connie? Connie Shepherd? Sorry. *Sutherland*." The expression of mixed shock and delight on Zoe Meade's face made Connie want to slap her.

Instead, she stood and smoothed her smock over her skirt, holding her temper in check. "Hello, Zoe."

Zoe continued to stare at her. "As I live and breathe. What are you doing here?"

"Working."

"Working as a shop girl?"

Connie glanced down at her smock. "It would appear so."

"My, my, my." Zoe looked around the shop and wrinkled her nose in distaste. "Well, I suppose you have to do what you have to do."

"I suppose so." Connie lifted her chin. "What can I help you with today, Zoe?"

"Just a jar of Pond's, please." Zoe giggled. "It seems so funny, having you wait on me."

It didn't seem particularly funny to Connie. But she let the comment pass, found the requested product on the shelf, and carried it to the counter.

"Will there be anything else?"

"No, thanks." Zoe said. "Actually, there's one thing. Can you ask

Winston to telephone my mother? She had a question about some rumor she heard."

"What rumor?" Connie asked, annoyed. No doubt Drusilla Sutherland had been gossiping to her friend Sally Meade about their private affairs.

"Something about an investment? Heavens. I'm sure I don't know," Zoe snapped as she paid for her purchase. "Just have him give her a ring, will you? She's most eager to hear from him." With that, she swept out the door.

Connie relayed the message to Winston when she got home. "You might not have to worry that my having a job will tip off the neighborhood about the state of our finances," she added. "It sounds like your mother is broadcasting the news far and wide."

Win grunted but didn't say anything more. Instead he went into his study and shut the door.

Weeks passed. Connie came home weary and tired on the evenings she worked. One Tuesday, after taking over Scotty's care from Sonja, feeding him, and putting him to bed, she heated up some canned soup for herself and coaxed Winston to eat as well. He joined her but said nothing until she sat down to relax a bit with her own meal. Then, he started grumbling. He turned a red, bleary eye to her. "Why are you gone all the time?"

"I'm working. One of us has to."

He crumbled a cracker into his soup bowl. "It's embarrassing, having my wife out peddling in a drugstore."

"My 'peddling,' as you call it, is keeping us in soup and crackers."

He slammed down his spoon. "I suppose you think I'm not trying. I suppose you think you can do better without me."

Connie sighed. "I didn't say that. Although, I do think you could make more of an effort."

He shoved back his chair and stood, flushed and unsteady. He put a hand against the wall to brace himself.

Connie peered at him with concern. "Are you all right?"

He didn't answer, but he didn't need to. The smell of whiskey answered for him.

She sighed. "Tell me, Win. Do you have a better idea to keep us afloat than for me to work in a drugstore? Do you?"

He slumped back into his chair and put his head in his hands. After a long groan, he said, "I don't know why you stay with me."

"When you act like this, I don't know either."

She pushed back from the table, dumped her bowl in the sink, and went upstairs to bed. She lay motionless in the dark. After what seemed like hours, she heard the sound of the front door slamming shut behind her husband. She rolled over to lie on her side, pulled the blanket up over her shoulders and closed her eyes. Sleep ... she needed a good night's sleep. Tomorrow morning, things would be clearer. She'd be able to figure out where they'd gone wrong and what she could do to make it right.

❧ 26 ❧

A few weeks later, on a stormy Monday afternoon in March, Connie slumped in front of the library fireplace, staring into the flames. Lighting the fire had felt like an act of defiance, as the supply of wood had dwindled, and there was little money to buy more, but winter was almost over. She was so tired of feeling cold. Winston was out—where, she didn't know—and Scotty was playing contentedly on the floor.

In spite of the fire's warmth, she felt frozen and empty inside. On the end table beside her lay a letter from Aunt Pearl, its envelope torn in Connie's eagerness to open it. It had arrived that morning after Connie had finally confided her troubles. Her aunt had enclosed a small check, along with regret at not having more money to send her. *Most of my money is tied up in the farm*, she wrote. *I've spent the rest in coming here to India and helping Ruby's ministry.*

That part Connie understood. What she didn't understand was her aunt's lack of sympathy with her situation. She'd hoped for some encouragement, for some wise words of comfort, but had received only platitudes. *God will provide. Sometimes the answer is right in front of you. Take it step-by-step. Remember to sparkle!*

She stood and flung the letter into the fire. She was tired of hearing this God-will-provide stuff from everybody. If the answer was right in front of her, she couldn't see it. And she had zero intention of "sparkling" anytime soon.

The telephone rang, and she shot up a prayer of gratitude that at least that utility was still connected. She picked up the receiver.

"Hello?"

A moment of silence on the line was followed by a gruff male voice.

"Hello? Is this the Sutherlands?"

"It is."

"Connie?" A note of surprise entered the voice.

"Who is this?"

"George Carpenter."

"George?" Why was Gwen's husband calling?

"I—I was expecting your maid to answer."

"Just me, I'm afraid. What can I do for you?"

"I'm actually calling to talk to Win."

"I'm sorry, he's not here. He's gone out." *To the corner bar, most likely.*

"For how long?" George sounded annoyed.

"I don't know," she said.

"Oh. Well, it's urgent I speak with him."

You and a dozen others. Grimly, Connie thought of the stack of phone messages she'd piled on Winston's desk over the last few days— messages from angry people. Former clients, most likely. She doubted that her husband had answered a single one of them.

"I'll tell him you called, George," she said.

"You do that." His unfriendly tone made her stomach contract. Annoyed strangers, she could understand, but George was supposed to be a friend.

She was about to hang up when she heard a muffled, shuffling sound, then Gwendolyn's bright voice floated over the line.

"Con, dear, can I drive over? Will you be at home?"

Connie swallowed. If George was angry with Winston, maybe Gwen wanted to read her the riot act, even break off their friendship. But she couldn't bring herself to ask, so she said, "Sure. Come on over."

She carried Scotty to the kitchen and gave him a bottle, then put the kettle on the stove. A half hour later, Gwendolyn's Cadillac splashed up the driveway.

"Look! Mama's friend is here," she said to Scotty as she pointed at the car. She choked up a little at the word "friend." She hadn't realized how lonely she'd been feeling.

"I felt I needed to speak to you in person," Gwen said after she'd shrugged out of her rain-spotted coat. "I'm sorry George was so rude to you. I'm afraid he's rather frantic that he can't reach Winston. Something about an investment?"

"Let's have some tea," Connie said. "I was just about to make myself a cup." She left Gwen in the library, bouncing Scotty on her Chanel-clad lap, and went into the kitchen. She returned with a tray of tea paraphernalia.

When they'd settled before the fire, teacups in hand, Scotty playing on the floor, Gwen got to the point of her visit.

"What's going on, Con? George only wants to ask Winston some questions."

"Everyone wants to ask Winston some questions," Connie said. "And they all sound angry. But he doesn't call them back, and they just get angrier. He won't talk to me about it. When I ask questions, he shuts me out."

Gwen's eyes reflected a mixture of sympathy and pity. "I'm sorry, darling. I know Winston keeps you in the dark, and I don't want you to worry about it. Honestly, it's not *that* much money—not so much we can't afford to do without it until Win can pay us back."

Connie's heart sank. Under the current circumstances, she could see no way they could pay the Carpenters back, much less the other investors hounding him—and now her—for money.

"I—I'm sorry," was all she could think of to say.

Gwen waved her hand. "Never mind. I really came here to talk about something more important. Moondrop Miracle."

"What?" Connie emerged from her daze, barely remembering the fanciful name she'd given to Feline De-Flaker.

"That stuff is magic," Gwendolyn said, pulling an empty bottle out of her handbag. "It's done wonders for my flaky winter skin. Do you have any more? I'd like to buy another bottle from you."

Connie stood and beckoned her friend to follow. "Come into the kitchen. I think I've got some in the pantry. I've been experimenting with it a bit, but nothing improves on Aunt Pearl's original formula."

"Ingrid allows you to meddle in her kitchen?" Gwendolyn joked as they walked down the hallway to the back of the house.

Connie sighed. "Ingrid's gone, I'm sorry to say. We had to let her go. Through no fault of her own, of course."

Gwendolyn frowned. "Oh, Connie, have things gotten that bad? I'd heard rumors, but I didn't believe them. I'm so sorry."

Rumors like I'm working in a drugstore? Connie looked at the floor. "It's been one thing after another. Winston made some bad investments. Then he used all our savings and insurance to cover the losses, even my inheritance from my parents, but it wasn't enough. If he could have gotten another job, he would have earned it all back. I know he would have. If there's one thing he knows, it's how to make money. But he hasn't been able to get another job. And now it seems he's given up." She gave Gwendolyn a pleading look. "You won't tell George all this, will you? It would damage Win's pride to think George knew. He will pay George back, every cent he's owed. Eventually."

"Goodness, being out of work is nothing to be ashamed of," Gwendolyn said. "And it's hardly a secret. Not a day goes by that a bank doesn't close or a major firm doesn't go belly-up. But of course, I won't say anything to George." She touched Connie's hand. "You're not the only one, you know. The Meades have been struggling as well. I saw Zoe on the street the other day, and she didn't look well at all. Kind of down-at-heel, you know. She and her mother have moved in with a grandmother or great-aunt or something."

"Oh, no. I'm surprised to hear it," Connie said, remembering the humiliating condescension of Zoe's visit to the drugstore. "And sorry, too," she added, a bit insincerely. "But it's nothing new. Thanks to that high-stakes-gambler father of hers, her family's fortunes have rocketed up and plummeted down ever since we were girls. Remember how Zoe'd wear a brand-new fur stole to school one week, then have to borrow lunch money from us the next? The Meades will bounce back. They always do."

"Maybe." Gwen shrugged. "I hope so, for Zoe's sake."

"Perhaps I should drop her a note."

"Perhaps you should. She's always been so jealous of you. It might make her feel better if she knew ..." Gwendolyn stopped abruptly. Faint red circles rose in her cheeks. "Sorry, Con. How tactless of me."

"If she knew that she and I are in the same boat?" Connie finished. "Don't worry about that, Gwen. She knows." She briefly related the story of Zoe's drugstore visit. "Believe me, she was perfectly giddy to see me reduced to working as a shopgirl."

Gwen nibbled her lower lip. "I heard. Zoe told us you'd taken a job at a drugstore, but I confess, I thought she must have been mistaken."

"Not mistaken."

Gwen looked at her a moment, then said briskly, "Well, you're sure to make a great success of it then. You needn't worry about what Zoe or anyone else thinks. Anyway, back to Moondrop Miracle, how about I take three bottles? Two for me and one for my mother. I know she'll love it as much as I do."

Connie's shoulders slumped. "Gwen, you don't have to—"

"I want to," her friend said firmly.

Connie pulled the last three bottles of Moondrop Miracle from the pantry and set them on the table. "This is all I have left. You're welcome to it."

"What do I owe you?"

"Oh, I can't charge you for it," Connie said, embarrassed. "You're my close friend. I can't possibly take your money."

Gwendolyn insisted. "I'll write you a check immediately." She reached into her handbag and pulled out a leather-bound checkbook and a silver fountain pen.

"I can't take money from you," Connie said, shaking her head. "It wouldn't be right."

"You will take my money, Connie." Gwen picked up one of the bottles and held it up to the light, swirling it so the transparent green liquid sparkled. "Moondrop Miracle is worth every penny and more." She set the bottle down, scribbled on the check, and tore it from the pad with a flourish.

Connie looked at the figure on the check, and pride flared in her chest, followed quickly by humiliation. Yes, they needed the money. But it went against everything in her character to accept charity.

As if reading her mind, Gwen said quietly, "Just take it, Con. If you want to consider it a loan, go ahead. But I won't accept a nickel of it back. I believe in Moondrop Miracle, and I believe in you."

Tears pressed against Connie's throat as she reluctantly took the check and folded it. Gwen believed in her. She didn't want to offend her dear friend by continuing to refuse, though privately she vowed to pay back every cent. She'd figure out a way.

Gwendolyn stowed the checkbook and pen in her handbag and snapped it shut.

"You really should consider selling Moondrop Miracle, Con. It's great stuff. And try getting it carried in some stores," she suggested. "It's a top-drawer product, as good as anything I've ever found at Marshall Field. Aim for the top, for the carriage trade. That's where the money is."

"But I don't know the first thing about selling," Connie scoffed.

"Sure you do," Gwen said. "I've seen you sell plenty of dinner reservations and raffle tickets on behalf of our dear old school."

"Oh, but that's different," Connie protested. "That's not selling. That's fund-raising."

"How is it different? In either case, you're convincing people to open their wallets in order to get something they perceive as having value."

"I suppose so," Connie said doubtfully. "But as for getting it carried in stores, I wouldn't know where to begin."

"Everything's learnable," Gwen said. "Anyway, think about it. I've got to run."

Connie saw Gwen to her car, then returned to the warm library. She gazed at the glowing embers, lost in thought. Was this what Aunt Pearl had meant by the answer being right in front of her? Was this the next step? Would Moondrop Miracle prove to be the answer to her prayer?

27

After Gwendolyn's visit and her purchase of Moondrop Miracle, Aunt Pearl's words about the Lord providing scrolled through Connie's mind for days. Was Moondrop Miracle somehow connected to that provision? Ingrid, too, had always been good at letting the peace of God rule in her heart. Connie wanted that peace. She wanted to find out what it was that made difficult burdens easy to bear for Ingrid and Aunt Pearl. Although she doubted both women's easy conviction that the Lord would provide for her, the following Sunday, Connie determined to go to church. It would be good for them all, she decided, to think about bigger things than just themselves.

She hadn't been back to St. Lucian's since Scotty's christening and, before that, her parents' funeral service. Now, the elegant city church seemed too far of a drive, and she wasn't eager to encounter people she knew, friends of her parents, who'd grasp her hand and look deeply into her eyes and ask in low voices about how she was doing.

So, instead of going to St. Lucian's, she bundled up Scotty in his stroller and walked down the snowy sidewalk to the small church in the neighborhood that Ingrid had recommended. When she'd asked Winston, "Want to come along with us?" he'd shaken his head silently without lifting his gaze from the newspaper. He remained slouched in his chair unshaven, still dressed in his lounging robe and slippers.

Connie pushed Scotty's carriage down the street, mincing along the icy sidewalk, warm in her sable coat. At least she could hold her head up about the coat. Wrapped in sable, she needn't worry that people would know she and Win were poor as the proverbial church mice. Appearances had been important to the well-heeled parishioners at St. Lucian's, and she assumed it would matter here in the neighborhood church as well. *People can be so judgmental,* she thought, cringing at the memory that she herself had spent many a church service scrutinizing not the state of her soul, but the trim and tailoring on a neighbor's hat.

She wheeled the carriage up the curved brick sidewalk of the quaint English country-style church. The heavy wooden door swung open, and a gray-suited usher greeted her with a smile and a warm handshake.

"Come in," he said heartily. "Come in out of the cold. You're welcome to leave the carriage here in the vestibule."

Connie lifted a drowsy Scotty out of the carriage. The usher hoisted the contraption up the steps and set it next to the brick wall of the vestibule near a steam radiator. "It'll be nice and toasty for the little fellow after the service."

"Thank you," she said with a smile of gratitude, mildly surprised at the usher's friendliness.

The small sanctuary was filled almost to capacity. The usher helped her find a seat with room to lay Scotty on the pew next to her. She spotted Ingrid seated across the room, flanked by several young people whom she guessed were her children, including Sonja. Ingrid grinned and waved. Connie nodded, then looked away. No waving ever took place at St. Lucian's—and very little smiling.

Connie had never considered herself a religious person, but as the service progressed, she found the organ music comforting, the hymns inspiring, and the pastor eloquent. But suddenly the text of his sermon brought her up short.

"'Humble yourselves in the sight of the Lord, and He will lift you up,'" the pastor quoted from the Book of James. He glanced at his notes. "In the words of the great Charles Spurgeon, "If you claim to believe in Christ, yet you go on living a light, frivolous, giddy life, your faith is belief in a lie."

In the words "frivolous and giddy life," Connie thought of her own life.

The pastor continued, "Repentance is as essential to salvation as faith; indeed there is no faith without repentance."

Something stirred deep within Connie's chest. Feeling desperate, she bowed her head and poured out her heart to God. She'd been going about it all wrong, looking for peace first and not finding it, because she hadn't humbled her pride. Now she admitted she couldn't continue moving forward under her own power. That was what Aunt Pearl and Ingrid had that she lacked: genuine repentance. In place of their pride, there was peace.

In desperation she prayed to the Lord for guidance. For some pathway out of her and Winston's problems. No answer came to her immediately, no bright light or angel choir. But she did feel a sense of peace that, in spite of her circumstances, everything would turn out for the best. And if it didn't, that she'd have help to be strong enough to cope with whatever came.

After the service, several people in the congregation welcomed her warmly, smiling at Scotty and introducing themselves in a friendlier manner than she'd ever experienced at St. Lucian's, where the social hour seemed more focused on stylish people seeing and being seen. A jovial woman invited her to join them in the church hall for coffee. Connie started to beg off, eager to get home and think about the experience she'd just had. But then Ingrid bustled up with her children.

"So glad to see you here today, Mrs. Sudderland. And you, little Scotty. You remember Sonja. These are my boys, Carl and Magnus."

Sonja reached for the baby.

"Hello, Scotty. May I hold him?"

"I suppose that would be all right." Connie handed Scotty to the girl, who instinctively began to rock him. He sucked his thumb contentedly.

In the church hall, the family and Connie took seats around a table. The ladies sipped coffee from thick white china cups while the boys nibbled at cookies. Ingrid slid a piece of paper toward Connie.

"Here is a notice about our upcoming neighborhood working-women's club meeting," she said. "Is two weeks from Saturday. We mostly socialize, but we have a speaker and we buy and sell some things to raise funds for the needy."

"Do you? That's nice." Connie, watching Sonja hold her son, was only half listening.

"I think you should come."

Connie glanced at the flyer. "Maybe," she said, just to be polite, although the prospect held little interest for her.

"I think you should come and *speak*," Ingrid said, a little more forcefully.

"Me? Speak? What would I speak about?"

"We invite speakers who talk to the ladies about interesting things. You could talk about Moondrop Miracle, about how your aunt gave you the recipe and you turned it into something special. Have some bottles on hand to sell. Maybe give away some little samples for free, so ladies can know what it's like."

"Oh, I don't know ..." she demurred. "I hardly think I'd have anything of interest to say. And ingredients cost money." *Money I don't have.*

"I think what you do with Moondrop Miracle is inspiring," Ingrid said. "Something brewed up in your own kitchen. I'll bet plenty of ladies will be wanting to buy some, after they sample it." Ingrid tapped her index finger on the table as if driving home a point. "You have to think long-term, if you want your business to succeed."

"My business?" Connie hadn't thought of herself as a business-woman before, but clearly that's what Ingrid saw.

Ingrid shrugged. "You have to have samples," she said sensibly. "Is cost of doing business."

That got Connie's attention. If she could sell some bottles of Moondrop Miracle to the church ladies, perhaps she could bring in a little extra money to pay the electric bill. "Do you really think they'd be interested?"

"The ladies in our community would snap it up." Ingrid paused. "Of course, the proceeds would go to the needy. Is fund-raiser, after all."

Connie's face heated at her own presumption that she'd get to keep the profits. "Of course," she said.

"But think of how many ladies will learn about Moondrop Miracle who would never otherwise know about it." Ingrid leaned forward eagerly. "You'll want to give out samples, and the ladies will want to buy some to take home, too. You better bring plenty. I'd say fifty bottles should do it. Big ones for selling, little ones for sampling."

Connie felt dizzy. "That much? But I can't possibly make fifty bottles of Moondrop Miracle in a week."

"Of course you can. We will help you. Won't we, Sonja?"

Over Scotty's head, Sonja nodded.

"I'll think about it," Connie promised.

She said good-bye to Ingrid and Sonja, bundled Scotty into the radiator-warmed carriage, and walked down the sidewalk through thickly falling snow, contemplating. On the one hand, she didn't see herself promoting Moondrop Miracle at all, much less to a crowd of working-class women like Ingrid. On the other hand, doing so could let people know about the product, and maybe they'd recommend it to their friends. Maybe eventually Connie could earn a little extra cash that her family so badly needed. By the time she turned onto her street, she'd determined to ask Mr. Dornbusch to let her have the relevant Saturday off.

Approaching her house, she saw that the Bromleys next door had sent their handyman, Leroy, to shovel out the Sutherlands' drive. He was just finishing up as she approached. Cheeks burning, she waved her thanks, and he waved back with a broad grin. Inside the house, she settled Scotty in his playpen, then telephoned Mary Bromley to thank her.

"Don't mention it." Mary sounded sympathetic. But Connie felt driven to explain.

"We—we're short on help at the moment, you see."

"Yes, Leroy mentioned that you'd let Sam go."

Connie swallowed. "Anyway, my husband has been meaning to get to the shoveling. He has been, um, rather ill a lot this season." She couldn't bear to have the neighbors thinking Winston was a drunkard, all evidence to the contrary.

"I'm sorry to hear about his poor health," Mary said. "It's no trouble for Leroy to do it. I'll ask him to keep an eye out."

Connie's cheeks burned with shame. She recoiled from pity from anyone, including—maybe especially—from neighbors. "You're very kind, but please don't put Leroy to any trouble. I hate to create extra work for him." *And I can't afford to pay him either.* Who knew it would be so hard to accept a kind gesture?

After hanging up the telephone, she sat at the kitchen table with her notebook and pen and a cup of tea. She still thought selling Moondrop Miracle beyond her circle of friends was a harebrained idea. But what would it hurt to try? If she was going to make a success of this venture, she had to make a plan.

She needed ingredients. To buy ingredients, she needed money. And to get money, she needed to keep her job at the drugstore. Life would be hectic, to say the least.

❧ 28 ❧

The following Monday, like army recruits on their first day of basic training, Ingrid, Sonja, and Sonja's friend Joleen lined up in the Sutherland kitchen while Connie paced back and forth in front of them like a drill sergeant.

"All right, ladies," she said in her most authoritative tone. "Thanks for coming over this morning. We need fifty bottles of Moondrop Miracle for the working women's club by the end of the day."

"Plus samples," Ingrid added.

"We need to follow these instructions to the letter." Connie waved Aunt Pearl's formula over her head with a flourish. "No deviations. No getting creative. The instructions need to be followed exactly. Any questions?"

Joleen glanced at the bright floral apron wrapped over her dainty dress. "Does this thing come in stripes? Stripes are more flattering."

"Yoleen, focus," Ingrid snapped.

Sonja took the paper from Connie and read it over. "You've made this before, right, Mrs. Sutherland?"

"Only once, last Christmas," Connie admitted. "But with your mother's help, it turned out well. I'm sure we can do it again."

"We made it together," Ingrid added with a grin. "Is always better to work on things together."

"That's right." Connie returned her smile. Dear Ingrid!

Joleen, reading over Sonja's shoulder, pointed to the paper. "What's dicing?"

Sonja turned to her friend. "It means cutting up into little squares. You know, like *dice?* Like we use in Bunco?" At the girl's blank expression, Sonja sighed. "Joleen, don't you remember anything from domestic science class in high school?"

Her friend shrugged. "I must have been sick the day they taught dicing."

Connie snatched the paper back. "Here, I'll do the dicing. While I'm doing that, can somebody put the water on to boil?"

Ingrid took charge of the girls. "Yoleen, fill that pot with water and turn the flame under the burner to high. Sonja, you chop up the herbs. I'll wash and sterilize the bottles."

Connie blinked at the large box she hadn't noticed before, filled with attractive commercial-grade bottles. She picked one up and examined it. "You have fifty of these? I thought we were using those vials I bought, the kind Aunt Pearl uses. Where did you find such pretty ones?"

Ingrid pressed her lips together, then said, "I have my sources." Connie chose not to inquire further but suspected Ingrid's moonshiner uncle was somehow involved. "We use your little miniature vials for the samples. Come on, girls, we get cracking."

By the end of the afternoon, the kitchen was an absolute mess. Pots had boiled over, forgotten pans had started smoking, glass jars had smashed on the tile floor. But fifty neatly labeled jars of Moondrop Miracle stood lined up like soldiers on the counters, along with as many samples poured into tiny vials.

"Thank you, ladies." Connie clasped her hands over her heart. "I couldn't have done it without your help. Now, take off your aprons, and let's go into the living room and relax with some cocoa."

Later, after Ingrid and the girls had gone home, Connie cleaned up the splattered kitchen as best she could. Then, she took the recipe upstairs and tucked it safely back among her wedding memorabilia, along with a whispered prayer that fifty jars of Moondrop Miracle would somehow, some way, help her put food on her family's table.

The following Saturday, seated on a folding chair beside a stark cinder-block wall in the church basement, Connie nervously sipped her tea, the white china cup rattling in the saucer. A church basement was not her natural habitat, and the assembled variety of women glancing at her with curiosity did not belong in her usual social circle. But things were different now, she reminded herself. In a few moments, she'd be the center of attention as she told the women about Moondrop Miracle and demonstrated how to use it. What if they laughed at her? Or worse, what if they felt sorry for her? From time to time she glanced over at Ingrid, who gave her a reassuring smile.

Finally, a matron in a heathery tweed suit and horn-rimmed glasses said, "Let's open our meeting, ladies." After running through a few parliamentary procedures and the reading of the minutes and the treasurer's report, she smiled at Connie.

"Today our special guest is Mrs. Winston Sutherland the Third. Mrs. Sutherland is a dear friend of our own Ingrid Swenson."

Several fluttery murmurs of appreciation sounded throughout the room.

"We've invited her here today to tell us about an exciting new product. Mrs. Sutherland?" The tweed-clad woman ceded the floor.

Connie stood and discreetly wiped her damp palms on her skirt. She walked to the front of the room to where a small table had been set up holding bottles of Moondrop Miracle. She lifted one.

"Moondrop Miracle is a skin tonic, but not just any skin tonic. It contains fenugreek, an exotic ingredient from India." She gave a talk about skin health that she'd picked up nearly word for word from one of Pearl's medical texts. "And the good news is, you'll each get a sample bottle here today." She had full faith that the quality would be appreciated and the women would come back for more.

To her astonishment, the women paid attention. One woman raised her hand.

"Does it work on eczema?"

"I don't know," Connie responded with honesty. "I'm not a doctor or a dermatologist, so that's who you should check with. But, in my opinion, it's worth a try. Maybe dab a little on your wrist first to make sure you don't have an allergic reaction."

Another woman asked, "Does it cure blemishes?"

"It's done so for me," Sonja piped up. Connie tossed her a wink.

"It doesn't *cure* anything," Connie was careful to say. "But it will certainly help clear up your skin."

The ladies passed around the sample bottles, sniffing them and dabbing the tonic on the backs of their hands. As they made positive comments, Connie soon forgot her awkwardness and found she enjoyed answering all of the ladies' questions and concerns. The ladies were enthusiastic and promised to tell others about it.

By the end of the afternoon, every lady had her sample bottle of Moondrop Miracle. Several had bought up all of the stock she'd brought with her.

The next morning after the church service, Ingrid approached her and thrust an envelope into her hand. "Here."

"What's this?" Connie asked.

"I spoke to the head of our women's club," Ingrid said in a low voice. "I told her I knew of a family that could use the money from the meeting yesterday. And now I'm giving it to you."

"Oh, no. I can't take this money." Connie thrust the envelope at Ingrid, who crossed her arms without taking it.

"Yes, you can," Ingrid insisted. "You need it as much as anyone. Maybe more."

Much as Connie hated to accept charity, later that evening as she wrote out a check to the electric company, she felt a deep sense of relief. Gratitude toward the little club swelled in her heart. She vowed to pay the money back, and more, just as soon as she could.

Along with her gratitude, another feeling fluttered under her breastbone. A feeling of hope. Of possibility. The cash in the envelope told her that someone—even several someones, people who were not personal friends and felt under no obligation to make her feel good— wanted Moondrop Miracle and were willing to pay for it with their hard-earned cash.

Maybe she could keep the wolf from the door, after all.

❧ 29 ❧

A s word spread of the success of her presentation, invitations
began to trickle in from other local clubs and women's organi-
zations. Connie found herself gone from home often, leaving
Scotty with Sonja or Mrs. Bromley. The money she earned paid for
food and fuel and more ingredients, so she could make more bottles of
Moondrop Miracle, usually just in time for the next presentation.

Through it all, Winston complained about how often she was out,
complained about the mess in the kitchen, complained about the
hours she put in at the drugstore, earning money to keep them afloat
and buy more ingredients. But he didn't lift a finger to help. Increasingly he spent time away from home. He'd even managed to be out—
conveniently, Connie thought darkly—on the Monday afternoon in
April when his mother stepped out of the taxicab and onto the Sutherland doorstep. Connie willed her welcoming smile to stay in place.

In her letter, Drusilla had been vague about the length of her visit,
and Connie hadn't wanted to press, but from the startling quantity of
luggage that the taxi driver piled up in the hallway, it looked as if she
planned to stay permanently.

"Where's your maid?" the older woman said, looking around as if
she'd find Ingrid lurking behind the potted palm.

171

"I'm afraid that, due to Winston's job loss, we've had to economize on household help."

Drusilla made no comment to that. Instead, as Connie took her coat and hung it in a closet, she said, "I see you've done something different with your hair. It's shorter."

Connie started to thank her when the older woman sighed heavily.

"Never mind. It'll grow back."

Over tea, Drusilla recounted her experiences on the train journey—each one negative, everything from the too-salty scrambled eggs to the too-chatty seatmate.

"Surely you passed some gorgeous scenery," Connie said in an effort to lift the mood. "The springtime landscapes must have been beautiful to look at."

"Perhaps," her mother-in-law conceded, "but who could tell through windows that dirty?"

When they'd finished their tea, Connie gave Drusilla a tour of the house, which she'd only viewed in its unfinished state at the time of the wedding. Now her beady gaze took in the details of each of Connie's painstakingly decorated rooms with little commentary beyond, "It's quite a large place, isn't it? I hope it's not drafty."

In the nursery, she peered down at her grandson, sound asleep in his crib. "Nice to see the good old stock replenished again," she remarked, as if sizing up a prize steer at the county fair.

"And here's your room." Connie swung open the door to the guest room. "Your bath is attached. The nursery is next door, and we're at the end of the hall." A wail pierced the quiet. "That's the baby," she said unnecessarily. "I'll leave you to freshen up before dinner. I'm sorry we no longer have a housemaid to help you unpack your luggage."

"I suppose I can do it myself," Drusilla said, sounding aggrieved.

Leaving her mother-in-law to unpack and inspect her surroundings, Connie went to the nursery, picked up Scotty, and carried him down-stairs. In the kitchen she settled him into his playpen and gave him a toy to chew on. As she hoisted herself to the stove and ignited the burner under the kettle, she savored the comforting silence of the kitchen. How was she going to survive however many weeks—or months—Drusilla decided to stay?

Dinner that evening was a simple affair—pork chops and rice and canned peas. Connie's cooking skills were improving with practice, but not as quickly as she'd hoped. After dinner, the family gathered in the cozy library. Connie was so relieved to have Winston take over the chore of entertaining his mother that she didn't mind relinquishing the comfort of her favorite armchair to the older woman. As mother and son caught up on news about distant relations Connie didn't know, she snuggled her own little son on the sofa.

Presently, Drusilla brought out gifts she'd brought for the baby: an exquisite blue knitted coat trimmed with blue ribbon with a little cap and booties to match. Beautiful as the garments were, the memory of shopping with her mother for baby supplies and maternity clothes wrenched Connie's heart.

"Thank you so much, Mother Sutherland," she said. "They're perfect." Looking satisfied, Drusilla settled back into her armchair.

"I thought the child should have *some* nice things."

Connie breathed a silent prayer for patience. She was going to need it.

"And I understand you're working now, at a job." Drusilla's nose wrinkled slightly as though detecting a foul odor.

"I've taken a part-time job in a drugstore. And on the side I sell Moondrop Miracle."

"Moon what?"

"Moondrop Miracle. It's a skin treatment invented by my aunt, Pearl Russell. You met her at the wedding."

"Did I?"

"Yes. Anyway, she came up with this marvelous formula. Typically I brew up a big batch on Mondays, and bottle it. Then I make deliveries to customers' houses during the week, between shifts at the drugstore."

Drusilla lifted a skeptical eyebrow. "And you do all this by yourself?"

"Yes. Perhaps you'd like to help me while you're here."

"I think not." Drusilla touched her pearl necklace as if drawing strength from a talisman. "Gracious, how modern you are. Who takes care of the child while you're off doing that?" She made it sound as if

Connie were spending every afternoon betting on the ponies at Arlington Park.

"His father does, when he's able," Connie replied pointedly. "A young lady named Sonja takes care of him frequently. And Mrs. Bromley next door is on call as back-up." It had turned out that Mary Bromley was more than happy to care for Scotty during the hours that Connie worked, when Sonja was unavailable. The older woman had confessed that her only daughter and her husband had moved to California, taking her only grandchild with them. "I miss them so," she'd told Connie, her eyes moist. "Caring for your Scotty will be a comfort to me."

But now Drusilla bristled. "Well, thank goodness I've come," she declared. "At least now my grandson will have adequate care."

30

There was one upside to Drusilla's visit, as far as Connie could tell, and that was that Winston shaved, showered, and generally took care of himself when his mother was present. He even curbed his drinking somewhat. Although mother and son frequently engaged in hushed conversations from which Connie was excluded, she felt encouraged by seeing an improvement in his demeanor while his mother was around. Still, even with the crabbiest boss east of the Mississippi, she couldn't help but look forward to her shifts at the drugstore, if only to escape from home for a little while.

Connie was at the store alone one May evening, close to closing time, when the bell jangled over the door. Mr. Dornbusch had left early for an appointment, so she was alone in the store. She paused in counting the day's receipts, closed the cash-register drawer, and looked up as a tall, broad-shouldered man entered the shop. He was silhouetted against the setting sun pouring in through the plate-glass window. Connie shielded her eyes with her hand so she could see him. He was well-dressed, if a bit flashy for her taste, wearing a sharply tailored suit and a fedora pulled low over his thick dark eyebrows. He sauntered over to the counter where she stood.

"May I help you?" she said as he approached. A sense of apprehension enveloped her, and she wished Mr. Dornbusch had not left early.

He touched the brim of his fedora by way of greeting but did not remove it. His smile, though attractive, contained something she didn't trust. She was glad the counter stood between them.

"I hope you can. I'm looking for Mrs. Winston Sutherland." His voice was rich and resonant, his vowels pure Chicagoan.

"I am Mrs. Sutherland."

"My lucky day." He leaned closer and spread his hands on the counter. Multiple rings glittered. "Perhaps you can tell me where I can find your husband."

Something in his tone made her skin prickle. "My husband?"

"That's what I said."

"He's—he's not here."

The man gave a quiet chuckle. "I didn't think I would find him in a drugstore. But you see, I tried to find him at his home, and there was no answer. It's imperative that I speak with him, and I assumed his wife would know of his whereabouts."

"And you are ...?"

"A client of his." The man's black eyes bore into hers. "And lately it seems that he's been avoiding me."

She laughed nervously. "Avoiding you? Why, that's preposterous. Winston would never avoid a client."

"That's what I thought too. But as it turns out, he owes me some money. Quite a large amount, actually. So you see, it's of utmost importance that I find him. I came all the way out here to suburbia to find him, but when I rang the doorbell, nobody answered. I hate to think I drove all this way for nothing."

Panic slammed her chest. This man had been to their *home*? Her instincts screamed, *Run!* But she swallowed her fear and tried to keep her voice level. "Have—have you tried his club?"

The man's eyes narrowed. "His club?"

"The Saddle and Cycle Club. It's on Foster." She spoke quickly, knowing full well that Winston's club membership had lapsed and he'd been unable to afford to renew it. But since the club was located all the way in the city, it would get the man away from their town, at least for a while. And getting him away from her was her top priority at the moment, even though he might return angry after discovering he'd been tricked.

"I know where it is." The man regarded her for a long moment. Then he straightened. "When you see him, please tell him Louie Braccio is looking for him. He knows how to get in touch with me."

"I surely will," she chirped. She'd never heard the name Louie Braccio, but sheer instinct told her he was up to no good.

The man touched his hat again, then turned and left the shop. Connie hastened behind him, locked the door, flipped the sign to "Closed," and pulled down the shade, even though it wasn't quite yet closing time. She slumped against the door, trying to catch her breath, her mind swirling with questions. How had he known where she worked? Gracious, he'd been to her *house*?

She lurched in a panic toward the back office and gave the operator her home number. After a distressing number of rings, the phone was answered by an out-of-breath Drusilla.

"Sutherland residence."

"Oh, thank goodness, Mother Sutherland." Connie breathed. "Is everything all right? Is the baby safe?"

"Constance? Is that you?" Her mother-in-law sounded puzzled. "I was just returning with the baby from a stroll when I heard the telephone ringing as I came in. Is something the matter?"

Connie fought to regulate her voice. No sense in getting everyone in a panic. "No, everything's fine. It's just—may I speak to Winston?"

"He's stepped out. I sent him to the grocery for milk."

"All right. Well, if anyone rings the doorbell, don't answer it. I'll be home as soon as I can."

By the time she got home, Winston had returned. The three of them sat in the library, and Connie related Louie Braccio's visit and their conversation as best as she could remember it. By the time she'd finished, Winston's face had gone dead white. He flexed his fists and stared out the darkened bay window with glassy eyes.

"Winston, are you quite all right?" his mother said, alarmed.

"Fine." But he looked anything but fine.

Drusilla turned to Connie, her face contorted. "Tell us again, Constance. Who exactly is this Italian fellow?"

"I have no idea," Connie answered. "A client of Win's, he said."

Winston passed a hand over his face. "He's a loan shark, Mother."

Drusilla drew back in her armchair with a look of horror. "A loan shark! Why on earth would you go to a loan shark? Why not come to me, if you needed money?"

"I—I needed cash quickly." Winston's head dropped to his hands. "We've already borrowed so much from you, Mother, I couldn't bring myself to ask for more. I thought I'd be able to pay it back before now."

"With what?" Connie snapped. "A big win at the track?"

She'd intended the remark to be sarcastic, but one look at his face told her the suspicion was not far off the mark. "Oh, Win, how could you?"

Drusilla drew herself up. "What's done is done. What remains is to decide what we're going to do from here."

Normally Connie would have bristled at the commanding *we*, would have resented Drusilla's interference into what should be a private matter between husband and wife. But just then a wail sounded from upstairs. Her top priority was to make sure her child was safe and sound. *Let them hash it out*, she thought as she left the room.

As Connie tended to Scotty, Winston and Drusilla locked themselves in the library and held a hushed conversation that lasted late into the night. Connie fell asleep both dying to know what they were talking about and dreading finding out. When she awoke the next morning, Winston's side of the bed remained neat, as if he'd never come to bed. She dressed and hurried downstairs to find out what was going on. She froze in the foyer. It was filled with Drusilla's packed bags.

"I'm leaving, and I'm taking Winston with me," Drusilla announced. "He's quite ill, as anyone with half a mind to can see. Clearly, his fragile health requires a level of care and attention that he's unlikely to get here." Before Connie could respond, she continued, "There's quite a good hospital in Boston where he can recuperate and get a good long rest."

Connie found her words. "But what about me and the baby?" She turned to her husband, who stood silent and red-eyed beside his mother. "Win, don't leave like this."

"I need rest, Connie. I need ... I need rest."

You need to dry out, she thought. Perhaps a hospital stay was for the best, after all. He needed help, and if his mother was willing to pay for it, Connie could find no good reason to say no.

"We should come with you, Scotty and I."

"I don't think that's wise, Constance," Drusilla said. "Your presence will only agitate him further. Besides, you have your work. If and when the time comes that the doctors feel your presence will be beneficial, I will send for you."

She handed Connie an envelope containing a generous check, enough to cover the next couple of mortgage payments. "I understand you are in tight financial circumstances. At Winston's suggestion, I will take over the mortgage payments for the time being. If the situation continues unchanged in the future, I suggest we put the house in my name instead of yours, Constance, to secure ownership should your marriage not survive."

"Not survive?" Connie blurted, incredulous.

"Should circumstances continue to worsen," Drusilla droned, "I may send for young Scott to come and live with me as soon as he's old enough to leave his mother. The child needs a secure and stable home, and I am more than able to provide for him and give him a proper upbringing."

"My baby will never be old enough to leave his mother," Connie said scornfully. "So you can forget about that."

"We'll see."

Through the fanlight, Connie saw a taxi pull into the circular driveway. Soon the driver approached the doorway and rang the bell.

Panic rising in her chest, Connie whirled toward Winston. "I cannot believe that after all you've put us through, after all I've done to keep us afloat, you're abandoning ship."

Win lifted his hands "I'm not. I'm—I'm just—I need to get help."

"The drinking, the refusal to work—those were bad enough But now you're leaving. Letting your mother take over our house and breathe threats about taking Scotty away while you ... you just kowtow to her."

He looked miserable. "Please, baby. It's for the best. There are things you don't understand."

"Then explain them to me."

"We have a train to catch." Drusilla flung open the door and snapped orders to the taxi driver, who hoisted their luggage.

Winston leaned close and kissed her. "It'll be all right," he whispered. "I promise."

But as Connie watched the taillights of the taxi pull away, a shower of ice doused her heart. She doubted that anything would ever be all right again.

❧ 31 ❧

onnie had thought Winston's visit to his mother would last a few weeks, maybe a month or two at most. He needed time to dry out, to get his priorities straight, to figure out what he wanted to do with the rest of his life. But as spring turned to summer, it became apparent that he had no plans to return anytime soon. Meanwhile, Connie continued a steady round of shifts at the drugstore, making and delivering batches of Moondrop Miracle around the neighborhood, and trying to be both mother and father to Scotty. She relied on Ingrid, Sonja, and Mrs. Bromley more than ever to help her patch together her many tasks.

There were, thankfully, no further visits from Louie Braccio, though Connie remained on high alert for several weeks after Win left, anxious about every creak and thump at home, about every stranger who walked through the door of the pharmacy. Even though Braccio didn't turn up, the telephone sometimes rang late at night, and voices she didn't recognize asked for Winston—and sounded angry when she explained that he wasn't there.

Winston's letters to Connie were by turns cheerful, depressed, weary, and hopeful. But the one that startled her most arrived in the post one hot June morning. She read it in the kitchen while waiting for the coffee to brew.

I've begun looking for a job here in Boston, he wrote. *I think the East Coast is better suited to a man of my abilities than Chicago.*

She read the words over and over, feeling ill. He made no mention of her and Scotty moving to join him. No mention of putting the house up for sale. But surely that was his intention, to prepare her to leave everyone she knew and loved and move, lock, stock, and barrel, to Boston.

She made a feeble attempt to put the news in a positive light. Maybe Boston would be a nicer place to live than Chicago. Maybe the work there would be more suited to Win's talents. Maybe such a move would only be temporary, just until they could get back on their feet financially. In the meantime, she guessed she could make and sell Moondrop Miracle as easily in Boston as she could here. She'd have to start all over, finding new customers. But if she did it once, she could do it again.

But he hadn't asked her to move to Boston. Not yet. She thrust the letter into the wastebasket, slumped at the kitchen table, and buried her face in her hands. In truth, she didn't want to move to Boston. She didn't want to move anywhere. She wanted things to return to the way they had been before. She wanted her husband back—the strong, confident man who'd stood before the ornate altar at St. Lucian's and promised to stay with her forever. That man was nothing like the one who'd left her alone to bear their burdens.

Alone. The word had never rung so true. Would it really be so much better if he were home? Not if it meant him sitting around drinking all day, sunken in on himself in despair. He'd said his absence would be temporary. She'd assumed that meant he'd return, or that he'd find work elsewhere and send for her. But these were desperate times. One heard stories. Husbands who went out looking for work and disappeared. Husbands who went out to buy milk or bread and never came home.

That night she lay awake, listening to the clock tick, telling herself she needed to face facts. She had no one left to depend on. No capable housekeeper to take care of practical day-to-day matters. No strong male to fix things and reassure her, to tell her not worry her pretty head about important financial decisions. The prince wasn't coming to rescue her from the tower. If she didn't start worrying her pretty head, she was going to lose her home and maybe even her son.

The problem was, she didn't have what it would take to save anything.

She began to weep, her sobs reverberating in the stillness of her stately bedroom. How were she and Scotty going to get through this mess?

Winston's side of the bed was cold and empty. Who was she kidding? If he loved her, if he loved his son, he would be here. If he wanted to. If he loved them, he would want to.

Fresh grief welled up inside her, wave after wave. She missed her mother and her father. She longed for Aunt Pearl to come home, to give her some sort of guidance. Her aunt's platitudes circled around her heart. *One step at a time. The Lord will provide. Remember to sparkle.*

Gradually her sobs subsided. She stared glumly at the ceiling. Her "sparkle" had long since faded, so she could scratch that off the list. But she could still take one step at a time. And the Lord was providing, even if her life looked very different than it had just a few months ago.

Like a heavy blanket, realization settled on her heart. Security wasn't to be found in her husband or her father or her job at Mr. Dornbusch's drugstore, or random bottles of skin tonic. If any firm security was to be had, it would be found in her faith in God and the strength He gave her to make her way in this world.

She switched on the bedside lamp and sat up against the pillows. She reached for the Bible Aunt Pearl had given her, read the comforting words. A sense of peace penetrated her mind and permeated her soul. She read until dawn, then, feeling stronger, she washed her face and fixed her hair. Determination straightened her spine. No amount of wallowing was going to bring Winston back nor restore funds to their bank account. She had other things to think about now, more important things. She had a son to raise. And a business to run.

She went to Scotty's room and lifted her son from his crib and held him close.

"God will take care of us," she whispered. "God will take care of us." Then, she carried him downstairs, put him down in his playpen, tied on her apron, and got to work.

32

I f she were really going to make a go of this Moondrop Miracle business, she could no longer dabble. She needed to go all in. That week, she opened her pink notebook and reviewed all her lists. Lists of customers and prospects to telephone or visit. Ladies who'd expressed interest in Moondrop Miracle. Which supplies to purchase, if there was enough money left over to buy any at all. She telephoned everyone who'd ever bought Moondrop Miracle to ask them to consider placing another order. To her astonishment, most were eager to do so.

On a fresh page in the notebook, she carefully figured the costs of all the ingredients needed for Moondrop Miracle. She'd had some idea of costs, of course, but her thinking had been too hazy. Now she wrote down hard numbers: dollars, cents, prices per ounce. She found many of the necessary ingredients at a good price from a supply house recommended by Ingrid's cousin—no more depleting Aunt Pearl's stash. She added the cost of packaging: plain glass bottles and stoppers, the cheapest she could find without risking easy breakage or leaks. Labels, tags, ribbon. Another dollar to have some calling cards printed, neatly lettered on white cardstock. She even factored in the gasoline needed to make sales calls and deliveries. And then there was the cost of a mail-order advertisement and shipping materials. She totaled up all these expenses and figured out the cost per bottle, which helped her settle on a fair price, something her regular customers could afford that also allowed her to make a steady profit.

Gradually life fell into something of a routine. The drugstore was closed on Sundays, so that was the day Connie went to church. She spent the rest of the day playing with Scotty and trying to get household chores done before the busy week ahead. On Mondays, her regular day off, she ran a one-woman factory in her kitchen, brewing and bottling batches of Moondrop Miracle. The rest of the week, she felt as if she were running on a treadmill, from clerking at the drugstore during the day to making presentations to women's clubs in the evening, to processing orders for Moondrop Miracle late at night. The next week, she'd start the whole routine over again.

She felt stretched like a rubber band most of the time. But in the process, something inside her shifted. Now when she lay awake at night, instead of torturing her with memories of happier times and worries about tomorrow, her mind bubbled over with plans.

Early on a Monday morning in July, as she pulled out ingredients to start another batch of Moondrop Miracle while Scotty played happily in his playpen, a knock sounded at the kitchen door. Assuming it to be Sonja, come to watch little Scotty, she opened the door to see the friendly faces of both Sonja and her mother.

"Hello, you two. Ingrid!" Connie cried. "What a surprise! Come in, come in. Sonja, Scotty's been waiting for you."

The girl scooped the baby out of his playpen. He gurgled happily.

Ingrid shrugged off her white cardigan and hung it on a peg as easily as if she still worked for the Sutherlands, then reached into her purse and pulled out a white envelope.

"Is for you," she said, thrusting the envelope toward Connie. "Your Moondrop Miracle has been selling like crazy at Lotte's beauty parlor." Her wide blue eyes glistened with excitement.

"Goodness, I'd almost forgotten you'd taken some bottles there." Connie wiped her hands on her apron, took the envelope, and peeked inside. Gasping, she pulled out a stack of bills.

Ingrid grinned. "And Lotte wants to order more. A dozen more bottles, she said."

Connie shivered with delight. "My goodness. If it sold well there, it might do well at my own beauty salon. Well, my *former* beauty salon," she corrected. She hadn't had a proper haircut in months. Still, Ingrid's news made her feel proud and emboldened enough to try. "Anyway, I guess there's no harm in asking, is there?" She slipped the envelope into a kitchen drawer. "But as for a reorder, I'm afraid I'm out of stock at the moment. I was just about to start on a new batch. I have quite a few orders to fill already. Actual orders, not just samples." She filled Ingrid in on the presentations she'd been making.

Ingrid beamed. "Is mighty good news, Mrs. Sudderland. When more and more orders come in, you'll probably be needing some help in making so much of it."

Connie grinned. "I like how you say *when*, not *if*, as if demand is a foregone conclusion."

"It is."

"It was so nice having you and the girls to help me before," Connie admitted.

"Why don't you let me help you now?"

Connie clasped her hands in gratitude. "Oh, Ingrid, I'd love it. Can you spare the time?"

"Is my day off." Ingrid opened a drawer and pulled out a fresh apron. "I can stay until my boys are done with school. Be a pleasure to spend a day doing something besides sweeping up hair and doing Lotte's bidding."

The women worked side by side all morning long while Sonja cared for Scotty. By two o'clock, the table was covered with filled, capped, and labeled bottles. Connie found a cardboard box in the pantry and fitted twelve bottles into it for Ingrid to take to Lotte.

"Feel free to telephone me if you need more," Connie said. "No need for you to travel all the way out here to get it. Unless ... unless you'd like to come and help me make Moondrop Miracle every Monday." Her cheeks flamed at her own presumption. "I'll pay you out of the proceeds, of course," she added quickly.

"I'd like that, Mrs. Sudderland," Ingrid said. "I'd like to be a part of whatever it is you got going here."

As she had many times before, she said, "Please. Call me Connie."

They shook hands on it.

From then on Mondays, when Ingrid came to help her, became her favorite days. Not only did she appreciate the help, but she appreciated Ingrid's companionship in a way she never had when she was the employer and Ingrid the housekeeper. They talked and laughed as they worked. Ingrid doled out homespun wisdom and humor in equal parts, cheering Connie with hilarious stories about the ongoing drama at Lotte's beauty shop.

As the months rolled past, it became clearer than ever that Winston wasn't coming home anytime soon. She received an occasional note from him. He'd failed to find work in Boston, he told her, but he'd heard there were jobs available in the automobile industry in Detroit. Or on a fishing boat in the Gulf of Mexico. Or in the great pine forests of British Columbia.

Anywhere but Chicago.

Sometimes he enclosed a check. Not much, considering his mother's wealth, but often it was just enough to pay a bill or buy a new sleeper for Scotty, who grew so fast, Connie had a hard time keeping him adequately clothed.

But for all her hard work, she was still barely making ends meet.

"I keep telling you, Con," Gwen said when she came to pick up another order of Moondrop Miracle, "The carriage trade. That's where the money is. If you can break into a department store, you'll have it made."

One afternoon in October, Connie left Scotty in Sonja's care and took the train to the city. She mustered up her gumption, pushed open the revolving door of Marshall Field, and asked at the information desk for the buyer for cosmetics.

"One moment, please." While the clerk at the information desk dialed a telephone, Connie glanced around the main floor draped with autumn foliage and buzzing with shoppers. She'd often frequented the store as a customer. It felt strange now to be approaching it as a potential vendor. Her heart squeezed, remembering that final shopping trip with her mother.

The clerk hung up and told her where to find the buyer's office. The buyer for cosmetics, a man in his thirties with black patent-leather hair and a thin mustache, listened patiently to her spiel, then turned her down flat.

"Your product may be slightly interesting, but you don't appear to be a viable business." He sniffed, sounding bored. "We don't do business with mom-and-pop shops. We only deal with established manufacturers. Longstanding outfits with impeccable credit and unimpeachable character." He fiddled with his mustache and peered at her as if suspecting her of having the impeachable sort.

Connie gave him a smile that would melt ice in the Yukon. "But if you only deal with established manufacturers, Mr. Grant, how do any new products get into the market?"

The buyer was not to be moved. "Sorry." He shuffled papers on his desk, effectively dismissing her from his office. She closed the office door behind her. Her footsteps echoed down the hall to the elevator. She refused to be discouraged. Marshall Field wasn't the only elegant store, not by a long shot. Chicago was teeming with them.

However, a day spent trudging up and down the length of the State Street and Michigan Avenue shopping districts proved that the other fish in the high-end-retail sea were no more receptive to Moondrop Miracle. When she got off the train in her suburb, weary and discouraged, she decided to make one last stop at the top-drawer salon she used to frequent to see if Mrs. Gardner had had any luck selling her sample bottles.

"I'm pleased to say that we did," Mrs. Gardner said. Connie felt her spirits lift. "In fact, I know more salon owners would be interested in ordering some too. But you'll need to be prepared to fulfill substantial-sized orders. Are you capable of that? Also, you'll need to have all the proper paperwork and approvals in place for us to be able to order from you on a regular basis. We need to deal with established companies."

That phrase again. *Established companies.* But how did one become established if one couldn't get even a well-shod foot in the door?

"I'm prepared," Connie said with more confidence than she felt. "And I've begun the process of establishing a company." If contemplating it were part of that process. It was a stretch, but she'd do what she had to do to get this account. If this operation was ever going to move out of her kitchen, she needed to establish a bona fide company. She had no idea how to do so, but she knew someone who did. Her father's lawyer, Lloyd Deveare, had been a big help in settling her parents' estates. Surely he could help her with the legal end of setting up her business, or at the very least, refer her to someone who could.

❧ 33 ❧

L ater that week she took a day off from the drugstore, left Scotty in Sonja's care, and took the train into the Loop to meet with the lawyer. These days, she preferred taking the train to driving. She didn't want to use gasoline in the roadster or pay for parking in the city. Every cent mattered. But at least she still *had* her little car. It was more than a lot of people had and one of the few things she hadn't sold to make ends meet. Not long after Winston had lost his job, they'd sold his Nash sedan, but the Hudson had been a treasured gift from her father, the last tangible gift from him she still owned, and she couldn't bear to part with it. From a practical stand-point, she rationalized needing it to make deliveries to customers not reachable on the train or bus lines. And somewhere in Connie's heart, the roadster had become a symbol, a shred of hope to cling to.

From the train station, Connie walked to Madison Street to save taxi fare, even though the knife-sharp wind buffeted her face and whipped her hair into a tangle. She found the skyscraper containing the lawyer's office. She hadn't been back since the reading of her parents' wills, a steamy summer day so unlike this one, and the memory squeezed her heart.

She found Deveare and Associates on the directory board. As the elevator swept her to the tenth floor, she hastily checked her appearance in her mirrored compact. She found the correct office, approached a desk, and spoke to the secretary, a thin middle-aged woman.

"I'm here to see Mr. Deveare. I have an appointment."

"Your name?"

"Constance Sutherland."

The secretary glanced at her appointment book. "One moment please." The woman stood, walked to a closed door, knocked softly, and entered. Moments later, she emerged, followed by her employer. But instead of Lloyd Deveare, the man who came out of the office was much younger, attractive in a bookish sort of way, and also vaguely familiar.

The man approached Connie with a warm smile. "How do you do, Mrs. Sutherland. I'm Adam Deveare."

A spark of recognition ignited. She extended her gloved hand. "Of course, Mr. Deveare. We met a couple of years ago at the Carruthers' dinner party." That party seemed like a lifetime ago. So much had changed in the interim.

"That's right." His face lit up as he shook her hand. "I'm surprised you remembered."

She grinned. "I almost didn't recognize you. You weren't wearing eyeglasses that evening."

He laughed, and she remembered his delightful guffaw. "That's what I get for reading too much." His expression sobered. "I was very sorry to hear of Carruthers & Mullin's misfortunes. A tale all too common, I'm afraid, in these hard times." His eyes, smoky gray-green behind his glasses, held a look of genuine concern. "I trust your husband has landed on his feet."

"We're fine." Connie glanced away. She had no desire to discuss anyone's misfortunes, least of all her own. She had to remain positive, to look forward, not back. "I expected to meet with your father today. Is he here?"

He opened his hands in a gesture of apology. "Dad retired a couple of months ago. I've taken over the firm."

"Oh, I see."

"They ought to have told you that when you made your appointment."

"I must only have asked for Mr. Deveare. Which is you," she added clumsily, feeling oddly ruffled. "Well, in any case, it's nice to see you again."

"Shall we go into my office? Coffee, please, Miss Marshall." He ushered Connie toward the inner door. "Please take a seat." He motioned to a brass-studded leather chair across from his desk, then seated himself. "How can I help you today?"

Connie sat up straight in the leather chair. "I'd like to set up a company."

"A company?" His voice registered surprise, but he looked intrigued. She'd half expected him to scoff at her the way Winston would have and felt relieved when he didn't. "What kind of company?"

"I'm going to manufacture a skincare product." Connie's tongue almost tripped over the word "manufacture." It sounded so ... well, businesslike. Gathering her courage, she explained about Moondrop Miracle and its impressive qualities. "I've sold a few bottles here and there, but I've been told I need to establish a proper company if I want to start selling through major retailers and such. That's why I'm here. I'm hoping you can help me with the legal paperwork."

"Certainly. I'll be happy to do that." As the secretary returned with cups of coffee on a tray, he opened a desk drawer and pulled out a yellow legal pad. Then he picked up a fountain pen and uncapped it.

"What is the name of your company?"

"Pearlcon Enterprises." She felt a warm glow of pride as the name left her lips. It had taken her several sleepless hours to come up with it, and she liked how it sounded. Official and serious, like a real company, yet feminine at the same time. "You see, my aunt, who formulated the product in the first place, is named Pearl, and I'm Constance, so ..." She heard herself rambling and closed her lips.

"Pearlcon Enterprises is a good name," Adam agreed. "It makes it sound as if the company carries a full line of products, not just one."

"That's the plan," Connie said. She shifted in her chair. "In the future, I'd like to get Pearl working on some other things. Night cream, body lotion..." Blood rushed up her neck and burned in her cheeks. It seemed inappropriate somehow to be discussing something as personal as body lotion with a man as good-looking as Adam Deveare. "But for now, it's just the one product, Moondrop Miracle."

"Who are the owners of the company?"

"Myself and my aunt, Pearl Russell."

He glanced up in surprise. "Not your husband?"

"No, he ... No." She didn't care to elaborate.

Mr. Deveare set down his pen and leaned back in his chair. "Your husband does approve of your starting this company? You have his blessing?"

Connie lifted her chin. "I don't see how that's relevant."

"Forgive me." Adam leaned forward, his gray-green eyes on hers. "It's relevant because of financing. Very few banks will lend start-up money to a woman without her husband's signature. That's just the way things are." His voice sounded soothing, apologetic.

Connie fixed her gaze on the thick Turkish rug at her feet. With the shape their finances were in, no bank officer was going to give a loan application a second glance, husband or no husband. But Adam Deveare did not need to know that. She lifted her head and looked him in the eye.

"The company is privately funded." *Funded by the use of Aunt Pearl's ingredients, and the occasional sale to friends like Gwen, and the customers at Ingrid's cousin's beauty parlor, and the working women's club, and whatever leftover coins I can scrape together after I've bought food and paid the bills,* she added silently. But her gaze remained fixed on his, and at last he nodded and made a notation on his pad. Then, he tapped the pen on the desk in a rhythmic pattern that made her nervous.

"Are you going to employ a staff?"

"I have one part-time helper now," she said, thinking of Ingrid and their Monday sessions in the kitchen. "I suppose we'll need more help, sooner or later."

"And you have experience in the industry?"

She shifted in her chair. "I've been checking books out of the library every week on botany and herbal medicine, and also some dermatology textbooks. I've learned a lot about the skin, the way it's made, why it becomes unhealthy and when, and what you can do to keep it in the best possible condition. And next semester I'll be signing up for night classes in bookkeeping. Two evenings a week at a community college near my home." God bless Sonja, who'd agreed to babysit on the nights Connie went to class.

Adam stood and walked over to a bookcase. He scanned a shelf and pulled down a couple of volumes. "I recommend these as well," he said, handing them to her. "You may borrow them, if you like. They're books on sales and marketing. You're going to need those skills."

"So you're not just a lawyer, but a lending library as well?" she teased.

He grinned. "I specialize in business law. Helping small businesses like yours get off the ground is a particular interest of mine. I like to help where I can."

"Well, thank you. I'll be sure to read them." She slid the volumes into her handbag.

He returned to his seat and asked several more questions, jotting notes on the pad. She found him charming, professional, and serious about being of service.

Finally he pressed a button on a box on his desk and said "Miss Marshall" into the speaker. Moments later the door opened, and the secretary walked in.

"Yes, Mr. Deveare?"

Adam handed her his notes. "Will you please type up the usual incorporation forms in triplicate?" He turned to Connie. "A set for you, one for Mrs. Russell, and one for our file. It will only take a few minutes. Miss Marshall's a whiz on the typewriter."

He winked at the secretary, who smiled and retreated, closing the door behind her.

While they waited, Connie glanced around the office, which had received a fresh coat of paint and some updated furnishings since she'd sat here for the reading of her parents' wills. She forced the unwelcome memory out of her mind.

"I'm assuming some kind of official approval is needed for pharmaceutical products," she said. "Some kind of license, maybe? An inspection of the facilities?"

"Surprisingly, no." Adam adjusted the rim of his glasses. "As it happens, I've just been studying the matter for another client. According to the Pure Food and Drug Act, licensing is needed for all patent medicines, but skin tonic is not considered a patent medicine. It qualifies as a cosmetic product, and, at this time, cosmetics don't need approval. Although, frankly, I wish they did. Just recently there was a case where a woman was permanently blinded by wearing a certain brand of mascara."

Connie shuddered. "How awful."

"Cases like that make me wish the cosmetics industry were more tightly regulated. In the wake of that case making its way through the courts, the word on the street is that cosmetics licensing will be required soon enough. In the interim, we'll set your company up in a way that will make it relatively simple to comply with any future inspections and that sort of thing. If and when the time comes, we'll be ready to act."

Connie was grateful for his sensible advice—and liked his use of the word *we*. It make her feel less alone, as if someone were in her corner. Besides Pearl and Ingrid, of course. They cheered her on and encouraged her efforts, but neither of them had any real business experience. The support of a seasoned, experienced attorney like Adam Deveare made her feel more secure.

When Miss Marshall returned with the typed papers, he looked them over, then placed two sets in envelopes and handed them to Connie. "Take these home and go over them with Mrs. Russell. Then, each of you sign a set and mail them back, and we'll take care of the rest."

"My aunt is traveling in India. I expect her home soon. If she's delayed, I'll send the papers to her by express mail and ask her to return them as soon as possible." Connie stood. "Thank you for your help."

Adam guided her toward the door. He shook her hand warmly, smiling into her eyes. "It was my pleasure. And might I add that I admire you. It's not every day that I meet a woman courageous enough to sally forth with a business of her own. Especially in these challenging times. I wish you every success."

His smile felt genuine, personal, as if he truly cared about her and her little company. She felt protected and cared for, the way Winston had made her feel during the early days of their marriage. She liked the feeling very much—so much that her brain immediately flashed a danger signal. This man was her lawyer, not her beau. Not her husband. She immediately withdrew her hand.

"Good day, Mr. Deveare." She turned and walked toward the elevator.

On the train ride home from the city, Connie looked out at the passing scenery without taking it in. Her mind swirled with ideas. One more task could be crossed off the list. She was practically in business. In business! One minute she felt exhilarated, the next a bundle of nerves. Could she do this? She could. But how? At least she had Adam Deveare on her team now. The memory of his reassuring smile boosted her confidence. If only Winston had been as encouraging, she might have launched the business sooner and kept them from accruing debt.

The brisk walk home from the station through the crisp fall evening helped clear her mind. She had lots to think about. The next step was to figure out how to keep up with all the new orders that would roll in, as surely they would once word got out about the new company. She wasn't quite sure how word would get out, or how the orders would roll in, but she knew they would, and then she would need help. It felt premature to be thinking about hiring people. And yet, if the business took off, she'd have to. She couldn't keep doing everything herself.

34

Once all the paperwork was in place and she owned a properly registered company, Connie felt more confident about approaching potential customers with Moondrop Miracle. Still, she hadn't been able to secure any more appointments with any of the major department store buyers. *One step at a time*, Aunt Pearl's voice sang in her memory.

"Won't your aunt be surprised when she returns from India to find you're a big-time businesswoman," Ingrid crowed one afternoon as they worked in Connie's kitchen. "Has she said when she'll be coming back?"

"No. Her last letter said Aunt Ruby hasn't yet gained back her strength and can't yet return to her work at the mission. There's some question about whether Aunt Pearl will need to bring her back to the States."

"I continue to pray. I look forward to seeing Pearl again, too."

Connie's heart was touched by Ingrid's willingness to pray for Pearl and for Ruby, whom she didn't even know. She vowed to do better in that respect.

"I can't believe she's been gone almost a full year already. I miss her so much."

"I do, too. What a difference a year makes," Ingrid said.

"You can say that again." Connie had dropped hints in her letters about the changes that had taken place in her life while her aunt had been overseas, but she hadn't wanted to worry her unnecessarily. She'd have much explaining to do when Pearl got home.

The next day, in the spirit of one-step-at-a-time, she approached the humble shop of her employer, Mr. Dornbusch.

"It does wonders for all sorts of skin ailments," she explained, dabbing a little Moondrop Miracle on the back of his hand with a piece of cotton. "And it cleanses, tones, and clarifies, even on healthy skin."

Mr. Dornbusch looked skeptical. "You say you made it yourself? On your kitchen stove?"

"Yes. The active ingredient is fenugreek. I have many clients who love using it, and I'll be glad to get some testimonials for you."

He balked at first, but by mid-November he finally gave in to her repeated requests. Or badgering, as he called it.

"You may place a few bottles on the shelf, just to see how they do. On a consignment basis, mind you. And only for the Christmas season. And no fair pushing it on customers at the expense of the other vendors' products."

"Yes, sir."

Happily she gathered up some boughs of fir and tinsel and created an attractive Christmas-themed display on a table near the front of the store. A hand-lettered sign encouraged customers to buy small sample-sized bottles of Moondrop Miracle as inexpensive gifts or stocking stuffers. Hard times meant people were looking for economical gifts, and Connie was sure that once ladies had tried Moondrop Miracle for themselves, they'd be back to purchase a larger bottle later. She placed the full-size bottles on the shelf, right next to established products, nationally known lotions and cold creams and astringents. She stood back and gazed at the display with pride.

At first there were no takers, and she was worried about what Mr. Dornbusch would say. But as Christmas neared, customers stopped to take a closer look, picking up the bottles and holding them up to the light to see the liquid sparkle. One bold customer opened one to take a whiff and dab a drop onto her hand. Mr. Dornbusch's eyes bugged out at her presumption. When she left the shop without buying anything, he nearly exploded.

"Customers should not be allowed to open the merchandise if they're not going to buy," he sputtered.

Connie calmly picked up the bottle that the customer had left sampled. "Since this one's already been opened, let's make it a tester bottle that people can freely try without disturbing the rest." She wrote "tester" across the cap in bold ink.

Her boss rolled his eyes. "It's your money."

The small gamble paid off. When customers could see and smell the product, more bottles found their way to the cash register—and more money into Connie's handbag, which she then turned around and used to purchase more ingredients and supplies.

A few days before Christmas, a young boy entered the shop. He couldn't have been older than ten, wearing patched, faded overalls and a battered-looking newsboy cap. He looked around at the shelves in bewilderment.

"Can I help you find something?" Connie asked, prepared to direct him to the candy or toy aisle.

"I want to buy a Christmas present for my mother," he said.

His earnest expression tugged at her heart. Perhaps someday little Scotty would be buying a present for her. She hoped to become the kind of mother for whom he'd be willing to shell out his hard-earned allowance.

"What kinds of things does your mother like?" she asked the boy.

He shrugged.

"Do you think she'd like something like this?" She lifted one of the Moondrop Miracle bottles. "It's skin tonic for making her complexion pretty."

He wrinkled his nose and shook his head. She put the sample bottle back on the table.

"All right. Maybe some perfume?" She showed him where the perfume was displayed, but he shook his head at all of them.

"Well, let's find something else she might like."

Connie spent a happy and satisfying hour helping the boy choose the perfect Christmas present for his mother that he could afford, which turned out to be a deck of playing cards. As she carefully wrapped the precious gift, she tucked in a small sample bottle of Moondrop Miracle.

"This is my gift to your mother," she told the boy. "All I ask is that she try it and, if she likes it, to know she can get more here at Dornbusch's." She smiled and added, "Boys like you might not care much for skin tonic, but ladies do."

The boy's eyes grew big and round. "Gee, thanks, lady. I'll tell her."

There were no Christmas parties that year, no invitations, not even a lunch date with her friends. Gwen had sounded both apologetic and evasive when Connie had called to ask about it.

"I'm sorry, Con. We decided to do something different this year." But she didn't specify what the "something" was, and clearly Connie had been excluded. The rejection stung, but she could understand it. Whether intentionally or not, her husband had gambled with large sums of their money—and lost. How much money, Connie didn't know and didn't have the courage to ask. But it wouldn't have surprised her if their husbands had told them to cut her from their social plans.

Anyway, who had time for parties? She was too busy making and selling Moondrop Miracle to a growing list of customers.

"I can't explain it," she said one Monday to Ingrid as they brewed tonic. "I get so much satisfaction out of helping people. Who knew?"

By Christmas Eve, she'd nearly sold out of the small sample bottles and even the regular-size bottles at the drugstore and knew she'd have to spend at least part of her holiday making more. Mr. Dornbusch even looked on the verge of cheerful as he paid her the consignment fee.

"I'm impressed, Mrs. Sutherland," he said. "I'll be pleased to order more, and even bring it in as regular inventory instead of on consignment, if you like."

She left the store at the end of her shift feeling a glow of satisfaction she'd never felt before. The money she'd received for the consignment would go straight into her house payment, meaning she wouldn't have to accept any money from her mother-in-law this month.

But her glow was short-lived. As she approached her house, she noticed a long, dark car parked across the street. And from the driver's seat watching her were the black, beady eyes of Louie Braccio. A chill ran down her spine. The car sped away, but in that moment, Connie knew she couldn't live like this. She couldn't keep feeling fearful that Louie Braccio or one of his henchmen would come looking for Winston. Or for her.

She had to face facts. Winston might return to her someday. Or he might not. In any case, it was time to make a fresh start somewhere else. For herself and for her son. But where?

❦ 35 ❦

On a bright early-spring morning in 1931, Connie stood on the curving driveway of her fairy-tale house, bidding it good-bye. Green buds had just started to adorn the bare branches of the elm trees she loved so much, making them look lacy and delicate against the soft blue sky. Swallowing past a lump in her throat, she was ever grateful that Winston had had the foresight to put the house in her name, so that when it came time to sell it, she could do so legally. Little had she suspected that it would be in such awful circumstances, that he had virtually abandoned her. Virtually, she reasoned, because Winston still sent a note and a little money now and then, postmarked from different places on the continent. But not enough money to save the house, and she wouldn't stoop to letting her mother-in-law contribute to her expenses any longer than she had to. The less Connie put herself in Drusilla's debt, the better. So, the house was for sale, the contents up for auction, and Connie and Scotty on their way to begin a new life in an apartment on the North Side of the city.

Tears blurred her eyes and threatened to overflow. Gone were nearly all the tangible mementos that had belonged to her parents. But Connie couldn't think about that now. She needed the money too desperately to be caught up in sentimental feelings. Practically the only thing of value left from them was her car, the playful little roadster that now seemed so frivolous and impractical for her serious new life. Yet she couldn't stand to part with it, even though it would by necessity stay parked most of the time. Gasoline cost too much money. But it would come in handy for getting back and forth to her job at the drugstore, for making deliveries, and for the occasional trip out to Aunt Pearl's to stock up on ingredients. And hugs. How she missed Aunt Pearl's hugs! She could hardly wait for her aunt to come home.

"You all right, Mrs. Sudderland?" Ingrid had taken time off from her job at the beauty parlor to help her with the move. Now, she stood beside her holding a pink-cheeked Scotty in her arms.

Connie gave her former housekeeper a quick smile. "I'm fine. Thanks for looking after Scotty. You can both get in the car." Connie drew the collar of her coat around her neck—a plain but serviceable wool coat, her sable having gone to auction with the other luxuries— and touched her gloved hand to her chest, trying to still her tumbling emotions. She must be strong. Wasn't God watching over them both? That's what both Ingrid and Aunt Pearl had said, and what the Bible taught. In that moment, she chose to believe it.

She stepped back into the empty, echoing house and paused in the foyer, looking around. Everything was gone. The entire house stood clean and empty, ready for a new owner. That new owner hadn't been found yet, but Connie had faith someone would fall in love with her fairy-tale house and enjoy it just as she had.

She let her mind drift for a moment, memories scrolling through her mind like a newsreel. Win carrying her over the threshold as a bride—had it really been less than three years before? So much had happened since then. Gatherings with their friends—friends who had apparently dropped her from their social circle. Family dinners with her parents.

She gave one last glance over the rooms she'd loved, then turned and walked out, closing the door behind her. One last time, she turned the key in the lock. Then she lifted her suitcase and walked to the roadster, refusing to look longingly at the places where flowers she and Sam had planted were just now starting to sprout. Someone else would enjoy them now. It was time to enter a different world, a world where she would make a way for herself and Scotty. She was ready to face it. Still, she couldn't help feeling a pang of regret for what she was leaving behind.

On the drive to the new neighborhood, to the small furnished apartment she and Scotty would call home from now on, Connie mulled over her situation. She knew she'd miss the world she was leaving behind, yet she wasn't leaving. That former life had left her a long time ago. She felt impatient to face the future head-on, to conquer it before it conquered her, to make a good life for herself and her son. And when Win returned—if he returned—he could join them in the adventure.

✣ 36 ✣

Their new home was a tiny one-bedroom apartment on Sheridan Road. She parked in the designated area and paused for a moment to survey the building's exterior: a six-story brown brick edifice situated behind a small square lawn, still a bit snow-covered in the shady spots, and a patch of bare ground that she hoped might become a flowerbed.

Walking down the dim hallway of the second floor with Scotty in one arm and her suitcase in the other, she practically bumped into a young dark-haired woman about her age. The woman wore a paint-spattered smock and carried an empty wastebasket.

"You look lost," she said to Connie, smiling.

"I am, a little," Connie replied. "Can you show me which one is unit 2-B?"

The woman's face brightened. "You must be the new tenant."

Connie's face warmed. "I am."

"The landlady, Mrs. Helberg, said a lady with a child would be moving in. Helberg's a peach. You'll like her. And hello to you too." The woman's voice rose in pitch as she lifted Scotty's little hand and shook it gently. He stared wide-eyed at the stranger. Connie estimated her to be about her own age, although the events of the last couple of years made Connie feel much older.

Connie shifted his weight on her hip. "How do you do. I'm Connie Sutherland and this is my son, Scotty."

"I'm Lucinda Bricker. End of the hall." The young woman pointed. "Follow me. I'll show you the communal trash bin. It's over here near the stairs, and so is the laundry tub."

"Have you been painting?" Connie said, noting her new neighbor's stained smock.

"I'm an artist. Well, an art student. I have the rear apartment. It's not much to look at but it has the clearest northern light."

"I see."

After Lucinda emptied her wastebasket, she led the way to Connie's new apartment.

Connie shifted Scotty to her other hip, then unlocked the door with the key the rental agency had given her. She opened the door and stepped inside, swallowing back her disappointment at the drabness of the furnishings. At least everything looked clean. Shabby, but clean. And thankfully the landlady had included a crib, as Connie had requested, though she'd brought along his own little pillow, bed linens, and stuffed tiger to help him feel comfortable in their new home.

"Say, why don't you let me cook you dinner," Lucinda said, leaning against the door frame. "You must have had a long day, moving and all. I'm sure you're exhausted."

"We'd love to. Thank you." Connie suspected that the disheveled young woman knew more about painting than cooking, but it had been a difficult day and a little food and company would be welcome. They agreed on a time, and Connie retreated into her apartment.

After unpacking her and Scotty's meager belongings, setting up his crib, and settling him down for a nap, she took a bath in the cast-iron bathtub, then changed into fresh clothes. She spent some time exploring the contents of the kitchen cabinets, where she found utensils, a water pitcher, a coffee pot, and some plates and bowls. A rather skimpy set-up, but adequate for her needs.

Her most important items—the ingredients and equipment to make

Moondrop Miracle—she'd packed in the trunk of the roadster. While Scotty slept, she carried everything upstairs in two trips, then set up what would be her little skin-tonic factory for the foreseeable future.

It was while she was puttering in the kitchen that she became aware of a noise, a sort of high, thin wail. She checked on Scotty, who was sound asleep. Then she peeked out the kitchen window onto the fire escape, half expecting to see a stray kitten out on the ledge, or maybe a dog in search of scraps. There was nothing. She'd returned to her task when the sound came again, this time breaking into heartrending sobs. Not a child's sobs, but a woman's, evidently coming from the apartment next door, the sound carrying through the wall.

Connie pressed her hand against the yellow-painted plaster, unsure of what to do. The sorrowful sound that tore at her tender heart was issued by a perfect stranger. She felt torn between an impulse to hurry next door to introduce herself and offer comfort and the level-headedness of minding her own business. It also occurred to her that maybe her neighbor wouldn't appreciate making her acquaintance in such a state. She bowed her head and offered a quick prayer for the broken-hearted person next door. Then she woke up Scotty and dressed him, and they headed for Lucinda's apartment at the end of the hall. When she passed the apartment next door, she could no longer hear the crying.

Lucinda served spaghetti with tomato sauce and crusty French bread at a paint-stained wooden table in the midst of her cheerfully cluttered living room. Scotty perched on a chair atop a thick telephone directory and a Sears catalog. One dishtowel loosely secured him to the chair slats, while a second towel served as a makeshift bib.

"I could bring over his high chair," Connie offered, but Lucinda dismissed the idea.

"He seems happy with this arrangement, don't you think?" Indeed he did, having great fun playing with the unfamiliar strings coated in red sauce, even though most of his serving ended up on his face, hands, and bib instead of in his tummy.

"Is your family heritage Italian?" Connie ventured, striving to imitate the casual way Lucinda wound the long noodles around the tines of her fork.

"Oh, goodness no. I'm from Milwaukee," the young woman said. "My family's as German as they come. But spaghetti is cheap and filling."

Connie made a mental note of that fact. "It's tasty, too." After dinner, Lucinda gave Scotty some colored chalk and paper to play with while the ladies lingered over coffee.

"What do you plan to do when you finish art school?" Connie asked. "Teach?"

"I'm not sure. Believe it or not, I'd like to take a crack at commercial art. You know, magazine illustrations and such."

"What's unbelievable about that?"

Lucinda shrugged. "Most of my fellow students think I'm crazy for wanting to do commercial art. They're all starry-eyed about the purity and integrity of the *artiste*, dreaming of living in cold-water flats in Paris and drinking absinthe in cafes on the Left Bank. But I'd like to be able to afford to eat, thank you very much."

Connie laughed. "Paris doesn't sound so bad to me."

Lucinda smirked. "Most of them will just end up teaching the next generation of starry-eyed dreamers. Me, I want to do something with my art. But commercial art is a tough field to break into. I have to get up some samples, create a portfolio of real, professional work ... It's not enough to try to impress an art director with my superior shading techniques." She sipped her coffee. "How about you? What brought you to the city?"

"My husband is on the road a great deal," Connie said. "For work."

Lucinda nodded. "A lot of men are having to resort to working out of town these days."

Connie felt that the sooner she got off the subject of her marriage, the better. "I have a small company that makes a skin tonic called Moondrop Miracle."

"A company of your very own?" Lucinda sounded impressed.

Heat stole into Connie's cheeks. "Honestly, it's just myself and my aunt and one part-time helper. Hardly a real company. But people seem to like our product. We're slowly building a clientele."

Lucinda shrugged. "A product plus people who want to buy it sounds like a real company to me."

A nugget of an idea glinted at the back of Connie's mind. "Lucinda," she said, "you said you need to build a portfolio, right? What would you think of creating an advertisement for my company?"

Lucinda set down her cup. "Me?"

"I'm afraid I can't pay you much. But it will help you build up your credentials, and I'd pay you as much as I can afford."

Lucinda's eyes sparkled. "A homemade supper or two, and we'll call it even."

"Obviously you've never tasted my cooking. I'd better agree before you know what you've gotten yourself into." Connie stood. "If you can keep an eye on the baby for a minute, I'll go get a bottle of Moondrop Miracle so you can see what I'm talking about." When she returned with a sample bottle, Lucinda had gathered some pencils and a sketch pad. They sat up late into the night, talking and brainstorming, while Scotty slept on Lucinda's tattered sofa.

"I'm thinking of a straightforward ad," Connie said. "Something like, 'If you want clear and beautiful skin, buy Moondrop Miracle.'"

After a few false starts and various concepts considered then rejected, Lucinda sketched a pretty young woman with a dreamy look on her face, as if she were gazing at moonlight out a window.

"Perfect!" Connie exclaimed. "She looks like Juliet waiting for her Romeo."

"Except Juliet, being Italian, probably had dark hair, not blond," Lucinda said. "This woman looks more like ... well, like you."

Connie laughed. "I don't know about that, but she does suit the branding I had in mind." After reading the business books Adam Deveare had lent her, terms like *branding* and *market share* were becoming a natural part of her vocabulary. She studied the sketch. "This woman looks ... well, she looks like she's filled with hope."

The hour grew late. It wasn't until she hoisted her sleeping son and bid good-bye to their hostess that she remembered her sobbing neighbor. "I meant to ask you, do you know who lives in the apartment next door to mine?"

"Which side of you? 2-A is a reclusive old widower who listens to opera on his Victrola."

"No, on the other side." The wailing she'd heard hadn't been opera. She was sure of it.

"She's a teacher from the elementary school. Name's Miriam something. Shy little thing, pretty much keeps to herself. Why?"

"Just curious," Connie said. But in her heart she resolved to introduce herself to Miriam at the earliest opportunity, in case the woman needed a friend.

37

The advertisement that Lucinda designed, after many drafts and revisions and changes of direction, was submitted to two popular women's magazines, along with payment for space in the back pages—the cheapest ad space available. Then Connie, caught up as she was in the whirlwind that her life had become, promptly forgot all about them.

One chilly evening, she reciprocated Lucinda's dinner invitation by inviting her over for beef stew and baked potatoes. The stew recipe was Connie's favorite, one of the few of Ingrid's delicious dishes that she'd been able to replicate reasonably well on her own.

She also invited her next-door neighbor, Miriam Walters, whom she'd finally met one afternoon in the hallway. That day, when Connie introduced herself, the young woman had seemed cheerful and friendly. But later on, the sound of her sadness again seeped through the wall. Connie hoped that she and Lucinda would be able to form a friendship with Miriam and maybe provide some comfort, or at least distraction, to her aching heart. She was pleased when Miriam accepted the invitation.

In spite of Miriam's mousy appearance, to her surprise, she turned out to be a witty and engaging dinner guest who made Connie and

Lucinda chuckle at tales of the absurdities of the second-grade class she taught at the local elementary school. She told them stories of growing up dirt-poor in a large farming family and working her way through teacher's college as a waitress.

"I know it sounds odd, but even though we had next to nothing, we had so much fun. And then at teacher's college, I was surrounded by friends all the time. I never realized how hard it would be to live alone." She looked wistfully into her coffee cup, as if seeing happier times reflected there. "Chicago is nothing like where I grew up. It's nearly impossible to make ends meet on a first-year teacher's salary. Some months I have to choose between buying food and paying my rent on time. And sometimes, when I'm not at work, I don't know what to do with myself. It sounds pitiful, I know, but I get so lonely and homesick, all I can do is cry."

Tactfully Connie didn't mention that the sound of Miriam's misery carried through the wall. But now that she understood the reason, she vowed to help her new friend feel less lonely.

"You can always knock on my door," she said. "If I'm not out on sales calls or at work, you're welcome to come over. I'm sure Scotty would love to see a face besides mine once in a while."

"Oh, but you're so busy. I couldn't intrude on your time."

Connie shrugged. "If I'm busy, then I'll put you to work addressing envelopes or something. There are always little jobs that need doing." An idea clicked in her mind. "Say, if you'd be interested in earning a little extra money, I could really use some help selling Moondrop Miracle. Perhaps you wouldn't mind taking some sample bottles to school to see if any of your teacher friends might like to buy some. I can pay you a small commission on any bottles you sell."

Miriam's face lit up. "Really? Oh, I'm sure they'd like it." An expression of doubt crossed her face. "But I don't have any sales experience. I've never sold so much as a Girl Scout cookie."

"Maybe not," Connie said, "but you seem like a tender-hearted soul who's interested in people. I'll bet you were a great waitress."

Miriam grinned. "I was pretty good at getting people to order the special of the day."

"You see? That's sales," Connie said. "Look, if you like people and enjoy talking to them, that's the kind of person I'd like to have working with me. That's the Pearlcon kind of woman."

"The Pearlcon kind of woman," Lucinda repeated slowly. "I like it. Write it down. We might use it in an ad."

"Do you really mean it?" Miriam's face brightened. "I'll do it! I can put some bottles in the teacher's lounge and talk to them about it on our breaks."

Connie felt buoyed by her enthusiasm. "And if that goes well, maybe I can send you out to call on a few store accounts. That is, when you have time off from teaching during the summer and school breaks. You'd make some extra money, and I could really use the help."

By the end of the evening, Pearlcon had hired its first commissioned saleswoman.

❦ 38 ❧

S onja Swenson continued caring for Scotty at the new apartment
when Connie went to her job at the drugstore.

"I feel sorry that we no longer have a big yard for you and
Scotty to enjoy," Connie told the young woman. "I hate to think of you
two being cooped up in this tiny apartment all day."

"It's all right," Sonja assured her. "There's a park not far away where
we go when the weather's nice. And when it isn't, Miss Lucinda lets us
make a mess with her art supplies." An unexpected blessing of apartment living—a blessing that Connie dutifully noted in her pink notebook—was that Lucinda, who worked at home, was cheerfully willing
to keep an eye on Sonja and Scotty. She'd even been a back-up
babysitter for Scotty when Sonja was laid low with a cold. Connie felt
reassured that her son was well taken care of in her absence.

But soon it appeared the arrangement would be short-lived. In
March, Mr. Dornbusch sadly informed Connie that the drugstore
would be closing.

"We're simply not making ends meet," he explained as he handed
over her final pay, as well as the remaining stock of Moondrop Miracle
that had stood on his shelves. "I am sorry."

"I'm sorry, too," Connie said. But she wasn't—not really. She regretted the closing on Mr. Dornbusch's behalf. She'd grown surprisingly fond of the old curmudgeon. But the Moondrop Miracle business was growing so quickly that she had plenty of work to do, just keeping up. She kept Sonja on to watch Scotty, even though Connie was working at home, to give her time to focus on her tasks.

Connie and Sonja fell into the habit of taking a coffee break together every afternoon, enjoying some girl-talk. During their chats, Sonja sought Connie's advice on everything from makeup to boy problems.

"I wish I could move as gracefully as you do," she sighed, slumping in her chair.

"You can," Connie assured her. "Start by sitting up straight. Pretend you're a puppet with a string running from the top of your head down through your whole body, and someone's pulling on the string." Sonja sat up straighter. "Now, when you stand up, keep that string in mind. Pull your shoulders back and your hips slightly forward."

Sonja did as instructed, and Connie clapped. "That's right. Now walk."

At first the girl walked like a marionette, with clumsy and exaggerated movements, and both of them collapsed in gales of laughter as Scotty looked on, bemused. But soon enough, Sonja was walking as smoothly and gracefully as a runway model. Over time, Connie noticed that the girl began imitating the way she dressed and even got her hair cut in a similar wavy bob. Privately she felt both amused and flattered. She continued to offer tidbits of advice to help Sonja make the transition from awkward schoolgirl to confident woman.

By summer, the ads in the women's magazines had produced enough sales and income that Connie repeated them. Each day's mail brought a small stack of hand-addressed envelopes to the little apartment. Neatly folded dollar bills and creased money orders accompanied handwritten requests for Moondrop Miracle. After making sales calls on stores all day, Connie spent her evenings cooking and stirring the product by hand, then packaging the bottles to drop them off at the post office the next day or deliver them in her car.

Just before the Fourth of July, Aunt Pearl arrived back at her farm after her extended visit to India. Connie eagerly drove the roadster out to the farm with Scotty snuggled in the backseat. A folder on the front seat beside her held several important papers needing Pearl's signature, since she was a cofounder of Pearlcon and the inventor of Moondrop Miracle. Adam Deveare was leaving no detail to chance in making sure all the business arrangements were buttoned up.

As Connie approached the house, Pearl emerged onto the porch, swathed head to toe in brilliantly colored silks.

Connie parked and jumped from the car. "Look at you! You look like a rare tropical bird."

"You like?" Pearl turned around so Connie could see the full effect of her sari.

"It's extraordinary," she breathed, letting a fold of soft silk fall through her fingers.

"I've brought you one, too. Thought it would shake things up a little at the Junior League."

Her throat tightening, Connie flung her arms around her aunt. "I've missed you so much."

Pearl finished the hug, then swept a startled Scotty into her arms and squeezed him.

"Birdie," he pronounced, pointing at Pearl. "Birdie."

Pearl held him at arm's length. "You're *talking*."

"Once you get him started, you won't shut him up," Connie confirmed.

"I can't believe how big you've grown, little man," Pearl exclaimed.

"And I can't believe you're finally back," Connie said. "I was worried you'd decided to stay in India forever."

"It was magnificent," Pearl said, her eyes shining. "I can't wait to tell you all about it. And I loved getting reacquainted with Ruby. She's a marvel, I tell you. Her ministry has been extremely effective in spreading the gospel among young people."

"I've never had the opportunity to meet her," Connie said. "She was already working overseas by the time I was born."

"Maybe you'll get a chance to visit her someday," Pearl said, but Connie didn't see how such an extravagant trip would ever be possible. Not with everything that had happened since Pearl had been gone.

She embraced her aunt again. "You've lost weight. Have you been well?"

"A little tired, that's all. Travel takes its toll. I'm not as young as I used to be."

"But you don't regret going?" Connie said as they walked arm-in-arm into the farmhouse kitchen, Scotty toddling alongside.

"Oh, certainly not," Pearl breathed. "India is a beautiful country. I made some delightful friends, and I shall miss them very much. But nothing beats getting home to you and Scotty and my kittycats."

She disappeared into another room while Connie filled the teapot and pulled cups from the cupboard. When she returned, they sat together at the oilcloth-covered table.

"Now, tell me all about this new venture of ours."

While Scotty played on the floor with Pearl's cats, who'd grown fat and lazy in the neighbor's care, Connie filled in the blanks she'd left out of her letters. She explained about Winston's so-called travels, supposedly to find work.

"He drops a line once in a while—just a note here and there, with a bit of money if he has any. I miss him so much, Aunt Pearl. I wish he'd come home and see how Moondrop Miracle is succeeding. Who knows? Perhaps our little business will grow to the point of sustaining all of us, and he won't have to look for work so far away from home." *If that's indeed what he's doing*, she added silently. The Winston she knew would remain faithful to her, no matter how long they'd been apart. But then, the man who left her was not the Winston she knew.

"Work is often the best antidote for a grieving heart," Aunt Pearl said. She reached across the table and grasped Connie's hand. "Honey, I think you can do anything in this world that you want to do. And I want to help you. I'll sign these papers immediately. And before I left Bombay, I was able arrange a reliable and economical source of fenugreek. We won't have to worry about running out of our key ingredient."

Connie clapped her hands. "Oh, fantastic. That will be an enormous help. Thank you so much."

"And if it will help you in any way, sweetheart, I want you to have my savings to put toward the business, or toward anything you and Scotty need."

Gratitude swelled Connie's heart. "I don't want your money, Aunt Pearl. The only thing I want is your support and your expertise in mixing up Moondrop Miracle on a larger scale." She brought her aunt up-to-date on the sizeable orders she'd recently received from stores, as well as the smaller accounts she'd been servicing all along. She eagerly described Ingrid's involvement in the business, still at only one day a week, and the artist Lucinda who created ads, and the new saleswoman, Miriam, whose initial sales had proved that schoolteachers, too, cared about their complexions.

"My goodness! You have a regular empire going," Aunt Pearl crowed. "And all from your own kitchen table."

"Speaking of which... Now that Scotty and I have moved to a smaller place, I'm having trouble producing enough Moondrop Miracle from that tiny kitchen. When Ingrid comes on Mondays to help me, we're constantly bumping into each other. What would you think about doing the manufacturing out here at the farm? You have the proper equipment, more space for storage, and more elbow room for bottling, packaging, and shipping. What do you say?"

Pearl blinked rapidly. "Of course I'd do anything to help you, dear," she said, fidgeting with the silken edge of her sari, "but I can't possibly manage all those jobs by myself."

Connie laughed. "No, no, I didn't mean you had to do everything yourself. We'll hire employees, of course. Your job here, your chief strength, would be to develop ideas for new products. To tinker and experiment, as you have been." She turned serious. "But it would mean having others on your property all day, working out in the barn. You might not like that."

Pearl perked up immediately. "Not like that? But I'd *love* that! It gets awfully lonely sometimes, out here all by myself. I'd love to have people to talk to besides the cats. But what about you? Will you make the drive out every day?"

"No, I'll still be working from my apartment. It's more convenient to call on customers in the city. But we'll be in touch often. We'll talk every day on the telephone."

Aunt Pearl grinned. "Well. I guess we're in business."

"It's settled then. Someday, when we start making some real money, we'll put the profit into remodeling the barn into a factory. I don't think we'll have to tear it down completely—just remodel the interior to make it work for us and accommodate future employees." Her smile dimmed slightly. "Of course, that's still far off in the future."

"Maybe not as far off as you think." Pearl's face glowed. "I believe in you, Connie. I'm behind you every step of the way. And if turning my barn into a factory is the way to do it, then that's what we'll do."

"If you can provide the space, I can bring in people to help you do the work." Connie stood. "Let's go take a look at what we've got to work with, shall we?"

Wheeling Scotty in his stroller, they went out to the barn, which was even dustier and more decrepit than Connie remembered. "You've got a wood stove, which is something. But if you and other people are going to work in here year 'round, we'll have to get the place insulated and a more reliable heat source put in." She pulled her pink notebook from her handbag and jotted some notes.

Outside, tires crunched on the gravel drive. Peeking out the barn door, Connie saw a shiny late-model sedan.

"Are you expecting someone?" she said to Pearl.

"No."

To her surprise, Connie watched as Adam Deveare unfolded his long legs from the driver's seat. He stood and greeted her with a wave.

Connie started toward him. "What are you doing here?"

He grinned, dimples flashing at the corners of his mouth. "You'd mentioned you'd be bringing those papers by my office this afternoon after your aunt signed them. I decided to save you a trip and drive out here myself to see the place with my own eyes."

"This is it." Connie gestured to the barn, such as it was. She half expected Adam to scoff or criticize, as Winston would have done. Instead, he seemed to catch Connie's vision as she showed him around, offering comments and suggestions as to how the barn might be turned into a place to manufacture Moondrop Miracle. He and Aunt Pearl seemed to hit it off, too, exchanging ideas and enthusiasm. By the end of the afternoon, the three of them had compiled a long list of things that needed to be done to bring the barn up to standard.

"Of course, this is just a dream list. We can only afford to work on one improvement at a time, paying as we go." Connie said, surveying the list. "I'm afraid it's going to take forever."

"I'll help," Adam promised. "I may not look it, but underneath this attorney exterior, I'm pretty handy with a hammer and saw."

"Are you? Offer accepted." Connie smiled up at him. "You're always full of surprises."

"Can I entice you to stay to supper?" Pearl said.

"I need to get back to the city," Adam said regretfully. Connie and Pearl waved as he backed down the driveway.

Connie turned to her aunt. "I need to get going, too. This little fellow's had a long day."

"And so has his mother. It was very nice of that young lawyer to drive all the way out here with those papers so you didn't have to go to his office."

"Adam's been a big help in getting the company set up," Connie said. "I don't know what I would do without him."

"He thinks highly of you, too." Pearl's eyes held a twinkle. "He admires you."

"Aunt Pearl," Connie chided, feeling awkward. "I'm a married woman."

"I know," her aunt said. "I'm not suggesting anything improper. Only that it's nice to have good people on your side."

Connie agreed that Adam was a good person. But, goodness, if he felt attracted to Connie the way she felt attracted to him, that could only mean trouble. Privately, she determined that, fond as she was of Adam, she would keep her distance from him. They'd have to keep their friendship, if that's what this was, strictly confined to business matters.

As she loaded the sleeping Scotty into the car, Pearl touched her arm.

"I know you miss your husband," she said gently.

"We're doing all right, Scotty and I," Connie assured her aunt.

Frankly she found herself missing Winston less and less as time wore on. But she didn't want to say so out loud.

"It gets better, sweetheart. It really does."

"I know." Connie hugged her aunt. "It already has, now that you're home."

❧ 39 ❧

For the remainder of 1931 and into 1932, the fledgling Pearlcon Enterprises found its wings and made tentative attempts at getting off the ground. With Connie making sales calls around the city, often with Scotty bundled in the backseat, and Pearl mixing up the product in her barn out in Hoosier Grove, they were staying afloat, even making a profit, but at the cost of their time and energy. While the fairy-tale house had not yet sold, Moondrop Miracle was profitable enough to cover her rent, as well as make the most rudimentary improvements to the barn and hire two local women to package and ship the products. The next step was to hire an assistant for Pearl to relieve her of some of the manufacturing so she could concentrate on developing new products. As soon as possible, Connie would need to hire a similar helper for herself in Chicago. Handling all the sales and administrative work by herself was proving exhausting.

By the end of each workweek, she was more than ready to kick back and relax at the casual Friday-night suppers that had become a weekly routine for her, Lucinda, Miriam, and occasionally Ingrid. After work they'd gather in one or another of their apartments and share a meal, always something cheap and filling like spaghetti or scrambled eggs, with Scotty napping or inventing fun games with Lucinda's paints or Miriam's leftover school supplies. The women would laugh and talk and share battle stories from the week, as well as their hopes and dreams for the future.

Bit by bit, as Pearlcon grew, Connie shed her former life like a dress that no longer fit. In her diligent way she persevered, determined that no flaw in a batch of tonic nor glitch with a disgruntled customer would get the better of her. But she still didn't have the one thing that would make her life complete—her husband back home.

She'd written to Winston at what she thought was his current address, somewhere in Oklahoma, telling him she was earning a decent income now and that he could stop wandering the country looking for work. He could come home. She could support them both. But the letter came back stamped, "Addressee unknown."

With Pearl taking over the making of Moondrop Miracle, Connie no longer needed to work in the kitchen with Ingrid on Mondays. Even though that left her with more time to devote to sales, she found herself missing her friend. One summer morning at the end of a long week of sales calls, she had an idea. She took a streetcar from her apartment into the nearby Andersonville neighborhood. Following the directions she'd scribbled on a slip of paper, she located Lotte's beauty shop and pushed open the glass door. The shop hummed with noise and activity, very unlike the hushed, subdued atmosphere of the fancy salon Connie used to patronize. The hubbub quieted rapidly, however, as customers caught sight of Connie and turned curious faces in her direction.

A stout woman wearing a bright pink smock approached the reception desk, friendly but reserved. "May I help you?"

"Are you Lotte, by chance?"

"I am."

"I'm Constance Sutherland from Pearlcon Enterprises."

"Yes?" Lotte's expression remained neutral.

"I wanted to follow up with you on Moondrop Miracle to see if you had any questions or needed any replacement bottles. You see, I like to meet all of my customers in person, whenever possible. I believe in the personal touch."

All at once Lotte's face lit up and her demeanor softened. "You're the Moondrop Miracle lady? Why didn't you say so?" she exclaimed in the same delightfully lilting accent as Ingrid's. "My customers love the stuff. I want to order six more bottles."

Connie laughed. "That's wonderful to hear. I'll send you some right away." She glanced around the salon. "Is Ingrid Swenson available?"

Lotte kept her eyes on Connie as she turned her head and bellowed, "Ingrid, you got company."

Ingrid emerged from the back of the shop. Her pink smock and look of confusion matched those of her cousin.

"Mrs. Sudderland? What are you doing here? Is Scotty all right?"

"Yes, he's fine. I just came down here to introduce myself to Lotte and make sure she's happy with Moondrop Miracle."

"Oh, I'm happy, I'm happy," Lotte said.

"I'm so glad. Ingrid, is there perhaps someplace we can go to talk?"

"Sure thing." Ingrid said to her cousin, "Lotte, if you don't mind, I'll be taking my break now."

"Is fine." Lotte was still beaming at Connie.

Ingrid untied her smock and folded it neatly over the back of a chair. "There's a coffee shop just a few doors down where we can sit and talk in peace."

All eyes were on them as they left the shop. The buzzing began even before the door was closed.

Over coffee Connie said, "I've got a full-time job for you, if you want it."

Ingrid's deep blue eyes met hers. "I'm listening."

"As you know, Moondrop Miracle has gotten too big for my kitchen, especially now that we're living in that cramped apartment. So we've moved production out to Aunt Pearl's farm."

Ingrid nodded. "Is a fact. When I was up there on Mondays to help you, we were practically falling over each other." She paused. "Is probably a smart move. Although I miss our Mondays together."

"So do I," Connie said. "That's why I'm here."

Ingrid drew a deep breath. "So you needing a housekeeper again?"

"As a matter of fact, I do. But that's not what I'm here to talk about." Connie sipped her coffee. "Pearl is a dear, and she's a genius at coming up with creative ideas, but she's entirely too disorganized and scatterbrained to run a production facility. Her workflow systems are pure chaos, and I don't see that ever changing. We must try to instill some kind of order on paperwork, supplies, that sort of thing. In short, we need a good manager, someone to take charge of production. I'd like that person to be you."

"I see." Ingrid's face held a neutral expression, but her eyes shone. "Is good that you think of me."

"I couldn't think of anyone *but* you. I can't pay you much starting out, but I'll give you as much as I can. We've landed some good accounts, and with a few more like them, I can raise your salary soon." Connie bit her lower lip. "But the catch is that the factory's all the way out in Hoosier Grove. It needs to stay there, at least for now. It's the only place big enough without paying an exorbitant rent."

"I see." Ingrid's eyes lost a little of their glow.

"I know it's a terribly far trip for you. Maybe someday we can move someplace closer to the city, but I don't know when." When Ingrid didn't answer immediately, Connie prattled on. "The Milwaukee Road commuter line runs right out to Bartlett. We can leave Aunt Pearl's truck parked at the station to get you the rest of the way to Hoosier Grove." Connie smiled. "Or perhaps even her motorcycle."

Ingrid grinned. "Is a funny picture, me on a motorcycle." Then her expression clouded. "I'm sorry, Mrs. Sudderland." She sounded genuinely regretful. "I'd love to help you out, but I can't travel that far away from my family every day."

A spray of guilt washed over Connie. In her focus on her own needs, she'd neglected to consider Ingrid's other and more important responsibilities. *Again.* She reached for her wallet to pay for the coffee.

"Of course. I'm sorry, Ingrid, I didn't think it through. I'm afraid I've wasted your time."

Ingrid reached across the table and touched her hand. "No, you haven't." Her voice was surprisingly firm. "Is good you thought of me. You got a dream and is a good one. I got a dream, too, and it don't involve working in Lotte's beauty shop for the rest of my life."

"Oh?"

Ingrid's blue eyes looked straight into hers. "Mrs. Sudderland, may I say what's on my mind?"

"I wish you would."

Ingrid leaned forward, as if what she was about to say was confidential. "I know the perfect person to help your aunt run the factory. We've been friends our whole lives. Her name's Marietta Carlson. and she's an organizational wizard. You want something done, and done right, she's the person to call."

Hope rose in Connie's chest. "She sounds perfect. Is she looking for work? Do you think she'd be interested in the job?"

"I'm sure she would. She's currently unemployed and needs a brand-new start. Someplace where she can start fresh." Ingrid hesitated. "And there's the catch."

"What catch?"

"You see, she yust got out of yail."

Connie sat back. "Yale?" It took her a moment to realize that Ingrid wasn't referring to the prominent university, but to the penitentiary. "Oh. Jail."

"Now hear me out," Ingrid pleaded. "Marietta is a good person. She yust got caught up in a bad situation, that's all. They found some stolen goods in her apartment. Her no-good ex-boyfriend had put them there without her knowledge, but the yudge didn't believe her."

Connie inhaled. "But you do."

Ingrid nodded vigorously. "I do. As I said, I've known her all my life. Trouble is, with yail time on her record, she can't easily find a yob. She helps out some in Lotte's beauty shop, but there's not really a yob for her there. But I think she'd be perfect for helping your aunt out in Hoosier Grove. I know she would."

Connie thought for a moment, weighing this information in her mind. Then she said, "All right, I'll talk to Marietta. And to Pearl. If I think she's capable of handling responsibility and will be a good fit, and if Aunt Pearl agrees, we'll consider her for the position."

"Thank you." A slight frown creased Ingrid's forehead. "But what about Pearl? You don't think she'll feel like we're shunting her aside, will she? I'd hate for her to feel that way."

"Don't worry about Pearl," Connie said. "I'll keep her in charge of new product development, where she can tinker and invent to her heart's content. Pearlcon needs to offer more products than Moondrop

Miracle if we want to stay competitive. We'll keep a section of the barn as her laboratory. The rest will be used for manufacturing and shipping."

"Big plans," Ingrid said.

Connie nodded. "I hope Marietta will turn out to be a good fit for the production-manager job. Even so, that still leaves me without a business manager to help me manage the books and things."

Ingrid straightened in her chair. "For that you got me, Mrs. Sudderland."

Connie frowned. "But I thought you said you're not available."

"I said I can't travel to Hoosier Grove every day. As long as I can stay here in the city for work, I'd be happy to take on more responsibilities. I've got bookkeeping experience. I know the product backwards and forwards and upside-down. And you know I'm ten times more organized than you are."

Connie laughed. "You've got me there. You'd be willing to work for me full-time, not just on Mondays? At my kitchen table?"

"Of course I would," Ingrid said stoutly. "We started this thing. We got to see it through."

"Oh, Ingrid." Gratitude pressed against Connie's throat. "I knew you would stand by me." She laughed. "But you're never going to call me Connie, are you?"

"Probably not. It yust don't sit right on my tongue. Now, come on." Ingrid stood, suddenly taking charge. "We go find Marietta."

"Yes, Mrs. Swenson." Connie grinned. Together they walked out of the coffee shop and back up the street toward Lotte's beauty shop.

❧ 40 ❧

After meeting Marietta, Connie felt positive that she'd be a good fit for the factory. The woman had a forthright, cheerful manner as well as experience leading work crews in the prison laundry. A few days after their meeting, Connie drove her out to Hoosier Grove and introduced her to Aunt Pearl. After further discussion, Pearl agreed they should hire her on.

Marietta had an innate shrewdness about business matters. Pearl taught her how to make Moondrop Miracle, how to ladle the tonic into bottles, and how to box the bottles up for shipment. She had also hired an out-of-work Hoosier Grove man to make local deliveries in his truck and take mail-order shipments to the post office.

Back in Chicago, Ingrid began spending every weekday at Connie's kitchen table, updating the books and business records and showing Connie how to do it, too. They fell into a routine of going over everything on Friday afternoons, after which Ingrid would often stay for supper with the neighbors. She had an amazing aptitude for numbers and kept meticulous records. When she wasn't handling administrative details, she helped keep an eye on Scotty while Connie was out. She was turning out to be a boon companion and source of encouragement to Connie as well. Connie constantly marveled at Ingrid's good humor and can-do attitude, realizing with shame that she'd sorely underestimated her in her former role as housekeeper.

While Pearl and Marietta were at work in Hoosier Grove and Ingrid handled the books, Connie was the sales engine, the face of Pearlcon to potential clients. Day after day, she called on drugstores, department stores, beauty shops and boutiques—anyplace that might conceivably carry Moondrop Miracle.

As the months rolled on, word got around of the skin tonic's effectiveness. Women were asking for it by name, and retail accounts grew. A few more local Hoosier Grove women were hired, and, under Marietta's management, the manufacturing, bottling, and shipping operations flourished.

Connie lived scrupulously on her earnings and poured nearly every cent back into the business. It was not long before her meager profit swelled a little bit, and then a little bit more.

Her grand goal continued to be to achieve a concession inside the great department store, Marshall Field & Co. At last it looked like the proverbial doors of that elegant establishment were being cracked open for her.

"Your persistence has worn me down, Mrs. Sutherland," the buyer, Mr. Grant, told her on one miserably hot summer day. "I'm willing to give you a chance. Temporarily, mind you, to see if your product proves as popular with customers as you say it will. Although frankly," he added, "I don't see how you can possibly run a company on your own without your husband."

For a moment Connie couldn't formulate a response. Sweat dripped down her back in spite of the humming electric fan blowing the hot air around. She'd been to Mr. Grant's office at least three times, and every time, he had a different excuse. This one took the cake. She gathered her things and stood.

"What do you think I've been doing all along?" she said over her shoulder as she turned toward the door.

His eyes bulged. "Where are you going?"

"To serve my loyal clientele—the women who deserve my attention," she said. "I'm sorry, Mr. Grant. A luxury department store like yours isn't good enough for Moondrop Miracle. Good day."

Her repudiation of the snooty Mr. Grant gave Connie a brief sense of satisfaction. But by the time she reached her apartment building, her high dudgeon had been softened by prayer. The text of James 4:10 scrolled through her mind. "Humble yourselves in the sight of the Lord, and He will lift you up." Maybe wanting to have her product displayed in a grand department store had been a point of pride. Maybe serving the working-class women who shopped in Mr. Dornbusch's drugstore, and who attended Ingrid's club, was exactly what she was supposed to be doing. After all, women without much cash to spend on themselves still wanted to look and feel pretty. Maybe God didn't intend for Moondrop Miracle to reach the luxury market. If so, Connie decided firmly, she didn't want to either. She would learn to be content with whatever opportunities He gave her.

She pulled open the heavy front door of her building and trudged across the tiled vestibule, so preoccupied with her own thoughts that she nearly tripped over a young woman on her hands and knees, scrubbing the floor.

"Oh, excuse me." Connie stepped carefully around the freshly washed area. She stopped before the row of residents' mailboxes and fished in her purse for the key.

"Connie Shepherd?"

Startled, she looked down. The cleaning woman was staring at her.

"Do I know you?"

The woman stood and wiped her hands on her smock. "I'm Hilda. Hilda Schwarzenmuller."

Connie wracked her brain for a connection. The woman was about her age, quite pretty, with blond braids wrapped around her head and a clear, rosy complexion. Thanks to her relentless daily focus on skincare, Connie tended to notice people's complexions before anything else. Finally, she gave up. "I'm sorry, I don't ... Have we met?"

The young woman's smile dimmed slightly. "Hilda Schwarzenmuller," she repeated, with a little more emphasis than before. "I worked for your family for a year or so. Up until—until the accident."

"Oh, I see." A hazy, indistinct memory rushed to Connie's mind. A black-and-white maid's uniform. Soft footsteps on thick carpeting. A vague figure in the background of daily life on Astor Street, brandishing a duster or a polishing cloth. Heat rushed to her face. How could she have forgotten this person who'd spent her entire days tending to the Shepherds' needs? And yet it had been her mother who'd dealt most with the staff. To Connie, they had been merely interchangeable people hired to make life easier. This realization of her own youthful self-absorption now made her cringe.

"Hilda. Of course. I—I apologize. I didn't recognize you."

"That's all right," Hilda said graciously. "You got married and moved out not long after I was hired. Our paths didn't cross very often. Not at all, in fact, since the funeral."

Still, that's no excuse, Connie chided herself. She scratched around for a suitable response and finally landed on stating the obvious.

"You're working here now?"

Hilda glanced down at her bucket and scrub brush. "Yes. Mrs. Helberg hired me to help clean the building in exchange for rent." Her expression brightened. "But my real work is in a theater. Our play opened last week, called *Death Stalks the Capitalist.*"

"Oh, really?" It didn't sound like anything Connie had read about in the arts section of the *Tribune*.

Hilda's blue eyes sparkled. "You should come."

"Me? Why, I—"

"It's just a little neighborhood theater, practically around the corner," Hilda blurted. "I'll even give you a ticket. *Two* tickets, in case you want to bring a friend."

Connie took a step back. "Oh, you don't have to—"

"I *want* to." Hilda bit her lip. "You see, it's a brand-new theater company. My boyfriend wrote the script, the cast are mostly students, and we're having a little trouble getting up an audience."

"I see. You're needing some warm bodies to fill the chairs."

Hilda's mouth drooped. "Yes, I suppose you could put it that way. But you'll like it. It's a ground-breaking drama that sheds light on important current issues." She sounded as if she were reciting a description from a promotional poster.

In spite of her doubts about the entertainment value of a play focused on "important current issues," two nights later, Connie found herself seated on a wooden folding chair inside a shabby North Side storefront. The walls and ceiling had been painted black. A makeshift stage draped with heavy black curtains spanned one end of the space. While waiting for the curtain to rise, she scanned through a mimeographed program.

"That's funny," she murmured to Aunt Pearl, seated beside her, whom she'd talked into taking the extra ticket. "I thought Hilda said she was in the show, but I don't see her name on the program."

"Maybe she has a backstage role in the production." Aunt Pearl fanned herself with the program and glanced around at the audience, a motley assortment of students and other artfully disheveled types looking as though they'd only just left the easel or the writing desk. Connie became aware that she and Pearl stood out in their accustomed theatergoing attire of silk dresses and pearls.

"I assumed she was an actress," Connie said. "I guess not."

But ten minutes into the first act, there was Hilda, onstage, dressed in a ragged skirt and blouse, a kerchief wrapped around her head, her long blond braid extending down her back. Connie squinted at the program in the dim light. Next to her character's name, the cast member was billed not as Hilda Schwarzenmuller, but as "Hilly Crabtree."

She had trouble following the convoluted plot peppered with confusing Russian names. But however forgettable the play, Hilda's performance was outstanding. Winsome and tragic by turns, she carried the show as the sweet peasant girl in love with the greedy landowner's son.

After the final curtain, Connie and Aunt Pearl sought her out backstage.

"You were marvelous," Pearl gushed, grasping Hilda's hand in hers.

"Yes, you were," Connie echoed, carefully sidestepping any comments on the play itself. "I'm impressed. But who is Hilly Crabtree?" She pointed to the program.

"Oh, that." Hilda rolled her eyes. "My boyfriend Tony thought I ought to have a stage name. He thinks Hilda Schwarzenmuller sounds too clunky for the theater."

Privately Connie questioned whether Hilly Crabtree was any better.

Hilda glanced around, then pointed. "He's over there. Would you like to meet him?"

Connie spotted a skinny man engaged in animated conversation with another patron. His black turtleneck and pants blended so thoroughly into the black background that he appeared to be all head and hands, holding a cigarette and gesturing earnestly as he spoke.

"Oh, let's not bother him," Connie said quickly, not wanting to have to conjure up any insincere compliments about the script.

"Thanks to you, I'm sure the play will be a great success," Aunt Pearl said diplomatically to Hilda, "once word gets around."

Hilda pouted. "Unfortunately, the show's closing after this weekend." She brightened. "But we're already in rehearsal for a production of Tony's next play. It's a searing exposé of the Smoot-Hawley Bill."

"Sounds delightful," Connie lied. She didn't order tickets to the next production, but she did invite Hilda to supper the following week. Soon the young actress became a regular at the Friday-night suppers, laughing over plates of spaghetti with Connie, Lucinda, and Miriam. Together, the FruGals, as they came to call themselves, formed a support team of sorts, lifting one another's spirits and making near-poverty seem almost fun. Every so often Ingrid joined them too, when she didn't have to hurry home to her family.

"You know, Con," Hilda said at one such gathering not long after they'd met. "I could take some bottles of Moondrop Miracle around, show them to my theater friends. I bet it would be a big hit at the makeup table."

Connie lifted her hand to her heart, touched. "You'd do that for me?"

"Sure. Stage people are always looking for better ways to care for their complexions. All that heavy stage makeup takes a toll."

Hilda's hunch was accurate. As word of Moondrop Miracle's effectiveness at soothing ravaged skin spread from dressing room to dressing room, the tonic soon became a star in its own right among Chicago's theater community.

✥ 41 ✥

As often as she could during summer and fall of 1932, when the weather was fine, Connie brought Scotty with her out to the farm. He played happily with Pearl's cats and ran through the fields while his mother and great-aunt worked. Ingrid, meanwhile, ran the kitchen-table office back in Chicago.

One such Friday in early autumn, the Hoosier Grove telephone rang. Aunt Pearl picked it up in the barn and then patched the call through to Connie, who was in the farmhouse going over some shipping records with an employee.

"Constance Sutherland," she said into the mouthpiece. Ingrid's voice, sounding tense and hushed, came over the wire.

"Ingrid, what's wrong?" For an anxious moment Connie worried that maybe Louie Braccio or one of his henchman had returned to harass her. But no, she'd paid off that debt long ago.

"You have a visitor," Ingrid murmured ominously.

"Oh, for heaven's sake, just tell me."

When Ingrid told her who had come to visit, Connie ended the call and hurried out to the yard, where her son was petting one of Pearl's cats.

"Scotty, darling, come along. It's time to go." She notified Aunt

Pearl they were leaving, then drove back to the city as quickly as safety allowed. She paused a moment in the hallway outside her apartment, did what she could to tidy up her own appearance and her son's, then willed herself to smile and swept into the apartment.

"Why, Mother Sutherland," she said as gaily as she could. "What a delightful surprise!"

Drusilla Sutherland, looking slightly grayer and stouter but otherwise unchanged from her visit three years prior, stood from her seat on the shabby sofa.

"Hello, Constance. I'm in town for a reunion at my old school," the older woman said. "I'm staying with Sally Meade. But I thought I'd seize the opportunity for us to have a chat."

Connie's heart hammered. Had Drusilla come to tell her something about Winston—something terrible? Beneath her anxiety, she felt an unreasonable stab of annoyance upon realizing Ingrid had made herself scarce, leaving Connie to face her formidable mother-in-law alone. She would have appreciated some support.

"Scotty, this is your grandmother." She bent down to speak to her son, who stared wide-eyed at the stranger. "She's come all the way from Boston to see us. Go and say hello."

She nudged the boy toward Drusilla. Stiffly he held out his little hand as he'd been taught. "How do you do," he said solemnly.

"It's good to see you, young Scott," Drusilla returned the handshake. "Although in future you must remember that a gentleman always waits for a lady to extend her hand first." To Connie she said, "He has Winston's hair and eyes."

"He does," Connie retorted, "at least as far as I can remember Winston's appearance, having not seen him for—what has it been now?—three *years*?"

Tension crackled through the room.

"Now, Constance, there's no need to be bitter."

Connie placed a gentle hand on her son's copper curls. "Darling, run along to the bedroom and play with your trucks while Mama visits with your grandmother."

Scotty, only too happy to be released from this strange encounter, skipped out of the room.

Drusilla lifted an eyebrow. "There's only one bedroom? However do you manage?"

Connie laughed. "He's quite little. We happily share, as long as he doesn't leave his blocks on the floor for me to step on." She motioned for Drusilla to take a seat. "May I offer you a glass of water?"

"No, thank you. Your maid offered me some earlier."

Connie retreated to the kitchen to pour a glass for herself, momentarily wishing she had access to something stronger. "Ingrid? She's not my maid. She's my business manager."

Drusilla's voice registered faint surprise. "Your business manager? May I ask what sort of business you're engaged in?"

"Skin tonic. Moondrop Miracle."

"Oh, that," Drusilla said dismissively.

Connie raised her voice over the rush of the tap. "I've told you all about it in my letters. If you've read them."

"Of course I've read them," Drusilla snapped, "but I didn't realize you were serious."

"Quite serious." Connie returned to the living room. "In fact, Aunt Pearl and I have joined forces in a company we call Pearlcon."

"Pearlcon. How quaint." Drusilla sniffed. "And clearly it's been a successful endeavor, considering these opulent accommodations." She swiveled her head to survey the shabby apartment, including the piles of paperwork Ingrid had left on the kitchen table.

Connie cleared her throat. "What can I do for you, Mother Sutherland?" She determined to maintain her cool no matter how her guest provoked her. "Have you brought news of Winston?"

A look of disdain crossed Drusilla's face. "My son, it appears, has gone on a quest to 'find himself.'" She sounded disgusted. "When last I heard from him, he was pitching hay to cattle somewhere out west."

"Has he mentioned when he's planning to return to his wife and son?"

"You must be patient, Constance. Winston has endured a great deal of hardship and disappointment since your marriage. You can't expect him to bounce back overnight."

"*He's* endured hardship and disappointment?" Connie's anger threatened to boil over. "What about his wife? What about his child?

237

Surely three years is enough time to bounce back from just about anything."

"You've always been so demanding, Constance. If only you didn't put so much pressure on the poor man."

"Pressure?" The word came out strangled. Connie took a gulp of water to quell the bile rising in her throat. Then she said, "One generally does feel a bit of pressure when a man abandons his wife and child."

"Oh, Constance. Don't be so dramatic. He hasn't *abandoned* you. He's merely ... he's ..."

"Finding himself?" Connie interjected sarcastically. "I fear, Mother Sutherland, that you never approved of our marriage in the first place."

Drusilla cocked her head as she considered the statement. "It's true that I did think he could have made a more appropriate choice." *Like Zoe Meade*, Connie thought. "But what's done is done."

Connie'd had just about enough. "If you've no news of Winston, why are you here?"

"To see if you have enough money to live on."

"We do," Connie said stiffly. "We're getting by nicely."

"Well, then, the rest is simple enough," Drusilla said. "I've come to make arrangements about my grandson."

Connie's eyes narrowed. "What sort of arrangements?"

Drusilla straightened her spine. "It's time the boy came to stay with me."

❧ 42 ❧

Connie thought she hadn't heard correctly. "You want him to visit you? In Boston?" Her gut instinct was to refuse outright. Her little boy, all the way in Boston? On the other hand, Drusilla was the boy's grandmother; of course she'd want him to know her. Angling for time to think, she said, "This is sudden. Of course, we need to discuss it. But I'm sure a visit can be arranged." Her mind whirled. She'd have to take time off from work, which she could ill afford, but she certainly wasn't going to let him go all the way to Massachusetts on his own.

"I'm not talking about a visit, Constance. I want the boy to live with me."

Connie's gut contracted as if she'd been punched. "What are you saying? You've come to take him away from me?"

"What I'm saying, Constance, is that my grandson needs a better environment than this if he's going to thrive." Drusilla glanced with disdain around the shabby little apartment. "Does he even have proper playmates? Exposure to the right sort of people? Why, he doesn't even have his own bedroom in this place."

Connie sat in shock, open-mouthed. When she found her voice, she rasped, "How dare you? You don't even know him. You have no idea what he needs."

Drusilla released a sigh of longsuffering. "I can give the boy every advantage. He's going to need to start school soon. Is he even prepared? With all your running hither and yon, I doubt that you have time to adequately socialize him, much less suitably prepare him to begin his academic career. I will hire a tutor, to bring him up to speed with his peers."

"His academic career? He's three!" Connie fought for breath.

"Now, Constance," Drusilla replied calmly, "I anticipated you'd become hysterical. That's why I wanted to see you in person. Just hear me out. In time I'm sure you'll come to see that living with me is the only reasonable course of action. We have the child's future to think of."

"No." Connie stood. "You need to leave."

Drusilla opened her mouth. "I beg your—"

Connie shot up a prayer for strength. She chose her words carefully. "Mother Sutherland, I appreciate your interest in and concern for your grandson. I assure you, he is well taken care of. But I am his mother. Where he goes, I go. And I have no intention of going to Boston. My life is here. If you're going to threaten to take him away from me, you are not welcome here."

"Constance, be reasonable."

Connie pointed to the door. "Please leave, or I'll call the authorities."

The older woman stood, her eyes snapping with anger. "I'll leave. But you haven't heard the last of me on this subject." She gathered her purse and swept out the door.

Connie collapsed on the couch. Then, just as quickly, she leapt up, ran to the bedroom and swept a startled Scotty into her arms.

"My baby boy. Nobody's ever going to take you away from me."

43

An hour later, Connie still felt shaken, so she and Scotty went next door and knocked on Miriam's door.

"What happened to you?" Miriam said as she welcomed them into her apartment. "You look as if you've seen a ghost."

"A witch is more like it." As Miriam lit the burner under the tea kettle, Connie briefly related the conversation with Drusilla.

"So that's what was going on," Miriam said. "I heard loud voices, but I assumed you had the radio on. It's so unlike you to raise your voice. But it sounds as if you had good reason." She reached down and took Scotty's hand in hers. "Come with me, Scotty. Would you like some crayons to play with?"

The boy nodded. After settling him at the table with a coloring book she'd purloined from her classroom, Miriam settled onto the sofa next to Connie, teacups in hand.

"I haven't been a teacher for very long," she admitted, "but from things I've heard other teachers say, it seems custody disputes between parents and grandparents are not unknown. They're rare, but they do happen. Fortunately, most families are able to resolve the issue without getting the courts involved."

"The courts," Connie echoed, dismayed. "Oh, I don't think Drusilla would go so far as to pursue the matter in court. Do you?"

"I have no idea. I've never met the woman," Miriam said. "But if she took the trouble to travel all the way here to press her cause, you might want to talk to a lawyer, just in case."

"She didn't come just to see us," Connie clarified. "She's in town for her school reunion. She just didn't want to miss out on an opportunity to make our lives miserable."

Miriam settled back against a sofa cushion. "Then let's assume she's all bluster. Especially now that she's seen Scotty with her own eyes. Let's hope she realizes how young he still is, and that all that talk about school is way out of line."

"Let's hope so," Connie said. "She may try again in a year or two, when he truly is ready to begin school. But by then I'll be prepared. I'll have had time to think about it, about what's best for Scotty and his education. I can guarantee he won't be moving to Massachusetts. Unless, of course, he decides to go there for college."

"Maybe he'll be a Princeton man, like his father," Miriam said.

"That's in New Jersey. But it's the same thing. Way too far for his mama to even think about today." She patted Miriam's hand. "Thanks for talking all this through with me."

"What are friends for?" Miriam replied warmly. "You've done the same for me."

Feeling reassured, Connie slept well that night. The next day, she became so caught up in sales calls and Pearlcon business that she practically forgot all about Drusilla and her threats. So she was unprepared for the evening, a few weeks later, when she returned from a long day of sales calls to find in her mailbox an official-looking envelope bearing a Boston postmark. Her heart skipped a beat as she unfolded a legal-looking piece of paper with the words "Petition for Guardianship" splayed across the top.

Her legs buckled as she sat in a chair. The paper shook in her hands as she tried to focus on what it said. It was a petition for guardianship of one Winston Scott Sutherland IV, filed by Drusilla Sutherland. Cited under the "Reasons" heading, a few typed statements included "mother's work requires extended absences from the home" and "mother's business associates include a known ex-convict."

Connie fought down her panic and telephoned Adam Deveare. The next afternoon, she took the paper to his office.

"Now, Connie, you must remain calm," he said, reminding her of Drusilla despite his attempt to be reassuring.

"I will not remain calm," she shouted.

He laid a hand on her shoulder. "Let's not panic until we have all the facts. I'm not an expert in family law, but I have an associate who is. We can count on his involvement, if it's warranted."

"Of course it's warranted." She thrust the paper into his hands and flung herself into a chair, tugging off her gloves. She gave him several minutes to read through the document. His expression was unreadable.

"By 'ex-convict,' I assume she's referring to Marietta Carlson," he said. As a key advisor to Pearlcon, Adam had met Marietta a number of times and knew her story.

"Yes, of course. But how would Drusilla know anything about that? I'm quite sure I've never told her. I haven't talked to her about company matters at all ... not that she's ever shown the slightest interest. And as for my never being home, I need to earn a living, don't I? My boy is in excellent care."

"How she came to know is a mystery." He read the petition over, his face clouded. Suddenly his expression cleared. "The good news is, she's bluffing."

Connie bolted upright. "Bluffing? How do you know?"

He waved the paper. "This petition is not signed by a judge, nor has it been file-stamped by the court clerk." He handed it back to her. "It's a fake, not worth the paper it's printed on."

Relief mixed with anger rushed through Connie's veins. "But why would she do such a horrible thing to me?"

Adam leaned against his desk. "She sounds like an unhappy old woman who's just trying to scare you. If you feel confident that Scotty's happy, healthy, and being well cared for, then you needn't worry."

"My son couldn't be in better hands," Connie said with conviction.

"Then ignore it." He folded the paper and handed it back to her. "Without the backing of the courts, it doesn't require a response. And now, how about I treat you to lunch?"

In her elation that he had just vaporized the dreadful vision of losing her son, Connie accepted. What could possibly go wrong in a public restaurant? Over a delicious meal, she found herself laughing more than she had in a long time. Adam had a witty, self-deprecating sense of humor that she found very appealing. She enjoyed spending time with a man who could make her laugh. But as they parted ways, she sensed that he held her hand a little longer than usual, looked into her eyes a little too deeply. Her brain sent up red flags.

As for the petition, per Adam's advice, she didn't respond to it. He was correct. The matter came to nothing. *For the time being*, she reminded herself, worried about what other tricks Drusilla might have up her sleeve. But for now, Scotty was out of danger of being snapped up by his grandmother. *Like in "Little Red Riding Hood,"* thought Connie, *although* this *grandmother really is a wolf.* Thankfully the wolf had slunk back to its lair in Boston. Still, Connie didn't think she should get away with what she'd done. She mailed a strongly worded letter to her mother-in-law, ordering her to leave her family alone, but received only silence in return.

In the weeks after Drusilla's hoax, Connie had to fight the urge to contact Adam Deveare except when the needs of the business absolutely required it. Even then she tried to get Ingrid to do it. She just didn't trust herself and her feelings around him. Still, thoughts of Adam and the desire to see him cropped up with dismaying regularity. She knew she had to be disciplined, to keep her feelings in check, to remember she was a Christian woman of good character. She owed that much to God, to Winston, and to their son.

A few weeks later, as Connie sat on the sofa and scanned the evening paper, the name "Deveare" caught her eye. She was saddened to read an obituary for Lloyd Deveare, her parents' former lawyer. And, of course, Adam's father. The next day, Connie asked Ingrid to order flowers sent to the offices of Deveare and Associates. She carefully worded the accompanying message, to make clear it came from Pearlcon Enterprises with no hint of her personal feelings. While wanting to do the right thing, she had to make sure the gesture couldn't possibly be misconstrued as coming from her heart. Even though it most surely did.

❧ 44 ❧

In spite of the continuing Depression, the 1932 Christmas season was rewardingly lucrative for Pearlcon. With the price of Moondrop Miracle now out of reach for many women, Connie and Pearl had developed an economy line they called Opalesque, in honor of Connie's mother. Distributed through Main Street drugstores and supermarkets all across the country, Opalesque suited the needs and budget of working-class women and those living in straitened circumstances. Connie's instincts were right: even women with little extra money to spend wanted to improve their looks, to feel attractive, and to emulate in some tiny way the movie stars they watched on the silver screen.

"A woman might not be able to replace her shabby winter coat or worn pair of shoes," Connie told the retailers as part of her sales pitch, "but she can afford a bottle of Opalesque bubble bath."

Here and there, opportunities opened up, and she never failed to seize them. She'd been invited to sponsor a Pearlcon booth at the church Christmas fair, where a number of ladies purchased Moondrop Miracle for themselves and as gifts for their friends. The proceeds were donated to support the church's soup kitchen, and in the process, even more women were introduced to Pearlcon products.

Just before closing the company for the holidays, Connie and Ingrid met with Adam to make sure all the books were in order for the end-of-year accounting. Noting his black armband, Connie said, "We were all so sorry, Adam, to hear of your father's death."

"Thank you. We appreciated the flowers." He cleared his throat. Then he turned his attention to the records Ingrid had kept. After perusing them, he pronounced them in tip-top shape.

"You have a real knack for financial work, Ingrid. You're doing a fine job."

"Thank you." Ingrid's response was modest, but her glowing face revealed her deep pleasure at his remark.

As Adam and Ingrid talked about debits, credits, and amortizations, Connie inhaled the smell of him. Spicy, yet sweet, like gingerbread. She gave herself a mental shake. *Gingerbread. Oh, brother. I must be getting carried away by the spirit of the season.* She took a deliberate step back.

After a cheerful Christmas and rousing New Year spent at the farm with Scotty and Aunt Pearl, complete with a great fir tree decorated with popcorn balls and a raucous banging of pots to ring in 1933, Connie brought Scotty back to Chicago. Pulling up in front of the apartment building, she felt gloomy about the end of the holidays. Yet she also felt an odd sense of contentment. The winter break had gone well. Scotty had loved his presents and enjoyed sleigh rides and snowball fights with his young friends in Hoosier Grove. Best of all, they'd had time to snuggle together on the sofa as she read aloud the Christmas story. That meant more to Connie than any present she could possibly have received.

Although experience had taught her not to count on anything for sure, Connie felt reasonably financially secure for the first time since Winston had lost all their money.

Winston. She still missed her husband deeply, especially in the depths of occasional sleepless nights. But the longing had faded from a sharp pain to a gentle ache. She'd long ago given up watching and waiting for his return, although she maintained a stalwart faith that it would happen. Someday. Once in a while, something would bring him to mind—a snippet of a song they used to dance to in their jazz-club days, or a whiff of the Burma-Shave he used to wear. She was forced to refer to the wedding photo sitting on her bureau to recall the details of his face. Perhaps, she thought sadly, contrary to the old adage, absence didn't really make the heart grow fonder, but caused the loving feelings to gradually fade from memory.

But if her yearning for her husband had dulled around the edges, so had the sharp blades of her anger lost their edge. She still had faith that someday, *someday*, he'd come home. At that time, they'd have to figure out the next step in their marriage, how to repair the damage and move forward. But unless he suddenly showed up on her doorstep, which seemed highly unlikely, that particular concern could be put off for a time in the foggy future. Now, she had a boy to raise and a company to run.

❧ 45 ❧

Throughout the winter of 1933, Pearlcon continued to expand. Pearl worked long hours in the laboratory, innovating and ultimately adding more products to the company's line. She was brimming with ideas: a healing balm, a cleansing cream, an after-bath lotion, all related to the original Moondrop Miracle. Not all of her ideas worked out, but once in a while she hit on a winner.

"You're a natural Edison," Connie told her aunt one afternoon over the telephone. "I wish I had half your talent and energy."

"But you, my dear, have the uncanny knack of figuring out ahead of time what customers want. And even better, what they'll pay for."

It was true. With her eye constantly on the market, on what would sell and what was capturing the public's attention, Connie made suggestions for products that would interest her customers, and, most of the time, she was proved right.

"Bottle by bottle and jar by jar, the Pearlcon empire is beginning to grow," crowed an article the local newspaper.

They both laughed at that. With just a handful of employees, a ramshackle barn for a factory, and a home office still headquartered on the kitchen table in Connie's cramped city apartment, "empire" was a stretch. Still, Pearlcon was earning them all a steady, if modest, income, and that was what mattered most.

That winter, all of Chicago was gearing up for the following summer's Century of Progress Exhibition. Connie read an article in the newspaper that listed the names of women serving on the women's planning committee. To her surprise, listed among the socialites and clubwomen who made up the committee, she noticed a familiar name from her past: Julia Harper. The daredevil of Rockingham School, turned staunch advocate for women's rights.

"Wouldn't it be marvelous if we could advertise Moondrop Miracle and other Pearlcon products at the Century of Progress?" she mused to Ingrid the next morning. "I'm sure we'd have an edge if Julia's on the committee."

"It wouldn't hurt to ask," Ingrid agreed.

Connie looked up her former schoolmate in the alumni directory, called Julia on the telephone, and wrangled herself an invitation to lunch.

"Connie Shepherd!" Julia said heartily, flinging wide the door to her Hyde Park apartment. "How delightful to see you." Taller than Connie to begin with, she cut an intimidating figure in her tweed suit and mannish brogues.

"You too, Julia. And it's Sutherland now," Connie reminded her.

"Oh, that's right, that's right. Please, have a seat." Julia swept some books and papers from the sofa in her cluttered living room and placed them on a nearby table next to a well-used portable typewriter. Connie shrugged out of her winter coat and gloves. Around Julia, at least, she didn't need to feel self-conscious about the coat's outdated style.

"I remember now. I attended your wedding, did I not? Quite the society bash, as I recall. And how is dear Winston doing these days? Holding his own at the investment firm?"

"He's no longer with Carruthers & Mullin. He's been ... traveling a lot these days. We have a son, Scott, who's three-and-a-half. And I've started a little business of my own."

That caught Julia's attention. "A businesswoman! Heading up your own concern? I'm impressed. Connie Shepherd, I never thought you had it in you."

Connie took no offense at the blunt remark. That was simply Julia's way. "Neither did I, but 'needs must,' as the Brits say."

"What's your line of work?"

"I make a skin tonic called Moondrop Miracle."

Julia's face fell. "Oh."

Connie cocked her head. "What, 'oh'?"

Julia shrugged. "Well, that's just a beauty product."

"What where you hoping I'd say?" Connie felt a trickle of indignation. "That I dig ditches? Build skyscrapers?"

"I thought you were going to say something interesting, like medicine or architecture or something. Something useful to the betterment of women."

"Moondrop Miracle *is* useful to the betterment of women," Connie said. "It improves their complexions."

"Oh, Connie." Julia sighed. "It's just that cosmetics are so ... so ..." She threw up her hands. "It's degrading for women to adorn themselves for the purpose of enticing a man."

"Oh, for heaven's sake, the purpose of Moondrop Miracle isn't to ..." Connie could see that argument was futile. "Well, anyway, I'm sorry to disappoint you," she concluded in a lighter tone than she felt. Who was Julia Harper to criticize her? *Don't*, she reminded herself. *Focus. You're here for a purpose.*

Julia reached across the sofa and touched her hand. "Don't misunderstand me, Connie. I am proud of you for starting a business of your own. Truly I am. If more women did that, maybe we wouldn't be so oppressed by the patriarchy. But I do wish you'd direct your considerable intelligence toward something more ... more useful to the cause."

Although Connie rather liked the "considerable intelligence" remark, she bristled at Julia's attitude. "It's *your* cause, Julia, not mine. At any rate, I'm afraid I've wasted your time." She started to stand.

Julia motioned her to sit. "Not at all. What is it you wanted to speak to me about?"

"I understand you're on the women's planning committee for the Century of Progress, and I was hoping you could help me get my product featured there in some way. Perhaps I could buy a sponsorship or put up an exhibit or—"

"I'm sorry, Con." Julia shook her head. "Truly I am. In spite of my personal opinion on cosmetics, I'd love to help you out as a woman business owner. But the women's committee has set a policy of not promoting beauty products."

"I see."

"The theme of the fair, in case you missed it, is *progress*. We feel that beauty products support too narrow a concept of women's appropriate role in society."

"I see," Connie said again, although she didn't. "Well, thank you for listening."

The former schoolmates parted amicably, if a bit mystified by one other's priorities. On the way home, Connie ruminated on their conversation, about the idea of keeping her femininity versus making it in a man's world. Did she really have to choose one over the other?

❦ 46 ❦

The Century of Progress Exposition opened with much fanfare in May of 1933, minus the longed-for Moondrop Miracle sponsorship that Connie had felt sure would have rocketed her company to a new level.

One sunny afternoon not long after the fair opened, she quit her work early to take Scotty there for a day's outing. As she was clearing her desk, the telephone rang.

"Catch you at a bad time?" Adam's clear, deep voice came over the line. "I wanted to talk over a few points of the contract Ingrid sent over yesterday."

"I'm sorry, Adam. Can it wait? I'm on my way to pick up Scotty. We're going to the fair."

"Lucky boy," Adam said. "I haven't seen it yet."

"Why don't you come with us?" Connie blurted impulsively, momentarily forgetting her resolution to steer clear of him outside of business matters. Mentally, she shook off her concerns. What could go wrong in the middle of a crowded park with her young son present?

"Do you mean it?" Adam's voice brightened.

"Of course. If the law will let you take an afternoon off."

And so the arrangements were made to meet at the front gate of the fairgrounds. Connie anticipated parking might be a problem, so she and Scotty took public transportation. Wrangling a fractious almost-four-year-old on the sweltering streetcar was no mean feat, but felt worth the struggle when they showed up to the gate to find Adam waiting for them, looking cool and dapper in a seersucker suit and straw hat.

Inside the gate, Connie and her son stood hand-in-hand, gazing up in wonder.

She said to her son, "This, darling, is the Avenue of Flags."

Scotty's eyes, round as dinner plates, drank in the colorful flags of many nations snapping in the breeze.

As the three of them strolled through the fair, dazzled by the sights and sounds, Connie stole little side glances at Adam. As her life and her business grew more complex, she found herself relying more and more on his legal expertise and advice. He was alert and protective concerning Pearlcon's business interests. She trusted him completely, and so did Aunt Pearl. Furthermore, she appreciated how he made her laugh when they were together. And he was very kind and attentive to Scotty.

If she weren't a married woman, she might also pay attention to the fact that he was very good-looking, with strong, well chiseled features, thick dark hair, and a few kindly, crinkly lines at the corners of his gray-green eyes.

But she *was* married. No matter how long Winston had been away, no matter how far he'd traveled or how irresponsibly he had behaved, he was still her husband. She still loved him. She couldn't bear the thought of divorce. He continued to write her sporadic letters and send money for Scotty, though his letters were arriving further and further apart.

The longer he stayed away, the more indistinct his face became in her memory.

And here, by contrast, was the extremely distinct face of Adam, freshly shaven and smelling spicy, as usual. With a sudden stab, Connie reminded herself to be careful around Adam. Very, very careful.

Perhaps she'd been stupid and reckless to invite him to join them. He mustn't get the slightest whiff that there was even the tiniest possibility of her becoming anything more to him than a valued client.

At lunchtime, they stopped to rest at a café table in *The Streets of Paris* section.

"*Bonjour, madame.*" A weary-sounding waitress approached the table wearing a white beret, black dress, and white ruffled apron that Connie supposed were meant to look Parisian. "Vould you lahk to see zee menu?"

Connie stifled a chuckle. Even with just one year of finishing-school French, she recognized a fake accent.

"*Merci,*" she said, playing along. "Menus, please, and we'll all have water, and—" She glanced up. Suddenly both she and the waitress froze, staring at one another in shocked silence. A crimson flush stole up the waitress's cheeks.

"Connie?"

"Zoe?"

For a moment, they continued to stare. Zoe's henna-red hair had now been bleached platinum blonde, but her brown eyes were unmistakable. At last Connie found her voice, if not her words. "What—? What—?" She gestured to the costume.

Zoe's screechy laugh sounded forced. "Oh, this? You'll never guess. Mother thought it would be a lark for us both to work at the fair for a few weeks. You know, something different to do, just for kicks." She giggled unconvincingly.

"Your... your mother works here, too?" Connie tried to picture Sally Meade in a French waitress costume, a vision she found impossible to conjure.

"Yes. I mean, no, not here. She takes tickets at the front gate. I got this job because, well, I can speak a little French. And it sounded fun, pretending to be a French girl all day."

"Oh."

Zoe Meade, waitressing in a French café at the fair? Connie's thoughts swirled. Had her friend gotten that desperate? She didn't know what to say, so she, too, laughed as if it were all a big joke, even though she didn't feel like laughing. Instead she remembered her manners.

"Zoe, this is Adam Deveare, our attorney. Adam, this is my friend, Miss Zoe Meade."

Polite greetings were exchanged.

"And how is Winston doing these days?" Zoe asked. "Someone said he's found a job that involves a great deal of travel."

Before Connie could answer, Scotty's attention was drawn to a passing clown. "Look, Mama," he shouted.

"That's sure something, isn't it, buddy?" Adam turned aside and engaged in animated conversation with the boy, giving Connie and Zoe a bit of privacy.

"This job is only temporary." Zoe lowered her voice. "Look, I'd appreciate it if you didn't say anything to the girls about this. I mean, they might not get the joke. You understand. I'll tell them all about it, of course, when the—the experiment is over. When we can all have a good laugh over it."

"An experiment. Of course." Connie didn't bother saying that she hadn't seen "the girls" in quite some time. A lifetime ago, it seemed. She no longer received invitations from the old crowd, and even if she did, she'd have no time to accept. The only one she'd kept in touch with was Gwendolyn, and last she'd heard, she and George were planning to move out West somewhere. Los Angeles, she thought.

Zoe glanced nervously across the crowd at an officious-looking man dressed in a *gendarme*'s uniform and leaned toward Connie. "Say, the manager will blow a gasket if he catches me chitchatting. Can I bring you something? Maybe a glass of milk for *le petit garçon*?" She smiled at Scotty. "He's getting so big. How old is he now?"

"Almost four." Connie cast a glance at her wristwatch. "Oh, dear, look at the time. I almost forgot, we have to—"

At that moment, Scotty gave a yelp, jumped off his chair, and pointed. "Mama, look! There's a bird lady!" He flapped his little arms like chicken wings. Several diners at adjoining tables snickered.

Connie looked over to where a woman wearing ostrich feathers and little else swayed to the music of an accordion. She gasped.

"That's the famous Sally Rand," Zoe said, a bit breathless. "You may have read about her in the papers."

Connie leaped to her feet and tried to divert her son's attention. "Look, Scotty. See the funny clown?"

"But I want to watch the bird lady," he whined.

Adam stood abruptly. "Come along, Scotty. We'll go to Treasure Island and feed the ducks in the lagoon." He grasped the boy's bony little shoulders to direct him away from the feathered spectacle. As they hurried away, Connie called over her shoulder, "Good to see you, Zoe. Let's stay in touch."

Adam made good on his promise about feeding the ducks. Then they boated across the lagoon, rode the Sky Ride, gawked at the pirate ship, and gaped at the towering Magic Mountain. Adam was kind, funny, and undeniably attractive. Connie couldn't remember the last time she'd had so much fun—and fun had been in short supply the last couple of years.

He drove them home in his car. From the back seat, Scotty chattered about all the grand and glorious sights they'd seen. But halfway home, he dozed off. The companionable silence was broken only by a jazzy piano composition playing quietly on the car radio. Adam touched the knob and turned up the volume.

"I'm crazy about this piece," he said. "It's called 'Rhapsody in Blue,' by some young chap called Gershwin."

She listened for a few moments to the syncopated rhythms. "I like it. It's different."

"Sure is. Gershwin was just in town, playing with the Chicago Symphony. I found out too late and I missed it. Otherwise I would have invited you."

"That's all right." She'd never been much of a music lover, unless she was dancing to it. But the fact that Adam loved it added yet another layer to his intriguing personality.

She sneaked a glance at his profile, his skin golden in the rays of the setting sun. Fighting a sudden urge to reach over and touch his hand, she clasped hers firmly in her lap.

Too soon, Adam pulled the car to the curb in front of Connie's building and got out. He circled around to her door and opened it, then opened the back door and bent to lift Scotty out.

He carried the boy upstairs to the apartment. After depositing him on his bed, he and Connie walked together to the front door. There they lingered.

"I should go," he said, turning his hat over in his hands.

"Yes. Morning comes early." But she found herself as reluctant to say good-night as he seemed to be. They stood in the open doorway for a long moment. Feeling his eyes on her face, she fixed her gaze on his top collar button. "Thank you for a lovely day."

"Thank you for letting me invite myself along." He leaned against the doorway. "Say, I hear there'll be a band concert in Grant Park on Saturday night. Perhaps you'd like to go?" It was a question more than a statement.

A breezy summer night. She and Adam seated on the lawn, listening to beautiful music under the stars. There was nothing she'd enjoy more.

She shook her head. "I'm sorry. I ... can't."

"We could take Scotty with us."

"No. I'm sorry."

"Of course. I understand."

But did he? If he knew how she felt about him, he wouldn't ask.

He took her hand in his and seemed to study it. "Connie, I—"

At that moment a door slammed somewhere down the hallway and the sound of footsteps approached. He dropped her hand and clapped his hat on his head.

"Well, good night."

"Good night."

As she got ready for bed, her mind was on Adam. Her conscience nagged at her. She tried to tell herself that she only liked him as a friend because he was fun to be with and was kind to her and Scotty. But deep down she knew that that wasn't the whole truth. And she remained a married woman, however flimsy she felt her marriage to be these days. She wasn't the kind of woman to break her vows. And it wasn't fair to Adam to let him think she might be that kind of woman.

She couldn't go out with Adam, not after today. They'd enjoyed each other's company a little too much. The thought made her sad, and she forced herself to push it from her mind, with only limited success.

But later, as she drifted off to sleep after reading a chapter of Agatha Christie, the image that stood out most in her mind was not of Adam but that last glimpse of her former classmate, standing in her beret and apron amid the flimsy Parisian storefronts, waving forlornly.

❦ 47 ❧

The next morning, Connie drove out to Hoosier Grove. She left Scotty on the farmhouse porch with the cats while she checked on things in the barn. At last she heard a roar and a sputtering sound coming up the drive, and she returned to the porch. Pearl rode up on her gleaming Indian motorcycle, sporting goggles, leather gloves, and a red plaid scarf over her housedress and apron. She killed the motor and slid off the saddle.

"Hello, you two. I didn't know you were coming out today." She gave each of her visitors a kiss on the cheek. "Had to make a quick delivery. That old sheriff can't get enough of Moondrop Miracle. Although he asked if we could call it something else. Something more manly that a fellow's coworkers wouldn't rib him about." She rolled her eyes.

"We can consider starting a men's line, I suppose." Connie coughed and waved away exhaust fumes. "You make deliveries on that thing?"

"Sure. Why not?"

"Me! Take me!" Scotty shouted, jumping up and down.

Pearl looked at Connie. "Do you mind?"

Connie sighed. "I suppose it's all right. Just once around the yard. *Slowly.*"

Pearl got Scotty situated on the bike, then climbed on behind him. She kick-started the engine, and he squealed with delight. Cats scattered every which way as the pair took a few turns around the barnyard. When they rumbled to a stop in front of the porch, Pearl lifted Scotty off the contraption, and he ran to his mother, eyes shining.

"Did you see, Mama? Did you see?"

"I saw," Connie said, sounding suitably impressed. "Now go play with the kitties, darling. Mama and Aunt Pearl have things to discuss."

As they sat on the porch, she told Pearl about her encounter with Zoe at the fair. "I was thinking maybe we could offer her a job, filing papers or something. What do you think?"

"Couldn't you use some help with sales?"

Connie wrinkled her nose. "I suppose so. But that would require Zoe and me to work closely together, and I don't think that's the best idea. Given our history, we're bound to grate on each other's nerves."

"And she wouldn't grate on mine?"

Connie bit her lower lip. "You're more tolerant than I am."

Pearl threw back her head and laughed. "Can't argue with you there." She gave her wicker chair a few slow rocks. "I guess it would be all right. Although, if she's one of your chums from that fancy school, she's probably not used to hard work."

"Difficult times have a way of making hard workers of all of us," Connie said. "Look at me."

Pearl's mouth quirked into a smile. "You have a point. Well, let's give her a job and see what she can do."

Connie stepped into the barn, a section of which was now brightly lit by overhead lights shining down over two new worktables. Around the tables stood a few employees—local Hoosier Grove women—who had been hired to help package and ship Moondrop Miracle. Connie felt a small rush of satisfaction at this achievement. At least the women had a decent space to work now, instead of the dusty, dimly lit space that had existed before. The other necessary improvements would come in time, as the company could afford it.

Connie stepped around the tables and greeted each employee by name, asking questions and truly listening to the answers. She wanted her employees to feel like valued members of a family, not cogs in a machine.

Marietta Carlson greeted her with a grin. "How you doing today, Mrs. Sutherland? And how's the little man?"

"We're both doing fine, Marietta. And so are you, I hear."

Indeed, under Marietta's competent management, the manufacturing, bottling, and shipping functions flourished. Marietta had earned Aunt Pearl's trust and respect, as well as her friendship.

On the way home from Hoosier Grove that evening, Connie made a brief stop at Zoe's grandmother's house to extend the offer of a job. Her former classmate's normally pinched face shone in gratitude under the bottle-blonde hair.

"You're too kind. I don't know if I could have lasted one more day on *Ze Streets of Paree*."

"The job's out in Hoosier Grove," Connie warned. "Do you still have a car?"

"No, but I don't mind taking the train. The commute will give me time to catch up on my reading." Connie was impressed that Zoe had taken on a gentler, more humble demeanor.

"That's the spirit!" She grinned as the two shook hands, sealing the deal. "Welcome aboard."

❧ 48 ❧

Time passed in a blur of constant activity. Winston continued to send money in varying amounts on a sporadic basis, often in an envelope with no return address. The postmarks ranged from Maine to New Mexico. Nowadays, there was seldom a note attached. Once in a while a few lines. *Hope you and the boy are well. Found a job here in Michigan.* Or Texas. Or Idaho. No job lasted very long, and never once did he hint at coming home or suggest his family join him.

But each time she received word from her husband, Connie thanked God he was still alive and fervently prayed for Jesus to watch over him. Early on, she'd also fervently prayed for his return to her, even though most people would tell her she was a fool to keep hoping. But if she were completely honest, that particular hope had started to fade in the light of Adam Deveare's smile—an unexpected development she tried very hard not to think about. Despite her resolve not to see him outside of work, he still managed to pop into her life on a more or less regular basis, dropping off a book he thought she'd find interesting or some little toy for Scotty, or making good on his promise to help with making repairs to the barn on weekends.

Scotty, meanwhile, seemed as happy as a little boy could be. Having no memory of the fairy-tale house, nor of his father, he had never mentioned either.

Connie noted how healthy and sun-kissed he looked from playing in the sun. He'd become the pampered pet of the Pearlcon staff, too. Whenever Connie brought him out to Hoosier Grove, Marietta and the other workers let him help with pasting labels and licking stamps, making him feel important and useful. He was always full of stories about the friends he made in Hoosier Grove and the games they played and his adventures on the farm. Friends his age were in short supply in their Chicago apartment building. He did, however, enjoy goofing around with Lucinda and Miriam and seemed quite enamored of the lovely Hilda.

One autumn evening, the telephone rang in the apartment. Aunt Pearl was on the end of the line. She sounded worried.

"I'm so sorry to have to say this, Connie, but I had to let Zoe go today."

"Zoe? Oh, no." Connie's heart sank. She shifted the receiver to her other ear. "Why? What happened?"

"She's been arriving at work intoxicated," Pearl said.

"At nine in the morning?" Connie couldn't believe it.

"Yes. It seems she's been keeping a flask in her purse and sipping from it on the train, all the way from Chicago. With another infusion at lunchtime, apparently."

"Oh, dear."

"I overlooked it the first few times. Finally I sat her down and told her it had to stop. It was starting to affect her work. And some of the other employees were beginning to notice erratic behavior and liquor on her breath."

"I see."

"I would have told you sooner, but you've been so busy with the Carson account ..."

"That's all right. Go on."

She heard Pearl take in air. "That's about all. This morning she was tipsy again, and got into a fierce argument with Marietta. She made some awful remarks about Marietta's prison record, within earshot of some other employees. So I had to let her go. I'm sorry."

"No, no, that's all right. You did the right thing, under the circumstances. I had no idea."

"I know she was your friend ..."

"It's all right, Aunt Pearl. I'm sure you had no choice. We'll start looking for a replacement right away."

After ending the call, Connie wondered if she should call Zoe to get her side of the story. In the end, she decided to write a note instead. She penned a brief message stating she was sorry that the job hadn't worked out and offering to provide a reference, should Zoe need one in getting another job. When she never heard back, she wasn't surprised.

One Friday evening in October, after the FruGals had finished dinner, she called Pearl to discuss plans for a pumpkin-decorating party for Scotty and his Hoosier Grove playmates. The telephone rang and rang. She tried the direct line to the barn. Unfortunately since it was outside of business hours, it, too, rang and rang.

"I'll keep trying," she promised Scotty before putting him to bed. The memory of how Connie's mother had sent her, all those years ago, to check on Pearl—an incident that had turned out to be totally unnecessary—now kept Connie from feeling overly concerned. Her aunt was no doubt playing cards over at the neighbor's or doing something equally harmless. But when, two hours later, her aunt still wasn't answering, she became alarmed.

"Operator, can you try again please?"

"No one's picking up," the operator reported, with excruciating obviousness, after several tries.

Connie's voice shook. She cleared her throat. "Could you please call the sheriff's office and ask them to send someone over to check on her?"

"Yes, ma'am. Please stand by for a response."

Connie sat by the telephone. She jumped when it rang.

"Ma'am, this is Sheriff Blake in Hoosier Grove." His voice was low and subdued. "I'm sorry to say there's been an accident. Your aunt took a nasty spill while riding her motorcycle. Apparently a head injury is involved. She's being transported by ambulance to Sherman Hospital in Elgin."

Connie's blood surged. "I'll come right away."

Leaving Scotty in Lucinda's care, she sped out to the regional hospital in Elgin as swiftly as she could without breaking the law. Unshed tears pressed against her vocal cords as she prayed the whole way. Prayers for the accident to have been less serious than the sheriff made it sound. For Pearl to hold on. For herself to have the strength to face something she wasn't ready for.

But she was too late. By the time she arrived, Aunt Pearl was dead.

As she wept over her aunt's still, gray form, all the grief and despair Connie had felt at the loss of her parents years before came flooding back. It was of little comfort to know that Pearl had died doing something she loved: riding her motorcycle. How would Connie ever manage without her beloved aunt's steady guidance and wisdom?

Dazed, she stumbled out to the white, sterile hallway and slumped against the wall. When her parents had died, Aunt Pearl had stepped in to take care of her. Who would take care of her now?

Lord, I can't do this alone.

Hearing footsteps fast approaching, she lifted her head to see Adam striding down the hall. She stood up straight.

"Adam. How did you—When did—" She couldn't seem to form an intelligible sentence.

"Ingrid called me after hearing the news from Lucinda. I'm so sorry, Connie. What can I do to help?"

She started to say something, but a sudden flood of grief overwhelmed her.

His arms wrapped around her. She laid her head against his shoulder. It felt so strong, strong enough to carry her burdens.

His voice against her hair was barely more than a breath. "It's all right, Connie. Everything's going to be all right."

His wool jacket was flecked with raindrops. The dampness felt cool against her cheek. When she'd recovered her composure somewhat, she straightened, embarrassed at the public display of emotion. But he did not let her go. Instead he grasped her shoulders, looking at her as though he had never seen her before.

"Connie, I—I think we need to talk."

She knew what he was going to say. She suppressed the shiver that touched her spine. "Don't, Adam. Not now."

Indeed, standing in a bustling hospital corridor with her deceased aunt lying just a few feet away gave her the perfect excuse to push him away. Even so, she fought a tremendous urge to slide her arms around his neck and pull him close. "Thank you for coming, but I'll be all right now. You don't have to stay with me."

"I'm not going anywhere." He spoke barely above a whisper. "I love you. Don't you see? I love you."

She stiffened and pulled away. "No, you don't. You mustn't." Her mind whirled with conflicting emotions. She turned her back to him. "Adam, please. I can't have this conversation. I've just lost my aunt. So if you wouldn't mind, please, just..." *Stay with me. Don't leave me here. I can't do this alone.* But what came out of her mouth was, "Just go."

He hesitated. "If you're sure."

Cold disappointment clutched at her heart. "I'm sure."

"You'll call if you need me."

"I will. Or ... someone will."

With a dejected air, he turned and walked away. Regret joined the grief in her belly as she watched the back of his jacket recede until he turned the corner. A small sob escaped her lips. Then she straightened and turned toward her aunt's room. There were things to be done, arrangements to be made.

One step at a time, she reminded herself. *One step at a time.*

❦ 49 ❦

C onnie stayed with Scotty at the farm for a few weeks, both of them despondent. It took her that long to put Pearl's personal affairs in order and make sure the factory and laboratory were in good hands. Over Scotty's protests, she found a good home for Pearl's cats on a neighboring farm.

"You can visit them often," the farmer promised as Scotty tearfully said good-bye to Edison and Newton and the others.

After offering her aunt's clothes to the women working in the factory, Connie boxed up the rest and took them to a charity shop in town that smelled of attics, a task that made her throat ache with unshed tears.

Marietta Carlson helped her every way she could with putting Pearl's laboratory in order. She had proven to be an excellent, diligent worker. Now, Connie put her in charge of the whole Hoosier Grove facility, in Pearl's stead, with a raise in pay to go with it.

"You might not realize how much talent you have," she told Marietta, "but God does. And so do I."

Marietta's face glowed with pride.

Connie tried without success to reach Winston at his last known address in Idaho and let him know of Pearl's death. Her letter was returned "Addressee unknown."

With Pearl gone, the company was deprived of her brilliant ability to think up new product ideas. That lack would have to be addressed eventually, but for now there was no rush. Thankfully, the current product lines were going strong.

While she was working in Hoosier Grove, Ingrid forwarded her the mail from Chicago. Going through the latest batch one afternoon, she opened a brief note of apology from Adam for what he called his inappropriate behavior at the hospital. In the note, he promised to never mention again that he loved her. He didn't deny loving her—just that he would never mention it again. Connie determined that any dealings with his office would be handled by Ingrid. Not until she heard that Adam had left for Berlin to work with an overseas client, his stateside accounts to be handled by an associate, did she relax about going near his office. She should have felt better knowing an ocean separated them. Instead, she felt a jumble of emotions: loneliness mixed with disappointment mixed with guilt and dismay that she, a married woman, should think these kinds of thoughts. *Lord, help me stay strong.*

When the funds from Pearl's estate came through, Connie planned to put them to work on not just jerry-rigging repairs to the old barn, but gutting it completely and building a new, modern factory. It would be Pearl's final legacy to the future that Moondrop Miracle had built. While Connie wasn't sure how long it would take for the money to clear, as soon as she could, she got busy with plans and blueprints.

Such an enormous undertaking once would have thrilled her under other circumstances, but now it made her feel exhausted and overwhelmed. She needed a break from work, but the relentless workload wouldn't let her take one.

When everything had been settled with the Hoosier Grove factory, Connie brought Scotty back to their apartment in the city. They still participated in the Friday-night suppers with the FruGals as often as they could, but even that had changed. Hilda had moved out, gone to California in search of work in the film industry, leaving behind both the skinny playwright boyfriend and the ridiculous stage name "Hilly

Crabtree." But Connie, Lucinda, Miriam, and Ingrid still formed a rock of support for each other.

After sending his note of apology, Adam tactfully stayed away. She missed him terribly. But a marriage vow was a marriage vow. Still, she kept his note tucked in her bedside table and pulled it out now and then when she couldn't sleep to remind herself that somewhere in the world was a man who truly cared for her.

In February of 1934, Connie finally decided it was time to move her corporate headquarters off her kitchen table. Now that she could afford it, she rented office space outside the apartment—a suite of rooms on the second floor of a charming older building, with "Pearlcon Enterprises" etched on the glass in the door.

She still brought a fair amount of work home with her, though. Taking care of Aunt Pearl's estate had caused her to fall behind on Pearlcon paperwork, and it had taken months to catch up. One frigid night, as her son finally slept after crying himself to sleep over missing Aunt Pearl, she took a seat at the kitchen table and opened a file. But she was too distracted and restless to concentrate. She threw down her pen, padded into the kitchen, and brewed herself a cup of tea. Her son would be young for such a short time, in the scheme of things. He was already four years old. In the fall, he'd start school, and before she knew it, he'd be all grown up. She'd heard an expression—the days were long but the years were short. At first, she'd thought it silly, but now she understood. First thing in the morning, she'd sit down with her boy and resume planning the party he'd been looking forward to before everything went haywire.

The jangle of the telephone made her jump. She rushed to lift the receiver before the noise woke Scotty.

"Hello?"

"It's me." Adam's voice came over the line, firm and sure. Her knees nearly buckled with happiness. "I'm back from Berlin."

She fought to control her voice. "I'm so glad. For how long?"

He didn't answer. Instead he said, "I'm wondering if I can come over for a little while. I'd like to talk to you about something."

"It's getting rather late," she said, even though it was only eight o'clock. "Can it wait until morning?"

"No."

"Sounds urgent."

"It is."

"A problem?"

"I don't think so. Well, possibly. I'll explain when I get there. I'm on your street."

She drew a deep breath. "All right. Just for a little while."

She spent the next few minutes pacing around the apartment, wondering what he planned to tell her and thinking about what she'd say. *He's your attorney*, she reminded herself. *Just your attorney. Coming over on attorney business.*

When he arrived at her door, dressed casually in an olive duffel coat over a sweater and slacks, he looked tall and fit. They shook hands warmly, and she invited him in.

"Coffee? I just made a fresh pot."

"Yes, please. Cream and sugar."

She retreated to the kitchen, grateful for a solid task with which to busy herself. She took her time. Coffee, china cup, matching saucer, quick pour of cream, two sugar cubes, just the way he liked it. While she worked, she called over to him, "How was Berlin?"

"My client work went well, but the city itself is ... well, disturbing is the only way to describe it."

She returned to the living room and handed him the cup and saucer. "What do you mean?"

"Germany has a new chancellor. A man named Adolph Hitler. He wrote a book called *Mein Kampf* that has a lot of people worried. The atmosphere over there is tense, to say the least. But I didn't come here to talk politics."

"What did you come for, then?" she asked lightly.

He didn't answer directly, stirring his coffee instead. "Where's Scotty?"

"Asleep."

"Sorry I missed seeing him. How's he handling Aunt Pearl's death?"

She shrugged. "Time heals all wounds, so they say. He's sad. He misses her. We both do." She paused. "He's been missing you as well. He often speaks of that day at the fair."

He looked at her intently. "And you? Have you been missing me too?"

She didn't trust herself to answer.

He paused as if searching for the right words. "Connie, I've been gone for months, but my feelings for you haven't changed. Not one bit. I still love you."

She turned away from him and looked out the window. "You promised never to bring that up again."

"That was before I went to Germany. Now... The future is uncertain. Peace may be fleeting. Life is short and precious, too precious to waste time. Connie." He set the cup and saucer on the table and grasped her shoulders, turning her to face him. His eyes bore into hers. "I want to be with you. I know you're not free to marry, but you need to face facts. You no longer have a marriage. Not a real one."

She had trouble catching her breath. She thought she might be sick. "It's real in the sight of God." She shook off his grasp and stood. "You need to leave. Now."

Adam stood as well. "Do you still love him?"

She hesitated. "He's my husband. He's Scotty's father."

His voice was surprisingly stern. "But you haven't seen him in years. He's been off riding the rails, or whatever it is he's doing. When's the last time you even heard from him?"

She bit her lower lip. "It was before Christmas."

"And here we are in February. By now you could be a widow, for all you know."

She lifted her hands in frustration. "But that's just it. I *don't* know. And until I have solid news, some concrete evidence, I have to believe he's okay. I have to believe he's coming back."

Adam lowered himself to the sofa and regarded her thoughtfully. "I love you, Connie. And I know you love me, too. It's insane for us to go on this way."

"I'm married."

"You keep saying that, but where is this husband of yours? Why does he stay away?"

"I don't know," she cried. "I've never known."

His gaze fixed on hers and glistened with unshed tears. At last he stood. "I'm sorry, Connie." He picked up his coat, turned, and walked out the door. She longed to go after him, to beg him not to leave, to stay and talk. But to what end? They could talk forever, endlessly talking, and they'd never reach a satisfactory conclusion. Never.

After he'd gone, she lay on the sofa, unable to summon the will to take herself up to bed. She did love him. Not with the giddy head-over-heels love she'd once felt for Winston, before everything went so wrong. But with the strong, steady love born of Adam's kindness and protection and support.

But her feelings didn't change the fact that she was married to Winston. She determined not to break her vows. Vows she'd made before God. The best thing she could do now was to let Adam go. To hope for the best for him, that he would find someone who was free to love him as much as he deserved. And she prayed for herself, too. For the strength to follow God's will for her little family.

As she prayed, she must have dozed off, because an unknown amount of time later, a loud banging on the door awakened her.

Adam. Had he returned?

Startled, she sprang from the sofa and eyed the door. If it was him, would she have the strength to send him packing, or would she fling her arms around his neck? *Oh, Adam.* She half hoped and half dreaded seeing him.

She hurried to the door, placed her hand on the knob, and breathed a prayer for strength. Then, she flung open the door.

And found herself staring into the older, thinner, more careworn but instantly recognizable face of her husband.

❦ 50 ❦

Her lungs stopped drawing air.

"Hello, Connie," Winston said, as casually as if he'd just come back from buying a newspaper at the corner store.

She lost all power of speech, her mouth slack. All the blood in her body rushed to her heart. She stood still, staring at him.

Finally she found her voice.

"What are you doing here?"

"I've come home."

She raised her arms with every intention of slugging him. Hard. Instead, as if by a force outside herself, her arms wrapped around his neck.

"I knew you'd come home. Deep down in my heart, I knew it."

This was the moment she'd longed for, prayed for. Even so, now that it was here, it felt nothing like she'd thought it would. She thought she'd weep with relief, or laugh with joy, or faint dead away, or *something*. She did none of those things. Underneath her startled astonishment, she felt ... nothing. Just an empty sort of numbness.

Feeling awkward, she stepped back and smoothed her dress.

He removed his hat and turned it in his hands. "May I come in?"

She took a deep breath and tried to calm her wild thoughts. She'd rehearsed many times what she'd say, what she'd do, if he ever showed up at her door. But now she was paralyzed, her thoughts swirling.

Standing right in front of her was her husband. For better or for worse, richer or poorer. The husband who had left her. The husband she ought to be overjoyed to see. The man she was no longer sure she wanted in her life.

"May I come in?" the familiar stranger repeated.

Somehow, she let him in and took his coat as if he were a guest and she the practiced hostess. When the blood pulsing in her veins had calmed a bit, she sat in a chair across from where he was seated on the sofa. They stared at each other.

The silence grew heavy. At last he said, "Gee, it's good to see you, Con. You look beautiful. Really beautiful."

She couldn't say the same for him. Deep lines ringed his mouth and surrounded his eyes, which still held their piercing green. He looked gaunt and leathery, more like a weather-beaten farmhand than the LaSalle Street financier he'd once been.

He glanced around the small apartment. "I was sad when you wrote that you'd finally sold the house."

"I knew you would be. We needed the money."

"Hard times." After a long moment he shrugged. "It was yours to sell."

"I didn't know if you were ever coming home. I thought you were gone for good."

"I'm sorry."

You're sorry? She tasted the bitter, metallic anger rising at the back of her throat. "How could you run off like you did? How could you leave me and, worse, your child, to fend for ourselves?"

He lifted his hands in a pleading gesture. "I've explained. I've written to you. I sent money, when I had it."

"*Occasionally*, and we appreciated it. Sometimes those few dollars were the only thing between us and the street. And half the time you didn't include a return address where we could reach you." She looked at him for a long moment, but he didn't respond. "I couldn't even reach you through your mother. Not that I was eager to keep in touch with her after that mean trick she pulled."

"What mean trick?"

"Oh, she didn't tell you?" Briefly Connie related the story of the fake petition that had terrified her before being so thoroughly debunked by Adam. "And I haven't heard a peep from her since. Who does she think she is, trying to take my son away from me?"

"*Our* son," he corrected quietly.

"Don't." She held up a hand as if stopping traffic.

He hesitated, then shook his head. "I hadn't heard she did that. But I can't say I'm surprised." His face drooped. "She's been diagnosed with senile dementia."

"Dementia." A sliver of understanding broke through the storm clouds in Connie's mind. "Well, that might explain why she'd go off half-cocked and attempt such a ridiculous stunt. Thank heaven I have a good lawyer watching out for me." Hot regret seared her heart as she thought of Adam.

Winston shrank back. "I'm sorry, Connie. I'm sorry for everything."

She drew herself up. "Sorry is not—"

"I need to say this," he pleaded. "Let me say it."

She waited.

He drew a deep breath. "I never should have left you. I never should have taken the coward's way out. I honestly thought you'd be better off without me. I was wrong."

"You were right," she snapped. "We are better off now than we ever were, Scotty and I. We may have a lot less money, no fine house, no fancy furniture. But we have something else. We have friends, real friends who don't value us for money or our social status, but have become like family to us. We have a thriving business. Above everything else, we have the Lord. If you'd never left, we might never have learned to depend on Him. But we did, and He came through for us." She paused for breath. "I'm not the same person I was before you left."

A light sparked behind Winston's weary eyes. "But that's good news. Don't you see? I'm not the same person I was, either. But it took years of drying out and then a few more years of riding the rails to make me see that."

"What do you mean?"

She listened quietly as he told her how he'd been fired from two jobs in Boston before leaving his mother's home and striking out on his own. How, despite his best efforts, he had failed to find anything more than temporary labor in cities from Scranton to Seattle. How he'd taken to riding the rails, just one more hobo in an army of hoboes. How he gambled and drank, drank and gambled, until washing up at an indigent mission right there in Chicago.

"They helped me turn my life around," he said. "They helped me clean up my act. Preached the gospel. And when I got better, they gave me a job working with other homeless fellows like myself." He shrugged. "They needed me. It felt good to be needed."

She finally found her tongue. "Needed you? I don't know what I'm supposed to say. *I* needed you. Scotty and I, *we* needed you. A boy needs his father."

"It didn't feel that way," he said. "Not really. After I lost all our money, I felt like I brought nothing but shame and hardship to you. Then it seemed like you were all set, building your business, earning your own way. I was nothing but a burden."

"That's not true."

"I hated the way you looked at me, like all you saw was failure and disappointment. I just couldn't face it anymore."

She swallowed. "I saw so much potential in you. It destroyed me to see you giving up."

He bolted his gaze to the floor. "How can I ask that you trust me ever again, or believe anything I tell you?"

"I don't know." Her head swam in exhausted disbelief. "We've been apart longer than we were together."

They were both silent, absorbing that thought. Then she said, "It's late. We're both exhausted. Neither of us can think clearly."

Nonetheless, they talked and talked and talked. They talked until the sky outside the apartment window started turning light. Dark circles ringed his eyes. Her heart ached for him, and for herself. They'd both grown so much older. So much time had been wasted. Or had it? For her part, she had a son she dearly loved and a fledgling business that was growing by the day. She'd used her time well. If any time had been wasted, it was his.

She stood up slowly, her legs cramped from sitting. "Hungry?"

"I'm used to it."

She went into the kitchen and fixed some fried eggs with bacon, buttered toast, and a pot of coffee. But when she set the food on the table, she found herself too disturbed to eat. She sat by, watching him eat and asking God to settle her emotions.

When he'd finished, she said, "Do you have a place to stay?"

He nodded. "I'm still at the mission. I have a room there."

"Go, get some sleep, and come back later this afternoon to see Scotty. I want to prepare him."

Win stood up from the table. For an awkward moment, he seemed unsure whether he should hug her good-bye. Apparently, he decided against it. "Until this afternoon, then."

She handed him his hat and watched his back retreat down the dim hallway. Then, head pounding, she headed for her room to take a bath and try to get some sleep before Scotty woke up.

Later that afternoon, Winston did return. When his father entered the room, Scotty rose from his seat on the sofa, as he'd been taught to do. Connie was proud of his manners. He was tall for his age. He'd lost his little-boy chubbiness and had wavy copper hair and clear green eyes, just like his father. He didn't remember his father, of course, and he shook hands politely. Connie had prepared him for what to expect. They exchanged a few words, father and son. Winston didn't linger, but he did promise to take Scotty out for ice cream later that week, and he kept his promise.

Maybe that's how we rebuild, thought Connie. *One kept promise followed by another kept promise. One step after another.*

Each day blurred into the next as Connie adjusted to the presence of her husband in her life. She didn't want to take him back easily. What she did want was to hold out and stay angry.

She'd been angry for so long, she didn't know how to let go. But deep down, she knew cherishing her anger was wrong. She prayed about it daily. If she were to let go of the anger, God would have to help her do it. Because she sure as heck wasn't able to do it on her own.

❧ 51 ❧

For the first several weeks after his return, Winston continued to live at the mission. There was so much to talk about, so much to work through. More than Connie had words for. If he'd been with other women, she didn't want to know. For her part, she refused to tell him about Adam. In truth, there was nothing to tell. She'd had feelings for Adam, but hadn't acted on them. That part of her life was over.

"You love me. You know you do," Winston insisted one evening in early April. He'd stayed for coffee after dropping off Scotty following a visit to the zoo. "After all, you didn't divorce me."

"I don't believe in divorce," was her crisp response. As for love, she didn't know her own feelings. Her chief emotion was anger, which floated up again and again like a dense fog, making it difficult to breathe and impossible to see things clearly.

By May she felt ready to let her husband move back in with her and Scotty, not because she longed for his company but because she felt it was the right thing to do. When he did, the apartment felt cramped with the three of them. As for his return to the marital bed, that took longer still. But Scotty seemed to enjoy having his father home. After a period of adjustment, Connie appreciated no longer bearing the burden of being a single parent. She hadn't recovered her loving feelings toward Winston, but she assumed those feelings would come in time.

"We should start thinking of buying another house," Winston said one morning at breakfast. "Not on the level of the old one, of course. We'll have to work our way back to that."

"I agree we need a larger place," Connie replied, scraping the butter knife across a slice of toast, "but buying a house is out of the question. We can't afford it. Your work at the mission, while admirable, pays very little." And any money he may have once stood to inherit from his mother was now being spent on the around-the-clock care she required at a genteel Massachusetts home for the aged.

"Besides," Connie continued, "I don't think we should consider buying a house until we're absolutely sure we have a future together."

He looked stricken. "Of course we do, baby. I'm not going anywhere. You have to trust me." But unlike the old Connie, the new Connie stood her ground. She didn't yet trust him. Maybe that trust would come with time, but for now, she wasn't taking any chances.

"About the job question," he said, stirring his coffee, "I've been thinking it's time for me to come on board at Pearlcon. With you." He said it as casually as if it were a foregone conclusion, as if she'd just been waiting for him to make up his mind.

Connie nearly choked on her scrambled eggs. "What? At Pearlcon? I'm not sure it's such a good idea."

"Why not?"

She rose from the table, filled a glass at the tap, and took a large sip of water to steady her roiling emotions. Pearlcon was her brainchild, her baby. Hers and Pearl's and Ingrid's. Not his.

"We're still patching our marriage back together," she said finally. "I don't know that trying to work together as well would be such a great idea."

"I think that's exactly what we need," he countered. "If we're going to be partners—true partners—then I'll need to understand all aspects of the family business."

She mulled this over. True, Pearlcon was a family business. But over the length of time Winston had been away, she'd stopped thinking of him as family. What would God want her to do?

"I'll pray about it," she promised.

One evening later in the week, she told him, "I've given it some thought. We're chronically short-staffed in production. I suppose you could start there. If you're certain you want to make a commitment to the business. And to me."

"I do," he said solemnly. "But I was thinking more of taking over the financial end of things."

"Oh, no," she said, startled. "That isn't going to happen. Ingrid is unsurpassed at keeping the ledgers and understanding profit and loss statements and all the rest. I have no intention of taking that responsibility away from her."

Winston smirked. "Quite a step up from being our housekeeper." When Connie didn't return his smile, he quickly added, "No slight against Ingrid, but I'm trained at finance. It's what I do best."

"It's what you *did*," she retorted, "before you lost many people's life savings, including ours."

A vein throbbed in Win's temple. "It's not my fault that the market turned sour."

"Be that as it may," Connie said, "you made some terrible investments. I had people hounding me after you disappeared. Bad people. Scary people."

"But that's all over, baby." He spread his hands in a gesture of appeal. "I swear. Those days are behind us."

"That may be, but for now, if you truly want to be involved in Pearl-con, then I need you to help Marietta with production and scheduling and leave the books to Ingrid."

In the end, he gave in. They decided that he'd start working at the Hoosier Grove facility the following week, under Marietta's direction. Marietta was strong enough to keep him in line, if such keeping were needed.

❧ 52 ❧

As May blossomed into June, then July, Connie and Winston continued to mend their ruptured marriage. At Pearlcon, business progressed normally. She worked at the Chicago headquarters, or went out making sales calls, and he spent all his time working at the Hoosier Grove facility, helping Marietta streamline the production and packaging processes. But he still made the hour-long drive home to Chicago every night, in a secondhand Model A they'd bought specifically for the purpose.

"I'll never leave you again," he said over and over. "You can trust me." And over time, she chose to believe him.

She did everything she could to put Adam out of her mind, even to the point of interviewing other law firms to handle Pearlcon's business. While it didn't seem fair to pull business from Deveare & Associates for no other reason than that she had inappropriate feelings for the head of the company, she knew instinctively that, for the sake of her heart and his, she needed to stay out of Adam's presence. In the end, though, none of the other firms came up to snuff. Instead, it was decided that Ingrid would continue handle all dealings with Deveare & Associates, thus minimizing Connie's contact with Adam.

Connie often marveled that Ingrid was coming into her own. She had a natural grace and professionalism that charmed customers and employees alike and earned their respect. Above all, she was dedicated to stewarding the firm's resources, keeping meticulous records and a close eye on income and spending, without relying on Connie for every little decision.

So, it surprised Connie when Ingrid telephoned her at home one morning before she'd even finished her breakfast. She jumped when the phone jangled. The morning had already been hectic, getting Scotty and herself up and dressed and fed. She couldn't count on Winston's help since he'd gone on a business trip to New York the previous day to check out a potential new bulk importer of raw ingredients.

"Aren't you the early bird," she teased when she heard Ingrid's voice come over the wire.

"I'm out at Hoosier Grove today." Ingrid said. "The workmen are here to put in the new flooring, and they get to work early, so I had to, as well."

"Oh, that's right." Connie caught her son's eye. "Eat your toast," she ordered, then added, "Not you, Ingrid. Scotty's dawdling over his breakfast. Why do you have to be there? Where is Marietta?"

"She's not here yet." Ingrid sounded aggrieved.

Connie checked her watch. "It's not like her to be late."

"She wouldn't be able to pay the workmen anyway. She doesn't handle the money. But that's the problem."

"What's the problem? You're talking in circles."

"Sorry." Ingrid drew a breath. "It's the workmen. Our agreement says the workers get paid the fee up front before they begin the work. I offered to write the foreman a check, but he says he'll only take cash. But we don't have any cash on hand."

"Of course we do," Connie said, relieved that the issue was easily fixable. "Winston put five thousand dollars in the safe last night. That should more than cover it. I had him withdraw it from the Chicago bank account yesterday and put it there specifically to pay the workers. I'm sorry, I forgot to mention it to you."

"That's all right." Ingrid's voice sounded more cheerful. "Hold on a moment while I check." There was a rustling noise as Ingrid set down the receiver. Connie used the pause to encourage Scotty to finish drinking his orange juice.

Several long minutes later, Ingrid came back on the line. "I think you should come out here. Come right away." Her voice shook a little.

"Why?" Connie's blood ran cold. She pushed back her chair and stood. From his seat at the table, Scotty stared up at her with interest. "You don't sound like yourself, Ingrid. Is something the matter?"

"Something is definitely the matter," Ingrid replied. "The five thousand dollars is not here."

"Of course it is." Connie grew agitated. "Winston knew the work crew would need it first thing this morning, so he said he'd drop it off, and then park at the Bartlett station and catch the eastbound train to New York to meet with that importing company. I remember his words very clearly." Her palms went clammy. She swallowed. "The money has to be there. Where else would he have put it?"

"He wouldn't have forgotten? He wouldn't have accidentally taken it to New York with him?"

Connie scoffed. "No one forgets five thousand dollars. Not even Winston." She paused to gather her thoughts. "Call Adam, and Abe Shriver too. Tell them what's going on and ask for advice. I'll try to reach Win at his hotel."

After ending the call, she asked the operator to connect her with Winston's hotel. The desk clerk confirmed his reservation but said he hadn't checked in yet. *That's all right*, she told herself as she ended the call. *It's still early. The train might have been delayed. Or he might have gone straight to the importer's office before checking into the hotel.* She dropped Scotty off at Lucinda's and made the long drive out to Hoosier Grove, praying the entire way. There must have been a good reason why Win hadn't put the money in the safe. Or perhaps he had, but someone else had taken it out. But who would do something like that?

When she arrived at the factory, she tried Winston's hotel again, without success.

"Ingrid, do you remember the name of the import company he was planning to meet with?"

Ingrid shook her head. "Perhaps it's written down on his desk somewhere. I'll check."

As soon as Adam and Abe Shriver, the company's outside CPA, arrived, she called a closed-door meeting with them and Ingrid in Aunt Pearl's former dining room in the farmhouse, now used as a conference room.

"Clearly the culprit is Marietta Carlson," Abe said confidently. "You've got to face the facts, Connie. I've told you before, I've never felt good about your letting an ex-con run your business. You need to let Marietta Carlson go, and then you need to prosecute."

Connie drew herself up. "I'll do no such thing. For one thing, she doesn't run the business. She runs one aspect of it, production, and does it very well. Second, and most important, you have no proof she touched the money. Zero. You have no proof of anything at all."

"Marietta doesn't have access to the safe," Ingrid added. "She doesn't know the combination to the lock. There's never been any reason to give it to her."

"Don't be so naïve," Abe said. "Criminals have ways of getting that information. And who else but a criminal would steal that money?"

Across the table, Ingrid sat in stony silence. Connie could tell her normally stoic friend she was on the verge of tears.

"Connie's right," Adam broke in. "We can't go around accusing people without some kind of evidence."

Grateful for Adam's support, Connie turned back to Abe.

"Marietta is an exemplary employee," Connie said. "I won't have her reputation besmirched in this way. We simply need to keep trying to reach Winston. He'll clear up the entire situation."

The accountant shrugged. "Suit yourself. But mind that the whole situation doesn't come back to haunt you later."

"Until we're able to get hold of Winston, we need to call Marietta," Adam said. "She may have seen something before she went home last night."

"I did try to reach her," Ingrid said. "She doesn't have a telephone, so I called Lotte and asked her to find her. I haven't heard back yet."

"Well, I'm sure everything will be cleared up when we do," Connie said with confidence. "Lotte is Ingrid's cousin, and she lives in Marietta's neighborhood," she added for the benefit of the men.

"What about the other employees?" Adam asked.

"Nobody but Winston, Connie, and I have access to the safe," Ingrid said. "Or even to the office. It was locked when I got here."

A tense thirty minutes had passed before the telephone rang and Lotte was on the line. Ingrid took the call in the farmhouse kitchen. When she returned to the dining room, she looked distinctly relieved.

"Lotte found Marietta home in bed," she reported. "She's sick with a sore throat and running a fever. She said her landlady was supposed to call and let us know."

"Thank goodness," Connie breathed. "Well, not about the fever," she added quickly. "Were you able to question Marietta?"

Ingrid nodded. "Marietta did confirm seeing Winston in the office yesterday evening, around closing time. She didn't see him put anything in the safe, although she could have missed it if he did. She wasn't paying particular attention. She did say one thing was strange, though."

"What's that?"

"She said she didn't know why you were asking, because you were with him," Ingrid said, looking at Connie.

"No, I wasn't. I was at home all evening. In the city."

"Then why would Marietta say she saw you?"

"Clearly she was mistaken."

Adam frowned. "So who was it she saw?"

"Let's call her back." Connie followed Ingrid to the telephone and waited while she put the call through to Marietta's landlady. Minutes later, Ingrid handed the receiver to Connie.

"Marietta, this is Connie Sutherland," she said. A fit of coughing came over the line. "I'm terribly sorry to bother you while you're sick, but I need to know why you told Ingrid I was with Mr. Sutherland last night in the factory office. As it happens, I was home in Chicago all evening."

"I'm sorry. I thought it was you," Marietta rasped. "The light was dim, and I was standing at a distance. When I saw a woman with blond hair, wearing a black coat and hat like yours, I assumed it was you."

Connie's blood chilled. Only one other woman she knew of had hair as blond as her own.

"Thank you, Marietta. Rest up and get well." She returned the receiver to the cradle, then returned to the conference room. "Adam." Her voice sounded unnaturally calm to her own ears.

"Yes?"

"Will you please go to the Bartlett depot and make sure Winston's car is parked there?"

"I'm sure it is, if he planned to take—"

"Please check," she interrupted. "It's a 1928 black Model A. There's a dent on the rear left bumper." *A dent caused by Scotty going a little too fast on his roller skates.* The memory made her throat spasm. She felt heavy in her spirit.

Adam left. Connie walked over to the barn, explained to the workmen that there'd been a misunderstanding, reassured them that she'd straighten things out with their boss, and sent them away.

When Adam returned, his face grave, Connie knew what he was going to say before he spoke.

Winston's Model A was not parked at the station. Clearly he had not taken the train to New York.

"It's possible he drove back to the city and caught the train at Union Station," she said weakly. But even as she spoke the words, she didn't believe they were true. A glance at the faces seated around the table told her no one else did, either.

Mechanically Connie telephoned the sheriff, explained the situation, and described the Model A to him. Then there was nothing to do but wait.

Later that night, when a knock sounded at her apartment door, she instinctively knew that the news would be bad.

❧

FOR THE SECOND TIME IN CONNIE'S LIFE, POLICEMEN SHOWED UP AT her door. But this time, she knew what they were going to say before they said it—not the details, but the bald fact of it. Before they said a word, she knew Winston was gone for good.

They'd found the Model A in Indiana. It had veered off the road at a high speed and crashed into a tree. Thankfully, no other vehicle had been involved.

He had not been alone, the officer said, twisting his hat in his hands. A Miss Zoe Meade was found in the passenger seat. She, too, had perished.

Recovered from the car was a large amount of cash. Did Mrs. Sutherland know the source of this cash?

Yes. Yes, she did.

Connie felt numb and disoriented at the news, but not especially surprised.

She wondered if the five thousand dollars stolen from the Pearlcon safe was all the money Winston had absconded with, or just the tip of the iceberg. Maybe he owed debts she didn't know about, unpaid debts to menacing people of Louie Braccio's ilk. Or maybe he hadn't needed to repay any debts at all, but had been planning all along to use the money to get out of town and start a new life. With Zoe.

She'd never know the truth. But the fact that the scandal was deepened even further by Zoe's involvement ... well, when all was said and done, that didn't surprise her, either.

June 1935
Hoosier Grove, Illinois

T he county commissioner wielded the scissors that cut the green ribbon stretched across the factory gate.

"In these uncertain economic times, it's gratifying to see a company thriving," he said. "Pearlcon will bring jobs and industry to Hoosier Grove that will help lift all of us out of the hard times."

Connie spoke next. "Today, we celebrate the grand opening of the new Pearlcon manufacturing facility. We are thankful to so many of you who have been with us every step of the way. My name is Constance Sutherland, and I am one of the founders of Pearlcon. The other founder was my aunt, Pearl Russell, without whom there never would have been Moondrop Miracle at all."

She made the crowd chuckle with the story of how Moondrop Miracle had started out as Feline De-Flaker. She explained how the money from Pearl's legacy went to completely refitting the old barn as an up-to-date factory. Not only was Connie able to hire construction labor cheaply and easily, but the job helped put food on the table of several local families as well—families whose livelihoods had been devastated by the Depression. The interior had been entirely cleaned out, whitewashed and fitted with new lighting, a heating system, four long tables, numerous cupboards, tile flooring, and several sinks. All the old fixtures and tables had been removed or refurbished. While the outside of the building still looked like a barn, the interior was no longer a jerry-rigged maze of splintered beams, dangling cords, and sawdust, but a safe, clean, modern factory.

She introduced her staff. "Mrs. Ingrid Swenson is our business manager, working closely with me at the Chicago headquarters. Miss Marietta Carlson, our head of production, is in charge of this factory. Miss Lucinda Bricker is our head of advertising, and Miss Miriam Walters is head of sales. And finally, Mr. Adam Deveare of Deveare and Associates, whose legal and business advice has been invaluable, all along the way." She smiled with gratitude at her loyal team as they acknowledged the crowd's applause.

"Next on our agenda is the ribbon-cutting ceremony, which will be followed by a tour of our facility."

The photographer gathered the management team and the commissioner together and took several photos. Ingrid held one end of the ribbon and Marietta the other, and they stretched it between then. Connie positioned little Scotty next to the commissioner and handed him a giant pair of scissors. The photographer snapped several photos, then Scotty cut the ribbon with a decisive slice. The crowd applauded.

"Everyone who wants to tour the facility, follow me," Marietta called out, and the crowd moved off.

After thanking the commissioner and other local dignitaries, Connie watched them head toward the humming hive of the factory. Adam came up beside her and slid his arm around her shoulders.

"Are you coming, darling?"

"In a minute," she said. "I just want to savor this moment."

"Don't take too long. You have a company to run."

She smiled up at him. "Yes, sir."

He kissed her lightly, then followed the crowd into the building. She stood silently, tears pricking her eyelids, thanking God for this moment. She still remembered the way her friends gathered around her, held her, comforted her after Winston's death. How nobody had called her a fool for trusting him. How everybody had admired her courage for trying.

She remembered how Adam had appeared in her doorway that evening, looking shaken and pale. How he'd held out his arms and how she'd stepped into them. How he'd whispered how sorry he was into her ear, told her he'd never wanted such a terrible thing to happen. But she knew, Adam was a good man. He'd always been a good man.

Her memory went back farther, to her Aunt Pearl. Through scrimping and hard work, all the debts owed by Winston had been paid off, down to the last penny. The feeling of freedom that came from not owing money to anyone, particularly anyone shady, couldn't be bought at any price.

She knew there would be more moments, good ones and sad ones, frustrating ones and gratifying ones. But through it all, one thing was certain. Adam and Scotty would be by her side. She had no doubt that she was exactly where God wanted her to be.

❧ 54 ❧

March 1988
Chicago, Illinois

From the podium, Sonja's voice pierced Connie's reverie.

" . . . someone you've been waiting all evening to hear from."

She bolted upright in her chair, realizing she'd missed most of what the other speakers had said. Glancing around at her tablemates, she saw every face staring at her, every face grinning.

Had she fallen asleep? Gracious, had she *snored?*

"Mrs. Sutherland, you're up next," Miss MacDonald stage-whispered in Connie's ear. "Are you ready?"

She glanced at her wristwatch, dismayed at the late hour. Goodness, the audience would be practically asleep by now. She should have been allowed to speak first and then gone straight home to bed.

Up on the platform, Sonja was still speaking.

"I owe a great debt of gratitude to Constance Sutherland," she said, "as do many of you." She paused, swallowed, and looked down at her notes. The audience was dead silent, as if they were holding their collective breath.

Connie looked around, wondering if this was her cue to stand and walk to the platform.

"I'll go first." Sonja cleared her throat.

First? First for what? What was Sonja rattling on about?

When she spoke again, her voice was thick with emotion.

"I first met Connie Sutherland when I was a teenager. So, a long, long time ago. My mother, God rest her soul, worked for the Sutherlands as a housekeeper, and I babysat their son, Scotty. I was there when Moondrop Miracle was first getting off the ground, when Mrs. Sutherland and my mother would brew it up at the kitchen stove. The FDA would have a few things to say about that today." Quiet chuckles rippled across the room as Sonja paused to take a sip of water.

Consternation bubbled in Connie's chest as she fluttered her index cards. *Hell's bells.* If Sonja were going to tell the whole history of Moondrop Miracle and Pearlcon, what would be left for Connie to say in her speech?

Sonja continued. "Because of Moondrop Miracle, my mother—an immigrant to this country, a single mother with only a smattering of education—eventually became vice-president of Pearlcon. Because of Moondrop Miracle, I was able to get a college education and pursue a career in education."

Not because of Moondrop Miracle, Connie wanted to protest, *because of Ingrid.* If it weren't for Ingrid's friendship and encouragement, not to mention her kitchen skills, there'd be no Moondrop Miracle at all. She must remember to work that into her speech.

With a stab, she felt the loss of her dear friend and colleague all over again. Sometimes, this getting-old business was no fun, as dear friends shuffled off this mortal coil before her.

Sonja was still speaking. "As I said, I personally owe Mrs. Sutherland a tremendous debt of gratitude. By way of example, she taught this gangly teenager how to carry herself with confidence, how to hold a conversation, and which fork to use for the salad course." More chuckles. "She even introduced me to John Atwater, the man who would later become my husband."

Connie glanced around the room to see if people were getting bored. Goodness, how Sonja was carrying on. A simple introduction would have sufficed. But the audience appeared to be hanging on her every word. Perhaps they all had later bedtimes than Connie did.

At long last Sonja took a deep breath and said, "And now, please join me ..." Connie began the somewhat laborious process of rising to her feet.

" ... in sharing your tributes to Constance Sutherland. Who's next?"

Connie felt a gentle pressure on her arm. She sat back down.

A student carried a portable microphone to the table next to hers and held it just under an elderly woman's chin. The woman had her back to Connie's table, but when she turned slightly, Connie could see her profile.

"I first met Connie Sutherland in the dark days of the Great Depression." The woman's creaky voice carried across the auditorium. Connie had a sudden flash of recognition. Miriam! Why, in the dim light she hadn't noticed her old friend sitting at the next table. "I was fresh out of teacher's college and working at my first posting in Chicago, having trouble making ends meet, and missing my family back in Iowa. Connie Sutherland picked me up, dusted me off, and put me to work selling Moondrop Miracle to supplement my meager teacher's pay." She turned her head to look at Constance. "Connie became my employer, but more than that, she became my lifeline ... and my friend. "

When Miriam had finished speaking, the audience burst into applause. She turned around slowly in her seat, and Connie reached across the aisle, grasped her friend's gnarled hand and squeezed it. "I love you," she mouthed. Miriam squeezed back.

Sonja spoke from the stage. "Who's next?"

All over the banquet room, people raised their hands. The student carried the microphone to an elegant woman dressed in a silk suit, her red hair swept up into a French roll. Connie didn't recognize her.

"My name is Nancy Stryker," she said. "You and I have never met, Mrs. Sutherland, but my grandmother was Marietta Carlson. Marietta had led a hard life, but because you and your Aunt Pearl and Mrs. Swenson gave her a chance—because you believed in her—I'm able to stand here today. You gave jobs to people who needed them—war widows, refugees, people down on their luck."

One by one, others stood to speak. An Illinois Supreme Court judge admitted that if it hadn't been for a job selling Moondrop Miracle during college, she might have had to drop out of law school. A business mogul credited the story of how Mrs. Sutherland turned a recipe for skin tonic into a worldwide cosmetics empire as the inspiration for the executive's own enterprise.

"She didn't think God wanted a world where a woman would have to break her back to support her family," the woman said. "She believed He used Moondrop Miracle as a vehicle to give women a chance. And I feel very humble and fortunate to have been one of those women."

Through it all, Constance sat quietly, poised, head up, facing the great throng whose eyes were upon her. In her youth, her hopes and dreams had centered around living a fashionable life in an impressive home with a rich and successful husband. But her dreams had been crushed, and in their place, the Lord had placed new ones. Better ones.

At last Sonja regained the crowd's attention.

"I'm afraid we have to draw this portion of the evening to a close. But if any others of you here also feel you owe a debt of gratitude to Constance Sutherland and Moondrop Miracle, please stand."

There was a great rustling as women all around the room stood to their feet. Tall women and short women. White, black, Asian, Latina, thin, plump, young, and no longer young.

"Ladies and gentlemen, may I present to you . . . Constance Shepherd Sutherland Deveare."

As applause rang all around her, Constance bowed her head, overwhelmed. She caught a movement out of the corner of her eye. And there was Scott, all dressed up in his black dinner jacket, still looking so distinguished, even in middle age, with his rugged jaw and green eyes. So like his father, at least in appearance. In his love, care, and protective attitude—so like his stepfather.

He bent down and touched her elbow, encouraging her to stand.

"When did you get here?" she exclaimed.

"I've been here all along. Come on, people are waiting."

"But you're supposed to be in Hong Kong."

Scott grinned down at her. "Hong Kong's doing fine without me. I'll tell you all about it later. Right now, this is your moment."

He helped his mother to her feet. Applause thundered throughout the cavernous room. She smiled and gave a gracious nod to the faceless crowd. Holding her son's arm, she walked steadily toward the platform. *One foot in front of the other.* When she reached the steps, Sonja gave her a steadying hand up, and then a long embrace while Scott stood to the side.

Constance stepped up to the podium. The applause died down. Her hand fluttered to her breastbone, and she sought to find her voice. "Thank you. Thank you all."

She was being honored. These people were here for her—all her old coworkers, employees, and friends. At least those who still could. They had come to encourage the Young Entrepreneurs—and to honor her. She must say something. She looked over the vast crowd of female faces, young and old.

She cleared her throat. "When I was a young girl, my Aunt Pearl used to tell me, 'Everything good comes from the Lord.' That was never more true than tonight."

She paused to collect her thoughts. "Long before I mixed up my very first batch of Moondrop Miracle—and that was a fiasco, let me tell you—God in His infinite wisdom had a plan. In the short term, His plan was to make a way for me to earn a living to support my son and myself. Soon it became clear that Pearlcon would grow to support other families, to help rescue many people out of the hard times of the Great Depression. But people helped us all along the way, too. It certainly helped us out when the great Hollywood actress Hilda Schwarzenmuller endorsed us and appeared as "Miss Moondrop Miracle" in our ad campaigns for many years." She paused. "You don't remember Hilda Schwartzenmuller? Forgive me. You'll recognize her by her professional name, Gilda Miller." A sigh of recognition ran through the audience.

A full glass of water sat on a table beside the podium. Must be for her. She took a sip, trying to moisten her throat and settle her voice. "Then in the 1940s, after the United States entered the war, Pearlcon received another great boon—a contract from the War Department to manufacture Moondrop Miracle for the military to treat burns and skin injuries."

She paused and smiled. "We did not call the product we sold to the military 'Moondrop Miracle.' It became 'Skin Remedy Number 702.'"

Polite laughter rippled through the banquet room.

"But through it all, God had a plan. His plan was to use my little company as a means to help women all over the world."

She looked out over the sea of faces looking up at her, eager and expectant.

"I truly believe He made us feminine for a reason. I definitely believe that women should pursue any career they wish. As we do that, we don't need to abandon who we are. Who God made us to be. If you want to know the secret of my success, this is it. Be whoever God made you to be. Honor Him, and the rest will fall into place."

Her mind flew to Ingrid, and Marietta, and the many people who'd come through for her over the years. "When it comes to finding people to work with you, there are two rules. One, do your best to find the right person for the job. And two, be willing to delegate authority to her when she's ready to handle it."

She thought of her mother, and of Aunt Pearl.

"Work hard. Keep your promises. Cherish those closest to you. Honor your vows. And, as Aunt Pearl said to me a long, long time ago, no matter what happens..." She paused to still the quiver in her voice. "No matter what happens, you must always remember to sparkle."

THE END

AUTHOR'S NOTE

Readers sometimes ask me how much of my stories are true. *Moondrop Miracle*, like my other novels, is a work of fiction, with invented characters, settings, and details. All of the primary characters and the entire plot are fictional.

Readers of my Roaring Twenties series may recall that Marshall Field & Company was a real department store in Chicago. (Today it is a Macy's.) Mr. Grant and Dot Rodgers, however, are fictional characters. The Drake and Palmer House Hotels are also genuine Chicago landmarks that are still in operation today.

The farming community of Hoosier Grove, Illinois, truly existed in the far northwestern reaches of Cook County. The area was settled in the nineteenth century by soldiers returning from the Blackhawk War who saw good potential in the rich, dark soil. Because several were Indiana natives, the name "Hoosier Grove" stuck. Following World War II, developers transformed most of the dairy farms into the postwar suburbs of Streamwood and Hanover Park, and the "Hoosier Grove" moniker faded among all but the old-timers. During the 1920s and 1930s, however, that name still would have been in use.

I modeled Aunt Pearl's barn loosely on the Hoosier Grove Barn. Built in 1888, the barn has been thoroughly renovated as an attractive venue for weddings and other events, under the auspices of the Streamwood Park District. From this sprang the story idea of refitting a barn for a different use. Everything else that happens in Hoosier Grove—including Sheriff Blake, Pearlcon Enterprises, and Pearl's abundant cats—are products of my imagination.

ALSO BY THIS AUTHOR

Thank you for reading! If you enjoyed *Moondrop Miracle*, you'll love Jennifer's Roaring Twenties series:

You're the Cream in My Coffee: In 1928, Marjorie Corrigan believes her first love was killed in the Great War ... until the day she sees him standing in a Chicago train station. Although the stranger insists he's not who she thinks he is, she becomes obsessed with finding out the truth.

Ain't Misbehavin': In Jazz Age Chicago, free-spirited Dot Rodgers sells hats at Marshall Field while struggling to get her singing career off the ground. Small-town businessman Charlie Corrigan carries scars from the Great War. As his fortunes climb with the stock market, it seems he's finally going to win Dot's love. But what happens when it all comes crashing down?

"The Violinist," a novella in ***The Highlanders: A Smitten Historical Romance Collection***. In 1915 Idaho, a homesick lumberjack despairs of ever seeing his Scottish homeland again, until a music teacher reaches a part of his heart he'd long ago locked away.

Be the first to hear when the next book's coming out! Sign up for Jennifer's newsletter at **https://jenniferlamontleo.com/**

ALSO BY THIS AUTHOR

Jennifer also hosts the podcast **A Sparkling Vintage Life**, celebrating the grace and charm of an earlier era. Give it a listen, or
subscribe wherever you get your podcasts.

Made in the USA
Columbia, SC
23 May 2021